AN ANTHOLOGY

A HellBound Books Publishing LLC Book
Houston TX

A HellBound Books LLC Publication

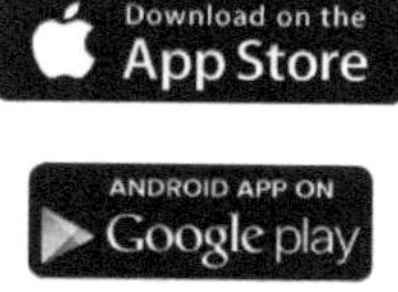

Printed in the United States of America

Contents

Foreword   5

Shape Shifting Priestess of the 1,000 Year War
Todd Sullivan   13

The Unholy Feast of the Witch's Heart
Timothy C Hobbs   81

The Flying Dentist
Mark Thomas   120

The Return of Mister Shovel
Andrew Post   171

Black Sun House
James B. Pepe   200

Subterranean Reptile Blues
Thomas Vaughn   216

The Last Screening
Edward Karpp   244

The Night of the Nails
Jaap Boekestein   267

Herman's Erotic Paradise
Lisa Alfano   281

Sin Eater from Hell
L.C. Holt   304

The Hills Have Votes
John Adam Gosham   327

The U.S. Coast Guard vs Lucifer's Horde
Brandon Cracraft   360

Undying Lust on a Dying Planet
M. Earl Smith   395

Axe Me No Questions
Sarah Cannavo   406

The Last VCR Made in Hell
James Gardner   449

King of the Tortured Dead
Bret McCormick   475

Carnal Harvest
James H Longmore   497

Other HellBound Books   **526**

Schlock! Horror! Foreword

What the hell is 'schlock?'

People who love words are constantly playing with definitions and variations on usage. I am no exception. The original meaning of the Yiddish word roughly approximated *trash* or *shoddy goods*. It was not a compliment to be called a schlockmeister. I decided long ago that schlock was not a bad word. I like it. To me it describes a certain type of raw, deceptively crude-seeming art, music, literature or cinema that more often than not defies any notion of good taste. I am a schlockmeister.

In 1966, when I was eight years old, I received my introduction to the battle between schlock and good taste.

It was a cool winter evening when my mother and her good friend, Marilyn, packed us four kids into the car and visited the Mansfield Twin Drive-In Theater in Fort Worth, Texas. The ladies wanted to see a pair of Doris Day movies; *Send Me No Flowers* and *Do Not Disturb*. We kids were an unfortunate obligation on the excursion. I'm sure the ladies would've preferred to hire a babysitter and see the films with their husbands, but those two were probably as excited about Doris Day as I was.

I stared out the rear window of the vehicle watching *The Seventh Voyage of Sinbad*, playing on the other screen. For the life of me I couldn't imagine why our mothers had not chosen the obviously superior entertainment at the other end of the drive-in. When the stop-motion creatures would appear, I'd add my own sound effects. That is until Mom told me to knock it off.

At intermission time my lesson in *taste* began. Halfway through the double bill, we ventured into the snack bar to purchase popcorn and allow those in need to use the facilities. While Mom and Marilyn herded the younger kids into the restroom, I waited by the door. It was here I received my first introduction to schlock. In a glass covered frame marked *Coming Soon*, was a delightfully garish poster for a flick called *Blood of Ghastly Horror*. Though I did not notice it at the time, this was also my introduction to Al Adamson, schlockmeister par excellence. I couldn't take my eyes off the poster and as soon as Mom returned I asked if we'd be seeing *that* movie.

"No!" Mom eyed the atrocity askance and stared me down in a manner implying I'd lost what little sense I may have previously possessed.

"Why not?"

"It's just…" she struggled for an appropriate descriptor. Her face wore the expression of disgust normally reserved for the unexpected discovery of a dirty diaper. Failing to think of a word suitably condemning, she settled for, "… trash!"

"What do you mean?" I was legitimately confused. I'd never before heard the word *trash* used in this context. Trash was what I carried to the curb on Tuesdays and Fridays. Did she mean they'd be throwing this wonderful artifact out for the garbage men? I'd have been glad to take it off their hands, free of charge! When I pressed for a fuller explanation, she told me to drop the matter, threatening to withhold my ration of popcorn.

It took persistence on my part to acquire further info on this enigma. Over the next few weeks, whenever I caught Mom in a good mood, I'd put forth a nonchalant enquiry. Finally, I had gathered the following knowledge: A) Good filmmakers, decent humans, went to a great deal of effort and expense to produce the sort of movies that promoted the values our family espoused. B) Some really sleazy bad guys would throw together inexpensive crap which appealed to the baser appetites of inferior humans. C) If I ever watched an abomination like *Blood of Ghastly Horror*, I would enter the ranks of sub-humans and lose what little standing I had in society. *(And I didn't want that, did I?)*

The meaning of the title remained a mystery. I'm pretty certain Mom was right on that point; it wasn't so much a title as a pastiche of trigger words. I remained intrigued by the idea that adults could actually earn money generating such wordplay. A foolhardy young lad, I imagined I was willing to risk being labelled a cretin, a mutant, a person with *poor taste*.

Time passed and I discovered the underground comics of Robert Crumb and others. I stumbled onto the cinematic perversions of Andy Milligan. I listened to the counter-culture music of Roky Erickson and The Thirteenth Floor Elevators. I even took in John Landis's first feature, *Schlock!* (Though, I still had no understanding of the word's etymology or connotation at the time.) I learned that even a fairly innocuous film like M.A. Ripps' *Bayou* could be reclassified as schlock by the inclusion of a single shot of nudity and a title change to the more lurid, *Poor White Trash*. The world seemed overflowing with forbidden fruit and I was inextricably drawn to it.

In 1979, I happened onto a book called *Kings of the Bs*. In it was a chapter dedicated to the career of one Sam Katzman. Here I got the low-down on the whole schlock thing. The author even called Sam a *schlockmeister*, but the moniker did not seem entirely derisive. I recognized Katzman's films. I'd grown up watching them. What's more, I still appreciated many of them even as an adult. Something in me longed to follow in the schlocky footsteps of Mr. Sam Katzman.

From 1984 until 1996 I wrote, produced and directed a slew of no-budget indie flicks for international home video distribution. The drive-ins had died, but the home video market created a demand for the same sort of schlocky fare. Instead of watching a movie or two a week, as Americans had for decades, many were watching five or more videos every weekend. Before I knew it, I had become one of the trash purveyors my mother warned me about on that chilly winter evening in 1966.

Today there is a solid niche market for films my mother's generation would have condemned. Even major Hollywood studies have journeyed onto turf previously ruled by only the meanest of schlockmeisters. It is common for modern viewers to rationalize their guilty cinematic pleasures by using such phrases as, "It's so bad, it's good!" or other non-sequiturs. To my way of thinking, you needn't explain or apologize. Schlock films are fruit of the same tree that gave us punk rock, body art, piercings, Picasso, underground comics, graffiti, taxidermy, carnival sideshows and literary oddities like the ones you'll find in this book.

Enjoy!

Bret McCormick, January 5, 2018, Bedford, Texas

SCHLOCK! HORROR!

Shape Shifting Priestess of the 1,000 Year War

Todd Sullivan

She mastered her dark powers and lived among unsuspecting humans!

Jung Min-Jeong leapt in her father's way, her tail swishing in agitation.

"You promised," she growled. She had been waiting for months, and the day had finally arrived. Today she turned two years old, and she would finally be taught how to shapeshift from a tiger to a human.

"I promised," her dad conceded, his eyes twinkling with amusement. "Where's your mother?"

"Still sleeping," Min-Jeong said. Her dad had appeared a week ago, and he and her mother had been mating in the den while Min-Jeong spent her days sleeping under the trees. But her dad never stayed long, and he usually left the same way he arrived: unexpectedly.

"Go wake her. She'll want to join us on this special day."

Min-Jeong tucked her tail beneath her body. She wanted her dad to herself before he left. He told the most wonderful stories about his time playing amongst the humans in the city in the valley, Gangneung.

"Does she have to come?" she asked. "And do I have to be the one to wake her?" she added.

Her dad barked out a laugh. "Yes to both questions." He playfully swiped her with his massive paw. "I'm not going to deal with your mother's wrath just because you're afraid of waking her."

He refused to go without her, so Min-Jeong darted through the trees, splattered across the creek running near the den, and poked her head into the mouth of the cave where her mom slept. She lay on her side, her chest rising and falling gently, her breathing deep, her eyes closed.

"Mommy." Min-Jeong spoke softly, hoping her mom would not hear and wake up. That way she could tell her dad that she at least tried but couldn't rouse her.

"Mommy," she repeated, "dad's set to take me to shapeshift for my birthday."

"So you caught him before he snuck away, did you?"

Her mom's guttural voice surprised Min-Jeong. Maybe she hadn't been sleeping at all. She rolled off of her side to her belly and began to lick the sleek, tawny and black coat covering her muscular body. Her pink tongue moved in long, slow arcs as she cleaned dirt from her coat. Min-Jeong bit back a yelp of impatience and glanced over her shoulder.

"Dad said we should probably get going early," she said, "before it gets too late in the evening."

Lying was a dangerous gambit with her mother. But the way her mom licked her paws, then lazily moved up to her forearms, made Min-Jeong think that this grooming session would take a long time.

"Did he?" Her mom paused, her bright amber eyes focused on Min-Jeong. Min-Jeong took a hesitant step out of the cave, and paused. She wanted to learn how to transform into a human, and her parents had promised her that they would teach her the secret of shapeshifting on her second birthday. Now neither of them seemed eager to begin. As a Han tiger, this was her birthright, and she had to show that she was mature enough to handle her bloodline's unique gift.

She didn't avert her gaze from her mother, though she didn't stare directly at her. Instead, she focused on the space above her mother's eyes, which was as much as she could do without initiating a challenge for dominance.

"Fine, then," her mom said after a moment. She yawned, her thick tongue extending between the sharp canines of her massive jaws. She rose to her paws and stretched her body tight, her head low, her tail high. Yawning one last time, she finally said, "Let's go see if your father is still waiting for us."

Min-Jeong followed her mother out of the cave and back across the creek to her father, who had laid down under a tree in the shade. He swiveled his ears at their approach, his white false eyes staring at them even as he gazed out at the horizon.

"Already itching to return to the realm of man?" her mom asked him.

"Something's afoot," he said. "Change is in the air in Han."

"Humans are nothing but trouble." Her mom followed his gaze to the broad river snaking down in the valley towards the ocean. "Nothing good comes of your playing in the city."

Her dad rose to his paws. "Experience comes of it, and that's always good." He winked at Min-Jeong.

"Your philosophy might impress your other mates, but it won't work on me. Nice words don't fill the belly, shelter from the elements, or protect from the sword and arrow."

They started through the forest down the gradual decline of the mountainside. Her mom walked on one side of Min-Jeong, and her father on the other. The sun hung low in the blue sky, its reign in the autumn months short as the season approached winter. The Seoraksan mountain range stretched from South Han to North Han. Her father claimed the valley where Gangneung City nestled as his territory, which stretched at least a hundred kilometers across.

"There's nothing more important than knowing," her father said to Min-Jeong. "That's how the Han tigers learned the art of shapeshifting. Generations ago, our ancestors were like the other animals of the forest. Intelligent in their own way, but not nearly smart enough to evade our greatest threat."

"Humans," her mom growled, long and low.

"Humans," her dad said, though without anger. "In this world, you're either the predator or the prey. Once, humans were the prey of tigers, but then man learned the art of magic weapons and gunpowder. They began to hunt us for our coats for clothing, and our bones and teeth and eyes for spell components."

"They were relentless," her mom said, "and cruel, leaving cubs without their mothers to keep them alive."

"The humans were clever," her father amended. "The tigers of Han were hunted almost to the brink of extinction until one of our kind journeyed far into foreign lands. A perilous journey this tiger endured, but when he came back, his orange fur had turned white, and his yellow eyes had become blue."

Min-Jeong rotated her ears to her father in curiosity. "A white tiger?" she breathed out in awe. "Does that really exist?"

"According to the legends," her mom said. "No one knows for sure."

"Your mom doesn't believe in the white tiger."

"I believe a tiger can be white," her mom said, "even if I've never seen one."

"But that's not the legend," her dad interjected. "That a white tiger can be born isn't the point." To Min-Jeong, he said, "A tiger's orange coat turns white when they've learned enough, and their eyes become blue with wisdom. Blue like the sky watching over the world learning all of the daily secrets of existence."

"Another type of shapeshifting?" Min-Jeong tried to picture such a tiger. How would it hide in the forests of green and brown?

The descent became steeper, and for several minutes they hopped down sudden falls and over jagged rocks until they reached the valley floor. In the distance, she spied Namdae River snaking through the land and cutting through Gangneung as it reached for the ocean surrounding the peninsula.

"The city of man," her mom said with a growl. "If there's any wisdom to learn from them, I can happily do without it and remain the color I am. Never underestimate humans," she told Min-Jeong.

They remained in the tall grass as they travelled forward, her parents keeping an eye out for threats.

"In small numbers, they're weak," her father said. "That's the key to battling them. We stay far up in the mountains, deep in the forests. It's not easy for humans to find us anymore, and if a large number of them dared to enter our territory, they'd be at our mercy."

"Unless it's tiger hunters," her mom warned her. "Even a handful of them can overpower a group of us. We may heal most wounds, but it's head injuries you have to worry about. Even with a regular weapon, if it lops this off," she swiped Min-Jeong's head, "you're not growing that back."

"Do you know how long a hunter would have to hack at our necks to cut off our heads?" her father asked in his deep voice, his tail swishing in amusement.

"Don't forget the muskets," her mom said. "They have poor range, and poor aim, but if you get hit in a vital area, say here," she tapped Min-Jeong's heart, "or here, or here," her paw touched her kidney, then stomach, "you're going to be slowed down considerably. You'll eventually heal, but you'll be easier prey for a killing stroke from a magic weapon."

"Be fast, stay alert, and it's no problem," her father cut in. "Here's the secret about magic weapons." He licked Min-Jeong's nose. "Since we're magic, we can smell them coming. So they're easy to avoid."

Min-Jeong's eyes opened wide in amazement. What did magic smell like? What did muskets and hunters look like?

The sun hung right above the trees, and a chill wind flowed down the mountainside as the evening deepened. Her parents took her to farms dotting the banks of Namdae River.

"The farmers are the lifeblood of the city, but they have the least amount of protection," her father said. "They're the easiest prey, especially for a novice like you."

The way her parents kept their tails low, and the sudden tenseness of their movement, made Min-Jeong think that they, too, were vulnerable off the mountainside.

"We should be quick," her mom said. She was a superior hunter to her father, and she spotted a middle-aged woman on one of the farms. Her parents abruptly stopped, and Min-Jeong swiveled her head from one side to the other.

"This is your first kill, and your first transformation," her mother said. "There is a process you must strictly abide to. When the woman is freshly killed, and her blood is still warm, you must eat the flesh from her face. Then you must consume her heart. Only then will you be able to take her appearance."

Min-Jeong nodded. "How long does the transformation last?"

"As long as you want it to," her father said. "Partial transformations are possible, but if you revert fully back to your tiger form, you'll have to start the process all over again with another human."

Min-Jeong tried to suppress her nervousness, but her tail whipped from side to side, giving her away. She had hunted swift-legged deer and red foxes and burrowing possums. The game today was a human, though, and she feared making a mistake. What if she failed? What if the woman got away and called for help? What if humans with their superior technology swarmed from the farmhouses and killed her?

Min-Jeong swallowed in a throat gone dry. Today was her second birthday. She was old enough now. Her parents must believe in her ability and trusted that she could make a clean kill. She couldn't disappoint her father. She wouldn't fail in front of her mother. And yet she stood there, staring at the farmer, the evening getting later, the wind coming down the mountain growing colder.

"You can do it." Her father nudged her, the mischievous twinkle back in his eyes. "Just stay focused, keep track of everything around you, and follow your instincts."

Glancing at her mother who had never taken her eyes off the woman, Min-Jeong started through the tall grass alone. She kept her belly low to the ground so that she would not be seen. The woman squatted in a row of cabbage, a floral headscarf wrapped tightly around her hair. The sharp smell of her sweat drifted in the soft breeze flowing off the river.

Min-Jeong's heartbeat picked up at the possibility of a chase. The farmer's stubby legs could not propel her across the ground very fast, but perhaps Min-Jeong was missing something. Some secret the woman concealed that would allow her to move faster back to the safety of the farmhouse.

Min-Jeong's anxiety increased as she neared the woman on silent paws. If she knew she came, she showed no sign of it. If other humans watched from the farmhouse, they did not reveal themselves. Closer Min-Jeong came, and closer, and then it was almost like an alarm sounded in her head.

Now!

Every instinct told her she had come close enough, and she leapt. The woman only issued a short cry of surprise as Min-Jeong knocked her over. Before she could say more, Min-Jeong ripped out her throat, her blood splattering the rich earth. As her parents had instructed, she ripped the flesh from the woman's face and swallowed the warm, thin skin in noisy slurps. After several attempts of clawing at the convulsing body trapped beneath her, she broke through the woman's ribcage, bent her muzzle down, and tore out the woman's heart to eat. Only then did the transformation begin.

Min-Jeong watched in awe as her beautiful orange and black fur receded from her flesh into a body imploding upon itself. Her muscles slimmed and tightened, her back straightened, and her tail wound itself into her hips. Her front paws stretched, curving into long, delicate fingers. Her powerful fangs receded into her gums.

Min-Jeong raised her new arms up to the evening sky and wriggled her toes in the grass. Her body was smooth except for the jet-black hair on her head, under her arms, and an orange patch of hair between her legs. Her parents, still in their tiger forms, bounded up to her and nudged her in the direction of Namdae River. She looked into the calm blue water at her new pale face still wet with blood, and her narrow black eyes.

"Is that me?" she whispered. Unable to form human words in their tiger throats, her parents only nodded. She had been so worried that something would go wrong, but she had committed the kill like a veteran. Pride swelled in her chest, and a wide smile spread her human lips.

The ground beneath her feet rumbled, and Min-Jeong stumbled. She stared at her parents, who growled long and low as the earth shook again. Min-Jeong dropped to her knees and pressed her belly to the mud along the riverbank. Small rocks scratched her pale skin, and she considered transforming back into a tiger. But her parents had said if she did a full transformation, she would have to find a new human to shapeshift into. She had just assumed this form, and she didn't want to let it go so quickly.

The decision came for her when a shriek reverberated through the mountains. The cry seemed to take root inside of Min-Jeong and gave rise to a terror that made her reflexively transform back into a tiger. Her parents came to her side as she wallowed in the mud in fear.

"We have to find cover," her dad said. "Quick!"

At her parents urging, Min-Jeong found her footing. Her mom darted ahead of them, her ears roving in different directions in search of attackers. But the shrieks didn't come from the farms around them. Instead they poured forth from the Seorraksan Mountains stretching into North Han. Her father's eyes never left the high peaks as he ran.

"Can it be that the rumors are true?" he said when they caught up to her mother. "The *Jeonha* of North Han actually did it."

A ball of flame erupted from one of North Han's peaks and raced across the evening sky. Min-Jeong followed the light of the flaming orb and watched it slam into the ocean. Giant waves rose up and steam bellowed into the air.

"The *Jeonha* has brought dragons to Han!" Awe and excitement filled her father's voice, and her mom swung towards him.

"Real dragons!" he said, and after the briefest of moments. "I have to see them!"

"Fool! Only a fool wishing for death goes *to see* dragons."

Her father shook his tawny head, his tail flicking wildly from side to side. "Don't you understand? If he bought dragons, he must be gearing up for war. And who would be caught in the middle of a war between North and South Han?"

Realization dawned in her mother's amber eyes. Even Min-Jeong understood the implication. Her father had long ago told her that the two Hans were technically still at war, even though neither had attacked each other for many decades. But if the fragile peace ended and North Han resumed the conflict with South Han, her father's domain on the border of both countries would get caught in the middle. His mates and his children spread throughout the mountains of Gangwan-do Province would be caught in a conflict between two massive armies, one of which had dragons.

"I'll collect several of my sons in the next few days," he said. "We must leave soon before snowfall covers the mountains."

"I'll go!" Min-Jeong could barely maintain her footing with the fear radiating through her, but if her father was going on an adventure, she wanted to go, too.

Her mom shook her head. "You don't have the experience. Plus," she looked at her father, "I will give birth to a new litter in three months. Min-Jeong must remain here just in case none of you come back and war truly begins."

Her father nodded. "Don't worry," he told Min-Jeong. "One day we'll play in the city together. But where I go now will be dangerous even for me, and there's too great a chance some of us won't return."

"Come back to the den with me, Min-Jeong," her mother commanded. Without a backwards glance, she started back up the mountainside. Her father winked at her, and went off towards the ocean. Min-Jeong stared after him until she lost sight of him in the underbrush. Then she turned and scampered after her mother.

Min-Jeong had been born in a litter of two. Her brother had died six months ago in Gangneung city when he'd snuck away from home not long after learning how to shapeshift. Her parents had waited to teach her until she'd matured further, but now she only thought of striking off with her father into North Han. When she caught up with her mother, she asked, "Where do my older brothers and step brothers live?"

"They're spread out through Gangwon-do Province," her mother said without pausing. "Each have their own territories and their own mates. Your father won't have to travel far to find them, though. At one point, we tigers were solitary unless we were mating. Now the head of the family keeps track of his children and their mates and their children. If the need ever arises, we can quickly form small groups, or even an army of our own."

An army of tigers? Min-Jeong could not imagine such a thing coming to pass.

When they reached the cave, her mom lay on the dirt floor. Now that they had returned to the den, some of the tension had left her. Min-Jeong felt the same. The dragons had stopped shrieking and shooting balls of fire into the ocean. The droning of crickets filled the night, and their familiar song comforted Min-Jeong. She looked around the wide, roomy cave, and wondered what it would be like when the cubs arrived. She had no experience with litters, but she only guessed that little brothers and sisters running under paw would be annoying.

Min-Jeong went to the edge of the cave and lay down, her head poking out of the rocky mouth. She assumed this position every night as days became weeks. Her mom hunted in the evenings, and Min-Jeong thought she seemed to be eating more. But her physical shape mostly remained the same, and she wondered if her mom was mistaken and wouldn't bear any cubs after all.

The dragon cries echoed through the Seorraksan mountains another two times over that first month. The sound, which had at first filled her with terror, now filled Min-Jeong with a mixture of fear and curiosity. What did dragons look like? Her mom had never seen one, though she knew of their description from old tales. Dragons appeared in the world slightly more often than white tigers, and her mom had an easier time accepting their reality over that of a blue eyed tiger.

At the end of the fourth week, Min-Jeong lifted her head. Someone approached the den on two feet. She looked back at her mother lying on her side, eyes closed. Min-Jeong rose to get a better look.

When she spotted a man carrying a bloodied tiger on his shoulders, she quickly woke her mother.

"So your father's returned," her mom said, her voice surprising Min-Jeong.

"I think so," Min-Jeong said. "But he has a tiger on his shoulder. It looks dead."

Her mom sighed long and low. Rising, she went deeper into the cave and returned with manmade tools in-between her teeth.

"Let's get this over with," she said in a low growl.

Together they met her father in his human form. They silently went to a cluster of mounds protruding from the side of the mountain. Her father laid the tiger down, took the shovel from her mother, and began to dig.

"I went with three of my sons," he said. "This was the only body I could bring back."

They had to wait until he buried her older brother and reverted back to his tiger form before they could speak to him.

"Was their sacrifice worth it?" her mom asked. "Did you learn anything of value?"

"The *Jeonha* of North Han only has a handful of dragons," her father said. "Powerful, yes, but he isn't sure if they are enough to guarantee a victory over South Han, so he waited. Perhaps too long."

Her father looked down the mountainside towards South Han. "There is a traitor of North Han whom he fears will sell dragons to South Han soon. I have to get to Gangneung City and infiltrate the government's inner circles to discover what's really going on."

"I'll go with you this time," Min-Jeong said, stepping forward.

"Silly little girl," her mother growled "Do you wish to join your brothers so soon in the afterlife? You will stay here to protect the next generation."

"No!" A low growl built up in Min-Jeong's chest, and she caught and held her mother's gaze. "I'm old enough, and I will go where I please."

The attack came faster than Min-Jeong could have ever anticipated. Her mother lashed out, her claws catching Min-Jeong in the flank and opening a long, bloody wound. She stumbled, but her mom wasn't done, and she swiped out and raked across Min-Jeong's chest, opening her flesh to the bone.

The pain seared through her, and Min-Jeong cried out as her mom came at her again. She latched her canines onto Min-Jeong's throat and pressed tightly on her jugular. With a little more force, she could break her neck.

"You will stay here," her mom said without releasing her, her voice muffled but clear enough to understand. "You will help protect the next generation. And after that, if you wish to throw your life away, that will be your decision."

Darkness slowly closed in on Min-Jeong as she struggled in her mother's grasp. From a far, far distance, she heard her father say, "I'm sorry, but she's right. We'll play together in the world of man one day. I promise."

His words swirled round and round in a vortex of shadows that rose up and claimed her consciousness.

***

When the dragons' roars echoed across the northern cities of South Han, the trees shook from the reverberations bouncing through the mountains.

Jung Min-Jeong, staring at her tawny reflection in the water swirling down the creek, lost her footing. She scrambled, her claws scraping on the wet rocks, and leapt into the mud.

Nearby, her brothers' high-pitched yowls floated across the tall grass from the den.

"Older sister! Where are you?"

A growl of frustration bubbled in Min-Jeong's chest. Her mother's litter had been born five months ago, and it was Min-Jeong's duty to look after them. She padded out of the mud and into the bright yellow canolas flowering around the creek.

"Older sister!" Their squeaky voices were impossible to ignore. "Have the dragons come down the mountains? Is the forest on fire?"

Min-Jeong looked up at the patches of evening sky visible through the closely standing trees. Birds that had returned for the spring flittered through the treetops, their sharp cries filling the air. Min-Jeong needed to get higher if she wanted to see the dragons' breath streak across South Han to slam into the sea. Her mom would scold her. Min-Jeong knew she should go back to the den to comfort her brothers. Sparks from dragon breath could start small fires in the green mountains of South Han. But that almost never happened, however, and her mom hadn't gone far to hunt.

Min-Jeong went to the nearest tree and leapt onto it. Her claws sank into the hard bark with each agile pounce up. Soon she was in the lower branches, and she scrambled up into the green leaves. Her mom often told her that she must also have monkey spirit in her because of her ability to climb trees. Min-Jeong employed the gift often when she wanted to escape a punishment for not doing what she'd been told.

She'd chosen one of the tallest trees near the den. The breeze's whisper through the leaves grew into a wail the higher she went until finally she stuck her head out of the boughs into the cool evening air. The sun's dying rays colored the sky in deep orange and red hues. She looked south at Gangnueng nestled in the mountains of Seoraksan, the stonewall surrounding the dense cluster of city buildings, and Namdae River cutting through its eastern section.

One day. How many times had she thought these same words? One day she would escape the watchful eyes of her mother, kill a human, and shapeshift out of her tiger form. Then she would find her father who hadn't come back in half a year, and play alongside him in the world of mortals.

The dragons' roars from North Han rumbled through Seoraksan mountains a second time and her heart raced. The *Jeonha* of North Han wanted South Han's attention before he commanded the fearsome winged beasts to belch the massive balls of flame across the country's coast.

"Min-Jeong! Where are you going?"

The voice startled her. She placed her paw too heavy on a branch, and it snapped. Min-Jeong scrambled for a hold, her claws digging into a studier bough. While the tree swayed by her sudden movement, she peered down through the shifting leaves but saw nothing.

"Min-Jeong. I know you can hear me!"

Her mom's voice sounded uncomfortably close. She must have climbed up in the tree after her. When Min-Jeong disobeyed her mom, she would deliver swift swipes that opened gaping wounds in Min-

Jeong. They would take hours to heal, and the pain would leave her weeping or unconscious. Her mom placed them strategically, knowing how to prolong Min-Jeong's agony without threatening any vital areas. When Min-Jeong angered her, her temper quickly unraveled into vicious attacks, and now Min-Jeong forced her to come up after her in a tree.

Again.

Min-Jeong was two and a half years old, but she maintained a slimmer frame than her mother's powerful one. She easily scaled the trees near the den while her mom struggled to pull her massive body up into the branches. This made her mom even angrier, and Min-Jeong knew that only by going all the way up to the highest boughs could she avoid her mom's wrath.

Usually, that was, for when her mom's blood boiled hot enough, she was capable of anything.

The high-pitched yowling of her brothers drifted up to her. She imagined them tripping over their paws as they emitted those awful whines while looking fearfully up the tree. They must have come out of the den and moved to the base of the trunk now that mom was back. The little brats seeing her punished by their mother humiliated her every time, another reason she wanted to avoid her.

Another roar, and a gale ripped through the forest as balls of flame raced across the sky beneath the clouds. The dragons lurked far away in the Seoraksan peaks of North Han. Min-Jeong thought she could almost make out the fearsome winged shapes of the mighty beasts as they belched out their powerful breath at the commands of the King of North Han.

Faint horns blew to alarm the citizens of Gangneung City as another set of flaming balls ripped above the mountains to fall far out into the ocean with an explosion of waves and steam. Then a third volley, and a fourth, and a fifth. The dragon roars before each new display shook the earth, and the heat from the giant balls warmed the mountainside. Min-Jeong's heart raced as she clung to the swaying branches. She glanced down to see if her mom had gotten closer but still did not see her.

The dragons finally quieted. The earth stopped rumbling, the gales from the dragon breath died back to the familiar wind sweeping through Seoraksan. Her brothers' yelps floated up to her at an even higher, more agitated pitch. The dragons horrified them as they once did her. She imagined the cubs scrambling around the tree trunk in terror. She looked down the thicket of leaves and saw two bright, shiny eyes gazing at her.

Min-Jeong let out her own yelp of surprise at seeing how her mom had snuck up on her. She clung to the bark only a dozen centimeters from her. She had actually made it all the way up the tree, and she bared her long, sharp canines at Min-Jeong. Min-Jeong tried to back away from her, but she had reached the top of the tree and had nowhere else to go.

"Come. Down. Now!" her mom commanded in a low growl.

Min-Jeong's heart raced. She looked to her left, and she looked to her right. It wasn't monkey spirit she needed, but squirrel spirit. She wondered if she could leap from this branch to the ones across from her as she always saw the squirrels do when they chased each other through the trees.

"Min-Jeong," her mom warned. "Don't even think about it."

Min-Jeong's fear made her pull back her lips in a strained smile. She crouched as best as she could in the leaves and calculated how hard she could push off to reach the next tree without breaking the branches. *Father,* she thought, *I'm finally coming to find you, and nothing is going to stop me this time.*

With a powerful thrust of her legs, she leapt. Branches snapped beneath her paws, and she tumbled through the air into the next tree. She slammed into the bark and struggled to find a grip as she fell through the boughs. To her relief, she caught hold and clung to the tree as it rocked back and forth under her momentum.

"Min-Jeong!"

Min-Jeong craned her head to look at her mother higher up in the other tree. For a moment, it seemed like her mother would leap, her body tense to pounce. But the branches suddenly broke under her too, and she fell through the leaves with a roar. She flailed for a hold, but her massive size made that impossible. She crashed through the branches until Min-Jeong lost sight of her in the darkness below. She thought she heard her hit the ground, and her brothers' yowling abruptly stopped, to be replaced by their squeaky voices.

"Mommy, are you okay?"

"Mommy, why did you fall?"

"Mommy, where's older sister?"

Min-Jeong became worried. With that kind of fall, her mom may have broken a leg if she tried to land on her feet. She'd be vulnerable for at least an hour as her body healed. If someone attacked the den now, she would have trouble defending the cubs.

Min-Jeong gazed down at the ground to see if her fear was correct, but the leaves obscured her vision. She clung to the tree and considered her options. If something threatened the litter, her mom's capacity for violence would probably thwart any attack. Her mom hadn't become the longest-lived female tiger in the province for nothing.

Min-Jeong climbed higher. When she neared the top of the tree, she peered at the thicket across from her, and pounced. The speed at which the tree raced at her immediately made her realize she overcompensated, and she braced herself as she crashed into the rough bark face first. Bright lights filled her vision, and she caught onto the branches before plunging to the forest floor. A brief bout of dizziness assailed her, the forest spinning around her. She breathed deeply in and out, waiting for her vision to settle, before leaping again. She landed in the next tree more gracefully. Or at least she didn't stop her momentum with her forehead. She was becoming more like the brown squirrels that played in the trees above her.

Min-Jeong grinned, tensed her muscles, and with a roar of excitement, leapt again. She crashed into the next tree's braches, immediately realized her confidence had been misplaced, and squealed as the branches snapped under her paws. She tumbled through the leaves whispering against her body. Her heart raced as she hit the ground hard and rolled down the side of the mountain. She slid to a stop moments later, and lay there in the shadows, stunned by the impact.

Her natural healing abilities quickly closed the scrapes opened on her flesh. Luckily, she had broken no bones. Their magic made them hard to kill, and she regained her feet moments later feeling as if nothing had happened. Min-Jeong gazed back up the steep slope where her mom and siblings remained. She shook her head.

What *was* mom so worried about?

Stretching her body taunt, Min-Jeong shook the grass and leaves from her fur. Then she ran down the rest of the mountain towards Namdae River. She approached the settlements along the edge of the river. Here, humans sparsely populated the area, and low walls of stone surrounded the farms.

The sun had almost disappeared from the sky, its bright crown just visible beyond the western mountains. Min-Jeong kept to the high grass and crept along the shadows, her belly low to the ground. She came to a small dwelling that seemed to be caving in upon itself. The smell of humans was strong, and she paused and listened closely to their voices floating out from their stone home. It sounded like four or five people inhabited the rooms inside. Her father's words came back to her. The best hunters are patient hunters. Wait and watch, and the prey will eventually leave itself vulnerable to you.

So Min-Jeong waited, and eventually the wooden door swung open and two young girls poked their heads out. The older of them, perhaps in her mid-teens, looked around for several seconds before she led her younger sister out towards the privy. She held a small sword in her free hand, which she kept in front of her, ready to use. Min-Jeong moved carefully in the cover of grass, placing her paws just right to minimize any noise amongst the fallen leaves and twigs littering the ground. The girls entered a tiny outhouse. The sound of urine splattering into a hole came to Min-Jeong, and the fresh smell of dung filled her snout. The older sister finished first, and stepped out of the outhouse to wait for her little sister.

Now!

Min-Jeong leapt from the surrounding grass, opened her mouth wide, and clamped her fangs into the girl's jugular. Only the smallest of cries escaped her lips before her windpipe was broken between Min-Jeong's powerful jaws. The girl weighed so little, and Min-Jeong easily dragged her into the woods. Death throes convulsed the girl's slender body, so Min-Jeong ripped out her throat, quickly ending the girl's life.

"Older sister!"

Min-Jeong lifted her head to the little girl staring directly at her, a look of horror twisting her face.

"Father! Mother! Help please! A tiger's taken older sister!"

The sister's shrieks rang through the night, and the wooden door of the farmhouse banged open. Min-Jeong grabbed the warm corpse between her jaws and darted across the flat ground back into the edge of the forest. Shouts and curses followed behind her, and a dagger wildly thrown hit the dirt meters from her. Min-Jeong paused and considered going back to take care of whoever hunted her, but the kill in her jaws was enough. The evening was getting late, and if she wanted to play in the city, she had to transform quickly and get on the way.

Min-Jeong dragged the body farther into the forest. Then, with it dangling in her mouth, she climbed a tree, a short, squat one this time, and settled into some of the thick branches. The humans didn't worry her, but she didn't want to attract the attention of other animals that might try and take her kill from her.

The girl was slender with little meat to her bones, and would do little to fill Min-Jeong's belly. She stared at the girl's beautiful pale face in satisfaction before ripping away the skin with the tips of her teeth. Her bites were delicate, and the flesh came up off the skull with light resistance as blood leaked down the leaves to streak the bark red. After she swallowed the skinned flesh, Min-Jeong broke the girl's ribcage to consume her heart.

Low hisses escaped from Min-Jeong's bloody mouth as the transformation began. Her beautiful orange and black fur slid beneath the follicles of her skin, leaving only an orange patch beneath her legs, and long black hair draping her shoulders. Her tail disappeared into her spine, and two breasts developed on her chest while her other two teats smoothed into her torso. Her muscles slimmed and her body straightened.

Her new form was petite, but she recognized the tiger strength and speed this body still held. Min-Jeong leapt from the branches to the ground on two little feet. She held her delicate hands up and wriggled her slender fingers. She touched her toned legs and flat stomach. The girl's simple brown dress had been ruined by blood and ripped apart by her fangs. Min-Jeong would need clothes if she wanted to play amongst the world of man.

Min-Jeong kept to the high grass as she crept along the edge of the forest towards another group of buildings outside the city walls. The brush irritated the soft skin of this body, and the bug bites raised red bumps along her pale flesh. She quickened her pace, and reached a small inn and drinking establishment. The low roofed building had its windows open to air out the sour odor of sweaty bodies gathered closely together in the warm spring evening.

Min-Jeong crept down the narrow lane leading to the inn and waited until she saw a group of men approach. They had swords on their belts and daggers tucked into their boots. They wore simple loose pants and shirts, and snug caps on each of their heads. A long metal tube with a leather strap was slung on each of their backs. Though Min-Jeong had never seen one before, she assumed these were the guns her parents had warned her of. Her father had called them muskets.

The men were dark skinned, and tendrils of gray smoke drifted from long pipes they puffed on as they walked down the road. Min-Jeong sniffed the sweet, heavy aroma emanating from them in delight. The world of man was as interesting as she thought it would be.

Two of the men walked ahead of the third, and she decided to take him first. Her parents had taught her that a partial transformation would mean that she could revert back to the human form without eating another heart. So she forced claws to slide from her nails, and she increased the muscle density in her arms and legs. A wide smile spread over her lips as a pleasurable thrill ran through her body.

Min-Jeong dropped to all fours and silently crept towards the man from behind. When she was less than a meter from him, so close that she could feel his body heat, she pounced, her heart racing at the kill. One powerful hand clasped tightly over his mouth while the other ripped out his throat. Blood spurted from the gaping wound to splash his comrades ahead of him. They both spun, their hands going to the hilts of their swords.

Min-Jeong leapt forward as their swords slid from their belts faster than she anticipated. Her momentum carried her too fast, and she plunged into the sudden stab the man directed at her. The blade slid into her side, but these weren't magic weapons. It stung but did little to slow her down. She cocked back her fist and slammed it into the man's face, crushing his nose with the power of the blow.

The last man sliced down upon her and chopped through her shoulder. That stung too, and Min-Jeong spun around and swiped the weapon from his grasp. The man turned and ran through the forest, and Min-Jeong followed him in quick pursuit. The kills had been exciting, but this hunt would be fun, and she wanted to drag it out.

The man fumbled with the musket on his back. He unslung it and went for a pouch bumping on his hip. He looked over his shoulder but did not see her in the shadows behind him even as she clearly saw him. He slid to a stop, dropped to his knee, and poured a black powder down the metal and wood tube. Min-Jeong snatched up a heavy branch as she descended upon him and swung it with all of her might at his head. The crack to his skull echoed in her ears, and the man fell backwards at the force of the blow.

Min-Jeong smiled in satisfaction at the kills. She'd suffered minor damage from the weapons, but too much blood stained her human skin. She stripped the smallest of the three, went down to the river, and submerged herself into the water. This body was overly sensitive to the cold, and when she came out moments later, she was shivering. She pulled on the loose pants and shirt and found them both to be way too big for her despite the man's smaller size. Once she got into the city, she would have to steal something better to clothe her female body.

Min-Jeong wrapped her long black hair into a tight bun and pulled the man's cap over it. Staring at her reflection in the clear water, she thought she no longer looked like a girl. Min-Jeong laughed, slapped the water to shatter the image, and turned towards Gangneung City. She walked through the forest until she reached the main road leading into the city.

The sun had now disappeared completely behind the mountains, and the sky was a deep blue, darkening to black. The first stars twinkled above her. She'd spent many nights staring at the shapes of the stars and trying to count them to see how high she could get. Of course, there were too many, but it kept her busy when her mom left her to guard the den. She turned and looked back at the mountains from where she'd come and wondered what her mom and siblings were doing. She wondered if she would ever see them again. Now that she was on this adventure, she did not want to stop. She wanted nothing more than to travel the roads of man as far as they would take her, and fill herself on experiences until she was bursting from life.

Gangneung's walls rose up above the trees. Min-Jeong scanned the rocky stone barrier where a guard stood sentry every dozen meters. A steady stream of people walked the road to the entrance, and gatekeepers inspected each individual entering the city. Min-Jeong paused, altered her direction, and slipped into the forest. If the gatekeepers asked her any questions, she wouldn't know how to answer.

Her father and siblings played in the city, but she wasn't sure how they actually managed to get past the front gates.

Min-Jeong crept through the forest while keeping track of each guard who paced the width of a meter, their eyes cast towards the trees. Pausing in the shadows, she strengthened her hands and pushed her claws from her fingers, the muscles in her arms and legs becoming denser. When the two nearest guards turned sharply to walk their short patrol on the battlements, Min-Jeong leapt onto the stone wall and quickly scaled over it. She rolled over the uneven battlement and dropped to the ground on the other side into Gangneung City.

The intense smell of humans living closely together washed over her. She never knew their odor could be so strong: the sharp stench of sweat and urine, the heavy odor of dung, the various scents of roasting meats, frying vegetables, fermented kimchi, and boiling rice. For several moments Min-Jeong breathe shallowly until it became bearable. The short, squat buildings left no room between them, and the narrow alley she stood in branched off in numerous directions. Voices drifted from behind open doors and windows. Children darted through the alleys on bare feet, their shrieks bouncing off the stone walls in the early evening. Dogs barking echoed in the alley, and when several mongrels rounded a corner behind Min-Jeong, they sniffed at her and growled, their hackles rising. Min-Jeong met the eyes of the pack leader and let out her own deep growl that rumbled long and low in her chest. The dog tucked its tail, lowered its eyes, and led its pack into another alley.

Min-Jeong wasn't sure which way to go, so she just started away from the wall through the alleys. The soft boots she wore were too big and flapped on her feet as she walked so that she often stumbled. She looked inside of homes in the narrow alleys, and residents stared back at her as she passed. Sometimes the stonewalls were so close that they brushed against her shoulders. Cats slipping through the shadows paused to stare closely at her. She could not understand them with these human ears, but she figured they saw her for what she was. So did the dogs that seemed as numerous as the humans. Solitary canines ran from her, but in packs she constantly had to stare down the leader before they moved on.

And then, without warning, she stepped out of an alley into a main avenue. Here, people pulled two wheeled wooden carts down a hard packed dirt lane. Stalls ran down both sides of the street where vendors sold meats, fruits and vegetables, dried fish, rice, household items, clothes, and more. For several moments Min-Jeong simply stared, her breath coming fast at this spectacle of man. Vendors called to people as they walked by to come try their fresh wares at the cheapest rates, and Min-Jeong sniffed the air hungrily. She hadn't eaten since the buck she shared with her brothers the day before, and her stomach rumbled.

In the distance, fireworks shot up into the air to brighten the evening sky in an explosion of lights. The people of Gangneung City didn't seem overly concerned with the dragon breath. North Han's *Jeonha* had ordered the beasts to display their power many times over the months, and like Min-Jeong, the people must have gotten over their terror of the giant balls of fire racing through the sky.

Min-Jeong walked towards the direction of the fireworks. The lane grew so dense with people that she walked shoulder to shoulder alongside them just to move forward. She had no money for any of the tasty snacks lining the street, so she maneuvered close to the stalls and waited for her chance. She did not stop, she did not slow down, but when an old woman sitting behind one of the food carts turned to grab a piece of black coal for the low fire in a dug pit, Min-Jeong darted a hand out and grabbed one of the pointy sticks spearing a multi-limbed meal. She held it close to her chest as she continued walking, and breathed slowly in and out until she had gotten several steps away without someone calling after her.

She looked at the snack closely but could not tell what it was. Most of its body was flat and wide, but it narrowed at both ends. One side seemed almost like a tail. The other side had half a dozen curled tentacles. When Min-Jeong bit into it, she had to really pull to break the rubbery meat between her teeth. She chewed with delight at the strange sharp taste of spices and tough flesh that filled her mouth. Something about it reminded her of Namdae River, and she thought that this must be seafood.

Seldom had Min-Jeong eaten the fish of the river. They were hard to catch in tiger form, and her mom rarely shapeshifted to human form because she didn't like going near human habitats. Her father had once or twice brought back seafood for them to eat while he still maintained the form of man. It'd been raw, of course, and not like this cooked meal that she happily ate now.

As Min-Jeong continued down the lane, she heard the shrill notes of flutes accompanied by drums and cymbals. The buildings pulled away from the street into a wide square, and here many people were gathered beneath cherry blossoms dropping white petals from their yawning branches. A stage in the center of the square held female dancers in flowing pink and blue *genjas*, an hourglass *janggu* slung around their shoulders. They beat one end of leather hide of the *janggu* with the mallet shaped *gungchae*, and tapped the other side with the thinner *yeolchae*. They danced in a circle, their pale young faces smiling out at the audience with bright red lips as their feet executed complicated maneuvers on the wooden stage.

Min-Jeong stared, rapt, and swayed to the music. She'd never seen anything like this, never knew humans could create such beauty. The young girls movements seemed so simple and yet with each sudden spin of their bodies, with each dip of their heads, with each tap of the drum, they revealed a skill that had probably taken their whole lives to master. And their faces were so young, like the one she wore now in her human form. Min-Jeong thought of the child who had cried out for this body that she had killed so that she could take its form. Just like the tiger cubs, the child had called the girl *older sister*. What was the life of this human female like before she ended it? Had she seen dances like this out here in this wide square? What had been her talents?

Min-Jeong shook her head. She was a tiger, and tigers killed humans to eat, just as humans killed this creature she ate now on a stick. All animals had language, and though Min-Jeong did not understand most of the words, she knew they existed in realities of their own just as special as man's world. Even the trees and flowers spoke a complex language to each other, their words floating on the wind over long distances.

This body she had taken as her own was simply who Min-Jeong was. Nature had given her the ability to transform, and had devised the way in which the power would be activated. She tore the rest of the cooked seafood off of the stick, chewed the rubbery flesh, and swallowed.

"You look like you're enjoying yourself."

Min-Jeong turned to the man speaking to her. He wore a blue *durumagi* with long almond colored sleeves draping his arms. A thin, bamboo *gat* perched on his head, the cylindrical, wide brimmed hat darkened to a coal black. His face was smooth, his eyes gentle, and a slight smile curved his lips. He carried a bamboo fan, spread wide, which he used to cool himself in the closely packed crowd of people gathered around the performance. An image of tigers poised to leap among white roses had been painted over the fan leaves. With a snap of his wrist, the man closed it, encasing the image in the fan's black, bamboo ribs.

The way he stared at Min-Jeong made her self-conscious. The jacket and pants he wore were finely made, and she reached out and fingered the silk material of the sleeve. She'd never touched anything softer, and suddenly she wanted it, wanted to wear something as wonderful as this outfit. But this square had too many humans. She would have to get this handsome man alone, and would have to kill him in such a way that his blood did not splatter the nice blue and almond colors.

She had chosen this girl because she seemed so pretty. Now, as the stranger smiled down at her, Min-Jeong wondered if he also found this slim body pleasant to look upon. In the hunters clothes she had stolen, and in this tight cap she wore on her head, she wondered if he even knew she was female.

Min-Jeong reached up a tentative hand and pulled the cap from her head. Long black hair, now free, tumbled down her face and shoulders to her back. The man's eyes opened slightly, and his smile widened.

"I thought I saw a beautiful face from the distance, but now I know it's so," he said in a soft voice. He bowed. "Please, allow me to introduce myself. My name is Hong Ji Ju. It is a pleasure to meet you."

Her skin warmed at the formal introduction. Is this how all human men talked to girls?

"I'm Jung Min-Jeong," she said quietly, and bowed.

"Do you come to the city often?"

Min-Jeong shook her head. "Not often, no." She looked around the crowded square. "It's so busy here. So many things to see. So many foods to eat."

"Are you still hungry? That squid was so small." He motioned to the bare stick. "I would love to treat you to a better meal."

Squid? Min-Jeong had it once when her father had brought it up the mountain. It had been raw and translucent with big black eyes. The meat on the stick had appeared nothing like that.

"Come," the man said. "My favorite eatery is just down that way."

Min-Jeong nodded, and walking side by side, they moved through the thick crowd of people. Their shoulders, often touching, warmed her each time. Her slender companion walked with a graceful stride down the dirt lane. People parted for him so that they got through easier. Min-Jeong wondered if he was someone important. Her father had told her about men like him, and how Gangneung's citizens respected government officials who held so much power with the stroke of the pen.

If only her mom could see her now. What would she think of her daughter walking with a handsome young human of importance? Her father had many female conquests among the humans. He even fathered kids with them, but her mom said they usually lived short lives. They had the blood of tigers but none of their speed or strength. They broke the law, fought, and died violent deaths.

Min-Jeong wondered what it would be like to sleep with a human male. What would it feel like to be on her back instead of four legs, for her legs to be spread and the man between them instead of behind her, panting and thrusting. She glanced up at Ji Ju and saw him staring down at her. Quickly she looked away, her face flushing.

Ji Ju led her to a squat woman with a shawl covering her hair. She stood behind a wooden stall, a big pot to her left. Around her were smaller pots, and on the counter were heavy black bowls. She bowed to Ji Ju and said, "My lord."

Ji Ju raised two fingers. "Grandmother, *o-jing-eo deop bap*, please."

The woman nodded, and set two bowls before them. She lifted the lid, scooped out ladles of white rice, and then scooped out round rolls of flesh covered in a bright red sauce that she placed on the side of the rice. Ji Ju dropped a bronze coin on the counter, and handed Min-Jeong one of the bowls. Min-Jeong held it with one hand and began to scoop the rice out with the other, but it was hot and scalded her fingers.

The woman behind the stall laughed.

"It's okay," Ji Ju said. Bringing her fingers to his lips, he blew on the burns, his breath cool and pleasant. When he released her, a sigh of disappointment escaped her.

"The spoon is easier to eat this with," he said, and handed her one.

She only looked at it, unsure how she should properly use it. She watched Ji Ju mix the food thoroughly, and she did the same. Then she spooned it into her mouth, and tears immediately formed in her eyes as the spicy red sauce bit into her tongue. The old woman reached for a metal container, poured water into a battered tin cup, and handed it to Min-Jeong.

"You never had it before?" she asked, and Min-Jeong shook her head.

"Will it be okay for you to eat?"

Min-Jeong was unsure. She tried it again, and the sharp sting assaulted her tongue and quickly rose up her throat into her nose. Ji Ju did not seem to be having a problem with it as he ate, and not wanting to disappoint him, she spooned more of the spicy food into her mouth and chewed. By the fourth spoonful, a light sweat had broken out on her forehead, and the old woman behind the counter handed her a stained towel.

"What are your plans for the evening?" Ji Ju asked her.

Min-Jeong shrugged. "I have none. I'm just in the city to play."

Ji Ju nodded. "This is what I thought. Then I would like to extend you an invitation. There is a social gathering happening in a treasury official's estate. All of the most powerful *yangbang* will be there enjoying themselves on food and alcohol. There will already be young girls to serve as companions for the men, but it would make me happy if you accompany me to the event." Ji Ju touched his heart. "I have been to these gatherings before, and none of the girls will be as beautiful as you."

Min-Jeong swallowed the last of the *o-jing-eo deop bap* and nodded enthusiastically. "Yes, yes, yes," she said. "I'd really like to go with you."

Ji Ju took her hands in his gentle grasp. "Thank you, Jung Min-Jeong." He held her eyes. "If you would permit me, I would like to rent you a *hanbok* for the occasion. There is a clothing shop nearby that I have heard has very good service. And I think you would enjoy wearing one of the many beautiful *hanbok* available there."

Min-Jeong followed Ji Ju once again. They turned off into one of the narrow alleys, and Min-Jeong and Ji Ju walked a short distance before stopping in front of a small store. A colored painting of a woman in a *hanbok* stood beside the door. Ji Ju knocked gently, and they stepped inside. A woman sitting on a stool poured a dark liquid into a crystal perfume bottle. When she saw them, she hastily set it aside, quickly stood, and bowed.

"You arrived early, my lord," she said.

"We will be going to the dinner meeting," Ji Ju said. "Please, take care of my little sister so that no other may rival her beauty at the gathering."

The woman approached Min-Jeong, who stared at her curiously. She touched Min-Jeong's legs, waist, butt, felt along her stomach and chest, and ran her fingers through her hair. "She is beautiful," she told Ji Ju, "but her outer shell is too rough. She will need time to become a true companion worthy of being at your side tonight.

"Give me one hour, and I will bring out of this coarse exterior the beautiful girl hiding just beneath the surface."

"I will return in an hour." Ji Ju bowed, and left. The woman led Min-Jeong to a bathing room one door over. There, she undid the hunting clothes Min-Jeong wore and ordered her to squat in a small tub. She said nothing about the flecks of dried blood streaking Min-Jeong's pale skin and hiding beneath her fingernails. She grabbed a towel and scented soap, patted her down with water, and began to gently scrub her skin.

Min-Jeong closed her eyes at the woman's ministrations. She cleaned her human body with deft fingers. She massaged her shoulders, back, arms and thighs, so that Min-Jeong made a noise close to purring. Her mom made her feel this way once with her tongue when she was still a cub. The persistent licking often lulled her to sleep. Her mom's fangs could rip apart the toughest flesh, but when she picked up a dozing Min-Jeong to put her in the safety of the den besides her brothers, their grip was soft like feathers. Nothing she'd experience since had felt as good as she did now under this woman's gentle attention.

The woman used more water when washing Min-Jeong's long black hair. It went well past her back when wet, and she added shampoo that smelled of apple and cherries.

"The scents will excite the lord when he draws close to you," the woman assured Min-Jeong. "Part of a girl's appeal is how she tantalizes all of a man's senses. You come from the farms on the outskirts of the city," the woman guessed, "but you are still so young, and your body has yet to be hardened by the spade and sun. Perhaps your parents plan to sell you to the government *kisaeng* schools." She squeezed Min-Jeong's breasts. "You will fetch a fair price, especially after being introduced in the lord's presence tonight.

"I know of this dinner meeting you go to. The men attending are the most powerful in the city, and you will catch many of their eyes. Tonight they will go to sleep dreaming about you." The woman stared closely at Min-Jeong. "There is something about you," she added. "He will not be the only man to gaze upon you in that way tonight. Especially after I'm done with you."

Min-Jeong didn't understand the woman's explanation. Her father had never mentioned the *kisaeng* to her. She did not mind the prospect of staying with Ji Ju for a while, however. He could introduce her to the wonders of the city. He had kind eyes and a handsome face, and as her first guide in the human world, he would be perfect. And when she became tired of him, she would leave him, or kill him, take his form, and learn about the city from the position of a man and a lord.

The woman rinsed Min-Jeong's hair and ushered her out of the tub. She wrapped her in a white cloth and led her back to the *hanbok* shop. While Min-Jeong stood naked before her, she placed the *dari sokgot* between her legs and tied a ribbon at her waist. She helped Min-Jeong put on three additional layers of undergarments before finally taking a bright red *chima* from the closet.

"It is pure silk," the woman assured Min-Jeong, "and delicate to the touch."

The dress opened up in the back, and she slipped it on Min-Jeong and tied it right above her breasts in the front. She took out a *jeogori* with bright orange sleeves, helped Min-Jeong into it, and added a green vest with red roses printed on it to go over the shirt. Min-Jeong slipped on red silk shoes, and when fully clothed, the woman made several adjustments before stepping back and looking Min-Jeong up and down with a critical eye.

"Your transformation is almost complete," she said. "Come."

She instructed her to sit on a stool in front of a counter with small brushes, combs, and round tins. Then she brushed her hair with long, careful strokes, and braided it. She applied heavy white makeup to Min-Jeong's face, mascara to her eyebrows and eyelids, and a bright red lipstick to her lips. They heard a knock at the *hanbok* shop.

"My lord, we are here. Come, please, and see."

Ji Ju stepped into the makeup shop and stopped abruptly upon seeing Min-Jeong. Slowly he exhaled as he stared at her. Then he bowed to the woman.

"You are indeed a master. You have shaped her raw beauty with elegance. I will have many offers from men to spend just moments in her presence at the dinner tonight."

He smiled. "I will be the most popular gentleman with you by my side. Truly, you are the most beautiful creature I have ever seen."

Was she truly so beautiful? She had wanted to play in the in Gangneung City for months, but what if she received too much attention? Tigers entered into the mortal world wearing human skins to blend in, not to stand out. The bath and clothes and makeup had been another shapeshifting, but instead of moving covertly through the mortal world, she may be putting herself further into the spotlight.

Min-Jeong shook her head. *She sounded like her mom!* She would not worry about this, and she would have fun tonight alongside Ji Ju. Her power rivaled any man's, anyway. How many had she killed tonight? Four? Her father claimed this valley between the mountains as his domain, so she, his daughter, was a tiger princess.

When they made to leave, the woman stopped them and picked up the small crystal bottle that Min-Jeong had seen her filling when she first arrived. It had a nozzle topping. "A gift before you go," she told Min-Jeong, and tucked away the bottle with a silk thread in the folds of the *hanbok.*

To Min-Jeong, she said, "This one has a different aroma than the one I already sprayed on you. It's for the night's most special of moments." She gave a knowing smile. "You'll know it when it arrives."

Min-Jeong bowed deeply to the woman and thanked her for her kindness. Then she followed Ji Ju out of the store. He would not allow her to walk on the dirt lane winding through the alleys in her new shoes. He ordered a child running past them to fetch two palanquins. Minutes later, wooden *gamas* rounded the corner, colorful ribbons hanging from their blue roofs. Two men wearing black hats and black vests over white shirts carried each palanquin. They stopped the litters in front of Ji Ju, who turned and helped Min-Jeong into the first one. He got into the second and gave the men directions to the dinner meeting. They lifted the carriage to their shoulders and quickly made their way through the narrow alleys back to the main lane running through Gangneung City.

The people in the densely packed street pushed each other aside to allow the porters to progress down the street. Many looked into the carriage in curiosity, and gasped when they saw Min-Jeong in all of her finery.

"Who is she?"

"There is no one as pretty in all of Gangneung."

"Any lord who has her as a companion tonight will indeed be a fortunate man."

Min-Jeong blushed, and averted her eyes from so many gazing at her. Finally, they arrived at the stone gates of a wide pavilion with red and yellow walls and a black steeple roof. The porters gently lowered the *gama*, and Ji Ju got out first to help Min-Jeong to her feet.

"We are here," he said, and waved his arm with an elaborate flourish. From behind the gate, Min-Jeong heard the lighter notes of *tungso* flitting through the stringed melodies of *ajaeng* and the sudden taps of the *janggu*. The guards flanking the gate wore long red overcoats and pants with black leather boots. They each held a *woldo* in their right hand, the polearm topped with a wicked curved blade. At their sides were strapped *hwandos* in black scabbards.

As Min-Jeong approached the guards, she noticed a strange scent in the air, and sniffed to identify it. The odor came from the weapons, and her nose suddenly twitching, she sneezed. The guards' eyes focused on her, and she smiled, but the curve of her lips felt awkward on her face.

"My lord," the guard said, "your guest tonight is only one?"

Ji Ju nodded. "But there are others in my party who may have already arrived."

The guard nodded. "As you know, security is tighter because the Jeonha of the North is believed to be plotting against us, and with so many high officials here we are all on the highest alert."

The guard trained his eyes directly on Min-Jeong.

"Tonight, only Gangneung citizens will be allowed inside. Does your young companion have official papers declaring her citizenship?"

"Of course," Ji Ju said, and removed a parchment from the inner folds of his blue *durumagi*. The same scent came from the letter, and Min-Jeong watched closely as Ji Ju handed it to the guard.

When had he gotten papers to allow her to enter the dinner meeting, she wondered. She blinked several times, her breath catching in her throat. The black script swirled in a continuous, hypnotic motion on the tan page. Min-Jeong glanced away, but when she looked back, the words continued their strange dance. She could not read, and her father had told her that writing was rare in the mortal world. But were the spindly characters supposed to move in that strange manner?

She looked at the guard to see if he was surprised by what took place in front of his eyes, but he showed no reaction. He only nodded, handed the parchment back to Ji Ju, and bowed.

The guards stepped aside, and Ji Ju led Min-Jeong through the gates. In the courtyard, cherry blossoms dropped white petals to create a soft carpet on the ground. Young women in yellow and pink *hanboks* played the music Min-Jeong had heard earlier, their heads bowed over the instruments, their faces pale and serene in the darkness. Men in silk *hanboks* covering a wide hue of colors gathered around and watched. Many of them wore *gats* similar to Ji Ju's, the bamboo top hats all black but varying in cylindrical lengths and brims.

As Ji Ju and Min-Jeong walked through the courtyard, one man glanced up and noticed Min-Jeong. He nudged his companion, who turned to look at her also. This man emitted a short gasp that caught the attention of the others. Soon they were all gazing at Min-Jeong, their eyes wide and full of admiration. Min-Jeong's lips pulled back from her teeth at so many stares directed at her. The unwanted attention brought her mom to mind.

Silly little girl, her mother's voice said in her head, *you have no idea what you're getting into. Come back to the forests and the mountains in your true form before it's too late.*

Then an image of her father blossomed in her thoughts. Wild and carefree, full of tales and experiences. Her father claimed the city and surrounding mountains as his domain. He was afraid of nothing, so why should she be?

Silly little girl, her mom's voice repeated in her head before fading away into silence.

When they reached the pavilion, another set of sentinels stood at the door. They wore blue overcoats with long white sleeves. They only had a *kal* in black scabbards at their waist that did not carry the same scent as the weapons the other guards wore. But Min-Jeong spied the narrow handle of a small handgun tucked into the sentries' belts. As before, they inquired about Min-Jeong's citizenship papers, which Ji Ju produced. She watched the words swirl hypnotically, and the sentry handed the parchment back to Ji Ju and bowed as he opened the door to allow them to enter the pavilion.

As soon as Min-Jeong stepped inside, she heard a booming laughter roll over the din of voices and music. The laughter was so loud and so full of mirth that she immediately looked to discover its source.

The pavilion's main room had four long rows of low tables. Men sat on embroidered cushions in front of platters of boiled meats and small bowls of side dishes. Green bottles of *soju* dotted the tables. Min-Jeong's father often brought the liquor with him to drink in the mountains, as well as *makeolli*, which Min-Jeong also saw on the tables in tin kettles. The men poured the rice wine into wide wooden bowls, a practice she'd never seen her father do since he drank it straight from the bottle.

Another clap of laughter rolled over the room, and Min-Jeong saw it spilled from a stout man in a bright yellow *gwanbok*. He sat at an elaborate wooden table, on a slightly raised dais at the head of the room. Two other men sat on either side of the table, and they poured his drinks when his cup emptied, and spoke with animated gestures causing him to laugh yet again. The *gat* he wore was different from the others, being rounded instead of cyclical, with flaps on the sides draping towards his ears. Personal guards in black armor stood at attention behind him. A red plume draped down the backs of their black helmets, and they clutched *kals* as their eyes roved across the officials dining in front of them.

"Some of my colleagues are seated nearby," Ji Ju said to Min-Jeong. "Follow me this way."

Min-Jeong nodded, and when she glanced at the stout man on the dais again, she saw he stared directly at her, a wide smile on his fleshy jowls.

Ji Ju led Min-Jeong to three men who paused in their conversation as Min-Jeon approached. They seemed quite older than Ji Ju. Whereas he had a slender body with a clean-shaven face, the three men had thicker waists and mustaches. One also had a beard neatly trimmed in a triangular shape. They wore different colored *hanboks* and black gats similar to Ji Ju's, and they pulled from long pipes that sent gray smoke curling into the air above their heads.

"Seniors," Ji Ju said with a deep bow. "It is an honor to see you here tonight."

"You've finally arrived," the bearded man said. "And you've brought the rarest of flowers as your companion." He puffed on his pipe, and expelled a funnel of fragrant smoke from between his lips.

"What is your name?" he asked her.

"Jung Min-Jeong." She bowed.

"How old are you?"

Min-Jeong hesitated. Someone asking her that question hadn't occurred to her, and she was unsure what age this female body should be. "Thirteen years old," she said.

He nodded in approval. "She is still in bloom," he said. "And no *kisaeng* here is as beautiful."

"You've done well," one of the other men said.

Ji Ju bowed. "Thank you, seniors."

"Sit down," the bearded man instructed them. Ji Ju helped Min-Jeong to a cushion, and sat down beside her. Only a handful of girls sat at the tables beside their companions, and the men at the surrounding tables all turned to stare at Min-Jeong. Her lips pulled back from her teeth again in a strained smile at their attention. The nearness of bodies and the four walls made the room feel too much like a cage despite its size.

The bearded man indicated the food on the table. "Eat your fill," he told her. "It's very delicious."

Min-Jeong looked at the assortment of side dishes surrounding a larger platter of boiled pork. She'd consumed more today than she normally ate up on the mountain where she had to share with her little brothers. The cubs had voracious appetites, and her mom made sure they got the lion's share of the meal. But today, Min-Jeong had eaten the flesh of humans as well as the food of humans, and despite the pleasant smell drifting from the boiled pork, she was not interested in sampling it.

"Here," Ji Ju said. "Try this."

He placed a wooden bowl in front of her, swirled the makgeolli in the bronze kettle, and poured it for her. Min-Jeong raised it to her lips and sniffed before tasting the sweet rice wine. It went down smoothly, and Min-Jeong's eyes opened wide in delight. She quickly emptied her bowl, and blinked several times as her head suddenly felt as if it would float off of her shoulders to the ceiling high above her.

The old men at the table laughed, and Ji Ju poured her another bowl before pouring one for himself. "Drink this one a little slower," he told her. "Makgeolli's sweet taste is both a blessing and a curse."

This time, she waited for Ji Ju to take a sip from his before she brought it to her lips. Her earlier apprehension had disappeared, and now the hall full of men, many of whom still gazed at her with open interest, seemed more inviting.

"She's the *kisaeng* of the evening," the bearded man said. "Everyone here will inquire about her services before the night is over."

Min-Jeong was unsure what he meant by that, but the makgeolli made her more bold, and she felt more like her father's daughter. She realized that she had gotten lucky in killing a young girl who was so attractive, and finding someone equally beautiful might be more difficult next time. Now she wanted to hold on to this female body for as long as possible.

"She's even caught the eye of Kim Sae Jun *Jeonha*, the seller of dragons," the other man at the table said with a nod in the direction of the dais. "He has not taken his eyes off of her in some time."

Min-Jeong turned to the stout man with the thunderous laugh. Indeed, he too stared at her, a pleasant smile curving his thick lips. He leaned over and spoke to one of the retainers sitting beside him. This man turned to Min-Jeong, nodded, and stood.

"And now it begins," the bearded man said to Ji Ju.

The retainer approached them, a strange twinkle in his dark eyes. By the time he arrived to the table, a blank, polite mask had replaced his bemused expression. The three older men and Ji Ju stood and bowed low to the retainer. Min-Jeong gained her feet a moment after the others, and offered a similar deep bow of her head.

"Gentlemen," the retainer said, "it would please Kim Sae Jun *Jeonha* greatly if he could have the company of your *kisaeng* for a short time. He has promised not to delay her for too long, but he would like to offer a toast to her incredible beauty."

"We would be honored," the bearded man said. "We will send her along in a moment after we educate her on the proper etiquette in the *Jeonha's* presence."

"What is her name so that I may inform Kim Sae Jun *Jeonha*?"

"Jung Min-Jeong," the bearded man replied.

"Thank you," the retainer said with a bow. "We look forward to her arrival."

When he left, they all sat down again.

"Min-Jeong," Ji Ju said, "Kim Sae Jun *Jeonha* is a very important man. He is the deposed brother of *Jeonha* of the North who threatens South Han with dragon fire."

Min-Jeong sat back, surprised. She glanced at the stout man on the dais again, who was listening to the retainer who had arrived back to his side. Opening his mouth, he issued another laugh that reverberated through the pavilion, and he clapped the man on his back.

"He is nothing like his brother," Ji Ju said, "but he has made many Western allies who will sell South Han dragons to match the might of North Han."

"Or at least, that is the rumor," the bearded man said, and inhaled deeply from his long pipe.

Ji Ju nodded. "There is much gossip these days," he agreed, "and picking through the tales for the truth isn't always as easy as it seems. It's said that currently there are plots underway to remove the *Jeonha* of the North from his throne and insert his brother in his place so that the two halves of this land will be reunited again."

Another bellow of laughter erupted from the *Jeonha*, and Ji Ju smiled.

"As I said, he's nothing like his brother. Kim Sae Jun *Jeonha* is a kind man who loves to laugh. He is renowned for enjoying practical jokes. It is why he's a perfect diplomat. He puts everyone he speaks with at immediate ease."

"He will be a great *Jeonha*," the old man at the table said.

Ji Ju touched Min-Jeong's hand. "It would please us greatly if you played a small joke on Kim Sae Jun *Jeonha* so that he will always remember us. What do you think? Are you up for the task?"

The idea made Min-Jeong giggle. "What should I do?" she asked the older men staring at her smoking their pipes.

Ji Ju tapped the perfume bottle secreted away in her *hanbok*. "Spray a little of this on him," he said, "so that he will smell like a *kisaeng* for the rest of the night. He'll find that very amusing."

Min-Jeong touched the crystal bottle in the folds of her *hanbok*. The woman at the shop hadn't sprayed this perfume on her, so she did not know what it smelled like. And even though she'd been called a *kisaeng* throughout the evening, she still did not fully grasp the word.

It didn't matter. A practical joke would be fun to play. She and her siblings used to play tricks on each other all the time when they were cubs. It was a way to sharpen their critical thinking skills and kill the hours when their mother left them to go hunting. Min-Jeong knew she could execute this act today on the *Jeonha* flawlessly.

She stood, smoothed out her *hanbok*, and walked towards the dais. Voices lowered as she passed tables. Men whispered questions to each other about her. The musicians began a faster song and Min-Jeong's heartbeat picked up along with the upbeat tempo. A large smile split Kim Sae Jun *Jeonha's* broad face. He patted his lap with fat fingers as she neared him. When she stood before him, Min-Jeong tilted her head shyly and the *Jeonha* roared with laughter.

"Forgive me, but there is nowhere else for you to sit but here." He patted his lap again and winked. "But don't worry, all of the diners will be witness so that your virtue remains preserved. For now."

Min-Jeong went closer to him but maintained a girlish reluctance. With another roar of laughter, the *Jeonha* reached over, took her by the waist, and pulled her to him. He lifted her up and sat her on his meaty thigh. "Such a small little thing," he said, bouncing her on his leg.

"Kim Sae Jun *Jeonha*!" she exclaimed. "You will make me fall into your dinner."

"And that will make it all the easier to eat you," he said. Another laugh bellowed from his red lips. "But I will not let you leave this perch so quickly. It's rare to have someone so lovely as you in my company, and I have known the pleasure of many *kisaeng*. None were as beautiful as you."

Min-Jeong covered a coy smile with one hand and placed her other over the crystal bottle tucked in her *hanbok*. "Kim Sae Jun *Jeonha*," she said, batting her lashes, "should we have a toast to your health?"

"Yes," the Jeonha said. He reached over and grabbed a tall dark bottle. "It's sake from the Land of the Rising Sun. I'm sure a rare brew such as this has never touched your lips before."

He poured the liquor into two glass cups so that the sake spilled over the sides into the small wooden boxes they sat in. Min-Jeong laughed with delight.

"It is too much," she said.

The *Jeonha* shook his head. "It's just the right amount," he replied. "Today you drink with the future *Jeonha* of North Han! And you, Jung Min-Jeong, the most lovely *kisaeng* ever to grace my vision, will always be free to play in my court as the *Jeonha's* companion. You will become a legend."

He handed her a glass, took his own, and raised it up into the air. Min-Jeong followed suit, but before they drank the sake, she swiftly freed the crystal perfume. With a laugh she said, "So that you'll remember me until next we meet, Kim Sae Jun *Jeonha*." She pressed the nozzle. Spray shot forth from the bottle in a fine mist into his face. Some of the mist wafted back into her nose, and Min-Jeong immediately doubled over.

Something wasn't right.

She heard both sake cups fall to the floor, the glass shattering. Min-Jeong slipped off the Kim Sae Jun *Jeonha's* lap to her knees as she gasped for air in a throat that had quickly become constricted. She opened her mouth to vomit, but nothing came out. She heard a commotion and glanced at the *Jeonha*. He too was doubled over, his face bright red, his mouth open in a large O, his eyes wide. The retainers at his sides had leapt to their feet and now held up the *Jeonha's* massive bulk. When he started to violently convulse, his thick limbs threw them from him.

The contents of the crystal perfume seemed swift and deadly. Min-Jeong realized that even though she had only inhaled a little, she would probably be in the same state as the *Jeonha* if it wasn't for her unnatural healing. Even now she felt the poison flushing from her system through her sweat. Opening her mouth wide, she desperately gulped down wonderful air. Finally she was able to vomit, and she threw up the food she'd eaten today, the digested brew of raw flesh and blood splattering the floor in front of the dais.

"The *Jeonha's* assassin is there. Arrest her!"

"Who were the men she was with? There, arrest them, too!"

Min-Jeong looked towards the table where Ji Ju sat. They had all stood, and the three old men suddenly released a cloud of gray smoke from their pursed lips as the guards rushed them. The guards screamed as their red coats went up in flames. Officials sitting around them jumped from their cushions and scattered to escape the expanding cloud and flailing guards.

Rough hands grabbed Min-Jeong and yanked her to her feet to face the sentinel who had been standing behind Kim Sae Jun *Jeonha*. The man's eyes were hard, dangerous, and he held a short sword to her throat that had the same peculiar smell she'd noticed on the other weapons. Attendants surrounded the *Jeonha*, but he no longer moved. Even without being close to him, Min-Jeong knew he had died.

"Who are you?" the guard barked at her. He pressed the sword against her throat, and a sudden burn made her hiss as the tip pierced her skin. Tears of pain filled her eyes, and her heart thudded with fear. Death lurked in the bright sheen of this magical blade.

The attendant with the strange twinkle in his eyes stood. He stared at her, a curious smile revealing his sharp teeth. With a shrug, he lashed out at the guard with a powerful blow, his hands growing claws right before it connected with the man to tear out the side of his face.

The guard holding Min-Jeong quickly spun her to the floor as he faced this new danger. He whipped out his sword, but the attendant was faster, and with two quick strikes he opened the man's jugular and almost decapitated him. Min-Jeong stared at him in shock, but the attendant grabbed her with hands covered with blood.

"We don't have time for questions." He yanked her towards the gray smoke that was just beginning to clear. He dove into the chaotic hustle of bodies as the officials ran around without any clear sense of which way the dangers laid. The attendant made use of that, and deftly slipped through them in his escape. More guards poured into the pavilion to shut off the exits, which only increased the panic of the officials.

The attendant pulled Min-Jeong into a hallway. They only took several steps before a guard appeared in front of them.

"I'm sorry, but no one can leave," he informed them, and drew his *hwando*.

"No apologies are necessary," the attendant replied and leapt at the man. He twisted just as the guard swiped out at him, and a splatter of blood slapped against the wall as the blade caught him across the chest. The attendant, gritting his teeth, emitted only a quiet growl.

The smell of magic drifted from the *hwando*. Min-Jeong swallowed as she steeled her courage and darted forward. She kept her eye on the blade and tried to dodge it as it whistled at her. The guard changed direction at the last moment, and it was only the attendant knocking her from her feet that kept the blade from biting into her neck. Instead, it sank into her shoulder, and she let out a massive roar of pain.

Desperation filled the attendant's face. Cursing, he transformed, the top half of his body growing orange and black hair as his clothes ripped away from the muscles filling his frame. Fear filled the guard's eyes at the beast bearing upon him, but he held his ground and stabbed forward again as the weretiger lunged for his throat. The blade slid into the beast's chest as its fangs ripped open the guard's jugular, and both of them crashed into the wall and crumpled to the ground.

Min-Jeong rushed forward. "Daddy!"

Her father tried to rise, but collapsed on his side to keep the *hwando* from plunging farther into his chest. Labored breath rattled in his massive body, and with great effort, he lifted his tiger head to look at Min-Jeong. When she tried to wrap her arms around him, tears streaming down her face, he knocked her away with his forehead.

"No time for tears," he growled at her, still able to speak in this partial form. "We're creatures of stealth. Remember that. Keep your head down, get out of here, and live to fight another day."

Blood dribbled from his mouth down his glossy coat. When she reached for him again, he nipped her with the tips of his teeth, breaking her skin. She drew back with a startled hiss.

"You fool, you hear the boots coming! But if the only way you'll get moving is if I do this, then so be it."

Her father lifted himself, then fell heavily, and the rest of the *hwando* plunged into his chest to its hilt. Just then, the door flew open, and a guard rushed into the hallway. He stopped abruptly at the sight of the massive weretiger, and he looked at Min-Jeong in confusion.

"What happened?" he asked her, his sword drawn and pointed at her father. "How did *that* get in here?"

"It attacked me," Min-Jeong said, "and that guard there fought the monster." She held out a shaking hand, her tears falling freely down her face. "Please, help me."

The guard nodded and reached out his hand to her. She grabbed it and extended her claws into his flesh. He opened his mouth to scream, but before he could issue a cry, she leapt on him, placed her lips to his lips, fastened her teeth on his tongue, jerked her head back, and ripped his tongue from his mouth. Red-hot anger flooded Min-Jeong, and swallowing his tongue, she plunged her claws into both sides of his chest. His ribs broke from the force of her attack. She ripped his heart from his chest, stuffed it into her mouth, chewed the tough muscles, and swallowed it almost whole. She had never done the ritual backwards, and hoped that it would not make a difference. She bent over him and ripped the skin from his face. She did this quickly, and to her relief, felt the soft curves of her body harden. Her breasts smoothed into her chest as the male organ blossomed between her legs. She tore off her *hanbok* and used it to wipe the blood from her face. Then she went to the guard her father had killed. His red overcoat hid some of the bloodstains splattering it, so she quickly stripped him and changed into his clothes. Min-Jeong did not know how many more humans she would have to kill tonight, but she knew who would be the last one to die.

Hong Ji Ju.

Min-Jeong crouched next to her father one last time. She buried her male nose into his fur and inhaled deeply. The familiar scent brought back memories of his visits to their den. Her father was an adventurer, a wanderer, but also a talker, and she cherished every word she'd eagerly listened to over the two years of her life. The humans had snuffed out a vibrant spirit, and she promised to make them suffer for that.

She went down the hallway in the opposite direction of the dining hall, opened the door, and stepped into the next room. Several guards stepped in from outside at the same time. They looked up at her as she entered, and gave her a slight bow, which she returned.

"We just received new orders from the captain of the grounds," he said. "The pavilion's been secured, but there's been no sighting of the *kisaeng* or the infiltrators she came here with."

Another guard interrupted him with a curse. "They're probably on the road back to North Han by now," he muttered. "That's where we should be. We're wasting our time here."

The first guard to speak shrugged. "The captain of the grounds isn't ready to admit that he let not one, but four assassins escape the house."

"Assassins who are magic users," the other said in a quiet voice. He glanced suspiciously over his shoulder. "They can get in and out of anywhere. That's why they were sent here to kill the *Jeonha*."

Tears filled the man's eyes, and he angrily blinked them away.

The first guard put his hand on his shoulder and nodded. "A good man has died. It is a sad day for South Han," he conceded. "Nevertheless, orders are orders." He looked at Min-Jeong. "Come, we're not to stop searching the grounds, even if it's fruitless at this point. Let's return to the main gate."

Min-Jeong nodded. She followed the men out into the night. The heady fragrance of cherry blossoms filled the spring air. She inhaled the earthy smell of the courtyard. She felt like she'd been in the rooms of man for weeks instead of hours, and she missed the green and brown smell of nature. She cast her eyes up to the shadowy mountains surrounding Gangneung City. She longed for the safety of the den as she walked besides these heavily armed guards.

Min-Jeong began a partial transformation in her legs as they neared the pavilion's perimeter. She tried to mask her changing gait so that the guards would not notice. When they reached the gate and the men spun on their heels to follow the path to the northern part of the courtyard, she leapt silently. The breeze whispered across her face, and she landed on a low roof across the main lane opposite the pavilion. Without pausing, she leapt again, and again. Finally, she paused and turned, letting out a breath that she hadn't realized she was holding. She could still see the steeple roof of the pavilion, the stone *giwa* rising high above the white cherry blossoms filling the courtyard. The voices of the guards carried in the night, but they did not change direction towards her. After several minutes she figured that she escaped unnoticed.

So they thought Hong Ji Ju and his three companions would be heading back to North Han? Min-Jeong had to discover if this was true, and there was one person in-particular who might have the answer to that question.

Dropping to the muddy ground, Min-Jeong quickly walked through the alley back to the main road running through the center of Gangneung. The night had gotten late, but people still filled the wide lane, and the stalls running along the side of the road bustled with customers. People glanced at her as she passed them by, and she heard excited whispers about a conflict that had broken out amongst the *yangban* in the pavilion's dinner event that evening. She didn't see other guards in red overcoats, and realized that most of the city forces must be at the pavilion following the orders of a captain who refused to admit that the assassins had slipped through his fingers.

When Min-Jeong once again saw the woman with the big black pot who sold her the *O-jing-eo deop bap*, she began to turn down the alley next to the wooden stall. The squat woman, her shawl wrapped tightly around her gray hair, called out to her.

"Soldier, just a moment. Are the rumors true?" she asked. "Has the seller of dragons been killed? Is Kim Sae Jun *Jeonha* dead?"

Other heads turned to Min-Jeong to hear her answer. She paused in the dim light of the mouth of the alley. "Yes," she said. "The *Jeonha* is dead."

The woman beat her chest with her calloused hands. "Now nothing will stop the North Han *Jusang Jeonha* from unleashing his dragons upon us all!"

Around her, murmurs of despair spread through the people gathered on the city street. Min-Jeong ducked into the shadows to avoid more questions. Soon she stood in front of the painting of the *hanbok*. An oil lantern had been lit to show that the shop was still open. The proprietor sat on a stool in front of a workbench, a long silver needle in her hand as she worked on a long bolt of cloth draped over the table.

Min-Jeong knocked gently on the door. The woman placed the long needle in a tray filled with needles and stood. When she saw Min-Jeong in the body of a guard in a deep red overcoat, she frowned. "May I help you find something, sir?"

Min-Jeong nodded. "*Ajumma*, may I come in? I have important matters to discuss with you about my coming wedding."

The woman looked past Min-Jeong. "Is your fiancée with you?" She focused on Min-Jeong again. "A man in official garb coming late at night to discuss wedding plans is indeed unusual."

Min-Jeong placed her hands on the door handle and pulled it open. The *hwando* tapped against the doorframe and the helmet scrapped against the low ceiling as she stepped into the small shop. This big body she wore filled the room so that only a handful of centimeters separated her from the woman.

"I am sorry to bother you so late," Min-Jeong said. "I will be married next week, and am in a rush."

The woman's eyes opened wide, and she laughed. "Next week! It is too soon. And until I speak to your wife, I will not be able to suggest matching *hanboks* for your special day."

Min-Jeong nodded. "My fiancée lost her father today and is in mourning." Fresh tears filled her eyes, and she blinked them away. "He was the light of her life, and now all she sees is darkness."

"That is indeed sad news," the woman said softly. "I will be gentle with her, but first she must come out, and then we can talk."

"Must she?" Min-Jeong nodded. "Then she will come out."

Min-Jeong's teeth sharpened to fangs so fast that they ripped apart her gums with a loud tearing. The woman gasped as Min-Jeong leapt at her. The woman clapped her hands and spoke a word. The long sewing needles erupted from the tray and impaled themselves into Min-Jeong's exposed flesh. She managed to adjust her trajectory so that the needles only slammed into the left side of her face, the longest of which impaled her eye with a soft plop.

Min-Jeong bit back the howl of pain that threatened to erupt from her as the vision in that eye went dark. *We're creatures of stealth,* her father had warned her in his final breath, and she planned on being the quietest of killers tonight.

Ignoring the pain radiating like pinpoints of fire through her body, she launched forward again. The short distance prevented the woman from casting another spell, and Min-Jeong wrapped a clawed hand around her throat and slammed her back against her wall. The woman opened her mouth to scream, but Min-Jeong tightened her grip, and the cry came out as strangled gasps from her lips.

"Where is he?" Min-Jeong hissed. She towered over the woman in this male form. The blood from her wounds and punctured eye dripped onto the woman's forehead and down her cheeks in steady rivulets. She loosened her grasp slightly so the woman could answer, but when a high-pitched scream issued forth, Min-Jeong tightened her fingers again, her claws digging into the woman's flesh.

"I'll snap your neck now if you try that again," she warned her. "Is Hong Ji Ju already on the road? Is he already headed to North Han?"

The woman's eyes widened further as her face increasingly turned pale blue. Min-Jeong came even closer until their noses touched. Ever so slightly, she loosened her hand around the woman's throat.

"Yes!" She gasped.

That was all she needed. They couldn't have gotten far in such a short amount of time. Now it was time to take a new form.

Min-Jeong slammed her free hand through the woman's chest and ripped out her heart as the woman convulsed against her. Quickly she consumed the leathery muscle, then ripped the skin off of the woman's face and swallowed the bloody pulp. After the transformation, she went to the shop next door, found water, and washed the blood away. She put on the simpliest *hanbok* she could find and left the building to hunt Ji Ju.

Min-Jeong stepped outside and saw several children staring at her from the windows of a building across the street. She placed her finger to her lips, and walked down the twisting alleys back to the main lane running through Gangneung. She started towards the main gate along with a steady stream of people finally leaving the city. When she reached the exit, she saw more guards silhouetted against the moonlight. They walked the battlements surrounding the city, their hands on the hilts of their weapons. She drifted close to the largest group of people going through the gate and kept her gaze on the ground. She felt eyes hot on her, though she did not know if this was her imagination or not. Ultimately, it didn't matter, for no one approached her, and she once again walked down the path leading through the forests of Gangwon-do Province to North Han.

Min-Jeong allowed distance to grow between her and the group she'd been shadowing, and when she was confident no one was keeping track of her, she slipped into the trees. Immediately, the sense of belonging overtook her, and she laid her hands on rough bark and inhaled the strong aroma of green leaves and fresh dirt. Min-Jeong would have liked nothing more than to transform back into her tiger form and roll around in the forest undergrowth. She wanted to splash her paws in a stream, wanted to run down a hill and leap into the air to feel the wind whip across her face and whiskers.

She missed home, but the den would never be the same. Her mother would be there waiting for her, and even her brothers whom, at this moment, she found herself also missing. But her father was dead, a magic blade through his chest. Even though the *hwando* had not struck her that fatal blow, she'd been deeply wounded all the same, and she bled in the form of tears that once again flooded her eyes. There could only be one salve that would lessen the pain of her wound: murder.

Min-Jeong kept to the cover of darkness beneath the trees as she followed the road north. She applied a slight shift to her eyes so that they could take in more light from the crescent moon and bright stars filling the sky. Her vision sharpened, and she moved swiftly through the darkness in search of her prey.

She found Ji Ju's party in less than an hour. Ji Ju had changed into a velvet colored *hanbok*, a dark *magoja* with long, puffy sleeves, and a tall black *gat* with a wider rim on his head. The three old men still wore the same *hanboks*, and they smoked their pipes as they walked. None of them bore visible weapons, though a short *kal* could be tucked away beneath their *hanboks*. She followed them on silent feet in the underbrush and waited for an opportunity to present itself.

One of the older men drifted to a tree and undid his pants to go to the bathroom. His companions slowed their pace but did not stop. Min-Jeong quickly scaled an adjacent tree, leapt to the branches high above the man, took a deep, steady breath, and dropped on top of him. She landed on his back, her hand instantly going around his mouth, her claws sinking into cheek and jaw.

The man uttered a muffled cry, but before he could do more, she sank her canines into his throat and jerked her head back, ripping through his jugular. With her other hand, she punched through his spine, grabbed his heart, and tore it out of him. Quickly she consumed it, then flayed the flesh from the man's face, stuffed it into her mouth, and swallowed down the pulpy skin.

By then, Ji Ju had stopped to turn and look back in her direction. "Older brother," he called out into the darkness, "are you done yet? We must make haste."

Min-Jeong looked at Ji Ju through the undergrowth as the transformation twisted her body.

She could not answer yet as she did not know how her voice would sound in the middle of the change.

Now the other two men stopped and joined Ji Ju.

"Lee Jae Young," the one with the beard said, "you're getting too old for these missions with the way your bladder runs."

"I'm okay," Min-Jeong said, the transformation complete. She wiped the blood from her face with the *hanbok*, but the shirt and jacket the man had been wearing were ruined. She would only have his pants to wear.

Min-Jeong looked through the leaves and saw Ji Ju and the remaining two men exchange glances.

"Older brother." Ji Ju approached the stand of trees Min-Jeong hid under. His hand pushed back his *magoja* and he clasped the hilt of a *kal* tucked into his *hanbok*.

"Remind me again what pass we will turn off on to reach Pyongyang."

"The pass?" Min-Jeong narrowed her eyes as she tried to recall every detail her father had told her of his journey into North Han. But he not been going to Pyongyang, had he? Weren't the dragons stationed near the demilitarized zone separating the two Hans?

Ji Ju approached her head on, while the two men split up, approaching her from the left and right. They must be aware of a deception, which would make killing them so much more difficult. A voice in her head sounding exactly like mother told her to retreat, to run up the mountainside to the nearby den and safety. But if she fled, Ji Ju would live. *No!* Min-Jeong could not allow that to happen, would not allow that to pass.

Hong Ji Ju would die tonight!

Sizing the three men up, Min-Jeong decided to take out the weakest one first. The bearded man smoking his pipe would probably be the strongest of the group and therefore best to be avoided until last. Ji Ju was slender like a reed, but there was something in his confidence, in the way he'd tricked her so casually that made her cautious of him. So she looked to her right at the man who had spoken the least, and she crept towards him. The underbrush scratched her chest and belly as she kept low to remain out of sight in the forest shadows.

Her prey stood under the trees and peered into the darkness. Min-Jeong tensed, then exploded from the underbrush, her claws outstretched, her canines fully grown. A sudden movement in the periphery of her vision caught her attention as the bearded man raced at her, opened his lips into a wide O, and bellowed forth a cloud of smoke.

"No, wait!" The other man cried out to him, his arms raising to shield himself. The cloud slammed into the both of them, enveloping them. The man's clothes went up in flames even as the heavy smoke burned Min-Jeong's skin and singed the hair from her body. A roar of pain erupted from her as she slammed into the man. She quickly rolled off of him, but she wore nothing flammable to catch on fire. The man's cries carried in the night as he flailed back and forth, slamming into the trees as a tiny inferno.

Min-Jeong roared a second time, her cry echoing through the mountains as she transformed completely into her tiger form. Ji Ju descended upon her, *kal* drawn. She leapt at him, but at the last moment he sidestepped and ran the tip of the blade along her side, opening a long gash along her flank. A terrible pain filled Min-Jeong and she roared again. She did not turn back to Ji Ju, however, and kept bounding through the trees away from him. The truth had finally dawned on her. If she did not escape, she would die. Her father would want her to live and fight another day.

As she ran through the trees, white ash covering her from the pipe smoke billowed up from her fur in explosive puffs. She heard the creek that bubbled down the mountainside near the den and veered off in that direction. Behind her, she heard the swift footsteps of Ji Ju and the bearded man tracking her. Blood flowed freely from her wound, and she left ash smeared against the leaves and the underbrush. Her passage couldn't be clearer to the men hunting her.

A white tiger running in the dark would never outrun its predators. Her only option was to kill, or be killed.

Min-Jeong spun around, bared her canines, and readied herself for her final, desperate counterattack. Ji Ju loomed right behind her, and the bearded man came upon her from her left. Min-Jeong roared again, but her cry was weak and strangled with fear and grief. Ji Ju raised his *kal* and leapt at her to strike, the point of the blade aimed for her throat.

Another roar, louder, stronger, and full of violence, tore through the mountains. Ji Ju swung his head in its direction and stumbled. The bearded man spun around to ward off the new attack, but he could not stop the massive tiger that leapt upon him, latched its canines into the side of his face, and ripped his head off his shoulders.

Ji Ju's mouth dropped open in horror, and Min-Jeong leapt. He cried out and tried to impale the *kal* into her chest. The strike came late, and he caught her shoulder while she caught him by the jugular. With a growl of rage, she tore his throat out. The force of her momentum slammed them both into a tree, and Min-Jeong hit the ground hard.

A gradual silence fell over the mountainside. Min-Jeong finally released Ji Ju's throat, her muzzle drenched in blood. She struggled to her feet and met her mother's gaze as her rapid breathing slowed. Somewhere in the distance, her brothers started to cry.

"The light of loss shines bright in your eyes, silly little girl. But your transformation is just beginning." Her mother turned from her and padded softly back to the den. "Perhaps the wisdom you learn will save us from the coming war. Go out into the world and become a legend, for one day you must become a true white tiger. You are free."

Free. How often had she longed for freedom over the last two years? Staring into space counting the infinite stars in boredom, she had ached to join her father at play in the city. But now her father was dead, South and North Han marched closer to war, and the world of man weighed heavily on Min-Jeong's shoulders. The fate of the tigers of South Han rested with her. She may have to transform many more times before she discovered how they could survive the coming war. A new white tiger must come into existence.

Min-Jeong lowered her head to Ji Ju's chest, tore it open, broke through his ribs, and consumed his heart. She skinned the flesh from his face next, swallowed, and let the magic transform her. The journey north would be dangerous, but this body should do.

For now.

The Unholy Feast of the Witch's Heart

Timothy C Hobbs

Her curse lasted 500 years and would not end until the Devil's meal had been served!

1.

Castle Hill
Edinburgh, Scotland 1537

Fat bubbled, sliding off the bone, dropping in greasy lumps on piles of crisp, burned flesh at the base of an execution stake. But Lady Janet Douglas felt pain no longer, her last breath and scream ending when blistering air and smoke filled her lungs with inevitable death.

Moments before, when the pyre ignited under torches, the crowd at Edinburgh Castle cheered and whooped, hands clapping in a macabre rhythm to the beat of "Witch, witch, witch . . . Burn, burn, burn!"

repeated over and over until shrill shrieks of agony from Lady Janet quieted the crowd. They watched her twitching body and open mouth gasping for air, her singed, sack cloth dress throwing sparks in dervish patterns, her hair igniting, sending the smell of burned corruption into a cold and misty night.

And then the show was over. Nothing remained but a smoldering form with patches of seared muscle and flesh clinging to blackened bone. The crowd dispersed disappointed Lady Janet suffered no more. A lone figure stood in the shadows of the castle's battlements, a man sent to watch the undeserved fate of an accused witch, a casualty of nothing more than political necessity, a woman charged with attempting to poison a king.

The man scrutinized the scene until flames were no more than pulsing embers, the body of what was once Lady Janet a withered, scorched rag doll. Satisfied all was finished, he mounted his horse and rode in haste toward the foothills of Angus Glens where a committee of barons and one man of God waited in the bowels of Glamis Castle for news of the lady's execution.

A frigid wind off the North Sea pushed relentlessly behind the rider, and by the time darkness gripped impartial ground between midnight and sunrise, guards at Glamis Castle opened the gate for the rider.

Inside, stone walls offered no warmth as the emissary made his way down a long, winding staircase to what served as both a prison and a room of torture. Four men raised their heads when the messenger entered.

"What news, Killearn?" one asked as he stretched his tired and chilled arms. "Is Lady Douglas gone?"

"That she is, Baron. Nothing left for carrion at sunrise but charred bones and bits of cooked flesh."

There issued a general murmur between the group seated around a rack. The elder of the group, Baron Lochlan, said, "May peace take her soul onward."

"Piss on your peace, Lochlan," said a baron named MacDonald. "The King ordered it. His will be done."

"The order was unjust," Lochlan said. "All of us gathered here know it. Lady Janet was no witch, no poisoner." He tapped the grooved, solid wood surface of the rack. "This being the only means to extract confessions from her kin." He then glanced at iron tongs terminating in pointed ends hanging on the stone wall beside other instruments of torture. "The rack and the Devil's Pinchers. Even you'd be hard pressed not to confess yourself or your sainted mother as a witch under the same duress, MacDonald."

MacDonald stood saying, "Be that as it may, King James harbored little love for the Douglas clan after Janet's brother Archibald kept the young King imprisoned all those years. A pox on the Douglases I say, guilty or no."

"Aye," the other man, Baron Guthrie, agreed, the preacher beside him remaining quiet.

"Gordon?" MacDonald asked the silent one. "What say a man of God, then?"

A pause filled the room with cold stillness as a monotonous drip of water echoed somewhere in the shadows. Gordon rose and walked around the rack, casting his gaze on all present, MacDonald the only man not lowering his eyes when Gordon's met his own. "What say I?" Gordon then glanced the other way, his eyes locking on the torture implements decorating the wall. "I say that Lady Janet had no part in her brother marrying a widowed queen, no say in the unjust treatment of James, our future lord and sovereign. Archibald's lust for power was not Lady Janet's doing or her desire." Gordon once again met MacDonald's icy stare. "Her confession to me was an undeserved sorrow for failing her King though she never did so."

"Pious mush, Gordon," MacDonald said with a sneer. "No one is innocent. She knew what her brother was up to. She shared his greed to be king and now has paid the price."

"And what of honor?" Gordon asked.

MacDonald let out a laugh. "Honor? Preacher, honor does not hold kingdoms on solid ground. Force does that, force and retribution to those who oppose the kingdom as the Douglas clan did."

"And yet she never confessed," Lochlan said. "Only her kin, unable to endure this rack and other torture, gave her up as a witch."

MacDonald snorted and sat back down. "Well, no matter, what's done is done, and King James will hold us in kind regard for our part in its doing."

Gordon glanced around the room and stopped at the sight of Killearn standing still near the shadows. "Did the lady say anything before dying?" he asked the young messenger.

"I heard nothing but her screams. But I was distant and could not hear all." Killearn lowered his head and added, "I did hear some of the crowd's talk as they left."

"And?" Gordon asked.

Killearn lifted his head, a look of dismay filling the recesses of his face. "I heard she cursed all responsible."

"Just like a witch then," MacDonald said with spite.

"And the curse?" Gordon asked.

"Something about darkness and wings," Killearn said. "The people I questioned had little desire to linger and explain, but from what I gathered, her curse had something to do with crows."

The room went silent for a long while. The sound of dripping water becoming exaggerated, unnerving all gathered there.

After awhile, Lochlan said, "And now here we congregate like a murder of crows. Nothing more than carrion ourselves, carrion waiting to pick the bones of Lady Janet, waiting to caw, caw, caw and preen over our good deed for King James."

MacDonald started to respond but found the words strangling his air.

"Killearn," Baron Guthrie, until now the most silent one of the group, said abruptly. "Go back to Edinburgh tomorrow. Recover any part of Lady Janet's remains not burned to ash or devoured by scavengers and incinerate them in the great furnace here at Glamis Hall." He glanced at the other men and added, "No part of that witch shall remain to haunt us while we live."

A ghoulish grin sliced MacDonald's face as he said, "Or after we die."

The monotonous noise of dripping water suddenly ceased replaced by the prominent rise of a strong, wailing wind buffeting the castle walls.

Gordon, gazing long and hard into the shadowy depths of the torture room, said, "May God show mercy for us, mercy for our souls."

* * *

Next morning a line of sleet blew across the North Sea, lacing Edinburgh in thin layers of ice. The execution site stood morbid, a solitary station of human ruin. Before Killearn arrived to gather any remains of Lady Janet Douglas, a young boy sifted through the growing deposits of ice.

Due to the inclement weather, no other soul stirred that morning, leaving the boy alone on his scavenging errand. An old woman had enlisted the boy, a kitchen apprentice at Edinburgh Castle, to gather something from the burned body. "Would you like a silver piece, boy?" the old hag-like woman had asked. The boy in answer, shaking his top-heavy red head yes, his eyes shining in the morning kitchen fires that had been started as part of his duties. The old woman slipped him a coin saying, "A tooth or a finger bone will do. Understand?" Again the boy nodded yes. "Stay away from larger bones like leg or arm or skull. And if anyone asks, you don't know me. Understand?" Another nod yes. "Good. Then be quick about it, boy. Before the kitchen crew awakes and comes down."

And as his numbed fingers examined the pile of charred flesh, ashes, and bones, the boy stopped suddenly, reached down and picked up a slender portion of a jointed finger bone. Only the tip and one knuckle segment remained still held together by bits of muscle and ligament. The boy smiled, carefully held the bone in his palm, and raced back to the castle where the old woman waited in the shadows of a wall nook next to stairs leading down to the kitchen. When the boy turned the corner, the old woman slid out of the gloom and extended her palm. The boy grinned and placed the slender finger bone in her hand. The old woman's eyes lit up and seemed to glow red, causing the boy to gasp and back away. The old woman's face took on a malevolent quality as she took out another coin and held it out to the boy. He carefully reached, then abruptly grabbed the coin and ran down the stone steps to the kitchen. The old woman voiced a subdued cackle as she slid the finger bone between her lips, smacked and then said, "Well done, boy. Well done."

* * *

Killearn arrived at the execution site long after the kitchen boy had left.

Breaking up accumulated ice, Killearn found more than he'd hoped for. "Will have to fill two bags," he said with disgust. "Bones don't burn well out in the open like this." An idea then struck him. "Not necessarily though," he thought with a broad smile. "I'll crack the larger ones into splinters. Only need one bag then."

And he did just that, filling a bag he'd brought along with what bones and ash remained of Lady Janet Douglas. When his task was almost done, Killearn saw one last item: a clump of something gray lying next to the charred pole. He picked up the piece and immediately dropped it, his body shivering with disgust when he realized it was the remains of Janet's heart. "God, but that's disgusting," he said out loud, the experience made even worse because the heart seemed to have held heat inside its boiled tissue from the execution fire. "But Baron Guthrie wants all, so . . ." Killearn suppressed a gag as he bent and swiftly moved the remains of the heart into the bag. He glanced around, found no other soul out on this freezing morning, then hooked the bag to his saddle, mounted, and rode back toward Glamis Castle never aware of a swift, dark shape following on the wind.

Once back at Glamis, Killearn opened the bag for Barons MacDonald, Lochlan, and Guthrie along with Preacher Gordon to examine in the lower torture room.

"A job well done, Killearn," Guthrie said as the others nodded in agreement. "Now we must dump all these remnants into the master furnace. The bones will crumble there for sure."

"Let me at least offer a prayer," Gordon said.

"A prayer?" MacDonald said through a cynical laugh. "For a witch?'

"For us mostly, mostly for forgiveness," Gordon said.

Lochlan frowned, "Let the preacher be, MacDonald. Nothing wrong in a prayer for Lady Janet or ourselves."

"Prayer will not help any of you." Startled, the five men turned their attention toward a voice in the deep shadows of the room.

"Who goes there?" MacDonald asked loudly. "Show yourself."

A dark shape undulated from the gloom and began to take form in between amoebic ripples.

"What devil's curse is this?" Guthrie asked as he and the others moved backward.

"One who knows all of you well," the shape announced as it solidified and glided forward surrounded in a misty, black swirl. The old woman who had enlisted the kitchen boy's assistance stood suspended in that mist before the men. "You have, all of you, unjustly murdered my Lady."

Lochlan squinted and said, "By God, I know you. Maldora Fain, nurse to Lady Janet from the day she was born."

"Aye, I was there when she took her first step . . . and I was there when the fire stole her last breath."

Lochlan studied the wizened face, long, bent nose, and cracked grin. "What business have you here?"

The matted grayness of Maldora's wild hair meshed with the swirling mist. "This," she said, holding out a slender finger bone. "The thing your man Killearn didn't find."

Ashamed of his growing fear, MacDonald marched forward and attempted to grab the bone, but the body of Maldora moved instantly to the side, leaving MacDonald grasping empty air. "Another witch," MacDonald said. "Taught Lady Janet all your dark ways?"

Maldora threw back her head and said, "Yes, I am a witch, but not my Lady."

"But she cursed us from the fire," Guthrie said.

"Was not her people heeded. The only words from my Lady were screams for death to release her pain. The curse was placed in a mouth already void of life. Placed there by me."

"Bah!" MacDonald spat out. "That bone means nothing." He raised the bag holding Janet's ruined body. "We have all here, all soon to be reduced to ashes."

Maldora laughed wildly, filling the hall with a chill beyond its familiar cold. "None of you will ever rest as long as I or the kin of Janet maintain this," she said and held out the finger bone. "No rest in the light of day, the gloom of night, or the moldy grave. You are forever cursed by your foul deed." All of a sudden, the bag holding Lady Janet's remains flew to Maldora's hand. The men hissed and backed further away as she dug inside and pulled out the gray lump of flesh once beating in Janet's chest. "Unless you can steal the bone from its rightful heir and feed them this," she declared and tossed the heart across the room where it landed with a wet thud in front of the five men. "You carrion, you Glamis Crows, will never embrace peace." Then Maldora was consumed by a massing, black mist and vanished.

"Witches," MacDonald whispered into the hushed room. "Satan take them all."

In the distance, a monotonous, maddening sound of dripping water once again echoed in the chamber.

2.
Calvary, Texas present day

Calvary, Texas is one of those small towns people pass through heading somewhere else. Any visitor who happens to stop for gas at the one pump station there can see the entirety of Calvary in one glimpse: a short, main street with post office/general store on one side and a drug store/ medical clinic on the other. As the visitor leaves, they will pass a demure Baptist Church and funeral home on the edge of town. Calvary also lacks public schools. A yellow bus transports the current twelve students to Walnut Wells about fifteen miles south down the road.

But for all its lackluster appeal, Calvary does profess to one business, envied by many in the State of Texas: **Henderson's Auto Salvage**.

Henderson's is the largest auto graveyard in Texas. In fact, if you live in Abilene and need a passenger door for your classic Pinto, or if you hail from the polar opposite direction in McAllen and are searching for a 1980 Pontiac Grand Prix carburetor, chances are Henderson's can mail you the goods. And customers are far from limited to the Lone Star State. From California to New Jersey to any other state, Henderson's inventory keeps a steady stream of orders coming in. "Biggest surprise for me," owner Mike Henderson admitted to a reporter from Texas Monthly, "was a 1969 Ford Maverick gas pedal assembly ordered from Melbourne, Australia." Mike spat a stream of Copenhagen before adding, "Hell fire, shipping cost more than the merchandise."

Truth be known, the five mile expanse of the salvage yard was larger than the remainder of Calvary's official county surveyed dimensions, and being that massive made it next to impossible to police the auto graveyard with any regularity. But the place consisted of so many damaged and abandoned vehicles, thievery was expected now and again. "Ain't about to hire a security agency to work twenty four seven at smoking cigs and swilling coffee laced with hooch. No way all them cars can be watched unless I hire the National Guard," Mike was glad to share with whoever asked. "Don't make a tinker's damn to me if I lose a part here or there. Me, my wife, and two kids can keep a good enough eye on the yard and still meet orders too."

But one additional aspect of trespassing existed, that being an occasional homeless body seeking a wrecked vehicle's interior for shelter. It would've made sense, even to Mike Henderson, for some of the homeless or railroad hobos to set up camp deep in the yard's interior. But the Henderson's were unaware if such a camp existed. They never saw a bonfire, found scattered trash, or discovered any indication such carousing went on. As for the occasional straggler, Mike held no animosity. In fact, if he or his family found someone sleeping in a car, they more than likely would give them food or offer clothes or blankets. "We all got hard times coming our way," Mike might say. "Don't think the good Lord wants us to turn our back on the needy."

And such was the case for Cullen Boley, who was roused from his slumber in the back seat of a wrecked Continental. "Well, at least you got good taste, mister."

The words buzzed in Cullen's subconscious for a moment before he jerked upright, uncertain for an instant as to where he was and how he came there. He rubbed his eyes, trying to focus on a figure standing outside the rear passenger window. When his vision finally cleared, Cullen was face to face with a girl appearing to be in her teens wearing dirty olive drab overalls, the upper portion of a grungy, short sleeve tee shirt surfacing above the overall's chest border. The girl smiled with amazingly white teeth as she touched the rim of a cap resting on a head of overflowing, dirty blonde curls, a logo on the cap promoting **Henderson's Auto Salvage**.

"You okay in there, mister?" she asked

Cullen patted his face briskly, opened the Lincoln's back door and slid out. "Fell asleep," he said groggily. "Didn't mean to trespass. I'll be on my way."

"Oh heck, mister, no need in hurrying off." The girl laughed a little and pointed in a circle. "There's so many wrecked vehicles, we don't mind anybody using them for shelter." She grinned then and added, "So long as they don't make it permanent."

The sun was at its midmorning station and a dull heat rose from it. "No, really," Cullen said as a fine line of perspiration covered his exposed arms. "I'm passing through. Needed a place to rest for a little while is all."

"Bet you're hungry though. Sure look on the thin side to me."

And Cullen did appear gaunt, his trek down from Colorado being hand to mouth, that hand mostly an empty one. He glanced down at his faded, soiled jeans, and felt embarrassed when rising body odor became quite evident from the under arms of his equally grubby western shirt. About the only item of clothing acceptable on this warm Texas morning were the relatively new tennis shoes he wore.

"Look, as I said, I'll be on my way." Cullen then started to walk away.

"Hey wait a minute," the girl said. "Why don't you stay here for the day? I'll bring you what's leftover from breakfast and then come back later with some supper. Looks like a little grub wouldn't hurt your feelings none."

Cullen stopped walking when his empty stomach growled at the mention of food. "You mean that, don't you?" he asked as he stared into the girl's dark eyes. "What about your mother and father? Won't they object to you helping a vagrant?"

"Vagrant? What's that?"

"You know, a drifter, no home no job."

The girl giggled, "Shoot, mister, my pa would chastise me if I didn't help you. Anytime I find someone out here on my rounds, I'm supposed to help out. Ma and Pa wouldn't have it no other way."

Cullen felt a slight suspicion ease up his spine, but it dissipated quickly. "Everybody can't be after you," he told himself. "Well," he then said to the girl. "If it's all right with your parents, I could use something to eat and another night's rest." His body odor seemed to escalate then. "But I'll be off tomorrow, I promise. I'm getting a bit gamey and will look for a homeless shelter down the road where I can bathe and pick up some clean clothes."

The girl giggled again. "You just stay put 'til I get back with the food. I can work something out with Pa about getting you washed up and in some clean clothes before you leave tomorrow."

"Oh, no, that would be asking too much."

"Won't hear of it," the girl said heading back down a line of stacked cars.

"Wait, what's your name?"

"Jane" came back to him from a distance as the girl's form disappeared around a tower of smashed metal.

The incident felt dreamlike to Cullen, like he would awaken any moment, his body aching and stiff from being cramped up in the back seat of the Continental. But when he returned to the car and leaned against its hard frame, he knew for certain he was awake. This wasn't the first time someone had helped him, but he was never certain how genuine their efforts were, not since all the madness started, not since last December at his Aunt Margaret Cameron's cabin, that night seeming longer removed now as he drifted back to it and the last words spoken by his only living relative.

3.
Gunnison, Colorado five moths earlier.

Due to a massive snow fall, Cullen's flight on a local puddle jumper was delayed for almost twelve hours, finally taking off and depositing him at a makeshift landing strip between Gunnison and Crested Butte. The ride to his Aunt's cabin came courtesy of her friend Macon Pike, one of the resident ranchers who happened to have an all weather Jeep made for besting frigid conditions.

"'Bout to give up on you, young man," Macon said.

Cullen stared at the older man vigorously working the Jeep's manual transmission along a road mostly obscured by ice and snow. Macon Pike resembled one of the prospectors settling Gunnison in the late 1800's: big, bushy beard laced with small ice shards, a large face round and red, massive head covered by an aviator cap complete with ear muffs, a bulbous body sheltered in layers of flannel and a heavy coat, and broad thighs wrapped in thick denim, the cuffs terminating in a pair of substantial work boots.

"Sorry about the delay," Cullen said. "Couldn't talk the Boulder pilot into taking a chance."

Macon laughed while grinding gears. "That'd be Bill Jackson. A more cowardly soul I've not yet met." He grinned and glanced at Cullen. "Kind of strange for a pilot."

"Well, anyway. I apologize."

"Not your doing, young man." Macon drove in silence for a bit before asking, "How long since you seen your Aunt Margaret?"

"Right after my parents died." Cullen's face took on a ragged look when he said it.

"Sad day for you. Cars can be treacherous things at times. Human frailty don't stand much of a chance in them."

Cullen shook off his melancholy. "Anyway, that's been five years ago." He stared out the passenger side of the windshield and followed the Jeep's meandering lights across the frozen ground. "Not that we'd lost touch. I spoke to Aunt Margaret several times over the years. Especially on holidays and her birthday." He turned his attention back to Macon. "Was surprised she wanted me to come down. She was very insistent about it."

"Margaret can be a pistol, that's for sure." Macon turned up a slight incline. "Don't think she's been feeling all that well lately."

"Oh, why so?"

"Ain't like her to have someone fill her grocery order and deliver it, or pick up her supplies at the hardware store. She always makes the trip into Gunnison no matter the weather. Told me keeping active was the secret to her ninety plus years." He laughed again saying, "Margaret never was specific about the number accompanying that ninety."

Cullen suddenly found it hard to remember what his aunt looked like. All the photos his mother possessed were of a much younger Margaret. "Well, I had some vacation time built up anyway." He looked out the window again and added, "Didn't count on this snowstorm though."

"Weathermen are useless around Gunnison," Macon said. "Whole town sits in a low valley. Plays hell with barometric pressure effects on cold fronts this time of year." A distant light materialized farther up the path. "Forgot what it is you do up there in Missouri."

"Work for the city water department. I regulate the purity." A smile crept over Cullen's face as his aunt's cabin came into view. "Keep Joplin's water safe to drink."

Macon pulled his Jeep to a halt in front of Margaret Cameron's cabin. "Well, here we are, young man. Safe and sound."

Cullen held out a pale, cold hand and Macon crushed it in his own massive gloved one. "Thanks for the ride, Mr. Pike," Cullen said wincing at the older man's grip.

"Don't mention it. Like I said, your Aunt's well thought of in Gunnison. Not a thing I or any other of her acquaintances wouldn't do for her." Macon released the handshake. "Margaret is a grand old dame, that's for sure. Now, let me help you with that luggage in the rear."

After delivering Cullen safely inside the cabin, Macon said goodnight and motioned for Cullen to follow him outside. "Your aunt's looking even paler than when I saw her in town two weeks past." Macon frowned and said, "Ollie Stinson down at the Food Mart told me your aunt looked haggard when he delivered her groceries a few days ago, but I had no idea Margaret was this down in the mouth." He looked directly at Cullen saying, "You see what you think after awhile, and if you need me to take her down to the hospital don't hesitate to call me day or night. Your aunt has my number but I'll give you my card just in case." Macon fought his layered clothing for a moment before pulling out a wallet, reaching inside and handing a business card to Cullen. "Day or night now," he repeated and then walked to his Jeep.

Cullen waved goodbye and then went back in the cabin glancing at the card as he did: **Macon Pike – Odd Jobs and Snow Clearing – Call ###-####**.

"Come in and close that door, Cullen," Margaret, blanket wrapped in an easy chair near a fireplace, said. "I swear, my blood gets thinner every year." She glanced at Cullen as he closed the front door. "Can't abide the cold like I used to."

Cullen took in the cabin's interior. The smell of burning wood mixed with a delicate trace of cooking spice warmed the room. A memory of being here after his parents' deaths brought a moment of emptiness. He recalled the interior layout—two bedrooms, a tiny kitchen and wood stove, and a living room with a fireplace, the largest room in the cabin.

He walked to his aunt and sat down in another chair across from her. "Your place still has that homey feel, Aunt Margaret." He took a deep breath and added, "Never could figure out how you kept the odor of cinnamon and nutmeg so prevalent in here."

Margaret smiled. "My secret," she said with a touch of mischief, then coughed a rattling, worrying cough.

Cullen scrutinized her frail face. He tried again to recall how his aunt appeared when he visited five years ago, but the picture wouldn't form. Still, he was certain she'd not appeared this ill. "How are you feeling?" Cullen asked. "You don't look well at all."

Margaret reached over to an end table by her chair, retrieved a pair of large spectacles and placed them on her much smaller head, creating an owl-like aspect. "Well, I can't say the same for you, Cullen. You look to be in the pink."

"Oh, I'm fine, Aunt Margaret. It's you I'm concerned with. Your phone call worried me enough, but your skin color distresses me, and that cough . . . Maybe I should call Mr. Pike and have him take us to the hospital and get you examined."

Margaret laughed slightly. "Why, you'll do no such thing. I'm doing quite well for my age, thank you very much." She glanced toward one of the side windows. "As I mentioned, I don't stand up well to cold weather like I use to."

A sudden chill seized Cullen and his body shook briefly. "Must have been colder than I noticed," he said, wrapping his arms around his chest. "You certain you're okay?"

"I really am. Promise." Margaret looked at Cullen for a moment before saying, "I'm so glad you came. I imagine my phone call sounded as if I'd become a dotty old maid."

"Not really. Seeing you now, I understand your concern, and I'm happy to come and help out." Cullen warmed from the burning fire and quit hugging himself. "You mentioned you wanted my help with getting your affairs in order. I suppose a lawyer would do a better job, but I know how you feel about family, so I don't mind."

Margaret smiled. "Sometimes my sister jumps right from your face." She sighed and removed her glasses, placing them back in their spot on the end table. "It's still difficult to believe Alice and Jason are gone. Why, I vividly recall their lovely wedding and . . ." She noticed Cullen's somber expression and stopped talking for a moment. "But then there's no use opening old injuries."

The fire cracked loudly as they sat in silence. Outside a wind rose and shook the cabin doors and windows.

Finally, Margaret said, "I have some left over soup and sandwiches if you're hungry. Still have a kettle on for tea as well."

Cullen got out of his chair, bent down, and affectionately placed a kiss on Margaret's cheek. "I'm more tired than hungry. I'll unpack and get ready for bed. I imagine you're ready for sleep as well."

A swift animation spread over Margaret's face. "Oh, no. I have so much to share with you. We mustn't waste a moment." She shivered and glanced uneasily at the front window and then stared at Cullen with pleading eyes. "Please, sit back down. Sleep can wait."

A hesitant smile occupied Cullen's face. "Well, certainly. I'm not all that tired anyway. I thought you might be."

Margaret ignored his comment and asked, "Did your mother ever tell you about the finger bone?"

"Huh?"

"I know it's an odd question. I only wondered if my sister Alice ever shared that story."

"Bone? I don't believe . . . Wait! Yes, I remember a story she'd tell me at bedtime every once and awhile." Cullen grinned. "It was supposed to be scary, but we laughed more than cringed."

A strange expression spread over Margaret's face. "Was it about a finger bone?"

"No, a soup bone. The story was about an old woman who found a soup bone in a ditch, brought it home and made a bowl of soup with it. Late that night when the old woman went to bed, the wind began to howl and this eerie voice spoke suddenly above the old woman's bed 'Where's my bone? I want my bone' the voice said growing loud and frightening. The old woman pulled the covers over her head as the voice continued 'I WANT MY BONE I WANT MY BONE', then mother would suddenly grab me and say 'GOT IT!'" Cullen beamed. "It never scared me, but it always surprised me, and mother . . ." He stopped talking when he saw the look of horror on Margaret's face.

"No," she said, her voice trembling. "That's not the story at all."

"I'm sorry, Aunt Margaret. I didn't mean to upset you." Cullen then asked, "What story are you talking about? Maybe I just forgot it."

"She never told you about our relatives in Scotland? Back in the time when James the Fifth was king?"

"You know, now that you mention it, mother did say something about us being kin to royalty. What she told me seems very distant though." Cullen frowned in thought. "Were we related to King James?"

Margaret seemed to pale even more under the firelight. "No, not to that monster. We were blood tied to the Douglases. Lady Janet and her brother Archibald."

"I'm afraid those names don't ring a bell. Were they important?"

"Archibald was the sixth Earl of Angus. He married James' widowed mother and acted as king when James was a child." Margaret pulled her blanket tighter. "James hated Archibald for that. When James grew to manhood he trumped up charges against Archibald and Janet."

"I know I would have remembered a tale as dark as this. What happened?"

"Archibald escaped, but Janet was not so fortunate. James accused her of attempting to poison him and of being a witch." Margaret stared at the blazing fireplace. "James condemned Janet to be burned at the stake."

Cullen felt a faint throb on his forehead and feared a headache would follow. "That's terrible. I had no idea."

"That's where the finger bone comes in."

Cullen had a sudden insight and asked, "Okay, Aunt Margaret, you've been pulling my leg, haven't you? I bet you're one sentence away from grabbing me and yelling 'GOT IT' like mother use to do." Cullen laughed, but his good humor dissipated when he saw Margaret's eyes tear up. "Of course, it's okay. It's rather fun if that's what you were up to."

"No, you don't understand," Margaret said as tears trickled down her cheeks. She pointed to the fireplace mantle and said, "That small, wooden box there, please take it down and open it."

Cullen got out of his chair and grabbed the box. There was a tiny lock securing the catch. "It's locked," he said.

Margaret fumbled under the blanket and eventually brought out a small key. "Here," she said, her tone suddenly nervous. "But you mustn't tarry. Open it, see what's inside and then lock it and give me back the key."

Cullen, now considering dementia as far as his aunt was concerned, decided to humor her. He took the key from her hand, opened the lock, and lifted the box's lid. And there, resting on a patch of red velvet, was a slender bone appearing to be that of a pinkie finger, its tip, first knuckle and the segment connected to its second knuckle still intact. The bone had yellowed over time, but there was no doubt as to what it was.

"Is this real?" Cullen asked himself as he started to touch the bone. A shuffling sound then halted his movements. The noise was uncanny and ominous and seemed to emanate by the cabin's front door. There soon followed a low mewling like a hushed chorus of crying intonations. A chill covered Cullen's skin when he heard "Ours, the finger, let us rest, give up the bone" materialize from the shadows by the front door. And when those shadows crept forward, Cullen jerked, dropping the box, the finger bone rolling out on the cabin floor.

"Quickly!" Margaret cried. "Pick it up and hand it to me quickly, Cullen!"

Cullen reached down hastily, put the finger back in the box and handed it to his aunt. The shadows advanced quicker as if desperate, the voices louder. "She's dying. Feed her the heart. Make her swallow." The ominous shades pressed forward and started to coalesce into definite shapes. Cullen felt a shriek rising when bodies emerged, bodies bearing some human lines mixed with something else, something hunched and heavy with dark appendages. "Wings!" Cullen's mind screamed. "Black wings!" And then the forming faces of dark, dense eyes, and noses more beak-like than flesh. There were five of them huddled in an approaching murky mass.

"Stop!" Margaret's shout crowded the cabin. She held up the box and made certain the creatures saw her lock it. "Not yet, you ghouls. Not while I still have life in my body! Not while I possess the bone!"

The malignant group slowed their progress, the voices becoming faint as they backed away. "Give us peace. Die now. Release us." And then the shadows faded, leaving Cullen to stare at an empty space by the cabin's front door.

Cullen felt dizzy and bewildered. What he'd witnessed could not be real. He tried to explain the event rationally—exhaustion maybe or an infectious state of hysteria brought on by his aunt's bizarre story. He rubbed his eyes and sat down hard in the chair. It took a moment for him to comprehend Margaret was gasping for air.

"Oh my God," he said and rushed to his aunt. He picked her up from the chair and rushed to her bedroom where he lay her down. The blanket slid away as he was moving her, and Margaret shook violently from chills as she struggled for breath. "What can I do?" Cullen asked. Margaret's face was blue, her lips purple. He started rubbing her arms and torso. "Try to relax," he said. "Breathe slower, Aunt Margaret. Slower." And eventually, she relaxed, her labored breathing slowing. "Good," Cullen said with relief. "I'm calling Mr. Pike this instant. You need to go the hospital as soon as possible."

Margaret, still gripping the wooden box with its grisly inhabitant locked away safely, shook her head no. Her wide eye stare softened and she said, "Not yet. You need to know the whole story . . . must be told."

"No, this is too much. You must be seen to." Cullen moved quickly from the bed and out of the room. He grabbed the phone receiver from its place on the wall and waited for a dial tone that never came, sharply clicking the cradle repeatedly to no avail.

"The lines are out because of the heavy snow." Margaret's voice drifted to Cullen.

"What? No phone service? But there has to be." Cullen continued clicking the phone cradle. "There has to be."

"Cullen, come back in here," Margaret said in a surprisingly calm tone.

Cullen finally dropped the receiver, leaving it to dangle in cold air. "Of course, my cell," he said and fumbled in his pants pocket, removing the cell and dialing, paying no attention to the No Service Found message.

"No service out here, Cullen," Margaret said.

Cullen let the cell drop to the floor. He wiped sweat from his forehead and tried to focus. "There has to be a way," he was telling himself when his thoughts were abruptly interrupted by Margaret's voice.

"There were five of them carrying out King James' orders. Three barons, one preacher, and a young knight who'd recently been given the title of baronet."

Cullen moved on trembling legs back to his aunt's bedroom. He stood in the doorway and leaned against the frame, his facial expression perplexed, his slumping body drained of its recent adrenalin rush.

"These five arranged for the torture of Lady Janet's closest relations since Janet never confessed under torment herself. And more than one of those relatives folded under pain, denouncing Lady Janet as a witch." Margaret sat upright now, her breathing slow and regular. "That was all the five needed, and

Janet's execution was arranged with full support of King James. Those who watched and cheered as Lady Janet burned swore Janet cursed the crowd and those five men who'd instigated the torture and false confessions condemning her to death. But that was not the case." Margaret's eyes gleamed as she continued, "Lady Janet Douglas was no witch. It was her old nurse Maldora Fain who practiced the black arts. Maldora Fain who cursed those five degenerate, power hungry men."

"What I saw . . . what I heard," Cullen said. "It wasn't real, Aunt Margaret. Only some sort of shared delusion." He rose from the chair and sat on the bed next to Margaret, covering her cold hand with his own warm one. "You are ill. We must get you into town. You still have a car, don't you?"

"Battery died weeks ago."

"I know there's a generator out in your shed. I can charge the battery with it."

Margaret frowned. "No fuel for it. Besides, I won't be here in the morning."

"Don't say that. I'm going outside to see what I can do about that car battery."

But as Cullen started to get up, Margaret grabbed his arm. "You must promise. You must promise me you'll take this," she pleaded as she shoved the wooden box under Cullen's hand. "They'll come for me if you don't. The bone must be possessed by one of our family like it was when Maldora gave it to our ancestor, a woman of the Douglas clan who would sire a line leading here, here to the last survivor of that line." Margaret's eyes grew wide as she pronounced, "You, Cullen! You're the only one left after me. The sole survivor of the Douglas clan."

Cullen felt repulsion for the object under his hand, but seeing the fear in his aunt's expression he softened. "Oh, Aunt Margaret. Can't you see this is just your illness talking." He smiled softly saying, "You even had me convinced. I thought I saw and heard those shadows, but it was only this morbid thing," he said and held the box up. "The night, the snow storm, my fatigue and concern for you, and the fact that you spin a very convincing horror story, but that's all this is." He reached for her hand adding with a slight laugh, "No telling where you got this old bone. Probably sold by some scoundrel like Mr. Pike for all I know."

"No," Margaret gasped reaching for the box. "No, you must promise. You . . ." Her face went ashen then and she fell back on the bed, one final, long expulsion of air leaving her lungs as she did.

"Aunt Margaret!" Cullen shouted. He felt her wrist for a pulse and found nothing. "Aunt Margaret!" he put an ear to her chest and found no heartbeat. Cullen then quickly moved her from the bed to the hard wood floor and started CPR, counting out the compressions between short breaths into her mouth. "Come on," he said out loud as he pressed down on her chest. "Come on!"

Cullen lost track of time then and eventually ceased his efforts to revive his aunt. He sat down by her cooling body and stared into her open, vacant eyes. "What a nightmare," he said. "I have to try and get to town and alert the authorities." He stood and headed to the front of the cabin when low voices stopped him dead in his tracks.

"Now, finally free. Feed her the heart." The shapes from earlier, those shades Cullen believed to be his beguiled imagination, appeared once again and slithered like spilled ink across the floor toward the dead woman in the bedroom. Bodies forming then receding, arms elongating into wings, hands to skeletal talons, faces melting back and forth between human and crow advancing swiftly.

At first, Cullen's instincts demanded he flee into the night and run as far away from these terrors as possible, but then a different emotion seized him, one of fury and revenge for an act hidden deep in his blood and bones and flesh, genetic memories as old and dark as the well of time. Images of a woman burning and men laughing in a cold, damp room of torture spilled into his brain as he rushed through the black mass of monstrous bodies screaming, "Nooooooooooo!" and then stumbled into the bedroom, stepped across the corpse of his aunt and grabbed the wooden box from the bed. He held it up as the shapes halted inside the bedroom doorway. "I promise you will never have this!" he yelled. "That as long as I live, you will never find peace. Never!"

One of the shadows moved forward and held out a cupped claw gripping a clump of gray matter. "Feed her this heart and give us the bone." A macabre grin twisted the chameleon countenance. "Give us the bone and leave before it's too late for you as well."

And for an instant, Cullen once again considered leaving the box and running away, but when he looked on his aunt's stricken expression of death, anger gripped him. Holding the box securely in his hand, he pushed forward through the things blocking his retreat, ran through the living room, pushed open the cabin's front door and hurried into a gloomy night embraced by the falling chill of snow.

4.
Calvary, Texas present day

It was near sunset when the girl returned with a large, foam takeout box. "Ma keeps a supply of these," she said holding out the container. "Sometimes one of us on day patrol take food along for the long haul." She looked over the piles of salvaged cars. "There's miles of this smashed metal to check out."

Cullen's memories of the weird night in his aunt's cabin vanished under the need for food. He took the container from the girl, slid down the side of the Continental and then sat on the ground.

"You'll need these," the girl said, handing him a sealed plastic bag containing a fork, spoon, napkin, and tiny squares of pepper and salt.

Cullen took the plastic utensils. "Thank you," he said peeling back the foam container's lid revealing a disgusting glob of food covering an equally disgusting piece of soggy toast. "What is this?" he asked, frowning.

"Never had shit on a shingle? At least that's what my pa calls it. Said that was the chief breakfast item on ship when he was in the Navy."

Cullen's lip shuddered as he took the plastic fork out of the plastic wrap and lifted up edges of the gray mass in the foam box. "Can't say that I have. What's in this stuff?"

"Oh, ground meat, gravy, boiled eggs, chicken innards, and pepper."

"Chicken innards?"

"Yeah, Ma cuts up boiled eggs, chicken livers, hearts, and gizzards, and throws them in the mix.

Hey, I know it looks like someone barfed up a load of Thanksgiving giblet gravy, but it's real tasty." The girl grinned impishly. "Give it a try." She then added with a slight giggle, "Everybody's got to eat a little shit in their lifetime."

Cullen slid the fork under the gray wad and lifted it to nose. He took a hard sniff and smelled nothing bad, only a meaty aroma laced in peppery tang. He raised his eyebrows and took a small bite. His palate immediately approved. "Damn sure tastes better than it looks," he said, shoveling the food.

"Glad you like it." The girl gazed at the waning light and said, "Should have brought you a flashlight." She shrugged and fumbled in one of her pockets, pulled out a disposable lighter and pitched it on the ground next to Cullen. "If you need to, it's okay to build a small fire. There's plenty of twigs and dry grass around the cars for you to use." She smiled and said, "Ain't got much in the way of rain this year so if you do make a fire be especially careful not to start a big one."

Between bites, Cullen picked up the lighter and shoved it in his shirt pocket. "Thanks again. Like I said, I'll be heading out in the morning."

"No rush. I'll be back later with some clean clothes and some body wipes." She wiggled her nose. "You don't exactly come over as springtime fresh."

"That would be great, but there's really no need. I can find some type of homeless shelter down the road."

"Like I said before, ain't no trouble." She shuffled off, raising a hand as she did.

Cullen grinned as he wiped what was left in the food container away with the last wedge of mushy toast. He then let out a satisfied moan, leaned back against the car and fell asleep within minutes.

In the middle of a nightmare complete with his dead aunt's eyes and a creeping group of monstrous crow things, Cullen awoke with a start. His stomach needled with pain, he stood on shaky legs and bent over gagging. It hit him then how the food might have been tainted. And about the time he was certain the shit on a shingle was about to exit both anal and oral cavities, a voice startled him, stopping the partially digested food's escape routes.

"Hey there," a low toned voice said. "You all right?"

Cullen rose and through watering eyes discovered the silhouette of a person wielding a flashlight, the beam falling directly on Cullen's pasty face. Twilight was ebbing by now and what little light remained illuminated nothing but shadowed outlines.

"The light," Cullen said, shielding his eyes.

"Sorry about that." The person came forward and sat the flashlight on the Continental's hood, a funnel of yellow light filling the area around Cullen. "I'm Mike Henderson, young fella. I own this salvage yard."

Cullen was about to speak but doubled over again before he could.

"You sick or something?" Henderson asked.

"Your daughter brought me some food." Cullen raised his head a little. "It didn't agree with me."

"Well, I ain't got no daughter. Have two sons who help me around the yard, and other than my wife and me, that's the only people around."

Cullen scowled in confusion and stared at the man standing close by. "Well, she said she was your daughter. Said you didn't mind a drifter sleeping in the cars as long as they didn't make it a permanent arrangement. She brought me food and said she'd be back later with some clean clothes."

"Don't have any notion who you're referring to, but whoever it was told you the truth about me not caring. Hell, we all need help now and again. I ain't about to refuse someone a place to sleep if they're decent about it. And I'd be happy to bring you a good meal and some clothes if you want."

Cullen gagged and spit up a small amount of food. "Lord no, I can't eat anything right now. That shit on a shingle your daughter brought me is having a disastrous affect."

Henderson came over and put a hand on Cullen's shoulder. "Like I said, I ain't got no daughter." He snickered a bit and added, "And we don't eat nothing like the crap I had in the Navy, no shit on a shingle no ways. Me and my wife and sons are vegetarians now. Have been for the last six years."

Cullen groaned, slid back down the car, and sat on the ground. "If it wasn't your daughter, why would she make up such a story and bring me that terrible food."

"You got me there." Henderson picked up his flashlight. "Tell you what, I'll go back down to the office and get some bicarb to treat your upset stomach. Can bring you some clothes if you still want some."

Cullen nodded yes. "Thanks, I'd appreciate that bicarb."

"Hate to leave you in the dark."

Cullen pulled out the disposable lighter the girl gave him. "The girl said I could make a small fire with this, but, since she's not your daughter, I don't know if you'd be agreeable to that."

"Well, as long as it's a small campfire, I got no objection." He started shining the light around the ground. "There're twigs all around here. I'll help you find some and get a fire going before I go after that other stuff."

And after a tiny campfire was constructed and lit, Henderson left Cullen alone and started his trip back to the salvage office. Cullen, his stomach still in throbbing knots, watched the silhouette move away until it vanished into the night.

Cullen moaned and lay doubled up on his side against the digestive distress plaguing him. His mind seemed bloated as the sickness continued with no relief. He could not force himself to vomit, which would have helped tremendously. Cullen even shoved fingers down his throat to cause a gagging reflex, but it didn't work. He was so miserable he moaned out loud and curled into a tighter ball.

"After all this time, finally got one of you Douglas clan to eat that damned heart."

Cullen glanced up at the figure standing by the campfire, its light outlining the girl who'd brought that terrible food. "What did you say? Eat what heart? Chicken hearts you said. Chicken hearts, livers, and gizzards." Cullen gagged loudly and dry heaved.

"I lied. Just got so damned tired of this thing your family put on mine." The form of the girl began to morph, swelling then receding, elongating then broadening until a hunched figure stood in her place. "Took longer to trail you than we expected," a harsh voice said.

Cullen stared at the hulking, black shape in amazement. "I don't understand."

"None of us believed you'd take on the mantle."

"Mantle?"

"The finger bone of Lady Douglas. Thought you'd see your aunt die and then bury her. Course we'd feed her that heart in between. You'd never know. She wouldn't have to be alive when we stuck it in her mouth. Course if one of you ever did eat it while alive, our curse would be broken for sure once we obtained the finger bone."

When he heard the rustle of something approaching, Cullen's mind suddenly cleared.

"We'd been keeping an eye on your aunt for years and were well prepared when her health started failing," the shape said. "Surprised us when she called on you though. Thought she might have been weary of it all . . . All the years guarding that bone, all the years keeping that secret." The rustling sound grew louder. "You're the last of your clan's line, but we were almost certain your aunt would spare you the task."

Voices growing from the shadows around Cullen seemed hideous and spiteful. "The bone. Find it. Burn it like she burned before. Set us free."

"Why don't you hand over that damned talisman and we'll be on our way to a long overdue rest," the shape by the fire said.

Cullen tried to stand and fell down. His face in the dirt, he felt something sharp probing his body. "Ahh," a voice said with pleasure. "I believe I've found what we came for." A sudden rush of airy whispers filled the air around Cullen when he felt the finger bone being pulled from him. He'd taken the bone out of its box, wrapped it tightly in the red velvet swath on which it lay, and shoved it where he felt no one would think to look —his underwear.

But, then again, these monsters were not hampered by any form of etiquette.

Cullen made a feeble attempt to grab the bone away from the talons holding it above the campfire. "Burn it now," the voices said in unison. "Then deal with him, the last Douglas heir."

The shape holding the bone now retained very little human characteristics, its back humped and weighted by thick wings, its face compressed into a crow's head with a horrible human smile. It held the finger bone high in the air and said, "No, better to take it back to Glamis Castle and destroy it where the curse was born." It then turned beady, black eyes on Cullen. "He'll die from the heart's poison. We need not worry over him."

The other shapes moved closer to the campfire, their mass separating into four distinct figures. Between his vision blurring and then clearing briefly, Cullen saw the faces of those who'd seen to it Lady Janet was unlawfully burned at the stake, the countenance of each being crow and man twisted together. Cullen wanted to scream but his organs were shutting down, his death visible under the watchful stares of the Glamis Crows, who lifted their raucous, victorious caws into a warm Texas night.

5.

Gunnison, Colorado present day

After the initial investigation into Margaret Cameron's death, the coroner ruling natural causes with no suspected foul play, it was Macon Pike who arranged the funeral and burial of his old friend.

"Can't figure out why her nephew run off like that," Macon said to the owner, chief mortician and funeral director Horace Green of Green's Mortuary. "And then to find out young Cullen died in Texas of food poisoning . . . what a shock." He put down the papers for the double service he'd signed on Mr. Green's desk. "Can't tell you how much I appreciate you holding off on Margaret's service when we were contacted by that fellow in Calvary, Texas."

"That being Mr. Henderson," Green said. "Runs the auto salvage where Cullen's body was found."

"Kindhearted man for sure. Found that airline ticket in Cullen's pocket leading him to Gunnison. Just luck Cullen kept that ticket stub, otherwise the poor boy wouldn't have been buried with his last relative."

"You sure that's what the boy would want. What about his parent's graves back in Missouri?"

"Nope, told me himself he wanted to keep company with his aunt because she had no one of her own."

"It's a shame both ways. Margaret was a fine woman."

"Indeed she was." Macon grinned and said, "A corker for sure."

"Well, that completes the business part of this. Don't worry about payment until Margaret's will is settled." Green opened a desk drawer and slid in the paperwork. "You being the executor, I'm certain this will be taken care of soon enough."

"And so it will." Macon got up from his chair. "Double service this Saturday then?"

"Yes, and it appears the weather forecast is on our side for once. Only sunshine predicted."

Macon smiled and said goodbye. He walked out of the funeral home and toward Gunnison Bank and Trust. Once there, he went to a small vault with one of the bank employees and opened Margaret Cameron's safety deposit box after he was left alone. He lifted a small bag out and untied its drawstring. His eyes fell on the finger bone and he smiled. "You pulled a quick one on them, Margaret. That decoy you kept in the box on the mantle fooled them sure enough. I was never convinced it would, but by God they went after your nephew like hounds after a fox." He held the bone up and studied it before saying, "Don't you worry, I'll put half of it in the bottom of your grave and half in Cullen's. I hated to lie about him wanting to be buried here with you, but it's one way to keep the talisman's magic strong." He put the bone back in the bag, tightened the drawstring, and slipped the bag in his coat pocket.

As Macon walked to his Jeep, part of the conversation he'd had on the phone with Mike Henderson resurfaced.

"Damned shame about that young fella," Henderson had said. "By the time I got back to the spot with some medicine and clothes, he was already dead. Never was sure where he got that spoiled food." The line had gone silent for a few moments before Henderson added, "Damnest thing was all the racket I heard walking back to the where the young fella was. Gave me goose bumps, all that creepy cawing noise and fluttering wings filling up the night. Hell, I never cared for crows no how."

Macon opened the Jeep's driver door, smiled a grim smile and thought, "Neither did my clan the Fains, especially my distant kin Maldora."

He drove in silence toward Gunnison Cemetery where he'd wait patiently until the sexton had both plots dug and ready.

6.

Glamis Castle, Scotland present day

The current owners of Glamis Castle closed most of the fortress due to maintenance costs, the torture room and prison in the bowels of the structure one of the first areas to be locked up and forgotten, that room now void of light, the wood and stone of its walls decrepit, its instruments of torture long removed to museums or on display in other, viable locations of the castle.

The five shapes materializing in that torture room did so in dank darkness, theirs a constant state of perpetual gloom, clammy air, and a yearning for tranquility. As the figures solidified in the murky shadows, black wings and eyes, talons and fingers, fleshy lips and crooked beaks formed a miasma of features monstrous to behold.

"There is no fire," the one once known as Baron Lochlan said.

"No fire, no light," what once walked the earth as Baron McDonald added.

The others, Baron Guthrie, the preacher Gordon, and the young baronet Killearn, mumbled their agreement and concerns.

"Matters not," the McDonald thing voiced as it snapped its talons, a dull glow of red then forming on the tips. "This unearthly fire will do. Now give up the bone, Killearn." The baronet creature shuffled over and held up the finger bone. "Place it in the furnace there," the MacDonald thing ordered, and the bone was set inside the cold, ancient ashes in the furnace near where the rack once rested. The MacDonald thing laid the fire from his talons on the finger bone and then stepped back, joining his fellow creatures.

"Now," the former preacher Gordon said in a hushed, raspy tone. "Now we can lift the curse and finally be forgiven."

The five huddled around the furnace and watched with lifeless eyes as the finger bone started to burn. Time passed and the bone glowed. Still more time went by and yet the bone remained solid, unharmed by the flame.

The five malefactors grew restless, flustered, and began to aggravate each other, fussing and pecking.

"Why does it not turn to ashes?'

"Why are we not changing to our restored human spirit forms?"

"Are we to be denied relief from the curse even now?"

Their raucous cries echoed in the empty room, the fire in the furnace soon dying, the changeling finger bone faintly glowing but unscathed.

Then silence filled the spot until deep in the gloom came the monotonous sound of dripping water, an eternal metronome for those not absolved, for those doomed to fly forever through the night, forever flapping black wings of damnation—the Glamis Crows.

The Flying Dentist
Mark Thomas

Real? Or just a hallucination? Who could explain this indestructible phantom?

1

Life is a big pile of feathers.

If you cleverly arrange those random bits of plumage you can create wings, which are marvels of natural technology, but if you're a complacent fuck-head, you'll stagger through life with little bits of fluff stuck to your pants, clutching an empty pillowcase.

I've always believed in making the best of any situation, even when it's extraordinarily unlikely that things will work out. Like my mom used to say, why be a feather duster when you can be a flying demon?

That philosophy certainly inspired my opioid-induced spasm of friendship with Curtis Weidman.

We met in a semi-private room at the new hospital. My lower right arm had been shattered in a clownish encounter with The Flying Dentist, and Weidman had been shot through his right humerus with additional damage to his rib cage and lung. We were lying in beds that were six inches too short, moaning for our next dose of pain killers, and unable to peel back the foil on our pudding cups with a single non-dominant hand.

It might seem like a bad patch of water to spawn a friendship, but that's the type of thing I'm talking about– wings or pillow—you need to make a choice.

Anyway, Weidman's injury wasn't the result of a bullet, as you might expect, he was shot with an *arrow*, a broad-bladed hunting missile designed to kill a moose at ninety yards. If it hadn't been slowed down by a couple of tree branches, a loose flap of Kevlar and two pieces of bone, it might have gone clear through his body, leaving a cleanly scoured hole an inch in diameter.

Weidman was the first police responder to a 911 call that indicated a neighbour was in the process of butchering his family. Distracted by the urgency of the situation, Curtis didn't cinch up his body armour as neatly as he probably should have. He and his partner charged into the house a little more quickly than was prudent. They found three victims, and at least one was still alive because she indicated that the person responsible (a deranged husband) was in the back yard. The partner attempted to truss up the witness, and Weidman went through the rear door while backup sirens filled the air.

The bow-shot felled Curtis while he was taking a third tentative step. Luckily the shaft of the arrow snapped as he fell to the ground, otherwise his arm might have been pinned to his side and he would have been easily finished off while writhing on the lawn. As it was, Weidman was able to defend himself, utilizing the clear-headed adrenaline rush that sometimes accompanies catastrophic injury.

Curtis realized that the shooter was in a wooden fort nestled in the crotch of a Stewartia tree in the back corner of the lot. The injured policeman crossed his legs, balanced his service revolver on the instep of his left foot and started blasting.

He was admonished for that later. Weidman's superiors figured that emptying a chamber in the general direction of some playground equipment, while aiming with his feet, was irresponsible even in those stressful circumstances. But the gunshots brought a quick crowd of reinforcements to the immediate area. There was a brief exchange of ammo including eleven more arrows and at least seventy bullets. When it was all over, Robin Hood was immobilized within his little rustic castle. A police marksman had crawled onto a neighbour's elevated pool deck and got him with a rapid series of blind shots through the rear plywood wall.

The three victims assaulted within the house all eventually died, but no civilians got injured in the ensuing crossfire, which is a little surprising. One of the shooter's super-arrows penetrated the door skin of a car parked in a cul-de-sac, over three hundred feet distant (small world—I happen to be dating the car owner). Weidman was the only policeman who got his uniform bloody.

Upon closer examination, the shooter's hideout turned out to be more like a hunting stand than a tree fort. The structure was a small, solid cube, with a trap door in the bottom and a horizontal slit in front, just spacious enough to track a target and discharge a weapon.

But the floor and front wall of the construction had been lined with pieces of diamond plate steel which isn't strictly necessary when your adversaries are suburban grazing quadrupeds. This person was clearly planning to shoot something that might shoot back. There were more pieces of loose steel lying on the floor as if he had originally planned to armour-plate all six walls of the interior.

The urge to butcher his family must have messed up the timing of his other messed-up obsessions.

Incidentally, there was no compelling reason for the man to attack his wife, sister-in-law and step-child, then howl loudly enough to garner three separate 911 calls, barricade himself in a military-grade play pen and shoot it out with the local tactical squad. His life was imperfect, but he didn't seem to be facing more obstacles than anyone else on the street. His wife wasn't sleeping her way through the neighbourhood, his debt load was high but not alarming, the sister-in-law was supposedly a little nosy, but countered that with a lot of free baby-sitting. A PET scan didn't show any physical brain abnormalities either (but I'd bet that says more about the current state of neurological science than the true state of William Tell's cortex.)

The man had a split-level in the suburbs, which suggests a pretty strong impulse to fit in. There was a tricycle in the driveway and a barbeque under the car port. He weeded the front walk and had a cement planter shaped like a smiling pig beside a decorative mailbox. In a way, his house was just like any other... except for the steel-reinforced pill box at the nethermost edge of his property.

Weidman, like everybody else, assumed that some specific grievance must have made him snap and it was only a matter of time before that personal agony was exposed.

But I recognized a binary life choice when I saw one. The sniper's nest and decorative mailbox had always coexisted in the man's psyche and he had symbolically chosen one over the other the day he shot Weidman. There didn't have to be some particular, toxic disappointment to trigger it. Actions like human-hunting don't evolve through a decipherable chain of cause and effect.

Here's an interesting side bar. Weidman's partner ended up on permanent disability because a victim fell apart in his hands during the rapid first aid survey. The killer had used a double-bladed field dressing knife called "The Eviscerator" to make shallow cuts in the body of his sister-in-law after he strangled her and it was just the stringy bits holding everything in place until the cop disturbed the arrangement. The experience qualified as Post Traumatic Stress because the officer was judged unfit to holster a weapon or even file papers afterwards.

Weidman, however, was back on light duty almost immediately after his hospital stay because his trauma was considered largely physical. He (and his wife) considered it unfair, probably because they had an insider's view of just how screwed up he was, but their opinions didn't transfer effectively to medical forms. That's important because this new shitty attitude was one of things that cemented our friendship.

Weidman got a bizarre surprise while he was attempting to recover in the hospital. His X-rays revealed a dark oval shadow in his humerus, completely unrelated to the arrow wound, just underneath the shoulder attachment. The dark spot meant there was fragile hollowness where there should have been bone and marrow. I heard two doctors give Curtis the good-bad news. If the cancer hadn't been discovered Curtis would have died soon, or at the very least had his arm and shoulder removed for containment.

That scrap of conversation creeped me out.

The stump of an arm can be fitted with a prosthesis and you can go for the Terminator look if you've got a little extra cash and ask them to leave coils of wire bulging where the real muscle tissue used to be. But you can't dress up the void of a missing shoulder. It's the kind of visual subtraction that makes one look inhuman.

But Weidman's cancerous humerus was quickly swapped with a sculpted piece of titanium and he didn't even need chemotherapy. According to the doctors, getting shot by a psychopath hiding in a pimped-out tree fort was an incredibly lucky break.

But for some reason, Weidman refused to see the specimen bottle as half full– and that's another thing that made us friends.

He didn't tell me much of that story himself. Most of what I just recounted was reported in the newspapers, and the rest I could figure out by the way his wife crossed her arms.

At first, when we were lying in our hospital beds, I didn't even realize Curtis was a cop, which is an indication of how much my own pain was distracting me. When you're in my line of work you tell yourself that you can recognize law enforcement types in any circumstance. Weidman had the neat little mustache, the regulation haircut, the gym-membership physique, and the blinkered outlook that should have immediately given him away as rank and file law enforcement. But I didn't clue in, even when a bunch of his look-alike friends filled the room for a visit.

We didn't fully appreciate it at the time, but Weidman and I shared a low-grade, non-specific paranoia that warped our perception of the world around us. We both chose to be in semi-private rooms, for example, calculating we were half as likely to die from institutional neglect if two people with stethoscopes hanging from their necks were obliged to walk through the door everyday.

And we both suspected the nurses were experimenting on us because they dropped off trays of food without waiting to see if we could actually feed ourselves.

We quickly reached an arrangement where I would crawl over to Weidman's bedside, and firmly hold the pudding cups from our dinner trays while he peeled back the foil lids. Then we could divide the spoils. We usually managed to remove our spoons from hygienic plastic sheaths with our teeth, but sometimes we had to tag-team those as well. I have to admit, I didn't treat Curtis fairly, at first. I would typically take *both* Cozy Shack Tapiocas and make Weidman eat a double dose of butterscotch (or even apple sauce) that looked like cat's vomit. He didn't like it, but I was in no mood to fuck around. I also regularly took Weidman's Jello and gave him my concrete oatmeal cookie in return.

Because I wasn't absolutely bedridden, I could do little favours for him throughout the day, and maybe I figured that hogging all of the decent snacks balanced the account.

The rough treatment probably did Weidman some good, anyway. I got the impression that he had been a bit of a bully before his near-death experience. The arrow plus cancer diagnosis was a healthy dose of humility; shaking him down for pudding just continued the good work.

Anyway, our biggest problem when we were roomies was physical pain management. Somehow, the nurses red-flagged us as potential addicts during our first night (the sobbing, threatening and pleading might have had something to do with it) and tightly controlled our intake of I.V. happy juice. So, Curtis had me take two hundred dollars from his wallet and buy Tylenol and Demoral capsules from some kid down the hall who had been hospitalized during a violent arrest but didn't hurt as much as he let on. I still didn't realize that Weidman was a cop, my impaired brain just figured he was resourceful, in a general way.

Goo wasn't dribbling from *my* side into a graduated plastic cup, so I was able to sidle down the hallway clutching a damp handful of bills and return with a plastic bag of pills and four more pudding cups. Weidman immediately swallowed an extra codeine caplet and I gobbled several of the morphine derivatives. Our differing drug abuse pathways was another indication we were meant to be buddies. I couldn't tolerate codeine because it made my tummy hurt, and morphine gave Curtis horrific nightmares featuring things like pin worms eating his penis.

Initially, our friendship was very utilitarian. Once, I took the pee bottle from between his legs and dumped it in the toilet just before his wife came for a visit. His legs would sometimes spasm and he thought it undignified to splash hot pee around while he was making small talk. But I insisted he repay the favour by taking his plastic fork and opening up an abscess on the small of my back before the pain made me hurl myself down the concrete steps by the elevator. It wasn't long, though, before our conversations didn't need ulterior motives to prop them up.

We were aware that nurses were available (and somewhat willing) to squeeze pustules, wipe up pee dribbles and even open stubborn food containers. But hospitals are busy places and we both reasoned, between mouthfuls of contraband painkillers, that if we squandered the nurse-visits on trivial things they wouldn't be available when we *really* needed them.

Curtis's wife didn't know what to make of me, even after I saved her husband's life.

She would always lean away when we talked, cross her arms, and generally position a lot of obstacles like chairs or stacks of bedpans between us. Her name was Kaerile, or something ridiculous like that, but Weidman called her "Kerry" so that's good enough for me. Anyway, she was young, *maybe* thirty, but had an intriguing grey streak in her reddish blond hair. She also had one slightly crooked front tooth, which I found strangely attractive. She was always thoroughly covered up, but morphine-induced X-ray vision informed me her body was beautiful underneath the protective layers.

Women, generally, find me creepy, so Kerry's standoffishness was familiar. Whenever she was in the room, I honestly tried not to leer at her with my robe hanging open, and I made an effort to be more superficially cheerful than her dopey husband.

Here's how I saved Weidman's life.

Well, to be completely honest, here's how I almost killed him through both direct action and neglect, then turned the tables at the last second and sort of pulled him back from the dark tunnel.

First of all, I didn't realize that Curtis had squirrelled away most of the codeine capsules purchased from the little shit-head two doors down. I had assumed he was downing the pain killers as quickly and indiscriminately as I was, like shooters of cheap rye at closing time, with pudding chasers. I hadn't noticed that his generalized depression had morphed into something more ominous until he ate a heaping handful of the capsules all at once and just sort of shut down.

I was blabbing on and on about something (the morphine had temporarily disabled my discretion) and I was angry when Weidman didn't grunt a response. So I told him to empty his own pee bottles from now on and I rolled my body elaborately away from him, just to be mean. He was still tethered to a bunch of drainage tubes and could barely shift from one bedsore to another.

There was no sound for a long time, then one of Curtis's machines gave a gentle, persistent beep. I rolled back towards him and saw his mouth pried open unnaturally and the whites of his eyes focussed on the ceiling light.

I hit the call button for the nurses' station then lumbered over to Weidman's bed, and dug two fingers into the place where the carotid artery should have been. I couldn't feel a pulse. I leaned close to his mouth but couldn't feel any breath.

Then I hollered as loud as I could and started to administer CPR. Unfortunately, I'd lost most of my vocal power as an odd side-effect of pain killer overuse. And, of course, I only had one useful arm.

Basically, I dropped left-handed hammer fists down on Curtis's rib cage like we were inside the octagon, then attempted feeble mouth to mouth resuscitation in between croaking cries for help.

Here's the thing.

My sense of time was badly distorted, but I'm positive it took much too long to get a response from the professionals. The bureaucratic screw-up we had irrationally feared was actually happening. I'd almost broken my good arm by the time an orderly happened to poke his head in, then it was code tapioca and all hell broke loose. Doctors were floating around the room and some of them seemed to be screaming angrily.

Curtis spent a day in intensive care, but insisted he be taken back to our room as soon as it was apparent that he wasn't going to die. I should have been discharged by that time but we seemed destined to re-unite. I broke a blood vessel in my injured arm by sneezing violently and a vascular surgeon had to be flown in to make my arm look like an arm again, rather than a wet purple garbage bag.

So we were in adjacent beds once more, but had been inexplicably switched to different sides of the room. Weidman could barely speak but he managed to call me over. "Peeeeeeter," he howled weakly like a ghost tempting me to join him on the other side. I didn't know what to expect when I lowered my right cheek close to his lips. I half expected him to bite off a chunk of meat and hork it back at me, but he only whispered "thank you" as his eyelids dropped like industrial window blinds. Then he slept for twenty-four hours.

Kerry never said "thank you," but I didn't hold it

against her. I understand how complicated some things are.

Our last few days as roomies ended up being full of candid personal conversation, and some people would have considered that healthy and normal. But we were a little embarrassed as we shook non-dominant hands and checked out.

Shortly after we were released from the hospital, Curtis and his wife Kerry wandered in to a café called "Bookbinders" where I was eating lunch with a woman named Pearl Swinghammer, who was my girlfriend/dental hygienist. Her car was the one hit by the high-test hunting arrow during Weidman's assault. For some reason, she didn't notice the damage. For weeks, she drove around with the thing waggling from the passenger door like a piece of alien genitalia. I pointed out the oversight in the hospital parking lot when she picked me up.

Anyway, Curtis plopped down at my table, grabbed a couple of onion rings and told me the latest news about my Flying Dentist.

2

Cole Hammond aspired to be the stereotypical loan shark you see in movies. He called himself "The Dentist" because he thought it conjured up a threatening image of someone who forcibly removed teeth. Hammond wore a fat silver ring with a human molar inset like a yellowing jewel, and he always pointed it out to acquaintances once he realized that people wouldn't voluntarily comment. He tried to give the impression that he regularly punched people's teeth out, then picked up the shattered enamel from the sidewalk and fashioned it into accessories.

I first met the guy a couple of years ago when I rented him some office space for a tax refund business. But he didn't have enough short-term capital, so that failed miserably. I leased him another space for a payday loan venture. Hammond screwed that up by lending money to a string of delinquent individuals who weren't impressed by his teeth-jewels. He wanted me to assist him collecting the bad debt file, but I told him I was too busy flossing my own incisors.

Hammond was always yapping about how connected he was with organized crime figures in Hamilton and Montreal, and swore that he would soon be welcomed back in the major leagues. He thought of himself as a professional baseball player who had been sent to a farm club to work on his slider. He was temporarily enduring the humiliation of our business relationship, but his time was coming. His time was always coming. Some unnamed rival would soon shit his pants in front of the boss then Hammond could leave people like me behind and re-enter the world of Escalades and custom-made shoes and strippers who paid attention.

The talk didn't impress me.

When The Dentist's pay day loan venture went belly up and his girlfriend kicked him out of her apartment, I assisted the downward spiral by renting Hammond a sleazy bachelor unit on the first floor of a poorly subdivided five-plex, so he could drink a case of Alberta Premium Rye and plan his next failure.

Pearl and Kerry noisily dragged chairs off to the side of our table and proceeded to discuss medical office politics. Kerry was the manager of a diabetic foot clinic and I guess that environment has as much intrigue as Pearl's orthodontist's. The women had previously met during hospital visits and I suspected they didn't like each other but that wasn't important now. They didn't understand our fascination with The Dentist, and wanted to avoid another rehash.

My last meeting with Hammond was almost fatal.

The Dentist had called me one morning saying he had a sure-thing business opportunity and wanted to invite me in at the earliest stage. He was already slur-talking, but I agreed to meet him because he was a couple of days late with his rent and I needed to serve him an eviction notice as a bit of friendly behaviour modification.

I didn't realize that Hammond had irrationally fastened on me as the root cause of his unhappiness. Sure, I'd screwed him with his last commercial lease, but no worse than any other desperate, greedy, mouth-breathing commercial tenant. His personal animus was illogical. But the point is, I was oblivious to the danger that awaited me until I was in no man's land, halfway up the front sidewalk.

I had parked the Silverado on a side street and walked to the five-plex because tenants' cars always overflowed the inadequate driveway. Hammond greeted me, in a manner of speaking, by stepping out onto the concrete veranda wearing a loosely-belted bath robe, and holding a hunting rifle. He swayed a little. The gun was pointed at the ground, not at me, and the stock was carelessly tucked under an armpit, but it was disconcerting, never-the-less. I pretended not to notice the partially concealed weapon and sauntered up the walk.

It was a difficult situation. Hammond appeared to be more than just drunk, he looked theatrically crazy and I found myself revisiting all of the mean-spirited things I had thought about him over the past couple of years and hoped he hadn't suddenly developed the ability to read minds. A strategic retreat would have been in order if there was anything to hide behind. As it was, I presented a large open target, even if the Alberta Premium rendered me somewhat fuzzy.

My shoes moved over the broken flagstones and I avoided eye contact as if The Dentist were some kind of animal that shouldn't be spooked. I was fantasy-planning to slink close enough to body check Hammond into the clapboard and beat him senseless with his own gun.

I extended a right hand, as if to shake, but froze at the sound of rapidly approaching police sirens. Then, Hammond surprised me by quickly whipping the gun barrel up and smashing my forearm with it. There was a loud crack and it was obvious one or both of the bones had been broken, even though I experienced that frightening pain-delay where a body part seems so detached that you almost wish it would start to hurt.

Instinctively, I shoved my left arm into Hammond's face and propelled him backwards into his shitty apartment. I heard him crash against a pressboard entertainment unit and I legged it across the lawn, with bits of arm swinging below my elbow like a forearm shaped bag. I climbed into the Silverado just as three police cruisers bumped onto Hammond's dirty patch of grass. Just minutes before my arrival, Hammond had discharged his weapon into the ceiling of his kitchenette and the upstairs tenant had called police.

I would have relished watching a couple of beefy cops jam their knees in Hammond's back as they cuffed him, but my arm was turning purple and still hadn't decided on its long-term attachment strategy, so I had to leave for the emergency ward before my mini adrenaline-rush faded.

At least I could be honest with the doctor at triage, a rarity in my work experience.

"He beat you with a gun barrel?" the woman asked incredulously, as she assigned me a spot with the next available orthopedic surgeon.

"Yeah," I admitted. The pain killers were starting to disorient me.

"Why didn't he just shoot you?"

"I've been wondering that myself," I said. Secretly, I didn't think he had the balls but there was no easy way to explain that to a stranger.

Weidman eventually described the full police confrontation for me. He wasn't present of course, because he was busy getting shot with a broad-bladed hunting arrow, but he had an eye-witness account from one of the officers involved, who ended up being assigned to the same trauma counseling group. All of those participants were compelled to elaborately revisit the events that fucked them up, so there were lots of juicy details.

Well, when the police cruisers were arranged in a tight semi circle, and six officers had disembarked, Hammond reappeared in the doorway, his robe a little looser and the hunting rifle in the ready position. The cops had their service revolvers balanced on squad car roofs and doorframes. Apparently, they followed protocol and gave Hammond an opportunity to put the gun down and get some pants on.

Hammond responded by firing four quick rounds then ducking back into his shit-cube. All six cops unloaded their weapons.

I knew that the encounter had been unusually violent because my first chore after being released from hospital was to personally assess the property damage for an insurance claim. Sections of the vinyl siding hung like crepe paper after a grade-eight prom, and the eavestroughs had been blown off the garage. Some of the facia on the *third* floor had been shredded and the angel-stone skirting the lower fifth of the building was pock marked and chipped.

It was impossible to count the bullet holes.

"What the hell happened?" I had asked Weidman. "Did The Dentist turn into some sort of mystic ninja and start running up the walls?"

"Funny you should say that," Weidman laughed. "The guy in my counseling group said the suspect grew wings and floated up near the roof line. He said he had to shoot him before his shadow infected the innocent."

"The guy's trying to get a disability," I snorted.

"It's not working. He's still on active duty."

Somehow, Hammond managed to escape. The delusional officer, Roger Foote, swore he made use of his newly sprouted wings and flew away, but three others were convinced he had burst through a permanently locked door, separating his living space from another tiny apartment, and left via that unit's rear door. Two cops chased a suspect down a dry creek bed for three miles only to discover they were pursuing the wrong guy—it was the tenant from the rear apartment, a sad piece of white trash named Gil Geneste, who had panicked at the combat noises.

Hammond was nowhere to be found.

The three nonpsychotic officers left on site made a search of Hammond's bachelor pad and determined that no one was hiding under the bed or in the laundry piles. There wasn't much area to inspect. Once additional officers arrived they went through the other four apartments pretty carefully.

Maybe The Dentist really had flown away.

The Bookbinder's waitress suddenly delivered a tray of imported Irish beers. Kerry must have ordered. She always drained a glass as if she needed it; Pearl wasn't a drinker but was determined to try for my sake. Weidman wasn't supposed to drink at all because of his medication but what can you do when a glass appears under your nose?

"What's the news?" I asked.

"Someone spotted The Flying Dentist in Brampton. An OPP officer made a traffic stop and recognized the face from APB circulars and called for backup."

"What kind of car was the guy driving?"

"A Lexus."

"Then it wasn't Hammond. If it was a Taurus with a missing passenger door and an 'I love Country Line Dancing' bumper sticker, it might have been him." Kerry and Pearl laughed loudly and for a moment I thought they had been following our conversation.

"You're right, it wasn't him. But the resemblance was close enough to warrant a trip to the station for fingerprints." Weidman was smiling. "Get this. The guy was a dentist. A real dentist. He runs a medical complex on Highway Ten. The name's Arcuri, and the business is legit."

The information about Hammond's doppelgänger was an interesting new wrinkle in the story fabric, but that's all. There was no new information about how Hammond had actually managed to elude the dragnet, and Weidman said that had become the subject of an internal investigation. A drunken, half-naked, delusional fuck-wit shouldn't have been able to outsmart several squad cars of trained officers, and fingers were being pointed.

"Hey," Kerry suddenly intruded into the conversation. "Remember to ask him."

"Oh yeah," Weidman said, "I need a favour. Me and Kerry are going away for the weekend and I need someone to stay in the house." He winced a little while talking as if he were trying to maintain his dignity during a rectal exam. Cops, in general, aren't very good at asking for help, and Weidman was a screwed-up sub set of that antisocial group.

He didn't need to explain why it was necessary for his house to be continuously occupied. He had already mentioned in a rambling hospital tirade that his neighbourhood was populated by a number of young people who had recently discovered the joys of breaking and entering, and policemen's houses weren't given a courtesy pass. There was nothing to do but hunker down and wait for the little hurtbags to get caught in the act. Unfortunately, that strategy was taking too long.

"Sure," I said.

Lunch eventually broke up and we walked towards the parking garage. We passed a glassed-in display at the entrance of the public library called "Shoes from the nineteen twenties." I'm sure it was supposed to inspire people to check out Fitzgerald or Faulkner. As we sauntered by, I noticed a pair of boots that tugged at something deep within my limbic system.

I'd never seen or heard of anything like them. They were labeled "Chestnut crushing" shoes, and they must have been worn to stomp vats of those common nuts into an edible paste, like you might crush grapes, if grapes were as hard as lumps of concrete. I found the odd-looking footwear absolutely fascinating. First of all, the shoes were enormous because they were supposed to be strapped over clunky work boots. A placard said they were size fifteen, which meant they were a perfect match for my own over-sized lumps if I wore thin socks. The uppers had flexible, overlapping metal shingles, like Venetian armor. And the soles! Attached to the underplate of each shoe were seven roughly serrated, gently curved mini-swords.

Each knife was formed from a piece of tapered angle iron, like a sturdy tent peg, and therefore double-bladed. Large notches had been carved into each edge so they resembled rows of monstrous teeth that certainly looked capable of turning tubs of chestnuts into unappetizing viscous sludge. They could have been the footwear lesser demons wore to force the corpses of sinners into little nooks of hell.

I had to have those shoes.

"I'm going to need a favour from you, as well," I said to Weidman. "Later this afternoon."

"Sure." He was eager to get out of my debt. "What do I have to do?"

"Kick a garbage can in the library."

***

I've been self-employed for most of my life.

The quasi-legitimate part of my portfolio involves property management for a family of Macedonian criminals named the Tripkos. It doesn't require a lot of time, but as far as any government agency is concerned it's the sole focus of my existence. My *real* job is to participate in insurance scams orchestrated by the same family. Usually, that involves starting fires with household chemicals.

I grew up in the golden era of industrial deregulation where wildly hazardous chemicals could be found in the supply closets of any medium-sized business. My all-time favourite is a paint deodorizer that smells like vanilla cake mix but will burst into flame if it is heated a few degrees above room temperature or mildly agitated. It was banned decades ago because it couldn't be safely transported, but I still have fifteen gallons of the stuff stored in a ventilated locker in a barn.

When the paint deodoriser is mixed with an industrial etching paste and a solvent that dilutes a boutique urethane product called "Xylene," a green fireball is produced. The etching paste has little shards of iron oxide in it, and those fragments of metal heat up rapidly when exposed to the air. It's sort of like old-fashioned oven cleaner, except it's strong enough to de-grease steel slabs in preparation for welding repairs. The temperature increase is more than enough to ignite the paint deodoriser and solvent.

If the three chemicals get splashed together they generate an effect worthy of an action movie. Of course, you can initiate the explosion remotely, but incriminating bits of the detonator will always be left behind, especially since this type of fire isn't long-lasting. I prefer a more primitive method of placing the chemicals in thin-walled plastic containers, which can be lobbed like grenades or simply allowed to chemically disintegrate. The only danger with my technique is getting your explosion a little early, in a jacket pocket or car trunk.

I selected a tall plastic garbage container near the first-floor library photocopier as the launch site.

My home-made bomb was contained within a clear plastic tube originally subdivided into three sections to dispense colorful bath salts. It was flimsy without the bath salts to support it, and had a two-part twist-off cap system that was perfect for this type of household arson project.

I photocopied some lease documents in a clumsy attempt to blend in with the other library patrons, although it was hardly necessary because everyone seemed preoccupied. The homeless guys were sitting on un-upholstered chairs reading the free papers and staff were pretending not to notice them. A bunch of young mothers were having exhausted conversations at the edge of a story-circle for pre-schoolers. Several university-aged students were shifting mounds of reference texts into cloth bookbags.

I pulled the bath salts bottle out of my pocket and twisted off lid number one. The secondary cover had a circular opening that could be twisted over any of the three sections. I maneuvered it over the etching paste, then reached my whole arm into the garbage can and nested the bottle, upright, in the waste. I had a paper in my hand as I withdrew it from the can, as if I was retrieving something thrown away by mistake, but that part of the little drama was pure paranoia. No one was paying attention.

Then I wandered out of the library and back to Bookbinder's café to get a coffee and Danish. Weidman was waiting at the counter, like we had arranged. We walked back into the library together, but the young woman at the desk politely informed me that food and drinks weren't allowed past the newspaper reading section. Weidman wandered in alone, and I stood by the circle of homeless guys, munching away.

Weidman saw the garbage can, and looked over at me for confirmation. I raised my Danish at him and smiled. He grabbed a corner of the can and pretended to lose his balance, giving it a violent shake. He looked back at me with a slightly puzzled expression on his face. I smiled at him again and he wandered back past the checkout desk without making further eye contact.

Now it was just a matter of waiting. I probably made the chemical bomb seem a little more unstable than it actually was when describing it earlier. Generally, the world isn't nearly as flammable as people expect. The unpredictable part of my mixture is the etching paste. It heats up rapidly when exposed to air, but that's when you're spreading it around on a piece of ship's steel. In an open bottle, the air exposure is minimal and temperature rise is agonizingly slow. If you give the bottle a vigorous shake, however, the reaction speeds up exponentially.

In this case, I waited about fifteen minutes, then there was a deep, muffled noise. *FLLLOOOM,* the garbage can said, like an angry goblin, and its plastic lid was launched into the air, chased by a roiling green ring of flame ten feet in diameter.

There was a loud secondary pop, that probably meant oxygen had exploded as a by-product of the chemical reaction, but I never paid enough attention in science class to fully understand the process.

The green circle of flame slowly floated to the ceiling where it boiled against the tiles for a few seconds then dissipated. A few sheets of burning copier paper floated like glowing snowflakes.

SHEEEEEE IT

The homeless guys were howling and quickly ran over to the garbage can, forgetting that they weren't supposed to mix with the other patrons. The toddlers in story circle were shrieking and the staff had all abandoned their positions to run in the direction of children's lit. The moms were frozen, staring open-mouthed at the bizarre fire-cloud, temporarily forgetting to be worried about their kids.

It took me seven or eight seconds to plant my ass on the check out desk, swing my feet over to the restricted-access side, walk into the glassed-in display area that contained this month's tribute to "Shoes of the Nineteen Twenties" and place the coveted chestnut crushing boots in a cloth bag.

3

Weidman introduced me to Roger Foote in a pancake house. Ostensibly, we met there so I could pick up a set of Curtis's house keys but there was something less innocent going on. Weidman called the other officer "Geek," and I thought it was incredibly unprofessional until Foote handed me his business card and I saw that the nickname was proudly included on it.

I didn't immediately recognize the name, but the little guy sitting opposite was the officer who claimed to have seen Cole Hammond sprout wings and fly across a north-end neighbourhood. I guess he and Weidman had become friendly during their counseling sessions. Foote didn't look crazy.

Geek suggested parking my Silverado on a side street in Weidman's neighbourhood, and I realized what was up: they didn't want me to scare away the pubescent burglars, they actually wanted me to have a confrontation when the little shitheads broke in.

That was fine, I guess. Most friends would have considered it unethical to place someone they cared about in danger, but we weren't friends in a conventional way. I wondered if Kerry approved of luring sociopathic teenagers into her home. Geek had given me his card so I could phone him personally if something went down, rather than phoning the 911 switchboard.

"Geek will take care of everything," Weidman said, and they both looked up at me with their heads tilted, like baby birds. I was never specifically told to club anyone with my cast. I told Weidman to enjoy himself and tried to adopt the body posture of someone who had everything under control.

***

I couldn't help myself.

I started snooping through Weidman's garage, almost as soon as I'd thrown my hockey bag into a guest bedroom. Perhaps it was because I didn't really know Weidman at all, and the best way to get inside someone's head is to look at all the shit they are in the process of discarding.

Most of my professional life has been spent sorting through the stuff people warehouse in their garages. The Tripkos and I have made a lot of money over the years by replacing skis, snow mobiles, riding lawn mowers, and golf clubs with the charred husks of stuff damaged in earlier fires and then re-burning everything in the new location.

But I digress.

In Weidman's garage, I hit psychological pay dirt almost immediately. I pulled two large Rubber-made containers off some over-sized metal shelves. The tubs were neatly labelled "everything proof suit," which piqued my curiosity. I opened them up and spread the contents over the floor. There were black, white and greyish clothing parts. It was difficult to see how everything was supposed to fit together, though, and I eventually had to consult an instruction manual.

Two years prior to being shot, Weidman had enthusiastically embraced all things violent, relating to his profession. He mentioned taking courses in Kingston and Washington where he learned to rappel from helicopters and ram buildings with armoured vehicles. Perhaps he thought it was possible to avoid whatever demons were chasing him by getting on the local SWAT team. The plan clearly hadn't worked because he was still wearing a patrolman's uniform when the broad-bladed hunting arrow pierced his trunk.

The super-suit must have been left over from that period of his life.

The paperwork referred to the whole getup as "incendiary armour" and it was labeled "PROTOTYPE" which might explain why I've never seen anything like it on the news. There was a thin, white, cottony inner-most layer that was meant to absorb sweat. Then there was a white, ribbed garment that had dozens of little water tubes running through it like a radiator, meant to keep the wearer comfortable underneath the outer protective layers. A small circulating pump tucked neatly underneath an arm. A network of overlapping black Kevlar pads seemed designed to cover all of one's fleshy bits and wrapped cleverly around hinge joints, ankles and neck. This part of the suit was divided into upper and lower body sections. Each part was bulky but shockingly light-weight. The shoes were small (eleven and a half) and were the only element that didn't expand to accommodate a wide range of body types.

The gloves were clever because delicate finger pouches allowed fine motor capabilities, but that inner arrangement was protected by thick rectangular slabs. There was a helmet with a squishy inner concussion-resistant bag and a thick, clear face shield.

The strangest component was the baggy, coarsely-knit greyish coverall that was draped over everything, including the helmet. There were no eye holes, but the mesh was loosely woven in the face area so that you could see through it. Apparently, it was designed to shed chemical splashes.

The literature also said that this thin, outermost sheath resisted penetration by knife or arrow tip, red hot nails and other types of shrapnel as well as flaming globs of phosphorous.

It was the type of protective gear you'd be eager to strap on if your job was to defuse bombs while under sniper fire. Weidman must have purchased it himself, dreaming of those glamourous assignments.

I loved the super-suit as much as a kid getting his first hockey sweater at Christmas. I quickly stripped down to my boxer-briefs and tried it on. The thin white long-john segment was delightful next to the skin. The tubed, radiator suit added girth to my arms so I looked like a pro-wrestler action toy. The upper body armor pulled on as easily as a sweatshirt, but looked like the horny carapace of some alien battle-crab. The armored pants were similar, they looked to be composed of a dozen discreet pieces but they were all strapped together and slipped on as smoothly as fleece pajamas. Then, I climbed into the greyish outermost layer. It had a zipper that started midway down the right thigh, made a lateral detour across the crotch, then up the chest past my left nipple and partially around the neck. It was the smoothest zipper I had ever encountered in my life.

I got the entire kit on as quickly as I could and stared at myself in the pitted, full length mirror Weidman had hung beside the connecting door to the house. At first, I was barely there. It was strange– the silvery outer layer blended with the mottled cement walls. I seemed to have a watery gray outline but no mass. Maybe it's the same principle as a "green screen" that makes some objects invisible during special effects filming.

When I was a kid, I used to read Flash Gordon comics. On one of the planets he visited, there were a race of clay people that used to camouflage themselves by pressing their lumpy bodies against the muddy walls of their environment. When Flash, or other unsuspecting intruders walked by, the clay people would peel themselves off the earthworks and kick the shit out of them.

Flash must have figured out how to best them, or the comic would have had a different title, but that isn't my point. I was now one of the monsters and I liked it. I experimented by shifting around and watched alien-me pop in and out of focus in the dirty mirror.

The last piece of my ensemble was, of course, the chestnut crushing boots that I had stolen from the library display. I'd brought them into Weidman's house in the hockey bag I used as overnight luggage. The bomb-suit came with a pair of stretchy Kevlar socks and I pulled them on, then slipped my feet into the steel boots and cinched up the straps.

Standing atop the serrated knives, I was a full seven feet tall, and enormously bulky within the layers of armour. I no longer fit in Weidman's mirror, and had to hunch down, bending my knees like a gigantic insect. I was delighted by my ferocious appearance. I even imagined that the air was full of insect-like whirrs and clicks.

Wait a minute. For once, the sound effects weren't coming from the theatre of my mind. The noises were real.

Someone was sawing a hole through the side door of Weidman's garage. As I stared at the interior of the metal door I saw a tiny, exploratory filament puncture the skin, like an egg tube looking for an unsuspecting host. Then suddenly, that initial guide was surrounded by a circular disc, about four inches in diameter. The entire head of the tool popped into the garage, then it was dragged back outside through the opening. There was a small pause, and a skinny hand reached through the hole and twisted upwards toward the deadbolt latch. Thin fingers strained like antennae until they located the interior lock mechanism, and snapped it to the right. Then the fingers disappeared.

There was another brief pause, the door was pushed open, and two young men displaced some grey backyard sky and walked inside. "Alright!" one of them said as he surveyed the mounds of stuff in Weidman's garage. One young man held an enormous electrical saw in front of his chest, like he was brandishing a futuristic machine gun. The tool was thick with protective cowlings and insulation, which perhaps explains why I didn't hear the break-in right away. He carefully placed the device on the cement floor, then straightened up.

I was invisible in my cement-colored armour, standing in front of the discoloured cement wall. I don't mean literally invisible– well, there was that odd effect where the two grey tones seemed to blend together– but the little criminals must have been so excited by the prospect of stealing cop stuff, or were so mentally unprepared to see a seven-foot, concrete-hued alien that I just didn't register. They looked at me several times, but gave no indication that they saw me.

Maybe they were just that stoned.

Eventually, I felt a little foolish and snicked towards them on my metal chestnut crushing boots.

As soon as I moved, they noticed me, and their terror was absolutely cartoonish.

I hadn't yet planned what to do when I encountered intruders, so I just grabbed the larger of the two by the throat and squeezed. The cast on my right forearm didn't affect finger movement. That hand became numb quickly, probably because of constricted blood flow, but the repaired radius and ulna were hanging in there.

When Weidman said that little shitheads were breaking into houses in his neighbourhood, I sort of assumed that it was fourteen-year-old punks riding a streak of beginner's luck. But these two were in their early twenties and the one I was strangling was fairly muscular. The scrawnier guy, whose upper arm fit through a four-inch circular opening, retreated through the door as soon as his shock dissipated. The person I was strangling thrashed around for almost six minutes before he turned purplish around the eyes and passed out.

I took a minute to catch my breath, then I stooped down and searched his pockets. He had a worn vinyl wallet that contained his drivers licence– home address on the opposite side of Weidman's street. "Jesus," I sighed. You don't take I.D. with you when you break into houses. What are they teaching them in school these days? I took a couple of deep breaths then crouched down and hoisted the burglar up onto my shoulders like a sleepy toddler and carried him through the open garage door. I had to duck down low to fit, but strangely enough, bending my legs made the muscles fire up and I felt powerful.

The thing that made me the happiest, though, was the sinuous comfort of the chestnut crushing boots. The metal soles were jointed and the heel flexed upwards with every stride. I was a little worried that they would get bogged down in softer surfaces, but there were enough points to distribute my weight nicely, and they provided healthy traction as I aerated the neighbourhood lawns.

I cut through the bushes along Weidman's driveway, angled across the enjoining patch of grass, then snicked down the deserted sidewalk with an unconscious garage-thief bouncing on my shoulders until I was opposite his bungalow.

I'm not really sure why I did this, but I bent down into a half squat, then straightened my legs, shoved upwards (damaged forearm be damned) and I propelled the guy into the middle of the street. If I were participating in an event at the criminal Olympics, that toss would easily qualify for the semi finals. On a sadder note, the young man landed cheek and shoulder first on the pavement and I experienced that groinal twinge that often accompanies witnessing a bad accident.

But I managed to overcome my squeamishness and snick back through the bushes and into the safety of Weidman's garage. There was no traffic on the street and no indication that anyone had seen me.

I removed the silver and black layers of the suit intending to neatly stow everything away in the tubs. Then I stripped off the ribbed layer that was supposed to function as a cooling radiator, and tried to figure out why my inner-most set of long-johns was dripping with sweat. After a brief inspection I realized that I hadn't turned the little pump on. I peeled off the sopping undies and rolled them into a ball. I would have to do a small wash load before I completed the re-packing job. I didn't want to risk killing the Weidmans with a toxic damp underwear marinade.

Back in my own clothes, I phoned Geek and told him I strangled the delinquent who had been expected to break into Weidman's house.

There was a noncommittal "Wooah" from Geek, who was initially unnerved by how fast everything went down. But after a few seconds he was more enthusiastic. "That's great work. Where is he?"

"I threw him in the middle of the road in front of his house."

"Oh." Geek was unsure again.

"I've got his wallet, and he left a kick-ass saw behind."

"I'll be there in five minutes."

Geek almost ran over the young man who was still lying in the street where I'd dumped him. Geek called an ambulance and the criminal was admitted to hospital with a fractured skull and separated shoulder. Later that evening, officer Foote officially registered charges, characterizing the crime as an armed home invasion, and reported that the intruder had injured himself running from the scene when he realized that the house wasn't deserted. Early the next morning, Geek would arrest the second burglar, hiding out in his grandmother's house, just a block away, near where I happened to have parked the Silverado. Both men left fingerprints on the saw, and it had been stolen, along with a trailer full of other contractor-grade tools, from another garage in the neighbourhood. The grandmother's house was packed with identifiable stolen goods, crude weapons, a toiletry bag full of hash, a shoe box full of money, drug paraphernalia, and a large Fed Ex container of counterfeit NBA hats.

But that was all in the near future.

During the evening of the break-in/assault, Geek led me through a witness statement that didn't contain any references to strangulation. Of course, I didn't mention wearing Weidman's camouflage super-suit, or knife-soled boots.

When that official business was over, I took the opportunity to ask Geek what the hell had happened during his recent confrontation with The Dentist.

"What do you mean?" he said innocently.

I explained my vested interest as a citizen who had been assaulted by the fugitive, as well as being the manager of the rental unit where the takedown had gone awry. I mentioned that I didn't have enough fingers and toes to count all the bullet holes when submitting a property damage claim to my insurance carrier.

"Oh," he said, a bit uncomfortable. "Two of the officers rolled underneath their cruiser to return fire, and they were aiming upwards, indiscriminately." He shrugged. "They're both under suspension right now." He made that last statement sound wistful.

"But you came through it okay," I goaded.

"I fired twice at an upstairs window. I thought it was an ambush, but the shadow I saw ended up being a floor lamp behind some curtains." He grimaced like he was experiencing a bowel blockage.

I was desperate to ask him if he *really* saw Cole Hammond sprout wings and float in front of the third-floor gables like a paunchy Peter Pan, but I didn't want to betray Weidman's confidence. Group therapy revelations might be protected by some sort of cop privilege and my inside knowledge might be considered a betrayal.

Geek and I parted company.

Our local paper has a reporter investigate every single 911 call, just in case one of the incidents has some sort of newsworthy twist. The assault on Weidman's garage apparently qualified, because it appeared on the front page two days later. The headline was "Goblin crimefighter likely spawned by salvia addiction."

I didn't see that particular story twist coming.

Both criminals had declared to police that they were attacked and pursued by a gigantic grey ghostlike creature with enormous claws. They must have mentioned it to some family members as well, because the story was circulating on social media sites. The men were avid drug users, so their version of events wasn't given much credence by investigators. But the reporter found a neighbour who corroborated the story. That person had reported a ten-foot high monster who melted, reappeared, then howled over the prostrate body of one of the criminals. That particular 911 call had initially been dismissed as a prank.

Someone must have been peeking at me through the curtains after all.

The reporter even photographed some claw-like gouges in a freshly repaired sidewalk slab. The news story was partly tongue-in-cheek, but there was a serious undertone. I was unaware that chewing salvia leaves had recently become trendy among Ormond's disaffected youth. The paper described the plant's hallucinogenic effect as "tactile synesthesia" and suggested ingestion of the drug as the most likely explanation for a group hallucination.

I wanted to ask Weidman about salvia use among police officers responding to weapons calls, but there never seemed to be a conversational entre. When he and Kerry returned from their love-weekend he had already read about my encounter in an on-line news service. Weidman was thrilled with the result. He wouldn't display his visceral joy in front of Kerry, but I could tell that the complex package of arrests, evidence, serious personal injury, and supernatural terror was exactly what he had coveted. Weidman couldn't stop smiling and couldn't stop thanking me.

I didn't mention that I'd already thanked myself, by placing the armored super-suit in the hockey bag I was lugging out of their house. The Rubbermaid containers on Weidman's garage shelves were now empty.

4

I have to explain something, or this next bit of the story is going to seem prohibitively strange.

First of all, I'm not a fighter. When I was

seventeen I ruined my right shoulder pushing a stolen BMW into a barn so Jeffery Tripko wouldn't go to jail, and that robbed my dominant arm of whatever power it once had. Now, if I were to lean over the table during Thanksgiving Day dinner and punch your grandmother in the face, it might leave a yellow bruise on her cheek, but that's about it.

My left hand isn't much better, though, so I can't blame everything on Jeffery. The physiology of punching is probably similar to throwing a baseball. Some scrawny little guys have hundred mile-an-hour fastballs, while beefier specimens like me can barely lob the ball to the plate.

That doesn't mean I haven't tried to be a badass. Over the past couple of decades, I have taken countless judo, karate, grappling, and MMA classes searching for the magic substitute for raw talent. Over all, it hasn't been a success, but I'd have to be a complete idiot not to have learned *something* during the thousands of instructional hours.

One MMA instructor taught me how to use a back fist to partially disguise my inability to throw a conventional punch. The technique is to bounce your knuckles off a person's upper lip shattering their nasal bones, and for some reason, my hand travels *back*wards with a fair amount of whippy, destructive force.

Another maneuver is called a "foot sweep," and it's fairly common in amateur wrestling. When an opponent shifts his weight, you kick out his moving support foot and he collapses. In practice, it's more dynamic than I just made it sound, in fact, the person cartwheels through the air when you get it just right. Five minutes after the grappling instructor showed it to the class, I had it mastered. Most people couldn't get it because they either waited until the foot was too firmly planted or struck while the person's weight was still balanced on the other leg. I could make anyone in the class look ridiculous after a few practice attempts.

My last technique doesn't have a name, as far as I'm aware. A Dutch karate instructor showed it to me when he saw that I had enough natural flexibility to do a front split. It's meant to be used when standing face to face with a belligerent person in tight quarters. Essentially, you pull straight down on any article of clothing. The person resists by pulling upward. That spasm of movement stops him from counterattacking for a fraction of a second. In that brief space of time you raise your size fifteen shoe above your right ear and drop the heel on the person's shoulder. The blow cleanly severs the collar bone and the person no longer cares if a drunken acquaintance said something inappropriate to his girlfriend. If you are young, slightly intoxicated, and angry at the world, you can footsweep the injured person into a table full of drinks, knuckle-rap him on the upper lip and then quickly drag your friend out the door.

The heel-dropping maneuver is shocking because the shoe just seems to materialize in the air. Of course, you have to be pretty loose in the hips to do what amounts to a standing split without throwing your upper body around to compensate.

I guess it's similar to the freakish ability that allows some underfed Cuban teenagers to throw that hundred mile an hour fastball. Of course, no one has offered me seven million dollars to break people's collar bones with my feet.

***

I was leaving Bookbinder's after an extended lunch, when a six/seventh model of an ordinary human approached me and said that if I didn't climb into the back seat of a mauve Chevy Malibu he would shoot me in the stomach. He had a hand hidden in a jacket pocket and there may have been enough room in there for a gun as well, so I cooperated. Whenever I find myself in a dangerous situation I tend to shut down, emotionally. It's not exactly heroic, but at least I'm not paralysed with dread.

So, I sat in the back of the mauve Chevy Malibu with a guy who may or may not shoot me in the stomach. The driver was a fat curly haired person who took three tries to enter a destination into a GPS unit attached to the dash. After a lot of sighing and squinting I knew we were taking a fifty-minute drive in the general direction of Toronto.

The guy in the back seat kept trying to taunt me. "Who'd you piss off?" he'd ask, and he seemed to genuinely want a response, it wasn't just rhetorical.

But even if I had been inclined to talk, I wouldn't have been able to answer the question. When you burn down garages and lease commercial real estate for a living you've encountered hundreds of people with poor impulse control so it's difficult to pick just one.

I remained quiet and avoided eye contact. That seemed to make my host's anger bubble a little more intensely and his questions evolved. "Hey, rod-boil, who'd you piss off?" Simmer simmer. "Hey, cock-cheese, who's angry? Hey, dick-sweat...." I risked a quick sideways glance. My antagonist seemed to know a lot about topical genital infections.

The traffic was a little thick and I quietly

suggested that the driver might want to take advantage of the diamond lane since we had two or more people in the car. The driver waited a couple of minutes to make it look like his own idea, then he shifted into the extreme left lane. There was a longish period of silence (if you discounted the "who was it?" chatter) then we turned northwest on Highway ten towards Brampton.

Eventually, we passed the welcome sign and ten minutes later bumped into to a nondescript commercial plaza near the arena. There was a suite of office spaces several stories high at one end, and a one-story series of stores at the other. The sign at the entranceway had the name Antonio Arcuri emblazoned on it.

What an odd coincidence. I was being taken at gunpoint to visit a person who had been mistaken for the last person who had physically assaulted me, Cole Hammond.

The Malibu drove around to the very back of the plaza where the blacktop sloped down to expose a service entrance. The driver got out and unlocked that door then we shuffled inside, me in the middle of a gangster sandwich. The little guy who wanted to shoot me and wasn't bothering to disguise it pulled out a cell phone and spoke briefly. "We're here." Pause. "Do you want to see him now, or should we just cut off his balls in the garbage room?" That was probably meant to disconcert me. I thought it was childish, but I kept my mouth shut on the million to one chance that the other end of the conversation involved the direction "don't cut off his balls unless he makes some smug little comment."

By way of explanation, I should say that I didn't feel particularly threatened at this point. The person who had built this neat little commercial/professional-use plaza and attached his name to the outside, couldn't shoot people, or slice off body parts. It's just not an effective long-term business model.

At the same time, I was also aware that people don't always act with their own best interests in mind. So, I had an exit strategy, if things got bad. The plan wasn't terribly detailed, but it involved *not* getting back in the Malibu with my new friends. I would create a scene in the midst of the biggest crowd I could muster within the building.

We took the elevator up four floors, walked around a corner and into an office. There was no waiting room, or secretarial space, just a big desk, and a lot of individual chairs for meetings and a decent amount of open area. A large picture window contained a view of Brampton's commercial district.

Cole Hammond sat behind the desk.

He stared at me for a few seconds. "Do you know what Mike Tyson did to Henry Tillman?"

I recognized Tyson's name as a boxer but Henry Tillman didn't ring any bells. "No," I said.

"Henry Tillman defeated Mike Tyson in the trials for the nineteen-eighty-three Pan American Games. When Tyson went pro he gave Tillman the opportunity for a rematch. Do you know what happened?"

"First round knockout?" I guessed.

He nodded and that was the end of our conversation. "Take him home," Hammond said to my escorts. I probably stood in the office as long as Tillman remained standing in his Tyson rematch. It was a surreal experience. I can only guess that Hammond really had been welcomed back into the organized crime fold and had re-assumed his old successful identity. He couldn't bear the thought of me witnessing his time in purgatory, and wanted to excise that unpleasant bit of reality.

I had been invited back, like Henry Tillman, for a brief glimpse at the successful incarnation before being dismissed forever.

"Home" was probably some cheesy euphemism for the place they dumped bodies.

We slumped back into the elevator and headed down. It stopped on floor number three where two nurses got on. The man who wanted to shoot me shuffled a little closer so that the ladies couldn't interfere.

As the little guy stepped sideways I swept his foot out of the way and his upper body pitched towards me. At the same time, I smacked him as hard as I could with the back of my left fist. There was a waist-high aluminum rail that went around the perimeter of the elevator and he struck it hard with his face on the way down. The contact made a hollow clunk that was a little sickening. The two nurses screamed and I ducked down and charged the driver. I didn't even have time to raise my fists, I just rammed the top of my head into his teeth and kept going. I scrambled for his hands and eventually found them. Thank God he wasn't holding a gun, he was clutching his key ring, and the individual keys were poking between his fingers and he was trying to jam the apparatus into my groin.

I yanked down on his arm and my size fifteen shoe materialized in the air beside his left ear. I sunk down a little as my heel dropped, trying to give gravity a power assist. The driver's clavicle made a loud popping sound as it sheared into two pieces. I wrestled the key ring out of his hand as he crumpled to the floor. The elevator door slid open again on floor number two and I walked quietly out into the hallway. The nurses were shrieking and a fed ex delivery guy who was waiting to board added some of his own noises.

I walked calmly to the end of the hall but as soon as I entered the stairway I sprinted down the last two flights to the lower maintenance level where we had entered. I found the garbage room door, went past the sticky recyclable containers and outside. I jumped into the Malibu and drove to the entranceway of the plaza. I didn't make the tires shriek like the nurses but I didn't dawdle, either. I waved a casual hand at the upper offices as I bumped the car back onto Highway Ten.

***

Back in Ormond, I was faced with an ethical dilemma. I wanted to call Weidman and his sidekick Geek and tell them that fugitive Cole Hammond had set up shop as the proprietor of a small medical centre in Brampton. But The Flying Dentist had eluded a police dragnet when he was an incompetent fuck-up, and now that he was re-connected and had a new/old identity that had already passed an OPP fingerprint check I was a little worried about my personal safety.

I suppose It's only fair to tell you how Hammond escaped. I wouldn't figure it out until the five-plex underwent another renovation two years in the future but there's no point in being coy now. The Dentist had constructed a false wall in the back of his bedroom closet with a clever hinged opening and bits of trim that artfully hid all of the seams. There was an irregular bit of wasted space there because of an air return duct and a toilet stack that had been installed during the building's initial subdivision. Hammond had jammed a reclining lawn chair into the cramped space, closed the door and simply waited for the police to leave. There was a pee jar, a freezer bag full of excrement and an empty butter tart package in the cavity along with the chair. Presumably, Hammond had an overnight bag packed and a water bottle in there as well.

For some reason, shooting me the finger from the back window of a limo wasn't good enough, Hammond had to blow up those unsatisfying years in a more theatrically puerile way.

At the time, though, I couldn't appreciate the convoluted, devious genius within Hammond's character, I only saw the immediate practical threat, as if it were an approaching thunderstorm.

Somehow, The Flying Dentist had turned years of incompetent failure completely around as if a horseshoe had been surgically implanted in his ass. I knew I had to deal with his threat, or I would spend my few remaining months on the planet nervously waiting to have my head beaten in with an Estwing roofing hammer, wielded by a cut-rate assassin chatting interminably about the appearance of my genitals.

I had to drive back to Brampton and get the confrontation over with.

Unfortunately, I had no idea where to find The Flying Dentist if he left his commercial nest, so I had to risk a childish stratagem. I looked up the number for Hammond/Arcuri's medical complex and called the general information number. I told a receptionist my name was Gil Geneste and wanted to talk to Mr. Arcuri about a personal matter.

I had no idea if Hammond had ever talked to his nearest neighbor in the five-plex, but he certainly knew the man's name and would be suspicious about the nature of the call. I was on hold for several minutes then the receptionist returned to say that Mr. Arcuri would be glad to meet me in his office, and would I like a car to pick me up?

I declined and asked how long Mr. Arcuri would be available at the complex. There was another longish wait then I was politely asked if I could meet Mr. Arcuri in his office at eight p.m. that evening. I said I would be delighted.

There were lots of directions about how to buzz into a building that was closed for business at that particular hour, and I pretended to listen carefully. I still had keys to the service entrance, the ones I had taken from the driver several hours earlier, and planned to enter (and hopefully leave) through the garbage room.

On the return trip, I drove the mauve Malibu rather than my Silverado. I loved my truck and if things went south I didn't want to bleed to death inside it.

I also put on Weidman's super-suit.

I didn't have the helmet on while I was driving, of course, because it would have looked silly and I wouldn't have fit in the vehicle. As it was, the layers of bullet-proof Kevlar elevated me like I was sitting on phonebooks. My head brushed the roof fabric of the Malibu and I had to twist my neck uncomfortably to see the roadway.

My feet toe-gripped the pedals within Kevlar socks; my chestnut crushing boots were on the passenger seat beside me.

I didn't have a plan incidentally, just a generalized hope that Weidman's suit really would stop bullets, arrows and globs of phosphorus until I could get my hands around Hammond's throat. I didn't own a gun, and it isn't easy to quickly get one in Canada. I might have been able to steal Weidman's service revolver, but I suspected that our seven-week friendship wouldn't shield me from the inevitable fallout.

I had to survive long enough to grab Hammond's throat… throat… throat… throat.

The Malibu made a funny noise and I glanced down at the speedometer. I was going more than forty kilometers over the limit, approaching the point where vehicles are automatically impounded at a roadside stop. I slowed down and had a vivid hallucination about The Flying Dentist being trapped in his office like a bird and flapping against the window and ceiling, just out of my reach.

Lately, I had been trying to cut back on the morphine, but I took a double dose just before getting behind the wheel. It probably wasn't wise.

Traffic thickened as I approached highway ten, then moved quickly all the way into Brampton. The little radiator pump hummed underneath my armpit and I could feel the water circulating through the ridges of my suit, like a secondary system of blood vessels.

I drove past the Arcuri building without stopping, just in case the police were still there investigating the bodies I had left in the elevator. I honestly thought the little guy who hit his head on the waist-high metal railing had been killed.

The dashboard clock indicated it was seven thirty.

The parking lot seemed absolutely deserted, so I

made a U-turn in a Macdonald's and drove back. I slowly went down the sloping blacktop to the rear of the building again. There were three cars parked near the garbage room service entrance. I stowed the Malibu far away from the others, in the corner of the lot against a neighbor's privacy fence.

Time to finish suiting up. I strapped into the chestnut crushing boots and got the helmet on, and covered up with the grey fabric. Then I opened up the trunk and constructed another bathsalt bomb with the paint deodorizer, solvent and etching paste that were stored in a vented carrying case. I figured a green ring of flame would make my entrance more dramatic.

It was a dark, overcast evening but strangely enough I could see very clearly through the helmet shield. The glass must have been designed for night vision. I opened the metal service door then tucked the key ring into a little pocket in the wrist of the suit. The designers had thought of everything.

Inside, there was an alarm panel, but it wasn't activated because The Flying Dentist hadn't yet left the building. I entered the lower floor hall, turned right and walked past the elevator to the stairway. I clicked my way up two floors before I realized that a security camera was tracking my progress. If a person was monitoring the live action, they would have the best story at the next company picnic.

At the fourth floor, I pushed the metal service door inward and listened carefully. I thought I heard voices mocking me, but that must have been nerves or the morphine. I strode, bent-kneed down the hall until I reached Hammond/Arcuri's door. I touched the handle and gently levered it down, which meant it was unlocked. Slowly, I allowed the handle to rise back to its original position.

Next, I removed the outer lid from the bathsalts container and violently shook the plastic tube. From past experience, I knew the contents would burst into flame as soon as I lobbed the bottle onto the office floor.

I pressed the door lever down, pushed against it, and the chemical bomb exploded in my hand. I could feel the initial heat from the etching paste, even through the protection of the high-tech gloves.

I staggered through the door, snagged a chestnut crushing spike on the carpet and fell to my knees as the green ring of flame rolled over my body and through the office.

There were five people in the room. With surprising clarity, I saw their rubbery faces register shock, but they weren't exactly incapacitated by it. By the time I lurched up to my feet, at least three of the men had pulled guns out of their jacket pockets and were firing indiscriminately. The noise, heightened by the morphine, was excruciating. I felt one bullet ring off the back of my helmet and several struck my legs and lower back.

Hammond hoisted his chubby body out of his chair, backed up against the window and fired at my chest point blank. I didn't even feel the first couple of shots, and thought the suit had absorbed the impact. But really, he had just cleanly missed. The next couple of bullets struck with surprising force and one hit me in the forearm, just above my cast, and the pain was intense.

One size-fifteen chestnut crushing boot clumped down on Hammond's desk top. I hoisted the rest of my oversized body up after it and reached my arms forward. Hammond had run out of ammunition and feinted towards a desk drawer where he probably kept an extra clip, but decided to duck out of the way instead. I pivoted on the desk top, the seven-inch blades attached to my soles augering into the veneer.

Hammond was moving towards the office door but I leapt awkwardly into the air and tackled him in the middle of the room. He managed to roll over on his back and draw his knees up and kick at me convulsively but I grabbed onto his neck and squeezed because my future existence depended on it.

The rest of the room was strangely silent, but I was almost afraid to look sideways and investigate why that might be. It was terrifying to imagine one of the men ripping my helmet free, pressing a gun muzzle against a temple and pulping my brain.

Thankfully, Hammond's body turned rubbery and I was able to stand and survey the scene.

Two of the men present were the people who had kidnapped me earlier in the day, the ones I had disabled in the elevator. The curly-haired man who had driven the Malibu had one arm in a sling and the shorter man who had threatened to castrate me, among other things, had a bandage wrapped around his head. I was shocked because I assumed they had been severely injured and would be occupying beds in intensive care or the morgue.

Two of the other men were strangers. They were young but haggard, wore green polo shirts under grey blazers, and had the badly damaged ears that are the by-product of significant wrestling practice.

All four had been shot, presumably in the frenetic crossfire when I was lurching towards The Dentist's desk. One of the wrestlers was definitely still alive because he was squirming, the others were either dead or unconscious, I didn't want to waste time finding out.

I ran like a mantis down the steps to the garbage room, out the door and across the parking lot. A man was walking his dog, letting the animal shit near a dumpster, and he turned around and sprinted in the opposite direction the instant he saw me. The animal just growled and finished its bowel movement.

5

The security video from Hammond's office wasn't immediately on the news. It had somehow been released to a YouTube account and only appeared on television after it had achieved internet notoriety. Pearl was the one who showed it to me originally, but I can't imagine she understood the significance. We were staying in Weidman's house, watering the plants while they were away for another weekend. I had managed to repack the super-suit in the rubber tubs while Pearl was administering to spider plants in the dining room.

She had turned on a kitchen T.V., seen a scrap of the video which was labeled "Goblin Avenger," then looked it up on a tablet that she always carried in her purse. She yelled at me to come look just as I was sliding the containers back home.

It was certainly a strange experience.

In the grainy video, my body seemed to disappear as it monster-stalked up the stairs, then reappear in fragments. I can only guess that the grey outer layer of the suit absorbed light in a peculiar way; my body didn't seem to cast shadows. Perhaps the color simply bled into the background cement and the camera equipment wasn't sophisticated enough to differentiate the two very similar tones. The effect was certainly ghostlike. There were no cameras in the hallway itself, so there was no photographic record of my botched entrance into the office. There were brief fuzzy glimpses of a shape entering and leaving the rear service door.

Various news outlets had originally reported the incident as a mob hit, not mentioning the shredded carpet and desktop, or the fact that four of the victims had actually shot each other.

Anthony Arcuri had died during the hit, as well as a cousin, Vincent, who was the curly-haired driver. The three others had survived their injuries but weren't yet making public statements. Arcuri's earlier iteration as Cole Hammond was either unknown or being supressed.

When Weidman and Kerry returned home, Pearl and I happened to be engaged in foreplay in their kitchen. I think I was moaning a little and didn't immediately notice the two frightened heads appear in the doorway.

"What the hell…"

I was tilted back in a kitchen chair and Pearl was scraping away at my teeth with her dental instruments. Her technique is full of suppressed violence and eight months ago I decided I loved her during a thorough cleaning. I remember my cheeks being wet after that encounter, and not being sure if the moisture was due to flecks of blood or tears of joy.

Pearl must have understood the sexual sadism underlying the attraction, but she was too polite to mention it.

We disentangled and greeted our bewildered hosts.

Kerry was eager to share two things with me.

The first was an apology card sent to Curtis by the man who had shot him with a hunting arrow two months ago. It was very childishly written because he had taken a round or two in the skull. "I very sorry," the note started out, and it was like a kid tearfully apologizing after saying something mean to his mom. The printing was a collection of shaky block letters scribed with a dark pencil. "I wanted to kill a great bird monster that haunted my family. I was saving my family as I slottered them. It is so foolish now. I very sorry."

"Do you think it's sincere?" Pearl asked.

"I don't know," Curtis said. "The lawyer may be prepping for future hearings. But it made me feel a little better about my own situation anyway."

"Yeah. You think *you've* got problems…" Kerry said, and her voice trailed away.

The second thing was a gift, an eagle feather that Curtis and Kerry had found while walking behind their B and B. It was strangely touching, because I have only received a handful of presents my entire life. I didn't notice the inscription on the quill until several days later because the letters were almost microscopic scratches that had been filled with a dark paste. I had to get the magnifying glass from my copy of The OED in order to decipher it. "And the goblins," I slowly read, "… they had not really been there at all?"

The Return of Mister Shovel
Andrew Post

When making a deal with the Devil, best cross your 't's and dot your 'i's!

Something new has been pinned to the cafeteria bulletin board. It's not the usual calls for roommates or students offering gently used futons to good homes. This new flyer has a picture: a black-and-white image of a lined, frowning face that needles passers-by with narrowed eyes. The way the leering subject is framed, it makes you think of the fine art class you took last semester. It's *American Gothic* but the pitchfork's replaced with a flat-blade coal shovel and without any soft-eyed wife, he stands alone in a fog-choked cemetery.

The text under the photo is too small for you to make out from where you're currently seated so you give it a read after finishing your oatmeal and orange juice. The page has been staked to the corkboard with enough force the thumbtack dimples the paper: a local filmmaker is seeking feedback on their independent horror film *The Return of Mister Shovel*. It's being shown tonight at nine o'clock, at an old picture-house walking distance from here. Those with constructive feedback, you read, will receive forty bucks.

You were planning on filling your four-day weekend renting movies to watch alone in your dorm room but getting *paid* to be an audience sounds much more appealing. You like to think you've decided to go because it'd help a fellow creative, but really it's the forty bucks that sways you. You know a guy on your floor who sells decent pot but your parents demand explanations—and substantiating receipts—following every withdrawal from your cash card. How your four-day weekend could suddenly improve, if still somewhat lonely, starts to take shape in your mind.

You leave the cafeteria into an overcast November morning. Making your way to your dorm, you skim the text exchanges with your ex. You don't know why you saved them. The word "never" had been used several times. You delete them. Maybe you'll meet someone at the movie tonight.

It's silent in the dorm. Each door stands closed with several of their dry-erase boards bearing scribbled happy thanksgiving messages. Your room feels strange without your roommate. Despite how little you've spoken, you miss them.

At eight you get dressed to go. Your phone will guide you. It also tells you to dress warm tonight and you heed its warning: coat, hat, and gloves. It's dark when you leave the building. You move along the campus's paved paths, passing through one orange pool of light to the next; each lamppost wears an aurora of misting rain, drifting gold dust.

When you do see other students who've also decided to remain, it becomes achingly apparent you're the only one who's not with friends. You would've gone home if your father hadn't said what he did. Not with family and not with friends, you are two-fold alone.

A group of girls coming the other way pause their laughter as they near and it restarts once behind you, louder than before. Like so many before, they find something amusing about you. You have never been able to pinpoint what this thing is; it's always scuttled from view when you've looked for it in a mirror.

Reaching the perimeter of the college's grounds, you feel like you're departing for a foreign land; it's been some time since you left. You cross at the corner and begin your journey toward the picture-house.

The streets shine with the rain, lights stretch to long smears that move when you move. Traffic is thin. The stoplights cycle for nobody. The rain's quiet pattering is oddly soothing. You don't wear headphones, to listen.

You glance inside a bar as you pass. The red-faced townies cackle, but they catch you looking and, as one, sneer. These are *their* refuges, places they can go unobserved by uppity college students. You continue on. The next bar has two men standing out front, smoking cigarettes. They suggest it's past your bedtime. You say nothing. They too laugh at your retreating back. It's only you and the drunks in town tonight. They've burned too many bridges and now only have alcohol—and fellow appreciators of alcohol—as final friends. You don't even have that. You regret letting things sour with your ex. You didn't think, at the time, the person-shaped vacuum walking with you now would be so loud.

You duck inside a bus stop enclosure to check your phone, unsure if you're still going the right way. When a bus rumbles up, you wave them on. The driver nods, mashes the gas, and douses you with a cloud of exhaust. The cool wind tosses it and you see, directly across the street, the entryway to a cemetery. A sign hangs over the chained gate: CLOSED FOR REMODELING. Each black bar of its tall fence bears a devil-tail spike. The street light only paints the closest gravemarkers. The rest are lost to the dark but you feel they are innumerable, standing solemn, stone, and unseen. Against a sky spanned with roiling gray, you make out the suggestion of a sharply slanted roof. The mausoleum, you assume.

Confirming you're going the right way, you pocket your phone, and step back out into the rain. As if waiting for you, the tolerable drizzling shifts and starts pelting you with heavy drops. You can hear them pecking the cemetery's carpet of dead leaves. Trying to banish the mental picture of a million tiny feet trampling the dead leaves only deepens its detail. You tell yourself it's your imagination when, next, you hear something suck a raspy breath for a scream that never comes. You pick up the pace—only because you're running late, of course.

The cemetery fence finally ends, giving way to the manicured yard of a small, dark-windowed church. The sign out front reads THE LORD IS WITH YOU EVERY STEP. You still look both ways before crossing. The theater stands up ahead, the only thing shining on the dark street.

The Endicott Picture-House marquee, jutting out over the sidewalk, is lit wax-yellow from within. The wedge-in letters, though, are not advertising *The Return of Mister Shovel.* You step under the marquee, out of the rain, and check the photo you took of the flyer. It's the right place, the right day, and the right time. But no one else is here. Behind the smudged glass of the box office stands only an empty chair.

You try the front doors but each holds fast, locked. Maybe rattling their glass panels caught someone's attention because you see a shape coming. Passing under a light the silhouette is given detail: a middle-aged man, dark hair and dark brown eyes, dressed in a hooded sweatshirt under a pin-striped blazer.

He looks out at the drowned rat, unlocks the door, and pushes it open an inch.

"Here for the *Mister Shovel* screening?"

"Yeah, sorry I'm late. Has it started already?"

"Not yet. Come on in."

The lobby is empty. Your first breath of the place is filled with its age; it makes you think of library basements or your bookish aunt's house. The blackened ghost of burnt popcorn haunts aggressively. The walls are hung with pleated red velvet, the floor carpeted to match. They're clearly serious about maintaining the old school vibe: every poster and lobby standee advertises films released before your parents were born.

He closes the door behind you and relocks it with a heavy ring of keys that, when done, he struggles to make his jeans pocket swallow. "Looks like scheduling this the day before Thanksgiving was a bad idea."

"No one else came?" Your voices carry and return to you changed.

"Nope. But it makes sense, given the holiday. Sucks, tonight was the only date available. *Rocky Horror* holds a permanent Friday slot and they're doing a Kubrick marathon the rest of the week so that left Thanksgiving Eve. Glad *somebody* showed up at least. Still up for it?"

You don't like the idea of being the only one here. You were hoping you sit in the back, let the other attendees give their assessments, and get an easy forty bucks never having to contribute. You've also never met this person. Though he seems friendly enough, you didn't tell anyone you were coming to this thing tonight. You try to think of an excuse to leave. But you're here, you put aside the time, what could (realistically) pull you away now?

He adds in your silence: "I don't mind an audience of one, if you don't."

"If you still want to show it," you say, "I'll watch it, sure."

Fellow lonely people are easy for you to spot. His desperation isn't well-hidden, either. But there's something else. Perhaps the film has leeched from him more than just its production costs. Tonight's turnout probably hasn't bolstered him to believe he'll be recognized as a noteworthy artist while still alive—if ever. Thankfully, you haven't experienced this bleakness yourself yet but you've heard enough about it—and seen it in some of your professors—to prematurely dread its arrival in your own creative life, whatever that'll end up being.

"Which one did it?" he says.

"Sorry?"

"Was it the flyer at the school, or the one at the Starbucks on Eighteenth?"

"The school."

"Are you a student there? You look like an art major—if you don't mind me saying, heh."

You peel off your rain-wet gloves. "I go there."

"Great place."

"I like it," you say.

"Great film program. Is that what you're . . . ?"

"Graphic design, actually. But I like movies."

He doesn't seem entirely pleased with your reply but his disappointment only shows briefly. "Cool, cool. I like movies too. Probably why I decided to make one, right?"

You smile to be polite while he laughs at his own joke.

He levels an open hand. "Phil Mayes. Director, writer, executive producer, and editor of this piece of cinema you're about to experience."

You take his hand, you shake, and you give your name.

"Nice to meet you," he says, releasing your hand. "It kind of threw me for a whirl. I would've figured offering to *pay* people to watch a film would draw a bigger crowd." He adds, blurting: "Don't feel guilty about that by the way. I *totally* understand. Pizza doesn't grow on trees. Say, you're cool to hang out afterward to give feedback, right?"

"I can stay for a while, yeah."

"We might be getting out of here pretty late, if that's okay. I could give you a lift after we're done. Are you staying on campus?"

"Thanks, but that's okay. I can walk. It's not far."

"Cool, cool. Well, let me know if you change your mind. Anyway, if you don't mind me getting kind of gushy here for a second: I *seriously* appreciate you taking the time." His gaze moves somewhere over your left shoulder. "I'm having trouble getting the audience to sympathize with Mister Shovel, I think. The few people I've showed the piece to so far didn't seem to connect with the piece. I mean, we wrapped three years ago, you'd think by now I'd have this thing figured out, but . . . that's how it goes sometimes. You're a design major, I'm sure you know what I mean." Before you can either confirm or deny this supposition he's already saying: "Maybe I'm too close to it, if that makes sense. Jeez, listen to me going on and on. What I mean is: a new set of eyes on this thing will *literally* help me out a ton. So, thanks in advance."

"No problem."

He claps his hands together. "So, shall we begin tonight's feature presentation?"

"Sure."

Crossing the lobby with him, your footsteps are muted by the high pile of the red carpeting.

"Neat place, right?" he says. "I really miss when theaters were like this, small, only one or two screens. Now they're the size of malls. Appropriate venue for *Mister Shovel*, I think. It has that throwback horror vibe. When people ask me to describe it, I tell them it's the love child of early Romero and Fritz Lang. But, spoiler alert, I do cater a little to modern film-goers toward the end with a little shaky cam."

At the far side of the lobby stand a set of heavy wooden doors with polished brass handles. He draws one open and gestures ahead with an outstretched arm. "After you."

"Thanks." You have to pass uncomfortably close to him. As you do, you notice, where his rolled up sleeve ends, he has a tattoo on his forearm. A simple thin-line cross, topped with an oval, almost like a one-legged stick person.

Inside, you're in awe. The ceiling has a large painstakingly detailed tableau of Greek gods in battle. A gold chain as thick as your arm keeps a massive chandeliers suspended. The stale air is twice as thick here but, again it isn't unpleasant. It's the kind of theater that has a balcony and curtains over the screen. You look for other people even though you've already been told it's only going to be you and Phil Mayes. There is no one else.

"Packed house, huh? Might have a hard time finding a seat."

You smile, again to be polite, and pick a row halfway back from the screen and halfway in, centrally positioned. Out of habit you make a note of the emergency exit door down at the front of the auditorium.

You shrug off your coat and drop it into the seat next to you. The seats are the kind that flip up when no one's sitting in them. Yours grates a sharp metallic note and a spring jabs at your tail-bone through the threadbare fabric.

Phil Mayes doesn't join you. You expected he might force you to share an armrest with him, but thankfully he remains at the aisle. He calls over to you:

"Do you want to use the restroom before we get started?"

"I'm okay right now."

"Are you sure? It's feature-length, not a short."

"Thanks, but I think I'm okay."

"Positive? Because talking about it has made *me* need to go, heh."

"I don't need to use the bathroom."

"Well, if you do, a good time to go is when Mister Graves says: 'These undead will stand as iron proof blah, blah, blah', no spoilers. If we were at my house watching this on my TV, I'd gladly pause it but here, I don't want to risk burning the print stopping midway through a reel."

"Okay." You reach over to your coat for your phone.

"Mind turning that off?"

"Sure."

"Sorry. I just want you to get the *full experience*, you know? Plus, feedback might be tough to give if you were texting or taking selfies."

You turn your phone off and give him a look as if to say: "Satisfied?"

"Okay, cool, I think we're set. Enjoy the film." He begins back up the gentle grade of the auditorium floor. His brief shadow, thrown long on the red carpet, is cut away when the lobby doors shut behind him.

At first it's uncomfortable being in here alone, a place that's designed to welcome a hundred at a time. You imagine the thousands that've filled this place over the years. Couples on dates with the boyfriend sighing with his chin on a fist; parents dragged to saccharine animated fare by their demanding spawn; a coven of housewives hoping a ninety-minute escape will dull the sting of the gray, flaccid thing their lives have become; self-professed film aficionados trying to resist blinking lest they miss something that might disappoint them. But at least they were all *with* someone, you think, scolding your inner cynic.

The lights dim and the curtains part in mincing shudders, ancient mechanisms whining. The screen bears duct tape patches in places. The projector clatters to life, flooding the screen with THE RETURN OF MISTER SHOVEL in a melting typeface. Though goofy, you feel it's appropriate for a horror movie made with the classics close in mind and heart.

Organ music, melancholy notes in a minor key, plays. Mister Graves, you read, will be played by Jacob Whipple and Philip Mayes Senior stars as the titular Mister Shovel. You almost laugh. Of *course* Phil cast his family in his movie.

We open on a graveyard, daytime. Like the image from the flyer, we're in a world of high contrast black-and-white. Shadows lay inky and deep behind each headstone. Whites—the sky and the shirt of the old man currently shuffling into frame—are bright as new paper.

You sit up straight when the camera pans to show the old man's apparent destination: a white stone mausoleum with a sharply slanted roof. But a lot of cemeteries have mausoleums, you tell yourself. And they probably don't differ much architecturally one to the next. We move around to gauge the old man's expression and we see the fence behind him, and its devil-tail spikes. Beyond the fence, fuzzily out of focus, stands the bus stop you'd stopped at not an hour ago. No big deal. If you were a filmmaker, you'd probably see this cemetery as a ripe place to shoot a horror movie as well. It certainly spooked you.

With a jarring cut, we meet the old man inside. By flashlight, he navigates the corridor, playing the beam about the walls. We see brass plaques of the dead and their individual slots, each lidded with a thick square of marble. The old man crunches a shriveling bouquet underfoot. The film's exposure makes it seem wherever the old man's flashlight ceases to shine that portion of the universe unmakes itself into total blackness. We follow him to a sturdy wooden door with iron bracings. The camera studies the side of the old man's face while he struggles with his keys. You see some resemblance to the Phil you know in the old man's aquiline nose and dark eyes. The old man unlocks the door and we catch up to him with another sloppy cut.

"You devil, why are you here at this ungodly hour, Mister Shovel?" someone demands to know, off-screen.

Mister Shovel (agitated): "The better question is, what are *you* doing here, Mister Graves? You frightened me half to death shouting out of the dark like that. Turn on a light, man!"

We hear a match spark and a heavy-faced man with thinning hair appears out of the murk, sitting behind columns of books piled on a desk. He wears a robe and a thick chain about his neck. Hanging from it is an amulet you suspect is made of shiny plastic because it swings weightlessly as he stands. Doing so, he bumps his head on the muff of a drooping boom mic.

Holding the match to a candle wick, Mister Graves says: "Is that better, you blind old cuss? Necromancers are supposed to be comfortable in darkness, are they not?"

Mister Shovel (admonishing): "We're not necromancers yet, Mister Graves."

Mister Graves (wry): "Yes, I know. Because you said we cannot begin our first round of experiments until we've assigned ourselves a protective spirit familiar. But I grow impatient, Mister Shovel."

Mister Shovel: "You read the same tome as I, Mister Graves. We cannot proceed without first creating a watcher to oversee our safety when we coax from the darkness new puppeteers for the vessels we lovingly offer."

Mister Graves (irritated): "I am aware. We drew straws and it was determined that *you*, Mister Shovel, would find us an innocent so we might shuck them free of their mortal coil to make our watcher. Still, I doubt we need be so careful; how worrisome can some little red imps truly be?"

Mister Shovel (incensed): "Quite worrisome! They are things most cruel. They count the minutes to be allowed to know what it is to have flesh and bone. They listen, even now, knowing what we delay to give them—and it enrages them! Can you not hear them scratching at your mind, Mister Graves? I can! And their impatience fuels my own, though . . . I fear I cannot bring myself to murder an innocent. Perhaps we should abandon this foolhardy pursuit altogether."

As Mister Graves storms around his desk to approach Mister Shovel with candle in hand, you notice a pair of corrective footwear peeks from under his robe. "Do not fear the darkness, Mister Shovel."

The screen flashes white, startling you. You're unsure but in that blinding millisecond, the words WATCH FOR US may've leaped across the screen.

Strange.

Mister Graves: "Abandon this pursuit, *now*? After we've come this far and studied so many long hours? No! Never! Besides, it's too late now anyway. While you were gone I started what you might call a preliminary experiment."

Mister Shovel (aghast): "Without a watcher? What if a demon leapt into you?"

Mister Graves: "But none did. Look, I am me, unoccupied and unchanged. Tremble not, Mister Shovel. It is but one small woman's body I've opened the door to. Come, our *guest* waits in the next room."

Mister Graves's robe flutters as he clumsily whirls to boldly charge from the room.

Cutting, we find ourselves in the same room with the furniture rearranged.

Mister Graves (loud): "Welcome to my laboratory."

Before them on the desk—now cleared of books via movie magic—is a dead body. The husk is shrunken-faced, lips retracting over a rictus of tall teeth. The dead woman's stare is glassy, but their eyes shine as if still wet. You're impressed because up until now you did not expect the makeup to be good. Maybe eschewing costume and lighting and everything else Phil Mayes sunk most of the budget into practical effects.

Mister Graves: "Behold, Mister Shovel, a cadaver most suitable for our maiden voyage into necromancy."

Mister Shovel: "I told you, Mister Graves, we need to assign a watcher *before* we attempt any sort of test. This way lies folly, man. We need an innocent, downy with purity, who will guard our mortal coils from inhabitation. The Devil's children may not be satisfied only occupying the rotten corpses we offer them—they may prefer *ours!*"

Mister Graves peers directly into the camera's lens—this time, unlike the accidental glance you noticed earlier, it feels on purpose. He tones: "Perhaps if we searched hard enough and lay our intentions bare we will stumble upon a willing candidate, a like-minded soul who can be taught wrenching power from an uncaring, fickle God is a pursuit most admirable."

As we slowly zoom in on Mister Graves's weepy old eyes staring down at you, another white flash. You jump. Words appear again but they vanish before you can read them all. Something ado ENDLESS SERVICE, maybe? Regardless, the unnecessary startle annoys you. You can tolerate the bad acting, almost enjoy it in a way, but the subliminal messages—which feel out of place—are starting to aggravate you and make you uneasy. You're not sure if it's the long hold on Mister Graves's eyes, but you feel the need to glance behind you.

The auditorium is still empty, every seat catching the light splashing back from the screen. The projector rattles on, throwing its beam out through one of three square holes high on the far back wall. From another, the silhouette of a head stares out but ducks from sight when you notice them. You imagine Phil Mayes is up there, watching to see how you're reacting. You want to catch him peeking and you stare at the hole for a few seconds but he doesn't reappear. The dialogue turns you forward again. "Rise, child of Enganar, and stand in your new body!"

With a Dutch angle so severe the picture is nearly vertical, Mister Graves raises his arms above his head and shouts: "Rise! This offered flesh is *yours* to command. Rise and give us secret truths and the wisdom of the damned! Take your mouthpiece, dark lord, and speak!"

The screen fills with a half-shut eyelid, drooping wrinkled and mottled over a bloodshot eye. The pupil yawns wide, a void carrying no flicker of life. You turn halfway in your seat, watching sidelong. Something doesn't feel right. The funhouse organ music has gone away, replaced with a stretching note of a violin, slowly bowed. A frail gasp trickles from the speakers, a cigarette burn dots the upper-right corner of the screen, and after a slight shiver in the film we're dropped into enveloping darkness. The only thing that lets you know you haven't been struck blind is the glowing emergency exit sign hanging in the gloom.

Mister Grave (growling): "These undead will stand as iron proof that God trusts only the select few with His power to restore life at their discretion—we have forced Him to give us that trust this night, Mister Shovel. The dead are ours to command."

Recalling this particular line signals an appropriate time to go use the bathroom, you stand to do so. You don't really need to go, but you feel you need a break from this. You grab your coat and sidle to the end of your row, keeping your back to the screen. Starting toward the lobby doors, you pass the many empty seats. You stumble when it appears one seat at the end of a row isn't empty. But it's only a play of the shadows, the flickering light chopping the dark of the cavernous into people-shapes. Behind you, the necromancers continue to squabble about watchers and inadvertent possession of the wrong vessels: theirs. "—we need someone to stand guard, combat them, someone as incorporeal as the would-be body-thieves themselves!"

Curiosity gets the better of you. You turn to face the screen.

In a wide shot, the necromancers watch the corpse sitting up, spasmodically lifting itself chest-first. Its head lolls too loosely for the neck not to be broken. Normally, movie gore doesn't bother you, but you're starting to feel hot and dizzy. Nevertheless, you can't look away.

The necromancers' reactions do not mirror one another. Mister Graves appears positively delighted while Mister Shovel presses a hand over his mouth, eyes wide.

You force yourself to turn away. In the lobby you squint at the change in light and reentering a world carrying the full spectrum of color. Directly ahead stand the front doors. The rain has let up. You decide you can live without the forty bucks and start to put your coat back on.

Someone's thundering down a staircase somewhere. A door marked employees only bangs open and Phil Mayes, panting, asks:

"Something wrong?"

"I was just going to use the bathroom. Mister Graves said that line, the one you said would mean a good time to go . . . so I thought I'd go."

"Should I turn up the heat?"

"I'm fine."

"Then why'd you put your coat back on?"

"I—"

"I told you to watch for that line as a test. For myself, I mean." Phil Mayes put his hands in his pockets and sighs. "Because if you could pull yourself from the film at that particular part, it means I didn't do my job. You're not enjoying it, are you?"

"I am," you say.

"Are you getting into it?"

You nod. "Did you film that opening part up the street? That cemetery looked familiar." By accident you glance at his arm, the one with the tattoo.

Phil Mayes rolls down his sleeves a little too nonchalantly. Apparently the inability to act carried down the family line. "My dad wasn't much of a thespian," he says, like he read your mind, "but I think the stilted delivery sometimes help build the mood. I just hope it doesn't come off as too Ed Wood-ish."

"That's your dad playing Mister Shovel?"

He nods, chin down. "Yep, that was Dad all right."

"Is he no longer—?"

An inhuman scream cuts its way out of the auditorium, dammed by the heavy doors. Only you jump. The shrill peal crescendos at an ear-splitting pitch before melting to a final plaintive moan.

Phil Mayes jerks his head to his right. "Well, bathroom's up the hall there."

He doesn't give you much room to get past him. You move up the hallway he indicated, feeling his stare hitting you in the back. You reach the bathroom. Inside there is very little light and the air has a coppery scent to it. There are no windows. You check to see if there's a deadbolt, like some bathrooms have, but there isn't one here. You stand in the bathroom, unsure what to do. The movie's noise bleeds in through the wall, more agonized screams. Your reflection in the mirror gives you a worried look. You still cannot pinpoint what's gotten you so anxious—the movie or its director. You decide you've seen enough, regardless, and that you'd very much like to go home now.

You open the bathroom door on Phil Mayes standing at the far end of the hallway. You feel his eyes on your front now as you approach. You watch your feet left, right, left, right, feet that feel numb in your shoes.

"Ready to head back in? I can fill you in on what you missed, afterward."

"Actually, I have to get going. I forgot I have a class tomorrow."

"You have a class tomorrow? On Thanksgiving?"

"I missed an exam," you stammer. "One of my professors, uh, decided to not go see her kids this year. She said I could come in and take it tomorrow morning. I forgot."

"Uh-huh. If you're not connecting with the film, just say so."

"It's not that, I just—"

"You don't have to lie. I'd appreciate it, though, if you watched the entire thing before calling my work garbage."

"I didn't call your movie garbage."

"Walking out is the same thing. And it's a film. I made a *film*, not a movie."

You say nothing. Your heart hammers in your chest.

"Sixty bucks. If you stay to the end. Deal?"

"I'm really sorry, but I really have to—"

He side-steps in front of you when you try to pass. "Two hundred. Come on, it'd mean the world to me."

You say, after a hesitation: "Let me see it."

His wallet is thick with cash. He must've truly believed he'd receive a better turnout. "See? I'm good for it."

You don't just see pot for your four-day weekend anymore. You see the myriad things your parents would demand you return if used the cash card on them. It's just a movie.

"Okay."

After giving you an unreadable stare, Phil Mayes turns and leads you back to the auditorium doors. You enter a room blasted with white light, a daytime scene is playing. Mister Shovel is pacing around the cemetery, his steps languid. He drags a shovel across the grass behind him. Weaving through the tombstones, the shovel connects with the corner of a grave-marker and elicits a sharp clang that stings your ears.

Phil Mayes, given an ashen pallor from his film, stands at the double doors, watching you. The hinge of your seat squeaks as you sit.

You keep your coat on. Your hand wraps your phone in your pocket. You watch Mister Shovel wander aimlessly around the cemetery. The camera isn't fixed like before; we move behind him wobbly and hand-held. Wind hitting the mic causes dropouts in the audio.

"Dad?" someone says from off-screen, the voice familiar to you. We nearly bump into the back of Mister Shovel when he stops to glare at his photographer. He regards the camera—looking right down at you, it feels.

Mister Shovel: "Why are you recording this?"

The Cameraman: "Can you explain what happened?"

"Well, it wasn't supposed to be that strong so soon, one. Two, I *told* Jacob we needed a watcher first but his idiot ass decided not to listen."

"Dad, stay in character. Jacob is Mister Graves."

"Jacob *was* Mister Graves. He's dead."

The Cameraman: "Not so loud. We're outside."

Mister Shovel: "You think I care what people hear? Too late now, they'll learn. Cat's clawing outta the bag as we speak." He shouts through the fence at a woman across the street, walking the same route you took to get here. "Hey. Do you know why cemeteries have fences? Old answer used to be 'Because people are always dying to get in' but now, 'fore long, they're gonna be trying to get *out*."

The woman quickens her pace. Mister Shovel scowls after her. He clangs his shovel against the fence. "Hey, I'm talking to you!"

Light out of the corner of your eye catches your attention. Over your shoulder you see Phil Mayes exiting the auditorium. The door shuts behind him.

The Cameraman: "Dad, come on, let's go back inside."

A cigarette burn winks while Mister Shovel drags his digging implement across the bars of the fence. *K-k-k-clang.* "We didn't have a watcher. We had no defense." He drags the shovel back the other way. *K-k-k-k-k-k-clang.* "We'll all be their puppets soon." *K-k-k-k-clang.* "We can't push 'em back now. They got a hundred for each one of us."

"Dad, stop, get yourself togeth—!"

The second cigarette burn hits, the words WATCHERS ARE FAMILY flicks by, and we're dumped back inside the mausoleum.

There are no artless cuts. The funhouse calliope music is gone. The camera jostles its way up a hallway. The hurrying cameraman's footfalls echo on the marble. When we pass a polished brass plaque, we catch a glimpse of Philip Mayes Junior with the camera on his shoulder. He looks terrified.

Something squeaks, close behind you. You shoot to standing. Two rows behind yours Phil Mayes, at some point, has returned to the auditorium. Your shadow eclipses him and he looks up at you, either hand clamped onto an armrest, saying:

"These seats could use some WD-40 I think, heh. Could you sit down please? I can't see."

"Is this thing about over?"

"Almost."

You remind yourself of the two hundred dollars and sit back down. You watch the film only insomuch as you're looking at it—on screen, we're turning a corner. We see Mister Shovel standing in front of a closed door, barred closed with a plank of wood. Taking his shovel in two hands, he leans an ear close. The cameraman's labored breathing fills your ears. Sudden pounding on the other side of the door makes Mister Shovel shirk back, the viewpoint wobbly as the cameraman, too, recoils.

"Dad, what are we gonna do?"

"I gotta put that thing down. If it jumps to me, you gotta take my head off."

"I don't think I could do that . . ."

"Then you'll have to find us a watcher. Will you do as I say?"

"Yes, Dad."

Clearly doubting his son will follow through on this order, Mister Shovel shakes his head, staring at the door as the thing inside continues beating against it. "We're not playing make-believe anymore. Goddamn stupid, anyway, thinking we could make a recruitment video."

"It might still work. People will see you're a good man."

Both men stop talking when, inside, the banging drops away. Silence.

"Stand back," Mister Shovel says. "I'm gonna go in."

Prying free the plank of wood wedging the door shut, Mister Shovel enters the laboratory. We're dragged into the room behind him. Looking over his shoulder, we scan the room. Mister Shovel curses and we move around him to see what he's found. A pair of corrective footwear lay attached to a shredded heap tangled in a soggy robe, shiny pools of darkness collecting in the folds of the cheap costume. Teeth in a ripped face part to gurgle painfully. Something shrieks from off-screen. We whip around with Mister Shovel as he brings up his makeshift weapon. A lithe shape barrels into him, low, and knocks the old man to the floor.

It becomes confusing to understand what's going on; the camera's all over the place. We catch a fleshless arm, a screaming mouth. Mister Shovel's teeth are dark with blood when he screams for his son to *do something, hurry*. The cameraman sobs, and continues to film Mister Shovel's ongoing savaging.

THIS DOESN'T HAVE TO HAPPEN AGAIN.

To your right, Phil Mayes is moving to take the last seat in your row. He doesn't look at you. His eyes are locked on the screen, face washed with the projected carnage. Tears shine on his cheek.

The speakers overload with the sound of a shovel clattering to the floor. We swing around—the door to the hallway stands as a white rectangle hanging in the dark. A storm of footfalls as we bolt toward it, the cameraman whimpering "I'm sorry" over and over. Inhuman shrieks follow us. We tumble out into the hallway. We pull the door closed behind us and bar it again, only catching a glimpse of our pursuer: reaching hands and milky eyes.

HELP US. SERVE US.

Filming the floor, the Cameraman pants and cries, whispering apologies. He gasps when the manic thundering on the door doubles; two sets of fists now.

Mister Shovel: "Boy, open the door. I'm all right."

The Cameraman: "I'll fix this, Dad. I'll find somebody."

Fade to black. You're shaking. As the credits roll, you force yourself to look down the row at Phil Mayes. Bent in half, he sits with his face pressed into his hands.

You stand and move the opposite direction, rushing toward the aisle. Phil Mayes's seat squeaks behind you. The double doors stand ahead, a blade of the lobby's light sneaking between them. To your left Phil moves up the opposite aisle. He stops when you stop and calls across:

"Dad needs our help. A watcher can help guide him back, so he can *return*—just as the title suggests. Help us make that happen. You can be in the sequel."

You take a step toward the lobby doors. Phil mirrors you. Again, he stops when you stop. "Please," he says, "I'll make it as fast and painless as possible."

"Stay away from me." You take your phone and mash the button to turn it back on.

Phil Mayes starts across the row toward you, latching onto the seatbacks to throw himself along. "I'll let you say goodbye to whoever you need. It won't be bad."

You turn and rush down the grade of the auditorium's sloped floor. The emergency exit stands just to the left of the screen that's currently listing Phil Mayes's many credits. You charge your palms against the door's push-bar but the door remains shut, chains rattling outside. Phil Mayes—climbing *over* the rows—almost closes the distance. He doesn't want to do this to you, but he must.

He latches onto your sleeve. You wrench free, your coat tearing. You sprint up the aisle, slam out through the lobby doors. Pushing them closed behind you, you only catch a glimpse of Phil Mayes in pursuit—reaching hands, blubbering mouth. "Please—!"

Flipping one of the lobby chairs over in front of the door, it only comes open an inch. Through the gap Phil Mayes begs:

"I tried to show him as a good man. He needs help."

Pressing yourself against the toppled chair, you see your phone is still taking its time turning back on. You rush for the front doors. None open. A kick to their glass panels only yields a crack and a possibly broken toe. Spotting a couple walking hand-in-hand across the street, you yell for help, fogging the glass with your screams. They either don't hear you or choose not to. The lobby doors bang open. You remain facing away, watching Phil Mayes kick aside the lobby chair over your reflection's shoulder—your breath fading on the glass makes him into a smudgy ghost. He stops halfway across the lobby, staring at your turned back. Your phone has finally woken up. You only manage to press the *9* before Phil Mayes swats it away, sending it bouncing across the carpet soundlessly.

He tries getting his hands around your neck. You bring up a fist, striking Phil under his chin. His head snaps back, his teeth clack together. He stumbles away, doubled over, clamping a hand over his mouth. Blood pushes through his fingers, the drops disappearing into the matching red carpet. Moaning wetly, he peels his hand away from his lips. Nestled in his bloody palm is a severed pink knot.

Phil Mayes (slurry, shocked): "My tongue . . ."

You charge at him, screaming. You knock him into the wall. Raising his arms to shield himself, he drops his bitten-off piece of tongue. Your knee rams into his stomach and he drops to the floor, moaning in a ball. You work a hand down into his pocket and tear free the jangling ring of keys. Trying each, you watch over your shoulder as Phil Mayes leaves a red handprint on the lobby standee pushing himself to standing, his gaze burning into you. One key works, twists. The blanching November air hits you as you shove your way out.

You don't look back. You run.

Your eyes sting. You cut through the little church's yard. THE LORD IS WITH YOU EVERY STEP, you're reminded, but feel this is not—at present—true.

You begin along the cemetery, arms and legs heavy, and hear something inside the fence trampling the soggy, dead leaves. At your ear metal connects with metal—and is dragged, matching your speed as you try to outrun it. *K-k-k-k-k-k-k-clang. K-k-k-k-k-k-clang.*

The cemetery fence ends and you hear a final crash as your pursuer reaches the limit of its cage. It continues running the piece of metal back and forth, volleying their rage after you. You run. Like in a nightmare, your burning lungs can only produce wheezing whispers that you yourself can barely hear: *"Help . . ."*

You reach the townie bars. It's dark inside the first, and the second. Banging on their doors only hurts your hands more. You're still wearing Phil Mayes's blood, you fleetingly notice.

You scramble across intersections, the lights cycling for nobody. You're all but certain your heart will explode. You reach the campus grounds and don't bother following the paved trails that needlessly weave only for the pleasing aesthetics—you run in a straight line across the grounds, moving under one orange pool of light, and again, until you're stumbling up the steps of your dorm building. You skin your palms on the rough concrete but you tear your way inside and throw yourself at the RA's office—finding an empty chair facing a dead computer screen. There isn't a phone. Your screams are hoarse now. No one answers; everyone has gone home for Thanksgiving and you are alone. You told Phil Mayes you live on campus. He will know where to find you.

You make it to your room and throw closed the door. You keep the lights off. You don't sleep. The only thing you hear during the night is some glass breaking, somewhere far away. Outside your window there's only the string of red lights on the interstate, people leaving town to be with family.

The night crawls on. Your breathing only returns to normal when the sun warms the far wall of your room. You've stared at the door the entire night, trying to keep your whimpering to the occasional whine you can't help. You've forgiven your ex, and your father. The release of these grudges is automatic; you wonder if your mind is performing some pre-death ritual of its own, privy to a future you are not. You want nothing more than to be around family.

It takes close to an hour to summon the courage to peek out into the hallway. Your desperate hello from a ruined throat only receives the droning buzz of florescent lights as a reply.

Moving down through the empty dorm building with a sculptor's knife in hand—the only weapon you could find among your roommate's things—you hesitate before stepping outside, watching for movement among the old oaks circling the quad. Orange leaves fall. No one passes among the trees. You don't know where to go for a phone. Yours is probably smashed to pieces, Phil Mayes clearing his connection to you should you send the police to the picture-house. To do so, you have to find someone. You can't stay here. You step out into the frosty morning, gripping the clay knife tight.

Moving toward the main building in the south part of the silent, fog-blanketed campus, you twitch at every innocent sound. You notice a red dot on the walkway, then another. A broken trail begins. You picture Phil Mayes, bleeding from the mouth, wandering around the school looking for you. Thinking maybe he decided to stick around to keep you from spoiling his *film*'s true intent, you hold the clay knife in two hands and follow the trail.

Turning a corner, you see, ahead, the glass door to the cafeteria lies in shards. The blood trail ends here, lost under the broken glass. Across the shadowy cafeteria—through the forest of upturned legs of flipped chairs—you spot the bulletin board. A bare portion of the corkboard shows, a new blank spot. A triangle of ripped paper is all that remains, dimpled by its thumbtack.

Black Sun House

James B. Pepe

**The darkness may speak with a thousand
tongues, but it doesn't stutter!**

LeDad stripped off his shirt, "Uncle" Joe dropped his Dickies, and I sat on the kitchen counter, drumming my high-top Chuck Taylors against the cabinet doors, as Uncle whined about having to smoke meth again out of a lightbulb because it made him feel ghetto.

"They got rose pipes at the Buffalo Nickle," Joe said. "Next to the Swishers behind the register. Can Cassi get me a rose pipe? Is there time?"

LeDad said nothing. He was drawing the Sigil on the kitchen floor with a fat sharpie. The product of seven-hundred pushups a day in Snake River Correctional, LeDad's back was solid, BMX bumpy, like the shell of a horseshoe crab. But no scars. No tats. Nothing. His skin was clean—a temple.

"Ghetto." Joe said. "'Get-to-the-capital—*Oh*' ghetto." He set a brass Zippo, a hollowed-out lightbulb, and an Eight-Ball of Lemon Drop on a crosshatched cutting board. "Like a low-life." He sighed. "Okay, ready, set . . . action! Hey, hey, hey—my Tubers." Uncle Joe waved at the smartphone perched on the microwave. "Riddle me this: You can rock with your Glock out; you can jam with your clam out." He thumb-hooked his Calvin Kleins and whipped them down, revealing a padlock dangling from his foreskin, Prince-Albert style. "But can you rock a lock—a Master Lock?" Uncle Elivesed his pelvis, gyrating, swinging his weighted dick like a morningstar on a chain. "Look at that shit, man. I mean, just look at that. Cassi, look."

I said nothing. I was reaching over for the cheapjack survival knife next to the moldy Mr. Coffee. LeDad used the blade for ceremonial purposes. I used its hollow handle to store dime bags of schwag and pieces of Halloween candy corn. I unscrewed the compass buttcap and emptied out a handful of high fructose.

"Yeah, hell yeah, everyone. We're back: the Black Sun House, in the house, uncensored, uncut, like me—your Uncle Joe." He gestured to his gravid dong. "And today we have a special show, so watch while you can. Admin's gonna block it quick, most Ricky Tick. Even 4chan can't handle this."

Joe pulled up his pants. His muffin-top gut oozed over his Pabst Blue Ribbon belt buckle like a swollen lip. "Oh, and hey—a brief shout out to Country Boy Bang, Southern Carolina makers of fine .45/410 ATF-legal inserts for military flare guns. My surplus Russian can now smoke a crow—*bang*—right off a wire. Nice, nice, nice."

LeDad finished the outer boundaries of the Sigil, a series of interlocking triangles and arches. They would serve as a container once he started licking our God into existence.

"So, before we get to any questions from our subscribers," Joe said. "Got a special shout-out for my homeboy, my Snake River cellmate; yes, our Magus, our very own Mad Arab—Brother LeDad, High Priest of the House. Love you, man, and that's no homo."

Rocking side to side on his hands and knees, LeDad stared at the Sigil, taking deep breaths, like a snorkeler preparing for a wreck dive. Our Magus rarely speaks, and even when he does, it's just a few clipped verbs: *Go, stop, get.* Real Spartan, like *Molon labe* ("Come take") Spartan. And that's a good thing, a safety issue. When LeDad speaks in complete sentences, the Egyptian listens.

Joe tapped the smartphone's screen, scrolling through the live-feed commentary. "Our first subscriber question is from *airsoft187*, who wants to know if he should buy a 9mm Lorcin listed on Craigslist for a $75; and I say, Mr. Soft, who cares: Those die-cast bricks stovepipe more than Santa Claus on a bad Christmas day. Get yourself a SIG if you want a straight man's nine. Next question."

Like a marathoner reaching for a baton, LeDad stretched out his right arm, and I handed him the survival knife, pommel first. The butt-cap compass was already spinning.

"Our next subscriber, *HeilGottParabellum*, says that he has an Oregon Trail Card, a curved penis, and the blood of three D-Block Peckerwoods on his hands; so, is this enough for membership to the House? And I say, once again, it's not up to me or even LeDad: Like the New Agers say, 'When the disciple is ready, the Master will appear.' This is the lesson of the Nigredo, the alchemy of the Black Sun. When the Egyptian anoints you, dick dog, you will know, and you will find us. Cassi, our newest member, case in point."

LeLad kissed the sawback blade, revealing his forked tongue, split halfway down the middle like the tail of a seal. He licked the knife edge, drawing blood, cutting the flesh notch even deeper. A cold jolt washed up my legs, as if I had fallen knee-deep into a freezing river. The ceremony was on. No turning back. I bit off the white tip of a candy corn; Joe crushed yellow meth with a rusty meat hammer.

"Our next viewer, *Romans13KJV*, says that we are 'cocksucking hell devils going to hell kingdom with king devil' and that Portland PD has been informed of our devil felonies. And, I say, *Romans*, when you made that report, could you accurately describe us? Go ahead; try again. Look closely. Before it gets blocked, watch this vid once, five times, ten—and it's weird, isn't it? We're just blurs. In fact, during tomorrow's commute, we're going to sit across from you on the Number 4 bus, and you'll be there, dicking with your phone, sweating, afraid to look up, trying to remember. And at home, you'll hit pause; hit 'Printscreen.' Cut-and-paste. But nothing, right? No screenshot. Blank, isn't it? Always blank. Crazy. And, for your sake, I hope you haven't downloaded this House file, not unless you want to learn, the hard way, why my God answers prayers. And yours? Yeah—"

Joe's right: We're slippery, on the move. Our first squat was an abandoned double-wide on the edge of a Sauvie Island cornfield. One Saturday, while Joe was giggle-sticking in the blackberry, watching nude grandmothers, brown as hush puppies, spike volleyballs on Collins Beach, the Magus and I walked the river shoreline. When LeDad's snaky tongue tasted the air, something Nessie-ish, like a disembodied alligator tail, swam against the current. The black thing stalked a sailboader who tacked into the wind.

We don't need much: A boarded-up cottage in the West Hills, a storage unit in Gresham, a listing 30-foot ketch on the Columbia. Someplace forgotten, someplace hidden—give us that and two months, and we will complete, record, and upload a Black Sun ceremony. When LeDad says, "on," our smartphone beeps and connects. No battery, no cord, no carrier plan. Just "on" and it's on.

God hates fat; God hates doubt. Mom's second and third Commandments, with the first being: *The finger points at you.* But what is it really, Mom—faith? A jack-in-the-box with a broken crank. No weasel, no pop. But Gnosis, knowledge, noetics—that is All, Mom, fuck All. If you could only see how LeDad, like a kid bobbing for apples, pounces on the Sigil, slathering it with bloody-tongue love, tracing its Spirograph curves; loving it, chowing down, going to town with a rug-munching passion, then you would truly understand that to know God is to love Him.

Because He wants to know you, too—inside and out.

"Damn. Goddamn," Joe said. "Look at that folks! Just look at that. Our Magus, swabbing the deck. Man sweats his prayers. Paint it. Paint the floor red, Brother."

Joe lit the Zippo, heating the lightbulb and rolling it like a glassblower, vaporizing the meth hit at the bottom. He bogartted through a bubble-tea straw until his right eye twitched.

"Damn. Oh, damn. Yes. Switchboard's lighting *up*. But first, a special thank you to Mr. Ngyuen Pham, who needs better locks. One kick and *pow*—the House was in like Flynn. Sir, Mr. Pham, your place has a mold problem, and the wood paneling is Starsky and Hutch, but I can see Mt. Hood from the kitchen. It's nice. When you get back from Hanoi, you'll find your junk mail in a neat pile in the hallway, next to a matchbook and a jerrycan. Read my post-it note; take it seriously. *Do not* come into the dining room. Just pour the gasoline, light it, and fucking run."

LeDad prostrated himself before the Sigil. He panted, tongue hanging out, drooling blood—eyes glassy. The room smelled like raw brisket.

"*PaganBlack* wants coffee with Cassi, and *Heilhipster42* wants an answer. First, *Pagan*, our Cassi is old enough to vote, but she has no time for relationships: She's married to the House; and, second, *Hipster*, keep watching, you little snot: This is the Named City, and *I* am Portland. Oh, and *JohnDugganEsquire* says that we are frauds, cut from the same cloth as Simon Magus, and that we must, as the Apostles Peter and John exhorted, 'Repent therefore of this thy wickedness, and pray God.' Simony? Dude, get it right. We don't bribe saints: We *are* saints, just like your Julian. You see, right now, while you're volunteering at the Food Bank, washing leper feet, your kid is in the garage with grandad's straight razor, a 12-gauge Orion flare gun, and the Sigil. So, put down that soup ladle, Mr.

Duggan. Hurry home. But remember to stop at the Chevron for a can of gas: You'll need it."

Uncle Joe loaded his Russian flare pistol, a crude slab-gripped thing, and flipped the breach shut. He pointed straight into the cell phone camera; I bit into a candy corn's orange middle.

I used to be stick-armed starving. After my first period, Mom started weighing out meal portions on a gram scale, like it was Peruvian flake, but she kept the good shit—the Chocadiles, the Ho-Hos, the Pepsis, the Triscuits, the Creamiscles—padlocked, all to herself. Bitch even had a mini-fridge. If I ever questioned my homeschooling (or, Christ forbid, said I was hungry), Mom would grab my throat. Squash me. Pin me against the sheetrock with her Jersey Cow chest.

Well, Mom, it's my turn: I got food. I got tribe. I sit at the left hand of the Father. The day I hoboed from Tacoma to Portland, I called you from inside the Polaris, a biker bar. Even over the speaker-blast of Swedish Death Metal and the crack of pool tables, I could still hear you screaming: *"How much do you weigh? Goddamnit, you little whore—you freak—tell me how much you weigh!"*

I asked if you were sorry for anything.

There was silence. And an answer: *"Having faith in you."*

Well, I still weigh 105 pounds. Never goes up or down. Maybe someday, Mom, I'll track you down, slice your face off, and eat it like sashimi with wasabi and pickled ginger. Someday soon.

"For those subscribers who have flare launchers," Joe said, "God's love be with you. For everyone else, just watching, too chicken, whatever: You're still screwed. When the Magus speaks—"

I flinched. The smartphone rang—an old-school, rotary-dial *triiiing*. Joe looked at me, wide-eyed, like a high-beamed deer.

This was my sixth ceremony. That phone never rang, not once.

As if caught out of uniform, Joe hurriedly stripped off his Dickies and boxers. His bare butt, his naked back, were hairy, almost baboonish. He touched the screen. "H-Hey." His voiced cracked. "Hey—?"

There was a click, a mic-test buzz, followed by the blatt of an acid-jazz flute. My vision blurred. The room got cold—fast. The hairs on my arms porcupined straight up. Then silence.

Joe went pale. He snarled, grabbed the lightbulb, and vaped hard. A whitish-gray smoke filled the room. He paced the kitchen *widdershins*, counterclockwise, stopping to breathe spittle in my face: "What's your problem, Cassi? You don't like boys, girls, China White—nothing. You just eat and watch. Always watching me. Are you a cop? Sometimes I think you're a cop. Goddamn-Fucking-A."

LeDad's split tongue undulated. He made a throat-slitting gesture, and a red mark, as thin as a garrote, traveled across his Adam's apple. Uncle Joe paced in circles, pawing at his face, knocking his padlocked pecker against the Whirlpool. The same red marks started forming on his cheeks, crawling up his brow, creating shapes, like he had fallen asleep on a roll of chicken wire.

"Okay," Joe said. "Okay. Brides to a bridegroom, Egyptian. We come. All the way. No stopping. On my mark."

"We—" LeDad gurgled.

"Say it, Brother. Fucking say it."

LeDad covered his eyes. Red tributaries dribbled down his chest, meeting in the cobblestones of his chiseled gut. "God—" He wheezed. "Oh, Dear God, we love You!"

Uncle Joe fired into the heart of the Sigil. The Russian flare gun boomed like a sawed-off, and the flare punched through the House floor as if it was ballistic jelly. Down, down, the flare tadpole-wriggled down, phasing through Prime Matter, through public domain, carrying our prayer, our cries to the Egyptian: *Hear us. We love you.*

Joe pranced about, fingering the holes of an invisible bagpipe. "*RazorBack10*: 'Is the Applegate a good combat folder?' I say yes.

VicksVaperRaver_vs_Prodigy: 'I wanna DJ your final show. Can I?' Go ahead, dude. Pop a xany. Roll a fatty. Smack my bitch."

"*Oooh, oooh--rah-haha/ Oooh, oooh--rah-haha/ Anti-Gold, anti-Grail/ See the Ship of Solomon/ watch it sail/ Or is this the White Ship?/ my mistake/ All aboard, Mr. Malory, 'for I am Faith.'/ Oooh, oooh--rah-haha.*"

I jumped off the counter. Joe and I stomped around the kitchen, knees high, like Sendak's "Wild Things." The third layer of a candy corn, the yellow base, melted on my tongue while the blooded ink of the Sigil expanded, contracted—breathed. He is the Egyptian. He is good, and He is coming. From a three-car garage in Lake Oswego, to a XXX jackin'-shack on Powell, fifteen Sigils from a fifteen House subscribers burned neon, as our collective flares ghosted 3000 miles down, past the Mesosphere, to the nickel-iron Ovum, the Earth's Inner Core, fertilizing it with devotion. Open the Gate, Egyptian. We love you.

"Anti-Life, hungry child/ Like a Strange Aeon on a Black & Mild/ suck the Nigredo from your throat/ Robe the Bride/ ride the Goat/ Oooh, oooh--rah-haha/ 'Ïa, Ïa'--ah-haha."

Something pricked my thighs. Behind me a falcon-faced man in a white shirt and black slacks gripped my bony hips as if this was a Conga line. His pink fingers ended in short talons; a lion's mane of blue feathers draped his shoulders. "Don't bond with this phase—the Nigredo," the Bird God whispered. "Flee to the Albedo. Oh, my little Rubedo, just run." The whisper became a chant. "Run, go—just fucking run; run, go—just fucking run; run, go . . ."

Ahead of me, Joe was jogging in circles backwards, slapping his fat gut, chanting in tongues, but the tongue wasn't his: It was LeDad's, severed. Joe held it between his teeth, whipping it back and forth like a pitbull on a jerky treat.

LeDad lay curled up, bleeding from a tongueless mouth, a butchered throat, while the Sigil pulsed, dilated—opened, revealing an endless meat well, a birth tube that helixed up from the stabilized Gate at the Earth's core. A blast of Artic air rushed out. LeDad fell in. I screamed, and our Magus was gone.

"Joe." I strained to join my "Uncle," but the Bird God held me back. "Joe!"

Uncle Joe spat out the tongue, and the moment it hit the linoleum, it began replicating by the dozen until the kitchen was filled with tongues that slithered, inch-wormed, and walked on their slits like little broomsticks from "The Sorcerer's

Apprentice." Joe reloaded the flare pistol and aimed it at me. He faced the smartphone.

"Hey, folks, Black Sun House appreciates your support. It's been a great year." The red marks on Joe's face and forehead now merged into a Humpty Dumpty pattern, as if he was cracked and badly glued together. "Come to Portland, folks. Bring the whole family, but don't let the tattooed baristas, the World Naked Bike Ride, the man-bun hipsters, or the nine months of rain get you down. They're just props and FX, a movie-set front, because the real City, the Named One, is me. I am Portland; you are Portland. This is His House. The Egyptian comes *longissima via*, the long way, and His name, among many, is—" Joe cocked the hammer. "Nyarlathotep."

Joe ate the muzzle and pulled the trigger. His head pumpkined into fifteen fragments. I counted them. They hung frozen in the air like a children's mobile. Then time restarted, and Joe dropped into the squish of tongues, who dutifully hauled him, like miniature pallbearers, to the edge of the hole and dumped him in, Master Lock and all.

I screamed. Down the street, on the corner of Johnson and Zann, a transformer blew with a white-light bang and a death-ray zap. The whole block went dark. Something touched my lips. I fainted headfirst into a bushel of severed tongues.

#

First, He leads us to Him.

Like that Sunday I woke up, stomach gurgling, beneath the St. John's Bridge, with two bits of Starbucks napkin shoved up my bloody nose. The night before, I had only managed to *spange* sixty cents on the I-84 exit ramp; and Donnie-D, my street sergeant, went all raped-ape in front of the other hobo Travelers, saying I should have tried harder, gone on blast, calling me a bull . . . dyke, a lazy . . . whore, straight-jabbing my nose with each word. But when he turned away to twist his dreads—smirking like the Fonz, just too-cool-for-school—my pocket Swiss opened up his cheek, wide the fuck open, with two diagonal slashes; and, suddenly, a crusty gutter punk was a gillman—a teenage Tweeker from the Black Lagoon. Donnie-D held his tattooed face and screamed. And then I ran. Left my pack behind and ran. Fuck this. Fuck everything.

I blacked out afterward. Seven hours, gone—plucked, like a k-hole. No money, no food, no tribe. Just me, shivering in the wet grass of Cathedral Park, with the bridge overhead, and the looping memory of Mom squeezing my jaw, daring me to call CPS.

What would it be like—? I remembered thinking. *To jump?* Off the St. John's. Into the Willamette. Down, down, two-hundred down. It would hurt, but it would be fast. And over. Over and done.

But in the crisscross of green bridge girders, every rivet became an unblinking eye, and every eye was watching me. The squeeze-toy shriek of gulls and the honk of coal barges became His voice, the command of the Egyptian, Aeon of the Named City. *Find me*, He said. *I'm waiting.* And in the rose bushes, I found His Sigil scrawled on a crumpled Taco Bell wrapper. I ate it, tearing the wax paper like flesh. For the first time ever, my stomach was full. My heart was light.

Then, He leads us to each other.

An anonymous sender kited the Sigil to LeDad while he was in solitary; he in turn kited it to Joe;

and, a year later, on my Sigil Day, I showed up at their table in the St. John's Flea Market, where they sold used DVDs, vintage Pez dispensers, stolen bicycle parts, and 440c "Super-Survive Zombocalypse!" survival knives by the crate load. I remember standing and staring at the two parolees like I had known them my whole life. I was a Cheshire Cat smile. I couldn't feel my body. My bones still resonated with the voice of God.

"Welcome, Sister," Joe had said. "To help Oregon homeless youth achieve that full, six-gill 'Dagon look,' we here at Uncle Joe's Black Sun House of Vintage recommend our six-inch survival model. Beats a Swiss Army. Every time."

And so I joined them at the table, pulling up a folding chair, as if I belonged there. Because I did.

#

The runic Glyph carved on the cabinet illuminated the kitchen with a faint aquarium glow. Climbing the walls, swarming the floor, the tongues infested the room like a frog plague, but they stopped at the Glyph's edge, where the Bird God sat on the counter, legs crossed. He scribbled notes on a clipboard and beckoned me with a clawed finger.

I stood on trembling knees. My clothes, brittle as damp newspaper, sloughed right off. Gluey tongues oozed over my bare feet.

"Is this the Albedo?" I asked. "The second Gnosis?"

The Bird God said nothing. He kept writing with his right hand and beckoning with his left.

"I didn't call you; I called Him," I pointed into the darkness behind me, the Gate that gushed subzero air. My skin goosepimpled; my breath steamed. The distant sound of a psycho fife-and-drum chorus grew stronger.

"I'm always hungry," I said. "I'm fat, lazy, selfish, stupid. I suck at algebra. I deserve this. Write that down. I'm a bad person. The Magus and Joe are gone. I deserve this. Just ask Mom."

Like Roman soldiers raising a siege engine, a wagon train of tongues lifted up the Zombocalypse survival knife, handing it to me, pommel first. The phosphorescent compass was no longer spinning. It pointed north.

"Look at this shit." I lifted up my left tit, exposing my ribs. "You see that? Good meat. Close to the bone. Take a slice. Eat."

The Bird God put down his stylus and shook his feathery head. His burning eyes—one gray, one black—looked sad.

"You're an Egyptian, too." I said. "Aren't you? What's your lineage, your sacred city? Say something. He's coming." From the Gate, laughter was erupting, raucous belly-shaking laughter, as Nyarlathotep crawled the walls of the tube, all the way up from Azathoth—the non-causal Cause, the many-named Mad Womb, the replicator at the bottom of this Alembic Universe.

"Take it." I offered my body. It was shaking. "Take your cut, Aeon. Eat. He's coming. I deserve this."

The Bird God hopped off the counter and stood at the boundary of the Glyph that divided the room into two halves. He held out his hands, palms up. To my back, the noise swelled, merged—*oompah-rattat-ahaha*—mutating into a single bridge-jumping shriek. The tongues began to stampede around the

Gate, counterclockwise, forming a vortex of wet meat, scudding hard against my shins.

"There's nothing else, is there? Tell me. Is there *anything* else? God, tell me where to fucking run!"

The tongues surged like a riptide. I stumbled, losing my footing. I reached out. The Bird God caught my hand. His grip was tight.

When I was a kid, I kept a stolen jar of Grey Poupon hidden in my closet, and at night I would sneak spoonfuls, pretending that each swallow was a rich bite of County Fair hotdog. Who the fuck does that? I deserve this, don't I? I chose this. *I chose this.*

The Gate irised shut. My ears rang. The kitchen was quiet. The tongues scuttled into the corners as if startled by a predator.

Footsteps. The clack of hard heels. A hand touched my lips.

"Cassi," a voice said. "Are you cold?"

Someone draped my bare shoulders with a burgundy robe. I couldn't see Him, but I caught a glimpse of a long-sleeved white shirt.

"Cassi," the voice said. "Are you hungry?"

Emerging from the shadows to my left, Joe's headless body cupped the puzzle pieces of his shattered skull. LeDad, sacrificial tongue in hand, flanked me on my right. I, in the center, straddled the threshold between two Strange Egyptian Aeons: Nyarlathotep and the Bird. My legs formed a perfect isosceles. The smartphone *tringed* one last time. It was my mother, asking me where I was and how much I weighed.

Something lodged in my trachea. I couldn't breathe, and I began coughing, holding my sides, hacking like a cat, until I vomited up a long drooly chuckle that just wouldn't stop, because it kept going, spiraling all the way back down to the Mad Womb itself. I pulled the robe tight and pointed the survival knife north, toward Tacoma, as if sighting a rifle.

"I'm in Portland, Mom." I said. "Come find me. I'm waiting."

Snickering into my sleeve, tasting the air with my tongue, I embraced the *Al-Khem*, the delicious alchemy, of a loving God's Egyptian arms.

Subterranean Reptile Blues
Thomas Vaughn

This underground movement draws its strength from a little chemical in the human brain!

After working thirty years in New York homicide you learn a few things. Rule number one is that everybody lies. That doesn't just apply to cons. I mean everybody lies. Our self-deception functions like a prison that we construct one piece of concrete at a time over many long years. Only these prisons are not designed to keep us in, but to keep the truth out. It usually works out all right, but sometimes the truth has a way of tunneling underneath that prison and threatens to bring the whole shithouse crashing down on our heads. That's what happened with The Strobe. I know what the newspapers said after we got done counting the bodies. Calling it a terrorist attack made a lot of sense. You find sixty-seven dead people in a trendy nightclub and you have to tell people something. The only thing you know for sure is that you can't tell them the truth.

What the reporters failed to mention was the fact that our problem began two days earlier in the tunnels under Red Hook. Some utility workers were checking the drainage system when they noticed the stench. At first they thought someone had set up a black-market slaughterhouse down there. Then they looked a little closer and called us.

"Holy Christ, Vaskov! Do you have to drive like your ass is on fire?" Valentina Vaskov was my partner. Her parents had migrated to New York from Kyrgyzstan when the uranium market went bust. She was a good partner. When the hustlers saw the chiseled features and long blonde hair they tried to work her, but they had a surprise coming. Vaskov was nobody's mark. She cut through lies like a blow torch through magnesium and carried a pair of .40s. She was hell with those .40s and could write her name on the wall at twenty yards firing with both hands.

"What's your problem, Stern? You want to live forever?" As she spoke one wheel popped on the sidewalk and we narrowly missed a stockbroker who splashed coffee on his shirt. Once we were back on the street she gunned it to the next light.

"No, but not every call is a goddamn suicide mission." She didn't drive like that out of necessity. We were headed to a crime scene, not pursuing suspects. She just needed the rush.

"I figured you would have learned to enjoy it by now."

"Enjoy what?"

"The way your balls contract. You don't have to play shy with me, Stern. You know you crave it." As the words left her mouth she threaded the needle between a taxi and a delivery truck with such precision that you couldn't have fit a red pubic hair between the vehicles.

When we got to the scene a pair of patrol cars had cordoned off the area. I already had a hunch about the victims. The mole people had been living under the city for decades. Sometimes when a person fell on hard times they would end up underground. They told themselves it was just a temporary setback, but then found the tunnels to their liking. It was cool and dark down there without all of the noise and hassle. They created these little makeshift villages from found materials. I figured someone had caught a razor after dipping into their neighbor's stash. That was the usual story. I couldn't have been further from the truth.

When the car came to an abrupt stop my partner gave me that cold smile, her eyes covered by wrap-around sunglasses. "There you go, Pops. All in one piece."

I stepped from the car. "You're a fucking psycho, Vaskov. That's why I love you."

After getting briefed by the patrol officers we made our way through the service tunnel with one of the security chiefs. The moles would tunnel through the cement or pry prices of sheet metal away from the walls, linking subway tunnels to drainage systems. We ducked through a hole in one of the access tunnels and found that we were treading on dirt. Our voices echoed off the walls and the sound of dripping water punctuated the silence. The flashlight beams revealed a litter of bottles, cans and scrap. There was a continual rain of debris from the surface so there was never any shortage of raw materials. Someone had spray-painted "Welcome to the end of line" above the opening. Any other day I would have called bullshit on that one. You might think you've come to the end of the line, but then you find that there's another rung down on the ladder. You can always go a little lower. But today the subway prophet had gotten it right.

"How many we got?" I asked the tunnel security agent.

"I stopped counting at three. That's your job."

I shook my head as the dream of watching the ballgame evaporated before my eyes. The more bodies you had the more time it took processing the scene. Vaskov smiled. She had a thing for carnage.

The subterranean township was comprised of about eight houses made from plywood, cinderblocks and burlap. Some of them were flattened while the others had at least one wall torn off. That's when I realized this wasn't going to be a normal case. The scene was at least a day old. The bodies had that smell of rotting fruit. The flesh wasn't falling off the bones yet, but they were emitting corpse gas.

Vaskov knelt over the first body and studied it. It was a skinny guy who looked to be in his mid-thirties, but age was hard to gauge with the moles. His face was turned to the side so she retrieved a pen from her pocket and elevated it toward my flashlight. "He took one in the head," she said.

"Yeah, but one what?" The hole was between the guy's eyes. You could see right into his brain where the tissue was perforated by bone fragments. It had hit him with explosive force. He must have been looking right at his assailant when the end came. His eyeballs were shrunken from dehydration and lips peeled back in a rictus grin. "That's at least two inches in diameter. Is there an exit wound?"

Vaskov carefully rolled the head back to the other side. "Nope," she said standing. "It looks like whatever did this went straight in, then right back out the way it came."

"You can't wait for the professionals?" I turned and saw Tom Kopchek leading a forensics team down the tunnel behind us. "I'd appreciate a little professional courtesy before you go tramping all over the crime scene." I ignored the irritation in his voice because I knew he was just claustrophobic. He was one of the few guys that had been in homicide longer than me.

"Hey Tom. You're going to have a field day cleaning this one."

He looked around and scowled. "What the hell happened? It looks a cyclone came through here."

His people were always neat and efficient. Within a few minutes they had counted seven dead. The wounds ranged from broken bones to limbs that looked like they had been amputated by a rusty chainsaw. The only common denominator was the hole in the head.

"What do you figure did that? A pick axe?"

Kopchek shook his head. "I don't think so. The wound doesn't look right. It's not deep enough. Plus, who could wield a weapon like that with such precision? Whoever it was they really wanted to scramble these boys' brains."

"Now this is disgusting." The words had come from Vaskov. I turned, idly wondering what type of atrocity would actually turn her stomach. She was standing near a side tunnel that branched into the drainage system. Her cuff was covering her nose. When we approached the smell hit us as well. It wasn't the smell of rotting flesh, but far worse. I had only run across it once in my life and it's not the kind of thing you forget. There was a puddle of slime on the floor that looked like it had been dumped from a rendering truck. It had an acrid smell that reminded one of a combination of battery acid and rotten chicken.

"Oh hell," I said and looked at Kopchek. He was one of the few guys old enough to remember. "You know what that is, don't you?"

"Christ, I thought we had seen the last of that," he replied.

"What is it?" asked Vaskov leaning forward, but I jerked her back by the shoulder.

"Don't touch it!"

"I wasn't planning on it, Pops. Either one of you boys want to let me in on the secret?"

"You're not going to believe it," I warned.

"Come on, Stern. You know how open-minded I am."

"When was it Tom? Was it 86 or 87?"

"87." Kopchek had eyes like a hawk and soon the beam of his flashlight came to rest on the bottle. I once saw him spot a pinprick of blood at thirty yards. You didn't even need luminal with that guy.

"I was just patrol back then. So was Tom. A contaminated batch of cheap wine came on the market. It was made by a defunct distillery on the other side of the river. Tenafly if I remember right. It had some type of toxin in it. When you drank it, it burned you up from the inside out."

"You're shitting me. I'm not a rookie so this better not be a prank."

"I wish it was," said Kopchek, kicking the bottle to reveal the label. "Yep. Tenafly Viper. We only found a small sample. It quickly vaporizes when it hits the air. Some type of contaminant had gotten in the batch and as it fermented it turned into pure raptinal."

"Raptinal? Never heard of it. Does it get you high?"

"Not exactly. It's an enzyme that speeds up the process of apoptosis—or programmed cell death. Every cell in the body is programed to die so that it can make way for new ones. This batch was so pure, once it hit human protean it started a chain reaction. Nothing could stop it. Total liquefaction took place in less than two minutes. It melted everything, even the bones. If that wasn't bad enough the neurological tissue goes last because it has a slower decay rate. You are conscious the whole time. You can feel yourself melting. I heard they died screaming."

"Damn," said Vaskov looking back at the viscous pool. "Why haven't I heard of it?"

I shrugged. "Well, New Yorkers drink a lot of wine. It wasn't like the folks who drank this particular brand meant anything. They were the dregs—just like these poor bastards. The city brass thought it might cause a panic. The Manhattan crowd pays up to thirty grand for one bottle. A story like this might have damaged the market."

Vaskov nodded. "That sounds about right. But what about all these victims? These moles maybe homeless, but they aren't weak. What kind of guy can tear someone's arm off? Do you think there's a connection?"

I shook my head at the thought. "Other than loosening your bowels when you see someone turn into a screaming blob of protoplasm, it shouldn't have affected anyone else down here. But to tell you the truth my gut tells me they're connected. Just when you think you've seen about every level of hell, some dumbass finds the key to a new chamber of horrors."

"Amen to that," said Kopchek. "I will send some samples over to Dr. Frankenstein."

"Frankenstein? I thought he retired. Hell, I thought he was dead. That guy must be ninety years old."

"Yeah. They keep him around as a special consultant. He's the one who isolated the enzyme back in 87. I'm sure he would like to have a look at this. If you're going to get some answers, he's your man."

The first break in the case came the following morning. A paid informant told us that a junkie named Roach had been in the mole enclave the night the killings went down. He wasn't hard to find. We spotted him in Green Point walking the streets and glancing over his shoulder. I knew he was a runner. By the look of him he was ready to bolt at the slightest provocation so I had Vaskov approach from the east. With her Victorian coat and black slacks he made her almost at once and took off. I was waiting for him just around the corner. I grabbed him by the shoulders and slammed him against the wall. He still had some fight in him so I shoved my forearm under his neck and pushed him up the wall, his legs kicking helplessly in the air. Then I stunned him with a liver shot.

"Damnit, Roach! You know I hate it when people run. I've got a bad knee." I let the poor bastard drop into a crumpled heap right as Vaskov knelt beside him and placed her taser against his neck. "Now the lady is going to ask you some questions, Roach, and you are going to talk. I should warn you, she's real trigger happy."

"I… I… I just mind my own business."

Vaskov smiled. "You know what a sadist is?" she asked. He glanced from me to her, trying to figure out which one of us scared him more. I looked up and saw some civil rights crusader shooting video on his phone. He got real nervous when I approached.

"This is a public place and I have every right to be here. This a clear case of police brutality." He was talking a good game, but I could see his resolve fading when I got close. I tend to have that effect on people. I took the phone from his hand, held it in front of his face, then crushed it. Splintered plastic and computer chips dropped to the sidewalk.

"You know, that's why I hate these iPhones. They just get so twitchy after an update. You never know what they're going to do." After that his survival instinct overcame his need for political action and he walked up the sidewalk like nothing had happened. When I got back to our witness he was going in and out of shock. I guess Vaskov had explained the concept of sadism.

"All right, Roach. We've got seven dead in the underground so we're not feeling real patient right now. So you either tell us what we want to know or my partner will cut your retinas out and hock them on the black market."

For a couple of seconds he just sputtered and blubbered. "It was Johnny the Reptile," he said at length.

Vaskov looked at me quizzically and I nodded. There wasn't a junkie or dealer in the city that didn't know Johnny the Reptile. He was a real degenerate, even by the standards of the street. He had these bulging eyes that kind of made you think of a lizard, but that's not why he got the nickname. Junk does something to your brain. It makes you cold. After a while you don't care about other people. They're just vending machines you use to get what you want. The Reptile never slept. He would hit the pipe until his chest was ready to explode then use the needle to even things out. The guy would do anything to get high. He stole and cheated. I heard he kidnapped runaways and tied them to beds, selling tickets to anyone who wanted to have a go. He was linked to at least five murders, but we could never pin anything on him because he was smart.

"So you're saying the Reptile did all of this? How?"

Roach closed his eyes, like he was going deep inside himself. Then he shuddered, not liking what he saw. "It was just like any other day," he began. "I had been out collecting cans. I wasn't looking for any trouble. I've been clean for six months."

"Bullshit," said Vaskov.

"I swear," he protested.

I looked at him a little closer. After enough time on the streets you get a feel for who's hitting the pipe. I realized he was telling the truth.

"Forget about that. Just tell us about the Reptile."

"Everyone was getting high, like they always do. But Johnny has this bottle of wine he found in the sewer. He says it was made back in the 1930s. He seems real proud of himself. But when he hits it, he gets all fucked up, you know. He starts spraying blood out of his mouth. Then his eyeballs and fingers… Everything gets all weird. It was like his flesh was quivering. It would start to melt from his bones, then it would kind of come back together. And he was screaming. We figured he was going to die so one of the boys went over and gave him a good kick in the ribs. You know how the Reptile is. When you get a chance to take a shot at him, you take it. He lay there quivering and convulsing for about an hour. I had forgotten all about him. Then all of the sudden he was back on his feet."

Here he stopped, searching our faces for some type of sign. "You're doing fine, Roach. Just keep talking," I coaxed.

"Well, he didn't look right. I mean, it looked like Johnny, but then these flaps came out on either side of his head, like one of those snakes from India." He gestured with his palms on either side of his head. "And you could see that he had gills along the side of his neck." Here he stopped. "Do I have to keep telling?"

"This is a load of shit," said Vaskov, but I put my hand on her shoulder.

"How did they die, Roach?"

"It was his tongue. He had this real hungry expression. You know how someone looks when they haven't turned on in a long time and they see a pile of rocks. That's the way he looked. His tongue just shot out of his mouth and went right inside their heads. It had a sharp spike on the tip. Some of the boys tried to fight, but his hands had become claws. And God, he was strong."

When he was done Vaskov sat back and rubbed her neck. "So you're telling me this guy turned into some type of super lizard with a spiked tongue? You must think we're pretty stupid."

"No! I'm giving it to you straight. I can't sleep or anything. I just keep seeing his face."

I helped Roach back to his feet. "So how did you get away?"

"I think it was an angel."

"Do you want to get punched again? I told you to cut the BS."

"No. He had me. I was in TJ's shack. He had just wasted TJ. I was lying there too scared to move. When it was my turn he just looked me over. It was almost like he was smelling me. Then he just walked away. Right before he left I saw an angel standing next to him. It was like a beautiful glowing lady. She had to be an angel. She saved me. That's the only thing it could be."

I brushed off his jacket. "You did okay, Roach. Now remember I hate chasing people. Next time I see you, make sure your guardian angel reminds you to put on the brakes."

As we started to walk away he called to me. "You believe me, don't you, Stern?" He had a desperate look on his face, like a man who can't decide if the nightmare is real or not. Sometimes men who are drowning in their own delusions need to drag you down with them.

When we got back to the car Vaskov looked hard at me. "Don't tell me you're buying this voodoo, Stern."

"Not the part about the guardian angel, but nothing surprises me when it comes to Johnny the Reptile."

"These homeless people disgust me. That guy is just a drugged-out scumbag. All that meth has trashed his brain."

"You're wrong about that. Roach is your typical schizoid. I remember when they hit the streets. We started seeing them in 1983. Reagan wasn't a big fan of housing the crazies at tax payers' expense. At first we didn't have a big homeless problem, then one day they were just there. They use whatever they can get their hands on to treat their symptoms. It took us almost ten years to round them all up and get them in jail."

"You sound like you're going soft."

"No. I call them like a see them."

"What about the Reptile. Is he another schizoid?"

"The Reptile is something else completely. For a while he specialized in the hot shot. He would spike the needles of his unsuspecting clientele with cyanide. At first I figured the motive was robbery. Then I realized he just liked watching people die. He would shoot up while their lights went out. He has this rich daddy who always makes sure sonny boy has a good attorney. Vice has been after him for years—a sexual deviant of the first order."

Vaskov checked her icy visage in the rearview mirror then turned the ignition. "You know, I almost hope he's telling the truth. To be honest, I was getting kind of bored. What was the name of that wine?"

"It's called Viper."

"Viper? Sounds like a good name for a killer. I like that. I'm looking forward to meeting this guy. I've been worrying that my trigger fingers were about to atrophy."

"You know something, Vaskov? You're the kind of woman that would eat her own children."

"With a little sage and garlic, Pops."

That's when the next call came in. It was only about five blocks north. The sound of panic in the patrolman's voice on the radio told us it was going to be bad. This time I didn't complain when Vaskov hit the pedal. We were the first unit to arrive on the scene. There was a crowd of people on one side of the street with looks of shock frozen on their faces. The rookie patrolman was standing next to an open manhole looking like his dead grandma had just crawled out of the sewer to lick his balls.

"It was a man and a woman. They were just a couple of Jesus freaks down here passing out fliers. I was checking their IDs when this cover gets knocked aside and something grabbed them. It had claws!"

I knelt by the hole and listened. I could hear the sound of chomping and slavering. It sounded like someone sucking the meat off the bones of an overcooked chicken. I pulled my .357 and stuck the patrolman's flashlight in my pocket.

"You going down there?" asked Vaskov.

"Yeah, unless you've got a better idea. Cover me while I am on the ladder. If you see anything, make it rain."

Vaskov pulled the .40s and pointed them at the hole as I descended. It was an access tunnel that connected to one of the aqueducts. The rungs of the ladder were coated in mud and difficult to grasp. The cement was cracked in places and the pungent ground seep smelled like feces mixed with bleach. Once I was on the ground I shined the light around the tunnel. The walls had been plastered with the two Jesus freaks. It looked like a Jackson Pollock painting. The body parts were all over the floor—arms, legs, torsos. I glanced up the tunnel and glimpsed a figure hunched in the shadows with something in its mouth. It had a human form, but its limbs were elongated beyond normal proportions. It had that unmistakable crouch of a predator over its prey. When it looked up and spit out a piece of flank I recognized the face.

"It's good to see you, Stern," he said in a voice that seemed to bubble up from his guts. Two flaps snapped into place along each side of his face and rattled in agitation. I was in no mood to talk so I leveled the .357 and lit the corridor with the blaze from my barrel. I got off one shot before he disappeared around a corner, but I know the bullet hit center mass. That's when I heard the rattle of Vaskov's .40s as she came up beside me. The bullets snapped and crackled around the opening that had swallowed Johnny the Reptile. When she had gone through half her mags she paused and we listened as the casings tinkled to the floor.

There was a long silence. Then Vaskov said, "That was weird."

"Yeah," I agreed.

"Did that guy have a tail?"

I didn't bother answering because I knew it wasn't really a question. She was still processing information. I shined the light around, finding one of the heads close to my feet. It was a girl. She looked like a nice kid. The emotion on her face was one of surprise, like she was on some type of rollercoaster. The hole came in through her right temple.

"I guess this is our boy's work," said Vaskov.

"Yeah, only there's one difference." I shined the light on a defleshed ribcage. "He has started eating his victims."

It wasn't long after that there was an uptick in calls. The moles were fleeing the underground and causing trouble. Everywhere you went there were homeless crazies babbling about monsters in the tunnels. Vaskov couldn't help herself and told the boys at the precinct we were after a guy called the Viper. The name stuck. If he had kept his activities confined to the sewers there is a good chance no one would have taken much notice. But when you start snatching civilians off the streets in broad daylight in front of a dozen people it arouses concern. The heat fell on us because the kind of people who shopped at Tiffany's and Saks were starting to feel the vibrations and that was unacceptable. And of course no one at the top wanted it leaked that we had known about raptinal for 30 years. I could feel the cards shuffling for a scapegoat. I wanted to make damn sure that I wasn't the one left holding the black queen.

The following day we paid a visit to Dr. Frankenstein. His real name was Leland Sykes. He had a reputation for reverse engineering bloody crime scenes and chemical analysis. He got the nickname after it was discovered he had a penchant for fondling dead bodies. You might be surprised at the eccentricities the department will tolerate in a talented forensics expert. He had his own office in the basement of the ME's building. It was immaculate and had no other decoration other than a large reprint of Dali's *Metamorphosis of Narcissus* hanging behind his desk. It had been a while since I had seen him. He had that stooped, leathery appearance that old people get. But his eyes belied sharp awareness.

"Hello, Stern. You are looking fit as ever. I always thought you should have been a prize fighter."

"Hey, Doc. I'm way too slow for that. This is my partner, Valentina Vaskov."

The old man turned his head slowly. "Oh, how charming. You are a lovely creature."

"Thanks, Dr. Sykes. I have heard a lot about you. They say you're the best. Were you able to work your magic on those samples?" Vaskov's flattery had the desired effect as the old man beamed at her through rheumy eyes.

"I think I might have something for you. I understand things are getting ugly. They're calling this one the Viper? That's a nice touch. He really is a naughty boy. I guess you already know you have another raptinal case."

"We figured that. What we can't figure is why the guy is still alive."

"Yes, I saw your preliminary report. That's a rather startling development. You know I can only speculate about that, but I will give you my best interpretation." He turned to a lighted panel on the wall, revealing the scans of several skulls. "As you can see a foreign object has been inserted into the cranium with explosive force, driving straight to the core of the brain. At first I assumed this was simply a means to terminate the victim's life, but then I noticed that something was missing."

"Missing?" queried Vaskov, closing in behind him.

"Yes. It appears that portions of the striatum and the substantia nigra have been sucked out of the head. The person who did this was not necessarily intending to kill the victim. He was after these portions of the brain. The fact that this extraction ended the person's life was simply ancillary."

Vaskov wrinkled her nose. "Why would he target that part of the brain?"

"My, you smell good," said Dr. Frankenstein, then turned back to the picture. "This is only speculation mind you, but I would suggest that this Viper of yours is feeding directly on human dopamine. This might explain how he has maintained corporeal integrity after ingesting the raptinal. You see, dopamine is a chemical that evolved in our predatory ancestors. It links pleasure to the act of hunting. It allows us to focus on prey and provides us with a sense of reward when we kill something good to eat. Given that this chemical is also crucial to coordinating the central nervous system, I think it is entirely possible that a subject with high dopamine levels might be able to develop enough cellular awareness to temporarily halt the process."

"Goddamn," I muttered shaking my head. "You said temporarily. Do you mean he will not be able to prevent himself from melting?"

"Well that depends. Raptinal is a powerful enzyme. You know we still cannot manufacture it. Just between you and me the defense department has been very interested in weaponizing it. Your friend's problem is that he will require larger and larger doses of dopamine to prevent total liquefaction. As long as he can get a steady supply, he might suspend the process indefinitely."

"Roach," I said to myself. "He left one man alive at the scene."

"All of your victims had just smoked a rather potent batch of methamphetamine, so their levels were probably elevated. Perhaps your survivor had not partaken."

"Damn. Well I guess he picked the right time to go clean."

"What about the Jesus freaks?" asked Vaskov.

"Yeah. Yesterday he snatched a couple of those street corner preachers off the sidewalk. They didn't look like the types to smoke or shoot."

"Don't underestimate the power of religious mania. There is little difference between spiritual indulgence and drug use from a biochemical perspective. Their fervent beliefs would have made them prime targets."

"Do you have any idea why he would be cannibalizing these victims?"

"I would surmise that he is attempting to replace the cells that he is shedding. That is a sign that he is becoming increasingly unstable. I would not be surprised if he required larger amounts of human protein to sustain himself."

I took a moment to absorb the doctor's words, then looked at Vaskov questioningly. She nodded. "Doc, there is one thing we left out of the reports."

The old man looked first to me, then to my partner. I saw his internal radar kick into high gear. "I am at your service. You can count on me for complete discretion."

"I got a look at him last night. Now I know this guy. It looked like him, but the bodily proportions were all wrong. He has some sort of spiked tongue that shoots through the victims' heads. And he looks like he is turning into some kind of snake monster—like something out of a B-horror movie."

Now it was the old man's turn to digest my words. I watched the gears turn in his head. He shuffled back to his desk and pensively caressed the Dali painting. "You know detectives… The human mind never ceases to amaze me. Would either of you know if this man has a fetish for serpents?"

"His nickname is The Reptile."

"Of course it is. I would say that one of the byproducts of his molecular instability is a certain malleability of form. What a unique case he is. As his cellular awareness develops he will probably assume different shapes. There is no telling what type of monstrosity he will produce if he goes on killing. It just goes to show you what a person can accomplish with a little imagination."

"And now for the big question," cooed Vaskov. "Stern shot him point blank yesterday. I know I hit him as well. How are we going to stop him?"

The old man took his eyes away from the painting and beamed at her. "Well one path would be to deprive him of his supply of prey. Once his own dopamine levels get low enough his cellular awareness will disintegrate. At that point the accelerated apoptosis will kick in and you will be left with nothing but a decaying pool of protoplasm."

"Unless we win the drug war overnight and close all of the churches that probably isn't going to happen. Any other suggestions?"

"Well, it's quite simple. Simply shut off his striatum. The rest of his organs are useless. I doubt they even exist at this point. My best advice is to blow his brains out."

After I pried Frankenstein's hands off my partner we exited the building. Once on the street we were greeted by a rush of people that remained oblivious to the monsters that dwelled right beneath their feet. "He seemed nice," said Vaskov.

"Yeah, don't go planning the wedding yet. He's just hoping to get you on the slab."

"Well, he's going to have to invent a youth serum because I intend to live a long time."

"I don't know, Vaskov. This case may not be the best way to increase your longevity."

"You need to have some faith, Pops."

"I've never really traded in faith. Pardon me for pointing this out, but you don't exactly seem like the praying type yourself."

"It depends on what you worship," she said patting the holsters beneath her coat. "My altar is gunpowder and lead."

Even as we were talking, our boy moved on a headshop in Green Point. It was one of those places that sold pipes and incense. Its alcoves were full of eastern shrines. Unfortunately the protective gaze of Vishnu couldn't defend the occupants from the Viper when he burst up through a weak subbasement. He came right through the floor like some kind of avenging demon. Those poor stoners never saw it coming. They sure picked the wrong time to find Nirvana. The fire department put out some bullshit about a gas explosion and I caught enough heat to wither the soul of any lesser man. As the lies piled up I knew the people at the top were getting desperate. It was then I realized the rulebook had to be tossed.

We finally caught a break from a buddy of mine in vice named Vic. I remembered him complaining about the massive influx of designer drugs into the club scene. After reviewing a map of the Viper's movements we saw a pattern. While driving the streets of Park Slope we ran across The Strobe. It wasn't really much of a nightclub, but a rental space for musicians and DJs who fancied themselves the new vanguard of the chemical intelligentsia. It was right in the Viper's path. As luck would have it a band calling itself Doorways of Perception was playing that night.

"Yeah, they fancy themselves techno-gurus of the new age," Vic intoned over the phone. He could have been promoted to homicide years ago, but had found the desperate underworld of vice more suited to his nature. "That's a rave—plain and simple. We usually don't hassle them because we catch too much heat from the top. Hell, the mayor's daughter will probably be there. A lot of the crowd will be slumming from the Hamptons. You would not believe the shit those kids put in their bodies. The one thing you can be sure is that everyone there will either be tripping or high."

That's what I needed to hear. All of those brain stems shining like the lights on a Christmas tree would function like a beacon for Johnny. He would hone in them like a flesh fly to an open wound. I decided to make it an undercover job. I figured me and Vaskov could handle Johnny, but just in case I asked for a SWAT team to be stationed down the street. The idea was to keep everything on the down-low. I wasn't sure what to expect from Johnny, but the guy had exceptional radar. One of the reasons no one had ever laid a significant case on him was the fact that he had a preternatural ability to sense traps.

When Vaskov picked me up she looked the part. She was wearing a red mini and had a matching streak dyed into her blonde hair. With the red-framed, wrap-around sunglasses she looked like a piece of modern art. I wore jeans and an old Molly Hatchet concert shirt.

"What the hell is up with you, Stern?" laughed Vaskov. "You look about as square as anyone could. They are going to make you in a second."

"That's where you're wrong, partner. Our undercover narcs are almost too slick. They're gonna think I'm some groovy old man who's off the chain for the night—some awkward throwback or failed experiment." I removed a couple of little pink pills from my pocket. Each was shaped like a grinning skull. I popped them in my mouth.

"What's that?" asked Vaskov.

"Ecstasy," I replied.

"Are you kidding me? You're going in there high?"

"Hell yeah. I want that bastard to come right at me. Besides, I'll have my guardian angel right beside me."

She studied me for a moment. "You know, I could miss."

"No you won't."

The doorman at The Strobe gave me a sideways glance, but when he got a load of Vaskov we had no trouble getting in. The place lived up to its name with a pulsing light display. The blacklights and glowsticks of a bygone era had been replaced by piercing, rhythmic lasers. Doorways of Perception was composed of three guys—two who played throbbing synthesizers and another who sawed away on an esraj. One of the synth players would occasionally chant incoherent poetry into the microphone. As Vic predicted the crowd was young and very high. There were at least two hundred people standing in clusters or dancing in intricate orbits.

Vaskov and I separated. It wasn't long before the boys started approaching her one at a time. She repelled them like pirates off of a Spanish galleon packed with stolen gold. I stood at the bar and nursed a beer, watching the crowd. They were mainly trust fund types. Their parents had made it during the crash by betting on the credit default swaps. While the rest of us took a ride they prospered. I thought about the moles under their feet scratching out a meager existence while they expanded their minds under the guiding throb of the Doorways of Perception. Things like this generally irritated me, but tonight I found myself drawn to them. They weren't really bad kids. It wasn't their fault the world was such shit. They were trying. Just because daddy made a living defending the corporation of death didn't mean they were bad people. Hell, they couldn't do any worse than my generation.

That's when I realized the ecstasy was kicking in.

"Hey, man," said a guy next to me. "I dig your shirt."

"Thanks," I said.

"It's totally ironic." I nodded in agreement, though I failed to see anything ironic about Molly Hatchet. "Is this your first time to a DOP concert?"

"Yeah," I replied. "A man can only deprive himself so long."

He looked like a nice guy—maybe twenty-five. I guess he was striking out with the girls so he was looking for another misfit.

"You seem kind of old to be here. No offense. I think it's cool."

"Actually, I am waiting on a friend of mine."

"Does he like to party?"

I have always believed in being honest. "He's strung out on a chemical called raptinal. In order to maintain his cellular integrity he is rampaging through the city spiking peoples brains and cannibalizing their bodies. He looks like a big snake. See, he can bend the shape of his body to whatever unconscious nightmare happens to be in his awareness. The boys downtown are calling him The Viper."

That was when the guy was done talking to me. "That is some of the spookiest shit I have ever heard. You should keep that to yourself. A head like that could crash the whole party. You shouldn't go off your meds like that."

As the guy lectured me I found myself swept up in the lights, amazed that a place like this could exist. The room was like a separate planet. The alien landscape around me continued to morph in unexpected ways as the bodies writhed and circled. When the screaming began I thought it was part of the show. I looked over and saw Shiva the Destroyer smashing up through the floor. His multiple arms seemed to embrace the dancers like lovers. Only instead of one head, I saw several writhing like some type of hydra. I was enraptured by the vision of the primal god ascending from hell to bring wisdom to his subjects. It wasn't until Vaskov started shooting that I came out the trance.

I don't know where Johnny came up with that shape. I guess he had imprinted on something he saw in the head shop, then added a few of his own improvements. Instead of one serpent head, there were seven or eight, each of which worked in conjunction with a massive arm. The claws gripped the dancers and held them while the spiked tongues shot through their skulls. I could hear the sucking sound over the music.

Vaskov's rounds peppered The Viper and I watched as the holes closed almost as fast as she could make them. One arm reached onto the stage and seized the esraj player and dragged him screaming into an open maw in the thing's belly. It bit off the top half of his body in one go. It was like a great white shark. That was Johnny. It was all about efficiency when it came to inflicting suffering. He had multiple dopamine siphons going while those massive jaws inhaled more human biomass. It was only then I became aware of the scale of his body. He was at least twelve feet tall and I had the impression that we could only see part of him sticking through the floor. The music died while the strobes continued to pulse. Most of the partiers started screaming, but there were a few that sat there gaping, wondering if this was real or part of some sick fantasy dredged from their unconscious.

I saw one of the serpent heads drop as a couple of Vaskov's rounds found a home. 'Where the hell is his brain?' I thought as I pulled the .357. I tried to draw a bead on one of the swaying heads, wishing I had a twelve gauge. Then Vaskov was beside me.

"How about this for a party, Pops?" she asked and jammed new clips into the forties.

I fired an ineffectual round. "Don't say I never take you anywhere."

I guess we should have briefed the SWAT boys. When they came through the door you could see the looks on their faces. They were not prepared for this. The floor was slick with blood while Johnny cracked one skull after another like a coconut crab. When he was done with one person the arm would fling them away. I was glad when the M-16s opened up and I saw another head drop. With so much lead in the air they were bound to hit something. But rather than run, Johnny lunged straight at them. They never had a chance to disperse and soon he was mauling them, his claws finding ways through their body armor. Vaskov cut loose with another volley. I couldn't figure it out. Did he have lots of brains?

That's when it hit me. "Johnny!" I yelled. All of the writhing serpent heads continued their deadly work except for one. When it turned, I recognized the eyes.

"Stern!" it yelled back in recognition. "You smell good Stern! I'm gonna eat your brain!"

The massive slug like body propelled itself across the room with surprising speed. Something bounced up against my shin and I looked down to see the severed head of a SWAT member still wearing his helmet. It must have been fresh because the mouth was still trying to form words. I am pretty sure he was saying "Hooyah!" It was fortunate that the first spike was not intended for me because I never saw it coming. It caught my friend at the bar as he crouched on the floor.

"I'm gonna eat your brain, Stern!" he kept yelling. After another volley from Vaskov I saw one of the heads explode, but not the one that was locked onto me. Johnny's pupils were vertically slitted like a snake's. I looked into his eyes and saw an expression of great satisfaction. He was enjoying this. But that's how it was with Johnny the Reptile. He thrived on chaos. I watched his jaw unhinge and could see the tip of the spiked tongue that was intended for me.

I don't think I was even aware of the round I fired. It was the only shot I landed the entire night. Johnny was smart, but he made one mistake. He should have hidden his original brain somewhere in that massive body. To maintain cellular integrity he needed a psyche. The round caught him between the eyes. The other heads dropped and that giant maw in his stomach vomited up the human gore that hadn't been digested.

Almost at once the raptinal went to work. I had never seen it melt someone in person. By this point Johnny must have weighed at least a ton. As the tissue boiled you could smell acrid flesh. Bit by bit he collapsed back into the hole as liquefied flesh bubbled up from the opening like the rim of a volcano. At first geysers of dead cells sprayed the ceiling, then gradually the tempest calmed and there was nothing but a gurgle coming from the subbasement. The Viper was dead. I holstered my weapon and looked around at the human debris scattered all over the floor. I was only dimly aware of Vaskov walking to the edge of the hole and looking down at what was left of Johnny. Haloed in the persistent strobe I could not help noticing just how beautiful she was. She had a kind of druggy glow about her. Then her smile faded into a look of vague sadness.

"I just realized something, Stern. No matter how long I live or what I do, I will never be happier than I am at this moment."

The Last Screening
Edward Karpp

A truly great horror film can really draw you in!

I feel concrete under my cheek and I can't open my eyes. I smell burning meat and something else. Hair? A loud rhythmic rumbling fills my head. Straining, I open my eyes a crack. I'm lying on the floor. It angles slightly downward toward my left. Streams of blood trickle down the concrete.

A man lies on the ground a few yards in front of me. Something is wrong with his blurry, red face. Behind him, out of focus, a tall black contraption is vibrating; I must be delirious because I see it's the contraption, not the man, that has a face. A face I recognize.

***

When I arrive at the Prism Theatre about twelve people are already in line. I take my place behind two middle-aged men in wool overcoats. It's five minutes to five. I told Dave to meet me at five, but I know he'll be at least 15 minutes late. As long as one of us is here on time, we should get our pick of seats. I feel an unexpected, electric surge of adrenaline. I'm looking forward to this even more than I anticipated.

The letters on the marquee spell out SPECIAL HALLOWEEN SCREENING! and FLESHCRAWLERS and STABBIES. The bottom line adds GUESTS! PRIZES! as if those are the names of more movies. The marquee is not yet lit, despite the October dimness and the overcast sky. I zip up my jacket and shove my hands in my jeans pockets. It's going to be a cold night.

Things have changed. When I was in high school, the curved letters spelling PRISM above the white grid of the marquee—now red—were a faded aqua color that matched the walls in the lobby. That was back during this place's first life as a movie theater, before it sat boarded-up for a decade, before it became a community church with marquee slogans like GOD'S RETIREMENT PLAN IS OUT OF THIS WORLD and FREE TRIP TO HEAVEN - DETAILS INSIDE. After that, it was vacant again for at least two years, and only reopened as a movie theater back in August. A movie theater in a small college town should not be a risky business proposition, but clearly I know more about stochastic differential equations—despite my last meeting with my dissertation advisor—than I know about business.

A teenaged couple falls in line behind me, the boy's arm around the girl's shoulder. I hear a quiet buzzing and turn back toward the marquee, whose lights are sputtering to life. When they reach full brightness—the white bulbs blazing around the white grid holding the movie titles, the letters of PRISM on top now bright scarlet—it feels as though all the light in the world has been sucked into that sign, and everything else is just a black void.

"There you are." I hear Dave's voice before I realize he is one of a group of people in silhouette walking past the ticket booth. I expected him to come from the other direction.

"Here I am," I confirm as he joins me in line. "You're not late."

"The lab shut down at four because Dr. Squires is flying to a conference tomorrow morning." Dave unshoulders his backpack and drops it to the sidewalk. It looks heavy. He hands me an off-brand cola and pulls out two burritos. "Yours has green salsa," he says. "Don't take the one that says red salsa." After a pause he adds, "Take the one that says green salsa."

By the time we finish eating, the line behind us stretches to the end of the block and around the corner of the dance apparel store next to the Vista. Dave follows my gaze and says, "It's going to be crowded." For my part, I feel satisfied, not annoyed, that two old horror movies can attract a good-sized crowd to an honest-to-God movie theater.

I check my phone. The signal is only at one bar. No notifications.

Flakes of snow drift in the light of the marquee. A man in a maroon suit unlocks the ticket booth and the college students at the front of the line swarm around the booth's curved window.

When Dave and I reach the ticket booth, I catch the name on the sixty-something ticket-trackers badge: Black. I wonder if he is the theater's new owner.

The sharp salty smell of popcorn overwhelms me as I enter the lobby, which is no longer painted aqua. The walls are dark red and there is gold trim around the small concession stand. The lobby has been refurbished but not expanded; there is still only room for maybe two dozen people on the carpet in front of the concession area.

The lobby still features four movie posters on the walls, their lighted frames now gold instead of gray steel. The poster for Fleshcrawlers, with its half-faced man reaching out toward the viewer, his fingers decaying into tiny blue metallic monsters, is familiar to me but the one for Stabbies is unfamiliar. It shows a huge knife lying on black velvet, an eyeball reflected in the blood covering the blade. The other two posters are for new movies I have no interest in seeing, The Diamond Trade and It Takes One to Know One.

"Medium popcorn and Whoppers," Dave tells me, walking to the curtains and the open doors leading into the auditorium.

I shake my head, knowing that he wants to get the perfect seat and that I won't complain about picking up his snacks. "Save a seat for me," I say, more to myself than to Dave, who is already gone.

In front of the concession stand, a college student, his back toward me, moves quickly in front of me and takes my spot in line. He wears a black jacket over his dark red t-shirt, and his long straight hair is dyed black. "Max?" I recognize him as a student from the spring semester.

He turns to see who said his name and he gives me a nod. There are three thin scars, barely visible, on his cheeks and lip, and a few more on his neck. In class I'd noticed scars as well, and had suspected he might be in the habit of cutting himself, but I never said anything. He turns away from me; I suppose I should be happy to get any kind of acknowledgement from him.

I pay for Dave's food and head through the doors into the auditorium. I'm full from the burrito, and I didn't have much appetite anyway. Dave will pay me back tomorrow; he probably already calculated the total, including sales tax, after glancing at the price list above the popcorn machine.

In the auditorium, Dave sits in the center seat of the fourth row, his backpack on the seat to his left. The theater is filling up. As I take the seat on Dave's right, I'm reminded of my impression from childhood that every cinema screen in the world faces the same direction.

"Look," Dave says, taking two VHS boxes from his backpack. The art on the Fleshcrawlers box reproduces the poster in the lobby. The Stabbies box art is the design I've seen a hundred times; it shows a screaming woman surrounded by short silhouettes holding knives. I wonder where the more abstract poster in the lobby came from and I think about asking Dave if he's seen it before, but he is already reading the box description. "Stabbies, 1983. When three college friends take a summer vacation to Redwood Island, their partying is interrupted by a vicious virus whose victims have the uncontrollable urge to brutally stab everyone in sight. Can the college students overcome the threat of the virus victims and survive until help comes? Watch in breathtaking suspense to find out who makes it out alive. Starring Linda Daniels, Ripley Cooper, and James Best from The Dukes of Hazzard."

Unsure whether he's reading to me or to himself, I don't say anything until he looks at me and asks, "Does that sound accurate? I don't remember any partying."

"And James Best is only in that one scene at the beginning in the marina." Dave looks at me and I think he's a little impressed. He usually assumes I don't know what I'm talking about.

The lights dim a little and more of the crowd settle into their seats. I estimate the auditorium is three-quarters full. Half of the people look to be college-aged or younger and half look to be at least forty, with Dave and me the only ones in the middle. I check my phone again, but now there is no service at all.

Dave puts the Stabbies box back into his backpack and examines the Fleshcrawlers box. Before he starts reading the description, there is a commotion to the left as two men walk down the aisle to the front of the theater. One man, in his early forties, wears a maroon suit matching the uniform that Black, the ticket-taker, was wearing, while the other man, a redhead in his late fifties, wears a denim jacket and jeans. The younger man carries a microphone. They reach the large open area between the red curtains and the empty first row of seats.

"Hello, hello," he says. "I would like to ask you all to settle in as quickly as possible so I can introduce our guest."

I look back to see that most of the audience is seated, but there are half a dozen people moving around or standing, many of them talking loudly to their neighbors.

The microphone squeals. "Okay," says the younger man, "Let's get started. My name is George Anderson. I'm the manager of the new Prism Theater. I have the pleasure of introducing Mr. Ryan Dakota. I'm sure you all recognize him from his supporting roles in both of our features here tonight, Fleshcrawlers and Stabbies."

The older man smiles broadly as Anderson hands him the microphone. His face is tan, with deep wrinkles. Though I don't recognize the actor's name, it's obvious that this is the goofy best friend from Fleshcrawlers, the one whose torso meets the business end of a jigsaw near the end of the movie. Dave gasps.

"Hello, and welcome," says Ryan Dakota to light applause. "Thanks for coming out. Mr. Anderson asked me to be kind of the host for this thing. We're going to show Stabbies first, and then of course Fleshcrawlers, but in between we're going to have a special treat. So get ready for that."

Dakota starts walking back and forth in front of the curtains. He seems satisfied to have the spotlight. "Now, most of you probably know that these are the only two films directed by Tucker Bates, a very talented filmmaker, which I can attest to. I was a close friend of Tucker's for most of the eighties, his closest friend, maybe. Tucker left the business after his difficulties financing his third movie. That would have been a doozy, I'm here to tell you. All about a silent movie with a deadly curse.

"Anyway, I lost touch with him after that, but I am positive he would be thrilled to see these movies, his labors of love, so well attended so many years later. So without further ado, we present to you the cinematic classic Stabbies, from 1983. Thanks, everyone." He and Anderson hurry toward the right side of the auditorium as the house lights fade off.

When the thick red curtain begins to part, I feel anticipation rising again. The screen fills with white light that dissolves into a series of shots showing rural small town locations, and I'm aware of Dave's hand on my arm. He is saying something to me but nothing registers because my attention is on the screen. I shoot a glance at him to shut him up, but he interprets it as a request to repeat himself. "Ryan Dakota is not in Stabbies."

"What?" I whisper.

"They're wrong. He's only in Fleshcrawlers."

"Okay," I say, trying to get across an air of finality, and it works at least temporarily because Dave turns his own attention to the screen.

On the screen, a preschool teacher stands in the center of her classroom, surrounded by a circle of four-year-olds sitting cross-legged on a plain blue rug. The children all have safety scissors and construction paper in front of them, but in front of a little pig-tailed girl sits a pair of the teacher's scissors, long and sharp. The girl picks them up and they glint in the fluorescent light. Suddenly she plunges the blades into the teacher's thigh, sending the teacher to the floor amid the screams of the other children. The pig-tailed girl stabs the teacher over and over while the other shrieking children run toward the classroom door. With one last stab, the girl plunges the blades into the teacher's right hand, pinning it to the rug as blood spreads outward from the body, turning the rug from blue to reddish-black.

Then the girl stands up and faces her classmates, a grim grin on her face.

The screen fills with the word STABBIES and the title credits start, to cheers of approval from the audience. Watching the opening sequence and the scene introducing the college students on the boat ride to Redwood Island, I'm reminded how efficiently the film has been made, how well Tucker Bates shot and cut his first film. The acting of most of the college students is pretty wooden, except for the lead girl, Traci, but the film differentiates its characters quickly and sends them on their way to the island in less than five minutes.

The students gather their camping gear and hurry along the boat dock until they are interrupted by the sheriff's voice calling out to them to warn them about wild hogs in the island's central forest. Brushing off the warning, the students make their way to the small village beyond the dock.

Some people in the audience start applauding, though nothing important appears to be happening onscreen. Then I see him: a young Ryan Dakota in the background, playing the proprietor of a bait and tackle shop arguing with a customer.

I lean over to Dave and whisper, "I guess you were wrong."

Shaking his head, Dave says, "He is *not* in this movie." He throws a handful of popcorn into his mouth.

Having learned not to argue with him, I try to enjoy the rest of the movie. Near the end, three of the college students are surrounded in the woods by six preschool kids infected with the virus. The preschoolers hold different sharp implements: a butcher knife, a pitchfork, a hatchet. The kid holding the butcher knife runs at one of the college women and buries the blade in her hand; blood gushes in a fountain, her pinky falls to the ground, and the rest of the fingers wiggle violently as she screams. The other kids jump on her and there is a frenzy of stabbing as they hack her body to pieces, all the while grinning as if the act of murder is scratching a hard-to-reach itch.

The remaining college students in the forest, Jill and her boyfriend Keith, turn back to back, armed only with tree branches. Keith starts swinging at the children, but then he looks at Jill, who suddenly has a grin on her face. She pushes one of the children down, grabs his axe, and starts hacking away at her boyfriend, a shocked, open-eyed expression on his blood-spattered face.

The audience audibly loves the scene, screaming and laughing, and then falling silent as the climax approaches. Onscreen, the surviving college student Traci, now wearing a bloody tank top and armed with the dead sheriff's pistol, jumps onto the only fishing boat left at the dock. She casts off the lines and runs to the pilot's cabin to start the boat, brushing aside the dead captain's body. She breaths a sigh of relief as the boat pulls away from the dock, but then she realizes there are three infected townspeople on the boat. I realize one of the townspeople is Ryan Dakota again, but I refrain from mentioning this fact to Dave.

Ryan Dakota's infected character only lasts a few seconds, ending up in the water. The final girl manages to fight off one of the other townspeople, who gets impaled by a harpoon gun, but the last infected man sneaks up on her from the top of the pilot's cabin. Armed with a long knife, he leaps at her, slashing her shoulder. She backs away until her legs are blocked by the outboard motor, at which point she aims the pistol shakily at the man. The man slowly approaches and I feel the same feeling I felt when watching the movie for the first time at two in the morning one Sunday at a sleepover with my friends: completely absorbed by the tension onscreen. The man seems to take forever to approach to the girl; the pistol trembles in her grip for what seems like minutes. Then she fires and the man's head bursts open. The audience cheers.

When the house lights come up after the end credits, the audience applauds. I look over my shoulder and the room seems less packed than it was at the beginning of the show, possibly because people have gotten up to use the bathrooms or visit the concession stand. There is no time to ask Dave if he wants to get past me, because Anderson and Dakota are hurrying back to the front of the auditorium, Dakota carrying a folding chair. The red curtains slide closed in front of the screen.

"Sorry for the low-tech presentation up here," Anderson says into his mike while Dakota unfolds his chair and takes a seat. Then he adds, "Wasn't that great?" After some applause, Anderson says, "Now we have a special treat. Who would like to win original one-sheets for Stabbies and Fleshcrawlers signed by Ryan Dakota?"

Anderson, still standing, holds up the two posters, though it is hard to see much of them as they both curl up from the bottom and Anderson appears incapable of deciding which poster he wants to put in front of the other. He announces that the posters will go to the two audience members who answer the most horror movie trivia questions, and that Dakota will be the quizmaster. At this announcement, Dave puts his empty popcorn bucket on the floor and sits up straight in his seat. I know I don't have a chance of winning with Dave in the audience but maybe I can get second place.

Anderson hands Dakota the mike. For the first group of questions, Dakota calls out character names and we're supposed to answer with the name of the right movie. Dakota says, "Sidney Prescott" and about half the people in the audience raise their hands, while a few yell out "Scream!" After admonishing everyone to raise their hands, Dakota continues. I know a few answers, like Brian Flagg in The Blob remake and Katherine McMichaels in From Beyond, and I get one point for identifying Dr. Channard in the second Hellraiser movie, but it's clear that others are much more knowledgeable than me. Of course, Dave does well. He gets five points for character names but I can hear his teeth grinding every time Dakota calls on someone else when Dave's hand is raised.

I'm certain I have no chance by the time two or three audience members, Dave among them, start listing actors who appeared in more than three Jess Franco movies so I leave the auditorium to find a toilet. The bathrooms were renovated at least as much as the rest of the theater, thank God, and the new urinals are now separated by steel dividers. Even though the bathroom is empty, I use the urinal farthest from the door.

When I'm done, I hear a loud squeal. The door to the stall directly to my left is slowly swinging open and I can see someone sitting in that stall. The man is completely still, his arms in bent positions as if he has been frozen while undoing his pants.

In a public restroom, you don't look at someone's face, but curiosity gets the better of me. This man's face is tilted downward, his graying hair is unkempt and his face is glistening with sweat. His mouth is open in what looks like the beginning of a scream, but his expression looks more like pain than fear.

Then I notice the blood trailing from the left corner of his mouth down his chin, and the red-brown stain on his pants that might be bloody vomit.

"I'll get help," I tell him, though I assume he won't respond. Maybe he's had a heart attack on the toilet. I hurry away from him and push at the bathroom door, which at the same time is being pulled from the outside. The ticket-taker, Black, opens the door and pushes past me. Wordlessly, Black rushes over to the open stall, so someone else must have reported the situation. Black motions for me to leave the bathroom.

Max stands in the lobby in front of the bathroom door, as if he were waiting for me. The other two people in the lobby are near the exit, searching for cell service. "You should go," Max tells me.

I walk down the aisle in the theater. The excitement about the trivia contest has died down. They are finishing with some kind of lightning round between Dave and a teenaged boy sitting three rows behind us. "It's a trick question," Dave is saying when I sit down. "Jason was born on Friday the thirteenth in June 1946 so he was fifty-seven years old in 2003 when Freddy vs. Jason came out. Freddy was born in 1942, of course."

"Well," says Dakota, "that's not exactly the answer we prepared, but, you know, it sounds correct, so you get the points. Let's give everyone a big hand for trivia. I think the winner is clear." He strides up the aisle to hand one poster to me; I pass it along to Dave. Dakota adds, "And this one to our runner-up." He hands the other poster to the teenager three rows back.

Dakota waves as he retreats up the aisle, and then the lights fade off and the curtains open again. Orchestral music swells as the screen fades from black to a wide helicopter shot of a university campus. Tucker Bates's second movie obviously had a higher budget than the first. After the helicopter shot, the camera prowls through the empty campus with its high concrete walls and angled concrete paths, the opening credits superimposed in bright blue letters. I relax back in my seat, and Dave does the same thing after rolling up the poster and sliding it under his seat.

Onscreen, two graduate students in their on-campus apartment are packing for winter break. Ben tells his friend Eric to catch his taxi or he'll miss his flight, and when Eric runs out the door he passes Ben's girlfriend Samantha, carrying a blue oxygen tank. Samantha has to stay at the university over the break to collect more data for her dissertation—the thought of which pushes me out of the movie because I remember all I have to do on my dissertation project before the end of the semester.

Fortunately, the horror on the screen starts quickly and my thoughts return to the story, where Samantha's advisor, played by a sweaty Cameron Mitchell, looks at his hand under the bright lights in his biology laboratory. The blood vessels in the hand are dark, pulsing, growing. Suddenly, a cyst inflates between the thumb and forefinger, bursting open in a red-black explosion of blood, to the excitement of the audience.

Behind the actor, a series of brains in glass containers begin to vibrate and pulse. Running into a bathroom in the lab, Mitchell grabs at a white towel, leaving bloody handprints on the terry cloth. Both hands are infected with something, the blood vessels swelling and pushing through the skin. He staggers to the stainless-steel sink and slams his hand against the mirror, leaving a trail of blood, and then he slides down to the bathroom floor. His body splayed out, the camera moves closer to his face; inside his eyes, dozens of tiny wormlike things slither.

I turn away instinctively from the eyeball scene, squeamish while still admiring the quality of the pre-CGI special effects. Turning toward Dave, I notice that his head has drooped and he appears to be asleep, though his eyes are open. The light from the screen grows brighter and I see the rivulet of blood and vomit on his chin. "Shit," I say quietly, and I grab his arm to shake him. His muscles feel tensed, hard as stone.

I turn around to see if I can get help from someone in the audience. There is a sudden blast of noise through the rumbling speakers and the theater vanishes into blackness. The last light I see is from a dull red EXIT sign flickering and fading away in the front of the auditorium to the right of the screen. Calling out would be useless because of the soundtrack's explosive crashing, and the music swelling up to amplify the crashing. I stand up and feel my way over the seats to my right, trying to get to the aisle and the exit door.

I become aware of something bulky in front of me before I feel hands grabbing my arms and pushing me hard down into a seat. My back twists as I lose balance. I reach out into the darkness to shove whoever was there but my hand only grazes a bit of cloth that feels like thick velvet. Then I push myself out of the chair and continue to the right; nobody blocks my way.

I stumble past the last seat and into the aisle. The exit door is somewhere ahead, to the right of the screen. I reach out, feel the curtain, sidestep, grab the steel bar to open the door. The bar moves up and down with a squeal but the door doesn't move.

I turn around and start upward toward the rear exit into the lobby. Nothing blocks my way. I pull my phone from my pocket. There is still no service. I tap the flashlight icon. It gives out just enough light to see where the rows of seats end. I hurry faster up the aisle.

White light blasts my eyes and I stumble. The light comes from the projector, below which I see the silhouettes of the audience scattered through the auditorium, all of them silent and frozen.

No, not all of them—there is a girl near the back row standing and then moving toward the far aisle.

One row in front of her, a man in the audience stands up, turns, and makes a quick motion with his right arm.

The girl falls back into a seat.

I hesitate for a second, considering whether to go back and get Dave, but after the girl has stopped moving I see motion elsewhere in the auditorium. About a dozen of the audience members, scattered randomly throughout the theater, stand up simultaneously. I can see a little better now that my eyes have adjusted to the projector light; I can tell that the people standing up are all men, and they are all wearing red. They move as one, raising small knives, pivoting toward the seated, unmoving audience members closest to them.

Adrenaline surges and I run toward the exit at the rear of the theater. I sense motion around me but it doesn't matter. I crash into the door to the concession area but it's locked tight. I feel something in my shoulder crack with the impact on the door.

Someone is behind me. I try to turn around but see only a white starburst as something hits the back of my head. "We need this one," a voice says, and I feel myself sliding down to the floor.

***

When I open my eyes, the movie screen fills my vision, a white rectangle fading to gray at the corners. The only sound I hear is a hum from the projector. I'm sitting in the front row, center seat. A man with a shaved head stands to my left, wearing a red t-shirt, holding a short-bladed knife in his right hand. Empty seats stretch to my right.

Dave is in the aisle to my right, prone, pulled toward the empty space in front of the screen by two other men wearing red t-shirts. I hear his shoes scraping the floor. I can't tell if he's conscious or unconscious. His eyes are open. His body is stiff.

I turn around—the man standing beside me tenses up but doesn't move—and see the two dozen or so audience members sitting frozen in their seats, their eyes open. The men wearing red are standing next to them with knives, just like the one guarding me.

There is a loud meaty thump as Dave is dropped to the floor in front of the screen. The men turn to walk up the aisle and I recognize them as George Anderson and Max. They stride up the aisle and disappear through the door, now obviously unlocked. I watch Dave but he is still. I can't see his eyes from my seat.

After a few minutes, the door opens. Max backs into the auditorium, pulling some kind of machine on a wheeled cart. Anderson appears on the other side of the machine, guiding it down the aisle, and I realize the machine is a big reel-to-reel movie projector, all black, that looks like it's from the days of silent films. I see a hammer and drill on the cart as well. Max and Anderson wheel the contraption in front of the screen, right next to Dave's body. Black stands back at the doors to the lobby.

Everything goes dark. Almost immediately, a much dimmer light glows, pale orange and flickering, from the black projector device. As the device's reels start spinning, its clicks and clacks accelerate until they become a steady hum.

The old machine projects a city street onto the cinema screen, an unsteady handheld shot. Skyscrapers rise up behind a figure that grows larger as it walks toward the camera. The figure drags an axe along the asphalt. Despite the image's muted colors, I see the figure has red hair and I recognize him as Ryan Dakota. He stares straight at the camera as he approaches.

Somehow he is now in the movie theater and no longer on the screen. He stands in front of the screen, leaning on the axe handle, scanning the audience and then looking at me. Shaking his head, he drags the axe toward Dave.

I want to say something but the knife is suddenly at my throat and slicing into my skin; any farther and it will cut my windpipe.

Anderson kneels in front of Dave and grabs his head, jerking it upward so Dave is prone facing the screen, his eyes wide open, his chin on the concrete.

Dakota raises the axe. I can see what's going to happen. All of us in the room can see what's going to happen.

I can't let him do it. The knife cuts deeper into my throat as I jerk away from the man beside me. Everything suddenly feels cold, and I feel blood dribbling down my shirt. I stumble toward Dave, grabbing the seats to help me push toward him, but my legs are no longer solid and I fall forward. I see Dakota swinging the axe. I see the axe blade pass in front of the projector light, its shadow massive on the screen. I see the blade fall and cleave Dave's skull parallel to his face, bisecting his head.

My trembling hand claws at the image of my friend's still body but reaching him is as impossible as if he were onscreen, just a random bloody shot, the aftermath of a horror movie.

The blade remains where it fell, separating the front of Dave's head from the back, until Dakota struggles to lift the axe again and the front of Dave's skull teeters and falls, blurring, fading to black.

***

I feel concrete underneath my cheek and I can't open my eyes. I smell burning meat and something else. Hair?

The vibrating contraption has Dave's face. That recognition brings me back to myself. Anderson has drilled a hole in my friend's forehead and placed the face and skull—eyes still open, one eyeball slipping down the inside of the skull—over the old projector's lens. The face is suspended on the front of the projector, bright light blasting from the third hole above the eyes.

"Do you see?" Dakota is saying. "Do you see?"

Onscreen, the city image fades to a darker interior shot, an almost colorless view of the inside of a movie theater, with the camera sitting right at the base of the screen and facing the audience. It's not the Vista—it's a much larger auditorium, more open, with many more seats—but the effect startles me, as if the movie screen to my left is a massive mirror.

In the projected image, there are about two dozen people in the audience, and beside each of the seated cinemagoers stands a man in a pale red shirt with a knife. The image jerks slightly and scratches flutter across it, as if the film were made in the twenties.

Max, Anderson, and Dakota are all facing the screen. They are expressionless. Dakota's eyes are closed.

"Do you see?" Dakota whispers.

On the screen, in that mirror cinema, the red-shirted men move quickly, simultaneously, their knives slashing patrons' throats. Dark gray blood gushes. The victims are frozen; they don't even slump in their chairs.

I want to scream out but I have no breath. I turn my head as far as I can to see what I know must be happening here in the Vista, triggered by the image onscreen. I catch the slashing motions in my peripheral vision, see the blood gushing, see all the frozen victims sitting silent in their chairs.

The three men still face the screen, Dakota's eyes closed. Then a rumbling starts, though it can't be from the old projector, which has no speakers. The scratchy image of the larger theater tilts on its side as the camera falls over. A glistening silver shape appears, roughly the shape of a man but much too tall and thin, its head nearly reaching the ceiling. The edges of the shape are either out of focus or the edges of its skin are flickering white and silver and black. It stoops. The black shifting thing where its head should be peers down and fills the screen, and like Dakota it is suddenly in the Vista, its head rising toward the ceiling, one thin arm reaching out.

The rumbling is louder now. It becomes rhythmic, like breathing. These men called the shape here but there is no controlling it. Its four fingers—now five, now six—slip through the air toward Dakota, touch his chest. He falls to his knees. I can't tell if he is alive or dead. Is this what he wanted?

The hands continue reaching out as the men in red make their way toward the screen. Fingers wrap around Anderson's waist and he falls backward. From my angle, it looks like his body is in two pieces, the top sliding bloodlessly away from the bottom. Max stumbles back against the projector and it tilts like the one in the larger cinema. The projector light flares. Something sizzles, crackles, catches fire.

The only thing that matters is moving away from the silver thing. I push myself backward. Another of its hands darts above me, impossibly long, and touches the man who cut my throat. I feel nothing as I watch him slide across the floor toward the light of the projector.

I can get away. I curl up and shift my knees, turning around toward the far wall. It's excruciating but I manage to put some distance between myself and the thing. Then I'm almost weightless. Somebody is helping me. I accelerate toward the wall, trying to see who has his arm around my waist. Max.

I open my mouth but I realize the silver fingers are behind his head. When they wrap around his face I feel an electric jolt passing from his body to mine. We are in the air, then falling horizontally, accelerating toward the screen. I push against Max's grip. His arm feels like a cold, wet strip of film. Everything grows colder. I no longer feel like I'm falling. There is no direction at all. All thought and feeling, all fear and anxiety, has been sucked into a freezing silver nothingness.

Then his arm is gone and there is just the rumbling sound, and then another sound like trees cracking and falling that grows louder and louder until I'm surrounded by fire and smoke.

***

The police believe me, eventually, after interviewing me twice in my hospital room and again after I return to my apartment. In any case, they believe I'm not responsible for what happened. My knife wound is effective as an alibi. I tell them everything I remember, including the shape coming out of the screen. They chalk it up to head trauma. At the last interview the detective tells me there is little evidence to work from. Bodies were found in the ashes of the gutted theater. No projector contraption, no knives, no axe. Nobody identified as the former actor Ryan Dakota.

Dakota survived. I'm sure of it. He survived, inside or outside the screen. That thought has kept me going. I'll find him. I'll find out who they were, how they did what they did, where they found Tucker Bates's final film.

It might take a long time to prepare, but I'll learn their secrets.

I had a long time to think, lying in the hospital. That's when I had the realization, lying in my hospital bed, listening to the oxygen hissing into my nostrils. They need to horrify. Personally horrify people, shock them deeply with a threat to their lives and the lives of people they care about.

I'll make them do it again. I will make it back there.

The Night of the Nails

Jaap Boekestein

A thousand cuts, a thousand pains, a thousand ecstasies in the embrace of the Bone God!

There are thirteen of you, but you are alone in the dark.

The stone slab under your naked body is unforgiving. The chill kisses your flesh, licks your bones, sucks on your marrow. Your muscles cramp but you don't dare to move.

Don't move, don't move.

Wait. Wait.

Waiting for the Bone God.

You hope you don't need to pee.

Don't think that!

Thirteen acolytes: maidens, virgins, sisters in name. Your whole life has lead up to this night.

In the morning, one of you will be accepted by

the Bone God as a new priestess.

All others will be dead.

Thirteen rooms in the temple, sealed for the night. No one gets in, or out. Except the Bone God, of course.

There were tears and hugs, at the goodbye ceremony. You have been together for years, serving the temple. Friendships, enmities, little dramas.

Tomorrow only one of you will be left. The others will be memories.

Will you survive or will you only be a name that will get emptier by the years?

It is dark. So dark. Not a big room, but very high, you think. You didn't see much when you entered the room. Just the stone altar –bed?– and the waiting darkness.

The rooms are hidden deep in the temple complex. They were always closed off and source of much speculation among the acolytes.

And now you are here, alone in the dark. Waiting for the Bone God.

Waiting, listening...

No, not really. The silence is too much to bear.

So you pray. Not for forgiveness, not for mercy. This is the Bone God! The Taker! He doesn't do forgiveness or mercy. You praise His name, chanting in your mind. You try to lose yourself in prayer, to reach that place where time and cold and hunger and pain and fear don't exist anymore. The emptiness, the waking bliss.

You fail.

No matter how many times you repeat the familiar words, no matter how hard you try to pull yourself into the addictive rhythm... You fail.

Your fear is too great.

Admit it!

You are afraid!

Afraid to die! Afraid to fail! Afraid for the Bone God Himself!

Will it hurt? Will He be terrible?

He is a God. He is the Bone God.

'Death' the peasants call Him. The Ender. The Last One.

He...

Maybe you ought to be afraid.

Yes, you should be afraid.

Certainly.

Worries, worries, all those worries in your mind.

You don't notice Him. Not at first.

How long is it before you realize you're floating in the air?

Suddenly you are aware the cold stone against the back of your skull is missing. Shoulders, arms, ass, legs, feet. All feel the emptiness beneath you... There is nothing!

You're in midair.

Falling, you brain shouts. *Falling!*

Madly you wave your arms, trying to hold on to something. Anything.

There is nothing.

But you're not falling.

You're floating. Like on water. A little bit like floating on water. Only it is on air.

Your heart races in your chest. Your eyes are big, but only see darkness. Your throat is dry.

He has come, you know. He has lifted you up or taken you away to somewhere else. Or...

It does not matter. He is here. You don't see or feel or hear Him, but you *know*. The Bone God is here.

And you weren't exactly greeting Him in the proper way, were you? Splashing around like a fish on dry land.

You start to pray, out loud, this time.

It really sounds like the whispering of a little lost girl.

Close your eyes, focus on your breathing, you tell yourself.

You do so. The words of the prayer now sound louder in the darkness.

Am I doing the right thing? Or is He displeased?

The worst thing is you don't know. You really don't. All the teaching, all the stories, they don't help you at all. You are clueless how to serve Him. So you pray.

Finally He touches you, for the very first time.

Something sharp rests –pushes– against your throat. Just under your chin.

You freeze, the words of the prayer die in your mouth.

Sharp, sharp, sharp! a part of your brain shouts. There is something sharp pushing against –but not breaking– your skin. You pull your head back, but the concentrated pressure on your vulnerable flesh follows relentlessly, pushing on and on, until you can't bend any further.

Have I done wrong? asks another part of your brain.

Your head is stretched back, all the way because there is nothing holding it up. Your body is rigid, your hands claw. (Still trying to find something to hang on to, don't they?)

Don't move, don't breathe, don't make a sound...

You are too afraid to swallow, fearing the movement will tear open your skin.

I can't make a mistake if I don't move. He won't push the stake through my throat, through my mouth and tongue and head and-

The nails flutter over your body. Your breasts, your belly, your legs. Quickly as jumping locusts, and they are gone. Like it never happened.

Shivers run from the tips of your toes toe the ends of your hairs.

Nails. *Finger*nails. As long as swords, longer maybe. Thin, yellow –you imagine– and sharp.

Suddenly you know what is pressing against your throat.

The sharp tip of a fingernail. *His* fingernail. The Bone God's.

He touched you. Is still touching you with His own flesh... Well, not flesh. Bone. If nails are some kind of bone. Some external kind of bones, maybe?

Tears? No, there are no tears in your eyes.

Fears? You fear plenty, but terror only is effective for so long. The fears are there, but somehow they are faded to the back. A nagging constant.

Somehow, weird enough, you feel an utter calmness descending on you.

I am here. All is now in His hands. He can do with me what He wants.

Having no choice feels very liberating. You don't have to think or to do anything. You only have to *be*. It is like you have discovered the ultimate truth: *just be*.

The pressure from your throat disappears. Like you've survived some kind of trial.

In utter silence His nails are back. Four, five? Six maybe? Probing, poking, touching you. They are long, so long! Long like a woman is tall, no like a man! You only feel the nails, not the fingers. They slide over your flesh. Smooth, bend, dry. Like the dead leaves of the long *avagar* shrub. Once someone –who?– showed you how to make an improvised flute from the white-yellow leaves. The peasants play those flutes on the Festival of the Dead.

You now understand why.

You should be afraid, shouldn't you?

You aren't.

He is here, the Bone God. He touches you.

If the God of Death touches you, what is left to fear?

The nails go everywhere. Your skull and face, your breasts and belly, but also your shoulders and back, your butt and legs and calves and heels. Up, down, high, low. Apparently there is no rhyme or reason. He scratches and pokes. The nails slide over your skin, get hooked in your long hair, or behind a shoulder or a knee.

You should be shuddering from revulsion, shouldn't you?

And shouting or crying from fear, don't you?

Maybe you are paralyzed by fear? Too afraid to be revolted? Being poked by an ancient God with scythe-like nails, in the dark?

You are not?

Little girl –No, you're a *woman*; you've bled... Young woman, this the Bone God. Death, the Ender, the Taker. And you're alone. Helpless. Subject to His mercy.

And He knows no mercy.

Then why are you so calm?

You shiver?

Good.

What?

Because... Because it tingles?

The nails, those ancient, wicked nails that have taken countless souls, you think they tickle?

He can sense your heresy. He can. Yes, He can.

He punishes you.

Wicked girl. Woman.

Nails, dozens of nails, appear invisible in the dark and pin you down on empty air. Nails on your outstretched arms and legs, nails on your forehead and cheeks. Those nails stay in place, just push and push, almost piercing your flesh.

The other nails scratch. Armies of nails march over the virgin fields of your naked skin, tearing, pulling, digging, scratching, leaving a trail of destruction.

Pain and shivers run through your body. High roads of fire, battlefields with armies of fighting spiked giants. You are like the Mother Goddess screaming in agony when the Bone God danced on her.

Except you don't feel agony. And you don't scream.

You gasp, hiss, but don't scream.

And about agony... Yesss, it hurtssss. But sneaking in the shadows of pain something else hides. A hot, wild feeling. The feeling of being alive. Of being touched. Of being the center or attention.

Nails on your breasts, your buttocks, under your feet, in hollows of your arms and knees. Scratching, digging, squeezing, pushing.

There is a rhythm now. There certainly is.

Still you don't scream. You try to move your body, in spite of the forest of nails pushing you down, you still want to move your body.

But why are you not trying to move away from the nails?

Do... Do you push yourself against the nails of the Bone God? Really? What are you doing, young woman? You are *challenging* Him? You think you can bear the pain He subjects you to? Your pride knows no limit!

Oh, you will be punished!

He doesn't stop. You had hoped for a quick resolve? A burst of anger? A quick end?

You will suffer for your hubris, young woman. You will suffer all night, if it pleases Him. You're nothing. A speck of dirt, a single candle in a hurricane, a mote of dust.

Nails dance, on and on. Sometimes they leave blood, a little, sometimes they leave scratches.

The fire in you burns. It is a steady glow, slowly getting hotter and hotter. There is pain too, but that is... That is like the surface of a deep ocean. The top layer is pain, but the deeper down you get, the hotter the water grows.

Fear? Fear has left long ago. Fear drowned. It left town, like a thief in the night. There is no fear anymore between you and the Bone God. No fear at all.

You grit your teeth, clench your fists. Sweat mixes with little droplets of blood. The pain is getting unbearable.

But you don't want to break. You are strong. You will show that damned, dirty-

The one nail stabs between your legs, right on that little, *very* sensitive bridge between your two holes. The front one and the back one, so to say.

It hurts like hell. You felt the nail go *in*! You shout it out.

Nails descend on your face like vipers. Three, four, six enter your mouth, push against your teeth and tongue and throat. Panicking you want to close your mouth, but you can't. Nails everywhere, you fight the reflex to vomit.

"Ugggh!"

Fear has returned.

On each of your cheeks lands a nail. So softly.

Soft, soft.

Do you notice them?

In the wood of pain, of nails pushing on a hundred spots against your flesh, of nails in your mouth, threatening to choke you, you feel those two butterfly wings—soft nails land.

Soft, soft. So evil.

They move, lightly caressing the skin of your cheeks. They move up, towards your eyes.

Soft, soft, up, up.

You fight, wrestle in your pointy chains. You don't care what gets pierced, where you bleed, what tears. You want to get your head away from those two soft nails slowing moving towards your eyes.

You know what will happen when they reach your eyes.

This is the Bone God. He likes to be feared. He doesn't like to be called damned, or dirty.

Tears run from your eyes. They don't stop the approaching nails. They slide through the water like the bow of a war galley.

They have reached your eyes. With all your might you keep them closed.

Please no! No! No!

Your eyes are pulled open, without mercy. Terrified you stare in the utter darkness, knowing the nails of the Bone God are hovering above your eyes. If He pushes, you will be blind. The razor-sharp nail will plunge into your eyes, cutting it open like a ripe melon, pushing deeper and deeper until blood and grey stuff oozes out. They will move around, maybe turn into hooks and pull your eyes from your skull.

You should not have called Him names.

At the same time His nails touch your eyes.

Ever so lightly. They rest on your eyeball, bathe in your tears.

They can push on any moment now.

Pierce your eyes.

The nails leave.

You can suddenly close your eyes.

Tears flow like a waterfall.

Relief from the deepest part of your soul. And something else. Something that had been hidden all those years. From the first scary story about the Bone God. From the first horrible sculpture.

The Bone God. You've known Him all your life. As the fifth daughter of your peasant parents, as the girl adopted by the temple. He has always been there with you. You never were alone.

I love You, you whisper in your mind.

You mean every word, there is no room for lies.

I love You.

Utter, unconditional devotion.

I love You. You don't say the words, but you know He hears them anyway. *Use me. Torture me. Kill me. I am Yours.*

Are you worthy? Probably not, but you will gladly die by His nails. The souls of the dead acolytes who don't become priestesses, go down in the dark, to serve in His palace made of rusty swords and rotten teeth. It is an honor, really. And you would gladly serve Him.

And maybe you will. The night is long. He can take your life when He sees fit. There is no hurry.

No hurry at all.

You are still pinned down, those horrible –sweet– nails against your wrists and ankles. Now only four remain, for every limb one. All other nails have disappeared soft and quiet like the summer wind.

The nails in your mouth? Gone. Gone, gone, gone!

Your tears are dried up, leaving tiny traces of salt on your cheeks, which you're unable to wipe away.

Once more He touches you, with His nails. But this time there is no poking, nor scratching. He touches you gently on your belly and your thighs. And your breasts and your face. Where you felt scratching and tearing, you now feel caresses.

You shiver. You sigh.

Oh, this is the Bone God. He has touched every man, woman and child. He knows bodies. He knows them like no other.

Nails. Long, yellow, crooked nails move over your body. All the right spots.

Unable to escape you suffer –such a sweet suffering– His attentions.

Oh temple maiden, you never had a lover. Your body and soul belong to Him.

Well, now He collects what is rightfully His.

Yes. Yesss, you shout out in your mind. A low moan escapes from your mouth.

Hanging in the air you wriggle, only to feel more, not to escape!

More and more of His nails join the fray. They touch you everywhere. Your back, your legs, your skull. Everywhere.

Your skin is on fire, your body is burning, your blood boils.

You've experienced pain by His touch of His

nails. Now you're experiencing pleasure. Which is just as overpowering and delightful.

Nails slide over the rim of your ears.

They kiss your lips.

They squeeze and scratch –a little– your rock-hard nipples.

They hold your ass, you breasts, spread your legs.

You willingly obey.

The nails slide over each other, making a clicking sound, when they move up at the inside of your wide open legs. You know where they are going.

You are so excited. A hot throbbing core of pure lust which is buried inside you, right there.

The nails have reached you womanhood. The tips turn little curls in the sweaty, wet pubic hairs. They pull, they open you up.

You are hanging there, being touched by the God of Death himself, and you are wet as the fields after the storm rains.

Almost hesitatingly one nail touches your hot, wet flesh.

It feels like a thousand hot kisses. You're are unable to breathe. Instinctively you open your legs even wider, pushing your lower body forwards.

The Bone God's nail, sharp, old, evil, enters you. Or maybe you push yourself around it.

A bit of both.

It is like a flaming sword sliding inside you, cutting you in half.

Sooooooo gooooood!

More nails follow. Crooked bone hooks. Entering your most secret spot. Flaming swords, each and every one of them.

He knows bodies. He knows them intimately. He is the Bone God. The Taker.

His nails inside you move. They push and scratch and reach parts of you, you never knew about.

Deep.

And hard.

And on and on.

Your whole body, all the nails, inside and outside your flesh, move in the same rhythm.

You cry out, beg for mercy, but He goes on and on, building the fire inside you.

You are going to be torn apart, or you will burn up. You feel so hot. You've never felt like this before. Never, ever!

The hot lust inside you wants to break free, but He doesn't allow it. He keeps on feeding it, but never unchains it. He is going to make you die from longing. Your heart will give up, your breath will die in your throat.

There is no conscious thought anymore. Just the red hot haze of eternal lust, the release that always will be just out of reach. The most cruel torture known to the Gods, the demons, and men.

You're flesh hanging as a rag on His nails. A plaything. A mere distraction, to be thrown aside as soon as He loses his interest.

But He keeps on torturing you. Feeding your lust. It will devour you, burn you up.

You still love Him?

Yes. More than ever.

You would die for Him?

Yes! Gladly!

And serve Him as the lowest of His servants, in his dark, desolate palace.

For all eternity, yes!

He does something. Twists his nails inside you just *so*.

The flood breaks through, exploding inside you.

You come and come. And keep coming. He makes that happen.

Your body convulses, you scream, look cross eyed, you drool and come. And keep coming.

The nails, those evil, divine nails, extract every spark of pleasure from your body.

You come and come, soiling His nails, dripping, soaked.

You die a thousand deaths.

...

You are alone when you wake up, laying on the stone slab.

You're exhausted.

You've been loved by the Bone God.

Voices outside the room. The stone door is pushed aside by strong hands.

Blinking you get up.

The kneeling servants and the morning sun greet the new priestess of the Bone God.

Naked, covered with scratches, old blood and dried up sweat you leave the room.

Your new life has just begun.

Herman's Erotic Paradise
Lisa Alfano

Seduced into a world that fulfilled his fondest dreams and his most terrifying nightmares!

February 3rd

Herman K. Bean was unspectacular in appearance. He was tall and lanky, standing six-four in his socks and weighing a buck-eighty. Shaggy brown hair, that refused to be tamed despite layers of hair gel, fell across his forehead. His nondescript brown eyes, hidden beneath thick lenses, and pockmarked face covered in the battle scars of a lost war with teenaged acne didn't make Herman a favorite with the ladies.

Herman spent his days and nights locked away in the cellar of his parents' summer home. The cellar, gray and damp and constructed of cement block walls, was his safe haven. He constructed an office in a far corner of the cellar, right next to the boiler, where he worked alone in the dimly lit cubby as a struggling video game creator. To the world, and especially to his father, twenty-seven year old Herman K. Bean was a privileged maladjusted millennial.

Herman didn't care what his parents thought, or anyone else, at least not anymore. He cared when he was younger, but in his haven below the frozen earth, he was safe from all the world's assholes. His parents were not innocent bystanders in Herman's mind. He blamed them for his present situation. After all, who names their only child Herman? Herman didn't give a shit that he was named after his paternal grandfather. If his parents had given him a normal moniker such as John or Tom, then life would've been different. Herman vocalized his opinion to his father often, or whenever his parents began pressuring Herman to move out.

"Did you think I'd grow up to be some popular jock with the name Herman? Did you even think of what you and mom were doing when you named me? You name a kid Herman and you might as well stick a neon hat on his head that flashes, 'NERD,' and while you're add it, just permanently attach at 'KICK MY ASS' sign to the back of my shirt. You set me up to be bullied and fail. So now you're stuck with me, dad."

Herman preferred the safe anonymity of electronic communication that his computers provided to that of human interaction. He found his life, void of human contact and bullying, to be quite satisfactory. He filled his days and nights surfing the Net, playing video games, and watching his favorite go-to since childhood; Star Trek. Herman dreamed of one day possessing a real-life holodeck like the one on the show.

His holodeck would be his personal paradise—Herman's Garden of Eden—a computer-generated utopian world that would reflect his particular tastes; an artificial world of safety where he would be able to exercise complete control. In his paradise he would never again face fear. He would talk to the computer-generated female beings in the holodeck without the hindrances of palpitations and odorous sweat. Herman wasn't crazy. He knew that a holodeck utopia, and everything within it, would still be, in all reality, an illusion; a world of dreams and light beams; of pure processed imagination—his imagination.

#

Herman hummed as his fingers tapped across his keyboard. He stopped at his favorite chat rooms. In these chat rooms he could interact with other people, not face-to-face, but through his keystrokes. They were faceless rooms; rooms void of sweaty palms, snickering women, and judgmental stares. He moved the cursor with his mouse and entered a Trekkie chat room. A pop-up for an upcoming sci-fi convention filled the screen. He shook his head. He had no desire to attend another convention. *Once was enough for me.*

Herman had attended a convention once, three years ago, but did not find the camaraderie that he had anticipated within the auditorium full of fellow Trekkies. No, Herman discovered soon after arriving at the venue that he was a nerd even amongst nerds. He was a man who didn't fit in with the living breathing world and he had made his peace with that.

Bored, he shifted in the swivel chair and maneuvered the mouse, ready to shut off his computer. Another advertisement flashed across his monitor. Herman leaned over his desk, ignoring the squealing seat. His face inches from the monitor, he reread the banner.

ENTER NOW TO WIN YOUR OWN REAL, PERSONAL, WORKING HOLODECK

"Impossible," Herman murmured, adjusting his glasses.

The bright red font flashed as the theme music from Star Trek played in the background; the loud, futuristic tones emanating through the powerful computer speakers on his desk.

"I know this is bullshit, but a model holodeck would be pretty awesome to add to my collection."

The ad promised a life-sized, working replica of the TNG holodeck. A man stood in the center of the holodeck to prove its size, outfitted in a classic Star Trek security personnel's uniform; bright red shirt with the tell-tale insignia emblazoned over the left breast, black pants, and the obligatory short black boots sporting small 1960's style heels.

"They should fire the ad agency that created this. TOS security personnel in a TNG holodeck," Herman said to the screen. "I guess they're going for the old joke that the red shirt in the landing party is always the first to die." He shrugged. "It's still pretty sweet, like an adult playhouse for nerds ... for me."

He clicked on the box, filled out the contest form, and promptly forgot about it.

February 5th

The rattling of a truck in the driveway interrupted Herman's solitude. He peered out of the cellar's crusty window. A large box truck, with no distinguishing markings, was parked in the driveway. Herman watched as an extremely tall man, dressed in a solid black uniform, walked across the snow-covered driveway carrying a large cardboard box. Herman's fingers gripped the edge of the scrap of black fabric tacked over the window, even though he knew that it was unnecessary as the filth on the small window pane was sufficient to conceal himself from the delivery man's view. The doorbell rang. The man did not wait for Herman to answer. He left the box on the front porch, retreated back into the tall cab of the truck, and disappeared down Lakeview Lane. Herman's fingers released their hold on the fabric. *I'm not expecting any new equipment.* Curiosity prevented him from returning to his desk and five minutes later he found himself standing on the front porch staring down at the box as the wet snow seeped through his dingy sock-clad feet. The label on the box, sporting his name: HERMAN K. BEAN in crimson.

"That's weird," he said, dragging the large, lightweight box through the snow and into the house.

There was no return address, no other distinguishing marks, not even the address of his parents' home, 13 Lakeview Lane, Barton, New Hampshire, on the box. He carried the box down the stairs into the dank and musty recess of the house and into his office in the far corner of the cellar. Using extreme caution he sliced through the clear packing tape and removed the envelope inside.

"Congratulations, Herman! You are the Grand Prize Winner of an Official Holodeck."

He ran an unsteady hand through his disheveled mane.

"Holy shit, I won."

He felt like a kid at Christmas as he tore into the box. The panels of the holodeck were made of wafer thin plastic and of a higher quality than Herman had anticipated. He delicately began to unfold each of the panels.

"It's too big for my office, but it will fit perfectly in the main part of the cellar."

The afternoon sun waned into the room as Herman assembled the walls of the holodeck, clicking each one firmly into place. The holodeck walls fit snug against the dingy concrete blocks of the cellar walls. Herman's fingers trembled as he ran them over the raised electrodes and projectors on the panels.

"Wow, it's so realistic. It looks identical to the one on the series."

He stood in the middle of his empty holodeck, squinting through his spectacles, battling with the fading sunlight and his poor vision, as he tried to read the small instruction manual."Log onto our website, personalize your world, and activate," the manual directed.

"Well, this will be fun," Herman said as he carried the manual into his office.

#

"Welcome to Holodecks for You. Please fill out the questionnaire below," he read. "Okay, I can do that."

He moved the cursor over the screen to the first category: *Choose your world.* His thoughts drifted to the weather outside his home; cold and snowy, not atypical for New Hampshire in February. Winters on Lake Bearing are harsh and the reason the houses surrounding Herman's home stood empty like rows of dark sentinels guarding the frozen lake. He longed to feel the warmth of the hot sun on his body and soft white sand between his toes. Herman rubbed the chill from his fingertips and clicked the tropical beach world option.

"Someplace where the days are long and the nights are short, unlike here where the days are short and dreary and the nights are black and endless," he murmured.

With a few more clicks he added palm trees and brightly colored parrots to his tropical paradise. He shuddered and quickly scrolled past the photo of the snakes.

"There will be *no* snakes in Herman's Garden of Eden."

He selected his attire: a floral shirt and linen shorts and downloaded his musical choices; Jimmy Buffett and other upbeat island type tunes. Herman spent the next several hours hunched over his keyboard meticulously choosing options from the vast catalog of scenarios and accessories. He laughed as he clicked the choices knowing that it was all pretend. *Real holodecks do not exist, but business is slow this time of year and I have plenty of spare time to waste.*

He reached the final category and hesitated. His palm began to sweat against the sleek curved computer mouse. *Can this imaginary world truly be a paradise if I am alone? But, this is my world and a woman in my holodeck will be programmed to like me. She won't mock or glare. She won't act as if I'm a pervert in training.*

"And I won't have to pay her to be with me," he said. "She won't be like Brittany Morrison."

He shook his head. He didn't like to think about Brittany. She was the first, and thus far the only girl, whom he had convinced to have sex with him. Convinced wasn't the correct word for his encounter with Brittany. No, he had paid her two hundred fifty dollars for ten minutes of pleasure his senior year of college. Pretty sorority girl, Brittany, was nothing more than a prostitute selling her body to him for money to buy a semester's worth of books. *She's a slut like all the rest of them.* These days Herman found his release with internet porn and his right hand. It was easier, less stressful, and far cheaper; and it suited him just fine.

"But, a 'real' woman in a holodeck, this definitely has possibilities. I won't have to pay her. I can create the woman in my holodeck to adore me. She will laugh at my jokes and lust after my lanky physique," he said to the monitor.

The mouse slipped from beneath his unsteady fingers. He wiped his sweaty palm on his jeans and clicked, "Yes," on the people option and selected a shapely blonde coed with big breasts and a brilliant smile.

With all of the selections completed, Herman hit the enter key on his keyboard and waited. A red alert siren wailed through the speakers as a flashing banner scrolled across the monitor screen. *Please accept the terms and conditions.* He began to scroll through the endless terms that filled his monitor screen.

"Oh, c'mon, this is going to take forever," he said impatiently to the screen. He hit the page down key and clicked the box marked "accept," eager to begin enjoying his holodeck. "No one ever reads this crap anyways."

He tapped the enter key again and waited. The screen flickered. "Congratulations, Herman K. Bean, on activating your special holodeck. Please proceed to your holodeck, secure the door, and press the blue button located on the far wall to begin your adventure." He smiled. He knew exactly where the blue button was located.

"Please enjoy your experience, Herman," a computerized voice said.

"I most certainly will," he replied.

#

The holodeck door shut behind Herman, clicking into the wall, like building blocks locking together, leaving him in pitch-blackness.

"Well, Herman, here goes nothing," he said.

He pressed the blue button and waited. The electrodes on the walls began to hum around him. Tiny projectors flickered and glowed, sending rainbow-colored hues rushing into the dark space. Millions of particles of color floated in the air above him before twirling like a wild tornado over him. He squinted to block out the blinding rays. The rush of wind and humming stopped as abruptly as it started.

Herman cracked opened his eyes; his breath catching in his lungs.

"I don't believe it," he whispered, his eyes absorbing his surroundings. "I don't fucking believe it. It's really real."

A tropical paradise surrounded Herman. He looked down at his thick wool socks, the damp cold concrete cellar floor was gone; his feet were sinking into mounds of soft white sand. Sunlight poured through the tops of palm trees that swayed back and forth in a gentle breeze overhead. His body felt warm from head to toe. Sweat dripped down the back of his neck and ran beneath his sweatshirt. He inhaled deeply. The air was salty and fresh. The sound of crashing waves filled his ears. *This is crazy.* He turned and stared. Crystal clear turquoise water filled the horizon. Gone were the dingy cinder block walls of the musty cellar; there was only blue sky and ocean as far as Herman could see. He yanked his heavy socks off, his toes squishing into the silky warm sand.

"It worked. I can't believe it. The son of a bitch actually works."

A folded floral shirt and shorts sat on a lounge chair a few feet away. He picked them up and ran a hand over the crisp linen material.

"They're exactly what I picked out. This is amazing," he said, discarding his sweatshirt and jeans for the new paradise attire. "This is better than Christmas. I'm never going to leave."

The familiar notes of a Jimmy Buffett song wafted through the air and that's when he heard her; a woman's voice, singing. Herman strained to make out her words. The singing was coming from within the dense green topiary behind him. *This is crazy.*

This can't be happening, but somehow it is and I'm going to enjoy it.

Herman pushed through the lush greenery. The singing grew louder, echoing hypnotically above the roaring waves. He hesitated. *Am I the guy in the red shirt?* He shook his head, chastising himself for his foolishness.

"I'm in my cellar and this is an illusion. It's not real. Relax and go with the flow for once, dude," he muttered to himself.

A multi-colored parrot cawed down at him from a tree limb. Herman stared up at it. It looked like a real parrot. He stroked a rubbery deep green leaf hanging from a low palm tree. *Everything looks so real; feels so real; smells so real.* He pressed on through the trees. He pushed aside a large palm leaf and he saw her; his inner geek bubbled up to the surface.

She sat on a bar stool at the counter of the tiki bar; blonde, beautiful, and curves in all of the right places. Long tanned legs swung casually from the stool as her plump red lips sucked on a straw emerging from a tall pink beverage. Herman's heart pounded faster in his chest. The front of his shorts tightened against a swelling erection and he found himself wishing that he was the straw between the blonde's lips. His clammy palms dripped as he stood, frozen in place, gawking at the buxom blonde … the blonde that he had created on his computer. *Thank you, God.*

He inhaled. "Relax, this is all an illusion. I created her," he whispered.

The blonde turned, her lips twitched, and expanded into a broad smile. Herman glanced over his shoulder, half-expecting to find some muscled male model standing behind him; no one. *No one is here except me, stupid. She is smiling at me. I programmed her to want me.*

"Hi there," she said, her voice low and seductive.

All saliva evaporated from his mouth leaving him parched and speechless. He swallowed hard, trying to regain his voice, unable to stop himself from ogling her toned legs. His eyes traveled up, pausing to admire her round breasts, before stopping on her heart shaped face. Her lips were even fuller and sexier than he had first thought. Her small nose had the exact right amount of tilt to it. His eyes locked with her eyes and his breath hitched in his lungs; two large pools of onyx, twinkled back at him. Herman had never imagined that black eyes could be so beautiful … and so sexy.

"Hey," he managed to choke out. "I'm Herman."

"Cool name. I've never met anyone named Herman before. I'm Eve." *Of course you are.* "You want to join me for a drink, Herman?" She jumped off the stool before he could respond; her breasts giving a healthy bounce.

"Thank you, God," he mouthed up to the blue sky.

She poured Herman a glass of the same pink liquid and handed it to him; her skin brushing the back of his hand as he took the glass from her. Heat coursed through his veins and his groin. He groaned inwardly and smiled. *Welcome to Herman's Garden of Eden. Instead of Adam and Eve, we have Herman and Eve. Nice, very nice, indeed.*

#

The afternoon was a whirlwind of laughter and splashing in the warm ocean waves. Eve laughed at his corny jokes and Herman ogled her luscious curves. He found himself enjoying Eve's company and enjoying her tiny pink striped bikini even more.

"What would you like to do now?" he asked, breathless from frolicking in the strong turquoise waves.

Eve grabbed his shoulders with her soft wet hands and offered up her lush lips to him. Herman took pleasure in licking the salt from her rose colored plumes before exploring her mouth. She pushed him away, giggled, and ran up the beach.

"Come on, Herman," she called out over her shoulder.

He caught her and they tumbled breathless onto the blanket spread out over the warm sand. Their wet and sandy limbs intertwined; the coarse sand crystals rubbing against their bare flesh. Herman made love to her right there in the open, all his worldly inhibitions gone. Eight minutes later, sated and exhausted, he rolled off of her. Eve's large round breasts pressed against his concave and hairless chest as she snuggled against him. Her long blonde locks tickled his arm as he cradled her head. *This is how it should be—no payment required.* He dozed off in the shadowed hues of the descending sun.

#

Herman woke up surrounded by darkness. The moon was hidden behind dense gray clouds; its outline a faint white shadow against the night sky. He shivered in the frosty night air and reached out for Eve, but his fingers found nothing. She was gone. He clamored to his feet, his eyes darting back and forth trying to adjust to the dark. His toes gripped the cold, wet ground. The silky white sand had disappeared along with Eve. Herman stood silent in the frozen, snow-covered tundra that replaced the warm beach. He strained his ears, desperate to hear the crashing waves in the darkness; empty, lifeless silence returned to his ears. He grabbed his thin floral shirt from the ground and pulled it over his head, wishing he had his sweatshirt instead.

"I guess the program ended. Nothing lasts forever. Oh well, I guess it's time to get back to reality," he said to the night.

He walked in the direction that he knew led to the holodeck door and his parents' cellar. Cold and tired, Herman was eager to get back to his office and warmer clothing. He squinted, his eyes fighting the darkness, and searched for the door.

"Where the hell is the damn door?"

The barren icy wasteland before him was obscuring the holodeck door's location from his vision. *What the hell? The damn holodeck must be malfunctioning and started a different program. If I press the blue button I can probably reset it or shut it off.* He cursed himself for not bringing the instruction manual with him. He, of all people, knew better. When it comes to computer programs, glitches are bound to occur.

"The blue button is on the far wall. So, that means it must be behind me." He spun around on his heels, finger pointing into the darkness. "It must be this way … about eight feet ahead. Yes, it should be right ahead. Go find the button, Herman, and get the hell out of here."

The terrain changed as he walked, morphing from a snowy, rocky wasteland into a dense forest, thick with pines and oaks, reminding Herman of the land surrounding his parents' lake house. The stagnant air smelled of musty leaves and pine needles. A low growling rose up from his left. Herman's feet halted. *What the hell was that? I didn't program any animals except for the stupid parrot.*

He waved his hands in front of him and trudged deeper into the forest trying to feel for the holodeck wall and the blue button. He shoved a pine bough aside with his left hand and used his right hand to try to disperse the thick blinding fog that descended around him. He walked deeper into the thicket of foliage with no sign of the wall or blue button. His bare feet landed in a frigid puddle and emerged chilled and covered in thick slimy mud.

"Oh, come on," he grumbled. "This sucks."

A faint hissing wafted up from a pile of leaves by his feet. Something slithered through the underbrush in front of him. He couldn't see the creatures clearly, but he knew there were several and they were circling his feet. His heart skipped as slimy muddy scales crawled over his bare feet and slithered up his legs; wrapping their cold cylindrical bodies around his ankles and calves.

"Oh, my God, oh God," he yelled and swatted at the creatures. "Snakes, fucking snakes," he screamed a high-pitched girly scream as he shook his legs in wild desperation.

A black snake sailed through the air and slammed into the trunk of a huge pine, its scaled body splattering against the bark on impact. The second snake refused to release its grip on Herman's leg. Herman held his breath, squeezed his eyes shut, and reached down and grabbed hold of the snake's tail; yanking it with all of his strength. The coiled creature slipped, inch by inch, from Herman's leg. He threw the snake with all of his might into the thick brush, the leaves crackled beneath the weight of the snake's body, as it landed with a muffled thud.

Herman picked up his pace, walking faster through the woods, his head snapping left and right, his heart palpitating as he frantically searched for the far wall; for the holodeck door; for the damn blue button; for the exit from hell.

"I just have to reset it. Once I reset it everything will be fine," he murmured to himself, trying to convince his pounding heart and anxious mind that all will be well.

His toes stubbed against an exposed tree root. "Shit, damn it, Shit, shit, shit." He hopped and cursed at the throbbing pain radiating up from his bruised digits.

A shadowed figure appeared in the trees ahead. Herman couldn't see the figure clearly; the fog too dense to see more than a few feet in front of him. He smiled, his shorts bulging subconsciously, *Eve.* He had forgotten all about his blonde beauty. Stepping carefully over the tree roots and rocks, he followed the shadowy figure deeper into the woods.

"Eve," he called out.

The figure didn't stop. It continued moving away deeper into the overgrown trees. The low rumbling growl of a beast grew louder behind Herman. *I can't turn back. I have to keep moving forward.* The snap of twigs and the crunching of leaves signaled that the beast, or something, was creeping closer; its footsteps padding against the underbrush of the forest. *It's hunting me.* Herman tossed a quick glance over his shoulder; nothing, nothing but the thick cloud of swirling fog. *Don't stop, keep going, those aren't the pitter patter of friendly little feet. It's a wolf, or something.* Herman didn't know what the 'or something' might be and he sure as hell wasn't going to stay and find out.

He marched forward, his head jerking back and forth, left and right, scanning the dense terrain; his palpitations graduating to rapid beats within his chest as desperation mounted with each pulse of fear that pumped through his veins. His eyes, weary from straining against the darkness and fog, searched for any visible confirmation of the beast stalking him, for the holodeck wall, and the elusive blue button.

#

Cool misty fog encircled Herman; encasing his body behind a veil of dreary gray precipitation, leaving his cheeks dripping with a frigid dampness. The shadowed figure now hidden from view, Herman continued walking and searching for Eve. She was nowhere to be found within the small holodeck. *Where the hell did she go? Where the hell is the holodeck wall?* He had somehow managed to lose her in the fog. Heavy breathing and menacing growls behind Herman alerted him that the beast had not lost sight of him in the fog.

"Keep moving, Herman. Screw Eve. She can fend for herself." He laughed soft and low at the absurdity of his comment. *What the hell am I talking about? She's not even real. None of this is real. I'm in a holodeck. I'm in my parents' cellar and there's nothing to be afraid of.* "I'm such a nerd."

His feet didn't share the confidence of his mind. Herman's body quaked as his unsteady feet kept moving forward, always forward; trudging through the underbrush. Branches lashed at his bare legs, slicing long thin gashes into the flesh on his calves. Hot liquid trickles of his blood ran down his legs. His flowered shirt snagged on briars tearing and leaving behind colorful swatches of fabric as a reward. His feet refused to stop moving forward. *The wall must be close ... and the blue button.* Time became a vague concept as he walked forward, leaving behind bits of linen dangling from offending razor sharp nubs of the thorny pricker bushes; specks of vibrant hues in the dark, colorless world. His feet ignored the cold and the pain and trudged forward; always forward.

The shadowy figure reappeared on a ridge, beyond a fallen tree, in front of Herman.

"Eve?" Herman whispered, not wanting the creature pursuing him from behind to hear.

The figure stopped and turned. Herman's eyes fought to focus through his fog speckled glasses. He wiped the dew from his lenses with his thumb. The rumbling growl rose from behind him, closer now. Herman ran towards the shadowed figure. The swell of decay infiltrated his nasal passages causing him to gag on the rancid aroma; his stomach wretched. *Something's wrong. This isn't right.* Herman grabbed onto the trunk of a giant oak to stop his forward momentum. The figure in front of him was too tall, much too tall, to be Eve. *But, who the hell is it?* Herman's heart pounded inside his chest, his breath wheezing, the nausea in his belly rising. *Who the hell is in my holodeck?*

The tall figure stepped out of the fog. Herman choked on his own saliva as terror flooded his mind. *What the hell is that?* Whatever stood in front of him, Herman knew it was not human, or at least it wasn't anymore. Its head, long and faceless; a black abyss where a face should have been. On its shoulders—if it was a man, it's where his shoulders would be located— were a pair of eyes; each 'shoulder' sported a single giant blood-red eye; each the diameter of a dinner plate. Thick oozing layers of jaundiced translucent flesh slid up and down over the creature's eyes. The giant rotted eyelids hypnotized Herman and made his skin crawl beneath the shredded remains of his floral shirt.

The creature's body was cloaked in a long, flowing black robe that hung like a loose-fitting skin. Herman couldn't see the creature's feet. The cloak covered them in drapes that reached out towards Herman. A mouth was in the center of the palm. Black lips, that reminded Herman of string licorice, outlined the mouth. The licorice lips twitched, curling upwards into a grotesque crooked smile, revealing rows of rotted teeth.

Sweat slid down Herman's forehead. The salty liquid stung his eyes, but he could not look away; could not force himself to cease gazing at the creature's hand; at the mouth grinning back at him. A black tongue, forked and shaped like a serpent's, emerged from between the rows of jagged teeth. Herman's body jerked back in horror, but his eyes remained focused on the mouth and the long black tongue licking the licorice lips and the surrounding decayed flesh of the palm. Herman hugged the tree tighter; his fingernails digging into the rough bark. He could not move, could not look away from the monstrosity as the creature glided towards him.

"Arghh," Herman gurgled, slumping to the ground as his weak legs collapsed. *Move, Herman; move or die.*

Herman crawled, like a dog on all fours, into the evergreens. *I have to get away. I have to hide; hide in the trees.* The creature's green festering fingers wrapped around Herman's right ankle; its powerful grip dragging Herman out from beneath the low-hanging boughs, the rough dirt scraping Herman's stomach as his fingers struggled to hold onto a sapling's trunk. Tepid pus slid over the bare flesh of Herman's ankle. He gulped hard to keep from vomiting. He scratched at the ground, clawing at the hard soil, trying in vain to get away from the creature's grasp; trying to stop his backward momentum towards the creature's mouths; trying to escape.

The creature's fingers increased their grip around Herman's ankle. A loud pop filled the lifeless air as the fingers crushed and snapped Herman's bones like dried toothpicks. A wave of intense agony soared through Herman's body. He fought against his waning consciousness as the pain shot up his leg and pierced his brain like a fiery spear. Herman opened his mouth and released a blood curdling scream; primal and intense—the scream of an animal about to die.

Hot raspy breath, reeking like rotted garbage, warmed the back of Herman's head. A long deep rolling growl in his left ear followed. Herman's body stiffened; the radiating pain in his ankle briefly taking a back seat. *The wolf has joined the party. I forgot about the fucking wolf.* Herman swatted at the mangy head hanging over his own. Yellow saliva, thick as snot, dripped into his sweaty hair. He forced himself to look up. A pair of onyx eyes rimmed in crimson glared down at him. Herman blinked, clearing the well of tears from beneath his eyelids.

The face staring down at him was not that of a wolf, but of a fleshless skull. Herman's eyes widened with terror. Long fangs emerged slowly from the black recess of the skull's mouth. The beast moved faster than Herman's mind could react. Sharp fangs ripped away the flesh on his left forearm. Red hot pain seared up Herman's arm as the attack continued; beastly teeth tearing away flesh and muscle, leaving behind strands of dangling bloody sinew.

Herman screamed. He had no words; all vocabulary vacated his mind. He reverted to his primal, Neanderthal roots of inarticulate grunts and screams. His body writhed and wiggled in agony as he attempted to free himself from the beast at his head and the creature holding his ankle. Herman lashed out between screams, kicking and punching at the two creatures; creatures that previously only existed in his worst, and most gruesome, nightmares.

Herman kicked with his good leg at the cloaked figure. The rows of razored teeth in the creature's mouth chomped down on Herman's flesh; chewing and swallowing chunks of his ankle. *Arghh.* Sweat and blood saturated Herman's dirt matted hair. Hot blood poured from his arm and ankle. He gritted his teeth and struck out again at the creature dining on his ankle. His foot connected, and sank, into the slimy flesh hidden beneath the black robe. Millions of tiny crawling sensations traveled up Herman's leg. He craned his neck. A thin beam of moonlight pierced the fog and glistened off of the slick white maggots drilling into his skin. Terror and despair rushed through him. His words flooded back as his body swayed back and forth along the thin line between fight and surrender.

"Arghh. It's eating me. Oh, God it's eating me."

The skeletal beast snapped at Herman's head. He swung his right arm up, blocking the beast's jaws, as it lunged in for another bite. Herman's fingers closed around a clump of hair hanging from the side of the beast's skull and pulled; long, thin strands of blonde hair filled his hand.

"No, no, what's this? Oh, no," Herman stammered, his raspy voice barely audible between his screams and the beast's growls.

The hand restraining Herman's ankle tugged with tremendous force and flipped Herman over with one swift, and extremely painful, motion. Herman landed hard on his back; *umpf;* a jagged tree stump impaling his lung. His heart pounded and he fought to breathe, as he felt his lung deflate in his chest, gurgling and drowning in the salty flavor of the blood pooling up in his mouth.

The growling beast hovered over Herman's face. He glared at the skeletal carnivore. A pink striped bikini top hung from the thin black layers of rotted flesh. *Eve?* Herman vomited; projecting blood and bile into the air and onto the shredded remains of his floral shirt.

"W-why? W-wh-why?" Herman whispered, fighting to remain conscious.

A deep throaty voice, cold as coal, reverberated around Herman; the voice making the ground and the air shudder. Herman closed his eyes, biting his lip to stifle some of the pain. *The creature in the robe.* "You agreed to this, Herman," the creature said.

"No," Herman protested weakly; spitting out blood and gasping for another laborious breath. "No, I didn't."

The creature laughed. "You agreed, Herman. You agreed to be hunted."

Herman tried to shake his head, but couldn't. His chest was heavy. He gritted his teeth and tilted his head up slightly. The bright colored flowers on his shirt were no longer visible. The fibers of the shirt had absorbed the blood that poured from his body; the remnants a solid shade of red. A triangular shaped, yellow patch of vomit lay over his heart. Herman dropped his head, too weak to move. The army of maggots, finished with his leg, now crawled over his torso. Their sharp teeth scraped away at the skin beneath the tattered remains of his shirt; burrowing into his body cavity and turning his body into a living cocoon. Herman pursed his bluing lips into a thin line as his insides moved and shifted beneath his pale flesh. *Resistance is futile, Herman.* He closed his eyes, too exhausted and in too much pain to fight any longer; wanting death; praying for death.

The raspy voice of the tall creature boomed around Herman. "You should have read the terms and conditions, Herman."

"I'm the guy in the red shirt after all," Herman gurgled with his final breath.

Sin Eater from Hell
L.C. Holt

**There is no hiding ... he smells your sins from
a mile away!**

Six P.M.

"Some things you don't forget," the old man said, stoking his pipe. "The eyes of my first love, the sound of her voice—these things have been lost to time."

"It's only natural," Lomax assured. "You've been alive a century plus one. A memory or two is bound to fade." *Why the hell am I here?* was what the attorney was actually thinking. *We could shoot the shit over the phone.* The only reason he'd dropped by was because the miser had mentioned adding an addendum to his will. Having redrafted the document to make himself sole beneficiary, Lomax was curious what the man had in mind.

"Listen," Hobbs said, an uncharacteristic curtness in his voice, "before I lose the nerve to tell you. I've kept this secret all my life. I can't keep it anymore." He paused, the carnival glass beside him casting shades of blue and green over his withered features. A dry fire crackled in the hearth. The house was otherwise dark. "My daddy built this place with money pilfered from the church. He was the reverend in this town before age stole his last breath. He was also a monster to me, my brother, and most of all my mother. She was fourteen when they married. Times were different then. I remember when I was a child, we used to keep a burlap bag of salt on the porch. Whenever she passed by, she'd lick her finger and get her some. One day he caught her, held her down, and shoved fistfuls into her mouth 'til she started foaming like a mad dog. He didn't spare the rod with us either. We'd get it just because we were there. He used to do revival meetings all over the south—be gone weeks at a time. It was during one of those trips I heard my mother one night screaming in her sleep. She came down the next morning with strands of white in her hair. That was the start of her decline. My daddy came home and saw the state she was in, asked what happened. She kept her lips sealed with him, but she told me. She said something had come into her room and had its way with her. I thought she was fooling 'til she started to show. This house as it is now is pretty far from the beaten track. Back then, it took the better part of an hour to get to town. My daddy—" The old man hesitated. "He thought my mother and brother had, I guess you could say, lain together.

When the baby was born, it seemed to confirm that. The child, you see, was deformed. The way it came out, my mother had no chance of surviving. It was—" The story was cut short by a scuffling in the wall. Hobbs' eyes skirted to the stairwell. "So sorry," he said. "Where was I?"

"Your mother died in childbirth."

"That's right, but the baby didn't, at least not at first. We used to have a box for kindling. My daddy put the newborn in it, wrapped it in chains, and gave it to me to bury. It was better, he said, for folks to think the child died with its mother than to see how horrible it looked. So I took it down cellar and buried it in the sacred earth of Coweta County."

"You buried it alive?"

Hobbs winced at the question. "I was thirteen-years-old. I didn't know no better, but that don't make it right. Life went on for awhile. My daddy played the part of the lamented husband. My brother took the brunt of his abuse 'til he upped and joined the navy. He died at the Battle of the Philippine Sea, June 1944. My daddy lived to be ninety-one, thriving the whole time. That's the nature of the world. The brave die while the weak and wicked go on and on and on. There is no order to things. No God. No Satan. Only us, and the horrors we create." His eyes locked on the stairwell. Something thumped on the plaster with enough force to knock an aged photo of his mother and father askew.

Damn rats, Lomax thought as Hobbs gave him an envelope which was only to be read on the day of his death. Considering his dwindling health—he had lost a leg to diabetes and most his vision to glaucoma—that day was speedily approaching. Setting his pipe aside, Hobbs rose on his prosthetic limb and hobbled to the kitchen. Another louder thwack sent a shower of plaster dust down from the ceiling.

"What the hell *is* that?" Lomax said as he pivoted to see a fissure forming at the floor and spreading upward. The impact which followed could hardly be called a thump. The photo jarred loose and shattered. Lomax was now on his feet, peering into the kitchen to see the old man with a gun to his temple. "What're you doing?" he demanded.

"I can't face it," the man replied. "I'm too weak. Too sick. Too—" He lowered his head and pulled the trigger.

Lomax winced as the wall beneath the staircase exploded, sending splinters of wood pulp flying. One struck him in the bridge of the nose, knocking off his glasses and causing his eyes to water. He was now on his hands and knees, lost in a short-sighted blur, his breath hitching on air thick with dust. A man-sized maw gaped in the drywall. He found his broken glasses and peered through to see a duplet of wiry arms unfolding from the dark gulf of a hidden doorway. A pair of long-fingered hands tipped in talons found purchase and pulled. From the shadowy cellar came a long, lean figure. Even with its shoulders slumped, it stood eight or nine feet tall. From the crest of its swollen scalp hung irregular tuffs of black hair. Its left eye bulged bloodshot. Its right was sown to a slit by seeping pus. It was naked, the latticework of its ribs chiseled in high relief to its protruding pelvis. Its arms and legs were twice the length of a normal man's. The same could be said of its sex, which jostled as it took one step, then another, traversing the room in a single gait. It wasn't until the beast was looming over Lomax that he realized its body was alive with creepy-crawlers. Spiders nested beneath its skin, burrowing dens between every furrow. Lice seethed in its knotted hair as worms slithered under its tongue.

"Wuh-what are you?" Lomax stuttered.

"Basilisk," the beast answered, each syllable riding on a fetid breath. From the blackness of its gums appeared hundreds of needlelike teeth, unsheathing like the claws of a cat. *"Greeed,"* it said as ropes of saliva dribbled onto the attorney's brow. A heartbeat later, it lunged—and that was the story of Sonny Lomax.

#

Six twenty-five P.M.

Brian was glad to be out of that monkey suit. He could only imagine how Faye must feel. Wedding dresses looked so heavy and cumbersome. They had just entered the police jurisdiction of Robinson Springs and were now perusing the twinkle light-embellished houses on their way to the quaint bed and breakfast where they'd spend their honeymoon. The newlyweds had first met three years prior when Brian was an assistant floor installer. He was laying linoleum at the dorm where she lived when their eyes met across the room. She was now a senior, majoring in history, while he manned an earth mover at the rock quarry. He was a roughneck and she the daughter of a city councilman. Their life together was going to be arduous, but love would see them through, or so they hoped.

"Honky-tonk," she said, pointing to an especially garish Christmas display. The B&B, by contrast, was elegant. They were soon pulling their bags from the back of Brian's pickup. A boy in a hooded coat stood pointing and talking to the grass a few yards away. By the time the two of them had reached the wraparound porch of the rambling Victorian, the front door had opened and out came a kindly old woman with blue helmet-hair.

"Sit," the boy could be heard saying. "Stay!"

The matron, whose name was Loreen Harper, said, "Don't mind him. He's just talking to his imaginary dog. I told him, 'Ansel, I'm not cleaning up after a filthy pet,' so he made one up." Cupping her hands around her mouth, she called for her grandson to come in out of the cold. He turned, a sodium lamp illuminating his slant eyes and flattened nose, two physical characteristics denoting Down syndrome.

"Say hello to our guests," Loreen prompted as he bounded up the steps.

"Hello," he said, and was gone a moment later.

"Cute," Faye crooned as they followed their host into the warm foyer. Through the living room door, she spied an enormous pipe organ. "Do you play?" she asked.

"I do indeed," Loreen replied. "Both here, and at the church." Handing Brian their room key, she winked, "There might be a little surprise for y'all upstairs. Have fun."

"Thanks," Brian said as they ascended. "Maybe she left us her French tickler," he said to Faye, who shushed him. Down the hall, they found the honeymoon suite. Faye took the key and motioned for the door. "Wait," Brian told her. "You can't just walk in."

"Uh? Oh." She rolled her eyes and offered herself to be carried. Brian swept her up and over the threshold, where they found a spacious room with its own fireplace. On the table by the bed they discovered their surprise—a bottle of Pinot Meunier chilling in a bucket of ice. "I hope you're not too disappointed," she said. "No sex toys."

"Would've been more fun. Now if only I had a corkscrew. That can be fixed. We passed a dollar store on the way here."

"Not so fast," she said, hooking him by the belt and pulling him forward.

"Silly me," he grinned, and kicked the door closed.

#

Seven P.M.

Moira had lusted for Lyle Burkett since they were in high school. After thirty-three years of unrequited love, it was he who came to her, asking if she'd mind keeping an eye on his house. Any funny business, he said, call me, but not at the station. Lyle was chief of police and his wife a backup dispatcher. She had friends in the department who might cover for her, he assumed. As for a definition of *funny business,* Moira needed none, not with the plumber's van at the curb and Joy wearing so skimpy a negligee.

"Hush!" she called to her corgis, who had been barking at the back door for what seemed like an hour. James Dean—the Pembroke Welsh—came plodding in first, followed by Elvis and Brando. They lingered at her feet, sniffing her slippers.

Moira, who was the local librarian, had garnered a reputation for being a spinster. (Either that or a lesbian.) In truth, she only had eyes for one man, and he was married to a chick half his age. Joy *was* gorgeous. That was undeniable. She had blonde hair, alabaster skin, and blue eyes flecked green. Moira, by comparison, was tall and angular with a hook nose and buck teeth. She was wearing plaid pajamas under a flannel robe tied at the waist with curlers in her hair. Joy had on a see-through teddy.

"Slut," Moira scoffed, the edge in her voice eliciting a bark from Brando. The dogs were now padding away. A moment later, they resumed their yapping, but by then, Moira was holding her cell phone, debating whether or not to warn Lyle. She chose to keep her word and composed a text. *He's here,* it read plainly.

Raising her binoculars, she was now in the bedroom with Joy and the plumber. They had yet to copulate, though it clearly wasn't far off. The distaste she felt was palpable. Some people had all the luck: born with a body to kill for, eyes like ice chips, and a smile so straight and clean it'd cause any man to swoon. It was a crime of the cosmos, she determined, that women like Joy could get anything they wanted while she remained a perpetual virgin. At forty-six, she had little hope of conceiving a child.

"Oh well," she said aloud, turning away from the window before things got sexual. That was one sight she didn't want to see. It was only then she realized the dogs had stopped barking. She crossed the bedroom, went down the hall, and pushed through the back door. Her Marlboros lay on the porch railing beside a tan Bic lighter. She picked up both and lit a cigarette to mull her lot in life. That's when she saw a flicker of fire through the treetops and a column of dark smoke rising against the night sky.

"Shit," she muttered, realizing the source of the fire must be Hobbs's house. She had left her cell on the bed, so she darted for the kitchen landline. The receiver was in her hand when the heady stench of rot stung her nostrils. Someone was in the house. She could feel their eyes upon her. A silhouette swelled in the dining room (too tall to be human) as a pair of gray two-toed feet stepped into the light, followed by a hulking form. The cigarette dangling from her mouth fell as her bladder voided. "Buh-Brando?" she murmured.

The corgi's leg twitched between the beast's teeth. It threw back its head, swallowing the last of the canine in a single gulp. Now she was its sole target. *"Envy,"* it growled as its incisors bisected her skull. What was left of her head squirted blood as it chewed, spitting out one curler. Then another.

And another.

And another.

#

Eight P.M.

Lyle had duties to fulfill, in spite of the rage incited by his neighbor's text. A blaze at Mr. Hobbs's place had reduced the four-story gabled mansion to smoldering embers. Murder was the most likely motive with a pinch of arson to cover it up. There was a gnawed leg in the driveway. It didn't take the deductive reasoning of Sherlock Holmes to determine the gam did not belong to Finneas. A run of the Beemer's plates revealed its owner to be Samuel Lomax, known in town as Sonny, a local probate attorney. The question was, who had killed him in so appalling a manner? Lyle was too angry to care.

The irony of his current situation was not lost. He'd traded in his wife of fifteen years for a younger model. Was her cheating divine retribution? Maybe so, but that didn't mean he had to bow to it, not after all the hours he'd spent in the gym, keeping himself sharp and in shape. He'd always known it would be a challenge maintaining her interest, but he thought between his libido and bank account that'd be easily accomplished. Perhaps he had underestimated his prowess, but then again, Joy had never been able to keep her thighs together, or so the rumor went. In his wild arrogance he assumed he could change her.

The county boys finally arrived with Sheriff Mullins leading the charge. With him on the scene, Lyle had an opportunity to break away. Luckily, his house was right through the woods, a ten-minute drive at most. Sure enough, a white work van was parked at the curb. Lyle inspected the clip of his pearl-handled Colt 9mm, kicked open the door of his cruiser, and crossed the lawn. He entered to find the living room lighted by a Christmas spruce, its ornaments sparkling red and green. There was a pair of discarded shit-kickers at the bottom of the stairs and a woman's ankle sock halfway up. Lyle followed a din of grunts into the bedroom, where he found a man's sallow ass thrusting. He cleared his throat, at which point the plumber's eyes grew saucer-wide, his lips working at words that wouldn't come.

Joy broke the silence by saying, "Don't overreact, Lyle. We were just—" Her reply was cut short by a gunshot to the carpet. "What the fuck are you doing?" she demanded.

"Marking my territory," Lyle said, turning back to the plumber—whose name was Denny Schofield. "Did you really think you could get away with this? Man, if so, you either have rocks in your head or brass in your balls. Judging from the way your lip's quivering, I think I know the answer." Denny said he was sorry. "If you got caught stealing a dilly-bar from the Dairy Queen, I might accept your apology, but you dipped your chip in my wife. Sorry don't cut it." He raised his pistol to the plumber's face. "I'm gonna ask you three questions. Answer them honestly, and you'll walk. How long has this been going on?" When Denny replied six months, Lyle inquired, "Who initiated it, you or her?"

"She did."

"I buy that," Lyle said. "Now listen to me, friend, if I let you leave up out of here are you gonna do this again?" He answered as predicted. No. "I don't believe that for a second, but still I'm gonna give you a head start. Get your naked ass out of my house." The plumber grabbed his clothes. "What'd I tell you? I said get your *naked* ass out of my house. Leave your wallet, leave your keys and phone, go on foot." Denny, at first confused, dropped everything and ran. "Alone at last," Lyle told his wife.

"Okay." She rolled her eyes. "What do you want?"

He put the gun to her head. "To see you beg," he grinned.

#

Eight-thirty P.M.

Never in a million years did Denny think he'd be running bare-assed down a dark country road on a chilled night with the chief of police pursuing him. It seemed appropriate that his dick would be his downfall. Denny, who had never broken the law, had broken many a-heart with his man-whoring. Unfortunately, the cop now breathing down his neck was immune to his innocent-eyed charm. Headlights rounded the corner half a mile down the road. A spotlight affixed to the cruiser's door scanned the tree line. Denny ran for cover, his boots thumping on the asphalt, then crunching on dead leaves and limbs. He kneeled behind a pine and prickle-bush, watching as the chief's vehicle idled this way. The searchlight found him trembling. The chief's amplified voice told him to come out and face the music. A countdown followed, ending with Denny on his feet, ambling into the road with his head lowered.

"You look like shit run over twice," Lyle said, getting out of his car. The engine purred, a pillar of white vapor rising from the rear. He had a set of cuffs in his hand and gouts of blood on his shirt. "Turn around," he ordered.

"Please—" Denny begged through chattering teeth, but the chief was unmoved. Seconds later, he was on his knees, his hands cuffed behind him. Lyle unholstered his Colt and showed it to the plumber, his fingers unfurling to reveal a name etched on its pearl grip.

"What's that say?" he asked.

" 'Cumie,' " Denny read.

"Unusual name, ain't it? Not one you hear often. I'm gonna tell you a little story about a fella named Prentiss Oakley. He was sheriff of Bienville Parish, Louisiana, but prior to that, he'd participated in one of the most important ambushes in American history. It was 1934. There was not a soul who didn't know the names Clyde Barrow and Bonnie Parker. Henderson Jordan, who was sheriff at the time, got word they were heading his way, and so he put together a posse which included Prentiss. They lay in wait until the Barrows' Ford came shimmying down the road, and then they jumped out and emptied every round they had into the car. Prentiss, being the first man there, got his pick of souvenirs. He took Barrow's gun, and when he died, it passed to his middle girl, and when she died, it passed to me. Prentiss Oakley was my grandfather, and this pistol was his prized possession. I imagine you're wondering how I know it's really Clyde Barrow's gun. I did some research, and come to find out, Clyde's mother's name was—"

"Cumie," Denny put together.

"That's right. So the question I have for you is, how honored are you to know your dick's about to get blown off by Clyde Barrow's gun?"

"No," Denny croaked. All the emotion of the past half hour was running down his cheeks in warm rivers. He could hear the chief laughing as his shoulders racked. Then, glancing up, the plumber saw something at first obscured by the cruiser's exhaust. A squall of chilly wind cleared the vapor, and now he could see in all its glory the spindly shape of a man watching the duo from beneath the road's only streetlamp. Was it a man? He looked

impossibly tall, his elongated arms too grotesque to be human.

The chief followed his quarry's gaze. "What the hell—" he murmured as it took one step, then another, gaining speed until it was loping toward them fast as a freight train. Lyle raised his storied weapon and fired, striking the beast square in the chest. An initial spurt of blood eased to a trickle. The unfazed creature caught Lyle by the arm and twisted, shredding every tendon from wrist to shoulder. The chief howled as it took his head and turned it round. Denny winced at the sound of the man's brittle neck breaking.

"*Wrath,*" the monster cried into the night.

If Denny had any hope of surviving, he'd have to get his hands in front of him. While the creature was preoccupied, he contorted his limbs, laboring to get them down and around his feet. He kept his eyes fixed on the beast, who was now chucking Lyle's body to and fro like a rag doll. Broad slashes of red blood hit the pavement and steamed, transforming the street into a canvas of macabre art. When the beast had bored of its exhibition, it tossed Burkett into the air, letting him fall to the ground with a watery *crack.* By then, Denny was in the cruiser, its warmth thawing his frozen flesh. He dropped the transmission into drive, but it was too late. Clawed hands exploded through the windshield. Talons dug into tender flesh, and now he was staring into the barbarian's pitted face.

"*Lust,*" it snarled as the feeding began.

Nine P.M.

Earl Scruggs was the groundskeeper of the First Baptist Church. He lived in a shanty out back full of gardening supplies and small engine parts. Tonight, he was lounging on his bed with a space heater humming near his feet. On TV, Jimmy Stewart was running through the streets of Bedford Falls, telling anyone who would listen Merry Christmas. Earl dug hungrily into the bag of Fritos balancing on his lap and shoveled a handful into his mouth. Several ended up either on his wife-beater or on the stained thighs of his blue jeans. As he gathered them up, he noticed the dry crackle of leaves outside.

"Son of a bitch," he said. Putting his chips aside, he went to the window and glanced out to see a shadow wandering the graveyard. He knew who it was—Ansel. "Little potato-head," he spat as he grabbed his coat and flashlight, and strode out into the cold.

The boy was standing under an oak tree when Earl found him, staring into its canopy. He shouted, "Ey!" at which point the boy took off in a hurry. What had been holding his attention so rapt? Earl hiked over, using his flashlight to examine the tree. Though mostly leafless, beards of Spanish moss swayed from every limb. Beyond that all he could see was gray bark seething with black spiders. Wait a second—the bark was supposed to be brown. He leaned closer and noticed that what he assumed was the oak's hide was actually a thin coat of sweating flesh. There was an animal hiding up there. He raised the beam to get a better look, a decision he'd soon regret. The light described an elephantine head and scarlet eye. Bestial features pulled into a salivating snarl revealing rows of hypodermic teeth.

"Oh God," Earl managed. "Jesus God," he repeated, then broke for the shanty. He could hear it pursuing, though he dared not turn until he was safely inside. The door had no lock, so he blocked it with a heavy shelf. The creature banged. The walls rattled. Never had Earl so wished for one of those new fangled phones. Screaming would have to suffice, and so he screamed until his throat was raw. There was a light on in the vestry. The reverend's office. Was Derwilliger so deaf he couldn't hear the roof being ripped off a corrugated steel shed? The heater had canted on its side and caught the bedding on fire. Earl was less afraid of flames than of the demon reaching in. It clutched his arm and pulled so hard the socket tore. He was yelling, not from fear but pain, his cries so loud they drowned out the beast's declaration.

"Sloth."

#

Nine-ten P.M.

"Reverend?" a voice called from the outer hall.

John Derwilliger shot bolt-upright. "Heidi," he said, not to her but to the guy between his legs. These late night trysts with Mark Gleeson, the church's music minister, were made possible by a baldfaced lie. Not a single song for Sunday services was ever selected during their evenings together, though plenty of sword swallowing was demonstrated. "Under the desk!" he ordered as the door opened. "Good evening," he told Heidi. "I didn't know you were coming by." She saw the bottle of Bacardi on the blotter. "Would you look at what I confiscated from Pat Welsh? Can you believe that rascal, bringing rum to a youth group?" In truth, the liquor was used to lubricate his lover's inhibitions. Gleeson put on a good front for the public, but get a stiff drink in him and he became a flaming queen. "So what can I do for you?" he asked.

According to Heidi, her boyfriend was having an affair with the chief of police's wife. "Denny didn't come home," she said. "I drove past the Burketts' place, and there was his van, parked outside. I don't know what else to do."

"You've done enough," he told the girl as he coaxed her into the hall. "A sweetheart like you could have her choice of eligible men. Let me tell you what my mother used to say. 'Never bet on a loser.' "

"So you're saying I should—"

"Drop him," the reverend advised. They were now in the foyer, heading for the door. "It might be difficult, but you've gotta do what you've gotta do."

"Okay," she said wanly. "Again I'm sorry for coming over so late. I know you're busy." He told her not to worry about it. A moment before leaving, she said, "And reverend—your fly's unzipped."

"Oh," he blushed. "Oh my. Thank you."

She left. Gleeson followed soon after, giving his forbidden lover a parting kiss. Another close call had been diverted. The last thing Derwilliger needed was to be outed by a teenager. If the ignorant asses in this town knew he was gay, they would automatically assume he was a child molester. Bacardi awaited, but first he had to lock up and turn off the lights. In the dreariness of the sanctuary, he saw the tremble of flames through the stained glass windows and wondered was Earl burning trash again? How many times did he have to tell that freeloader he was going to set the church on fire? With the new additions nearing completion, the last thing they needed was an insurance claim. Derwilliger switched the lights back on, went down the center aisle, and pushed open the door behind the baptismal pool.

The fire was immediately evident. It was coming from the groundskeeper's shack, which had been torn asunder and was now spitting smoke. Silhouetted by the flames was a creature, its head jostling back and forth as it tore mouthfuls of flesh from an animal on the ground. The man of the cloth called to Earl, which wasn't the smartest move seeing as how it alerted the behemoth to his presence. The monster stood up, and up, and up, a good nine feet from the tip of its toes to the crown of its head. *Impossible,* the reverend thought, though he couldn't deny the evidence of his eyes. The creature was now pointing a long taloned finger.

"Pride," it rasped as it broke for the door, leaping headstones as it went. He threw closed the portal and bolted the lock, his heart thrumming in his chest. A moment later, the beast's body slammed into the ingress, nearly taking it off its hinges. It was then that the reverend realized the animal at its feet had been Earl. Now *he* was to be made its next meal. He fled down the aisle as the door succumbed to the force behind it. Kneeling in the hall, he peered around a corner to see the beast lumbering into the sanctuary. It raised its head, sniffing the air before noticing a plaque commemorating the church's founder, Reverend Sigmund Hobbs. Its reaction was one of spleen. It ripped the plaque off the wall and threw it through the closest window. From there, it

launched into a childish tantrum, flipping pews and scoring the walls with its jagged claws.

Derwilliger seized the opportunity to slip into the basement. There was a secondary door on the other side of the cellar if he could navigate its pitch-blackness. He didn't hazard the lights for fear they would indicate his hiding place, and so carefully, blindly, he descended. He was not careful enough. His foot missed a step, and now he was tumbling end over end, his head striking the floor with a thud.

Then all was dark. All was silent.

Nine forty-five P.M.

There was nowhere Brian would rather be than in the arms of his fetching bride. The past three hours of love-making had made the years they waited worth it. "We should have pet names for each other," he suggested. "Something cutesy."

"What do you have in mind?"

"Can I call you the Areola Ayatollah?"

"Not if you expect me to answer." She glanced at the bottle of wine still cooling amid the melting ice. "You think that lady—Miss Harper—has a bottle opener?" He said he would check. "Don't be too long," she winked.

What should have been a simple trip turned out to be far more complicated. After sliding out of bed, Brian donned his jeans and a jacket and strode downstairs. He spied a liquor store on the corner, and headed that way, passing the First Baptist Church as he went. There was a coarse old woman, probably a parishioner of the aforementioned church, arguing with the clerk over the price of cognac. She was fit to be tied, refusing to concede no matter how adamantly the counter girl insisted that particular bottle was not on sale. It eventually went to the shelf, where the girl's case was vindicated. That didn't end the woman's prattling. She continued to fuss before finally leaving in a huff.

It wasn't until his return trip that Brian noticed the smell of smoke wafting from the west. He shrugged it off, more interested in getting in out of the chill than investigating what was most likely a barbecue. When he finally got back to the house, he saw Loreen on the porch, calling for her grandson. When Brian asked if everything was okay, she said, "He tends to wander. Usually it's easier to find him." Tying the polythene bag to his wrist, Brian followed her across the street, calling the boy's name the whole way.

The eastern flank of the church was cordoned off by a temporary chainlink fence. It must have given the work crew constructing the new fellowship hall a measure of comfort to know the equipment they left behind would survive the night unmolested. On the opposite side a bulkhead door leading to the building's basement swung open and a shambling man emerged. He was in a state of panic. "I don't have a key to this," he said of the gate. Then, motioning to the rear of the fence, "There's a gap they never fixed."

Ten P.M.

Seeing the smoldering shed and the splintered wood door, Brian wondered if there wasn't at least some truth to the reverend's story. Once they had freed Derwilliger from the construction site, the man dropped to his knees and thanked the Lord. Loreen had spotted her grandson in the graveyard. The reverend tried to stop her, but with Brian's aid she pushed him away. The nearer they grew to the boy, the more apprehensive Brian became. Ansel was edging toward a yawning grave, pointing and shouting for something to sit and stay. The hole had not been made by heavy equipment, but rather gouged by hand. Or claw. The tombstone looked as old as the town itself, the name upon it weatherworn.

Ebbe Row Hobbs, it read.

Even before he reached the grave, Brian knew the creature within was no imaginary dog. He could smell its putrid stench. What he beheld six feet below was far more terrifying than any specter his mind could've conjured. The ungodly fiend had ripped into the departed's coffin, and was now eating the remnants of bone and cloth that remained. This banquet was not the equal of its previous. It wasn't devouring its mother because the salt of sin had cured her meat. Rather, it was trying to make her a permanent part of it. It glanced up at Brian and Loreen, loosing a growl from the pit of its soul (if indeed it had one). They backed away as it rose, the distress Brian had recognized in its eye diminishing. He told Loreen to run.

When he turned to shoo her away, the massive creature lurched, seizing him by both sides with its prodigious hands. Claws tore into his down jacket, piercing fabric and flesh as it heaved him up and off the ground. From behind, Loreen let loose a scream, though all Brian could think of was his blushing bride. They'd come so close to happiness only to have it thwarted by a beast from Hell. Death seemed imminent until he remembered the bag dangling from his wrist. It was an effort, but he managed to labor through the pain of his punctured skin and tear open the gauze of plastic, closing his hand around the winged corkscrew. Aiming for the most obvious target, he drove the makeshift weapon into the beast's bulging eye and twisted. The creature stumbled, lost its footing, and toppled into the grave.

Brian landed on top of it, his head spinning. The fall forced the monster to loose its prey. Ansel, meanwhile, had pulled away from his grandmother and was now standing at the precipice, wiggling his finger and shouting, "Bad boy! Bad boy!" Brian's original assumption was correct. The basilisk was afraid of the child, his innocence being its greatest adversary. With the monster paralyzed, he struggled to free himself of the grave. What he didn't realize was that the reverend had commandeered the construction crew's cement truck and batter-rammed it through the fence. The mixer was now parallel to the maw, its drum turning. Derwilliger unfolded the chute, but he didn't know how to discharge the concrete. Brian, being a former mason, proffered the direction he needed.

Ansel held the demon at bay. It seemed eerily resigned to its fate. The cement splattered, first over the monster's feet, then its legs, then its torso. Brian couldn't believe how sedate it had become. Did it want to die? Or did it know this was only a temporary imprisonment? It studied the sky blindly, the stained corkscrew still protruding from its eye socket. As Derwilliger prayed and prayed and prayed, the mortar filled its mouth, its nose, then covered the balding crown of its head until nothing remained but the occasional air bubble. They filled the crevasse to brimming, hoping the weight would either crush or pin it permanently. By the time the final clod fell, Brian succumb to shock.

#

He would later remember the ambulance ride, though his first real memory was of Faye's fragrant hair in his face. It was the following morning. She was in bed beside him in a room that stank of antiseptic. His lacerations were sutured with no sign of permanent scarring. Raising her head, Faye asked, "Are you okay?"

He held her close. "I am now," he said.

"What happened?"

"I'll tell you about it later. First, let's get the hell out of this town."

The Hills Have Votes
John Adam Gosham

All they wanted was a liberal pep rally, but they chose the wrong county to hold it in ... a red county ... and it just got redder!

Fatima made a right turn and all at once felt lost. The road narrowed and the bush thickened. Within a mile, the pavement thinned to a crumbling membrane of asphalt. The gas gage wilted toward empty as the daylight waned.

"I don't think this is a good idea," Fatima said.

"What's the matter?" said Manuela in the passenger's seat. "Too grassroots for you?"

"No," Fatima said. "Not just that. It's this whole weekend. I mean, there are barely enough Dems in this district to outpace the third-party candidates, let alone the GOP. How many young voters are actually going to bother showing up?"

"That kind of attitude," Manuela said, "is the reason Democrats are dying off in these parts. We've got to mobilize the youth if we're going to get someplace," Manuela said.

"Yeah," Fatima said, "mobilize them to get out of here for someplace urban."

"You've got to be more committed to this party," Manuela said. "Besides, Wendell will be there."

"So?"

"So you've got a thing for him. I can tell."

"No you can't and no I don't. I like his skills as an organizer, and that's that."

Manuela smirked. "Maybe this weekend you can organize a little one-on-one time with him in the tent. Get a feel for the rest of his skill-set."

"Manny, if we could just stop—"

"You'll have to organize around Reuven and me," Manuela interrupted. "We get first dibs on the tent if everything goes as planned."

"No," Fatima sighed. "What I mean is we're actually going to have to stop somewhere, quick. We're almost out of gas. Do you know how far it is to the camp?"

"Dunno," Manuela said, stroking her phone. "The signage is shit around here. And Google Maps isn't giving me fuck-all."

"Well, keep your eyes peeled, okay?"

Fatima turned on the radio. From heavy static the news emerged, and it was all the same. The United States had officially exited NAFTA, prompting criticism on both sides of the aisle. There were reports of another US airstrike in Syria. The Democrats blustered about impeachment hearings. The POTUS was still on vacation at Mar-a-Lago. The news report was interrupted by Cardi B doing

'Bodak Yellow'; Manuela had plugged in her iPhone to the stereo jack.

"Enough of that," Manuela said. "Even being in the same state as him gives me the creeps."

Fatima felt a distressed gnawing in her stomach. The needle of the gas gage was pressing down on empty now. Just as she came to believe she was hearing the first sputters from the engine, the trees up ahead cleared on the north side of the road, revealing a weather-beaten, hand-painted sign. GAS.

Beneath the sign was a squat little building, more shack than store, painted a flaking white. Fatima eased the Yaris into the roadside clearing, slowing to a stop beside the singular pump. It was vintage, oblong and squarish with an analog meter. All that was missing was an out-of-order sign handwritten in marker on cardboard. Fatima got out of the car and reached for the nozzle.

"Hold it right there, ma'am."

The voice belonged to the rangy man emerging from the gas shack. He wore a white mechanic's one-piece smeared in motor-oil. The suit was unzipped down past his gut, over the curve of which strained a yellowing wife-beater. He pushed his scratched, murky glasses up on his nose and tugged at the bill of his Washington Redskins baseball cap.

"I can't have you pumping the old girl," he continued. "This here's full serve. You want it filled?"

"Please," Fatima said, "if possible."

The lanky attendant sidled up to the pump, drawing out the nozzle with his left hand, unscrewing the gas cap with his right. The pump whirred on.

"So," the attendant said, fixing his squint on Fatima. "Come quite a ways, haven't ya?"

"Y-yes," Fatima said. She saw that the flap of his breast pocket was embroidered with the name PURVIS.

"Where you headed?"

"We're looking for Sawyer's Bluff," Manuela said, stepping out of the car. "We're going there for the weekend."

"You're going the wrong way," the attendant deadpanned.

"Oh? Because the map said west from the turn…"

The attendant frowned. "That place got shut down a long while back. Why you wanna go messing up around there? This some kind of religious thing?"

Manuela scoffed. "No," she said. "It's a political thing. The Jr. Democrats' Campout."

"That so?" the attendant said. "In that case, you better go right back the way you came."

"And why is that?" Manuela asked.

"People like you," the attendant said, "go up that stretch of road and they never come back. Never used to be that way but now everything's going to hell around here as in the world abroad, if you get my drift. I hear things, especially of late. Things moving around, too loud to be harmless. There are voices, yes, but it's more than that. There's a mad dog out there, and I hear him howling. But it's not like the wolves howl. Just one voice, always the same. It's like it's calling out to me."

"Is that a threat?" Manuela asked. "Because we're not going to be threatened."

"No," the attendant said. "That's a warning. Go back where you came from if you want to live."

The pump stopped with a *thunk*.

"Thirty even," the attendant said. "Cash only, the way you're headed."

2.

A few miles up the road, Fatima and Manuela passed the Sawyer's Bluff sign. Grown over with foliage, it looked like someone had used it for target practice. A half-mile further, they found the turnoff into the camp. The tumbledown gates had been hung with a glossy banner: JR. DEMOCRATS' CAMPOUT.

"Oh wow," Manuela said. "They must have spent half the yearly budget on that sign."

Fatima parked between Reuven's red Jetta and an old-fashioned camper, the only other vehicles there. Reuven hurried over to receive them, curly brown mane bounding on the shoulders of his cabana shirt.

"Hey, Fatima! Hey, Manuela! Now the party's officially started."

"Hi, Reuven," Manuela said, springing out of the car and into Reuven's arms, pressing herself against him.

"Where is everybody?" Fatima asked.

"They're trickling in," Reuven said. "We've already got a great turnout. Come on. There are people I want you to meet."

Reuven led them over to a beat-up picnic table overlooking a fire-pit bordered with stones. Two men sat on the scarred tabletop, using the bench as a footrest. They wore horn-rimmed glasses, cut-off jeans and well-preened beards.

"Bruce and Julian," Reuven said, "meet Manuela and Fatima. Manuela and Fatima, this is Bruce and Julian."

"We're the Winnebago," said Julian, the slighter of the two men. "Pleased to meet you."

"And look who I brought with me," Reuven said, turning toward the sound of footsteps approaching the camp. "This guy doesn't need any introduction."

"Hi, Wendell," Manuela said, and then shot a suggestive glance at Fatima.

"Hello, Manuela," Wendell said, dropping to a knee to set down the bundle of firewood he was carrying. "Hey, Fatima. How was the drive up?"

"Fine," Manuela said. "Until we stopped for gas."

"Oh my god," Julian said. "You actually stopped at that place? You're so daring."

"Aren't we, though?" Manuela said, batting her eyes. "The gas guy was such a redneck—totally old-school racist. The cliché was almost as offensive as the racism. You could tell that Fatima's headscarf was making him really uncomfortable, and then he as much as told her to go back where she came from."

"Oh, no!" Bruce said.

"Yeah," Manuela said. "And when I called him on it, he totally tried to play it off with this don't-go-in-the-woods B-movie spiel just to backtrack on his bigotry."

"Pretty original cover, though," Wendell said, "for the predictable intolerance."

"I'm so sorry you had to experience that," Julian said. "Bruce wanted to stop at that place. He thought it was quaint. Now aren't you glad I talked you out of it, B?"

"Super glad," Bruce said. "I wouldn't have been as brassy as you two ladies. You're both very brave."

"I think we're all brave," Wendell said. "A handful of card-carrying Democrats coming out here into deep Republican country? Maybe we're just stupid. All the smart Jr. Dems stayed home."

"We're stupid *strong*," Reuven said. "We've got strength in numbers. There's a lot more people coming. So let's get that wood set up, okay? We want an impressive campfire to welcome everybody when they all start showing up."

3.

But no one else showed up.

By nightfall, after all their tents were pitched, the six Jr. Democrats sat around the fire pit in lawn chairs, steadying skewered marshmallows over the crackling flames. The exception was Reuven, who leaned on his tented forearms in a deep brood. When conversation fizzled, he vaulted up, gesticulating with his beer bottle.

"I'll tell you what it is," he said. "It's gerrymandering! Florida doesn't need a 28th congressional district. The Republicans hacked into the surrounding districts to make this one because they knew a win would be child's play, what with all the backwoods sons-of-the-soil this far north. Look how thick these thickets are. This is Republican territory. All those people who no-showed this weekend proved as much, the cowards. At least now we know who the true Democrats are!"

"True dat," Julian said.

"It's this type of unfettered Republican redistricting that's turning our party and our country to shit! They run roughshod over the small-d democratic process, all in the name of pushing a psychotic, geriatric, white supremacist tyrant's agenda. We're off bombing Syria and squabbling with the Russian mobster-in-chief while our own democracy gets sliced to ribbons from the inside! And where's that orange bastard all the while? The same place he is right now. In Mar-a-Lago, working on his short game. How long has he been there? Going on two full weeks? The going gets tough and then he ghosts!"

"Spooky," Manuela said, shining her iPhone flashlight up into her face and conjuring a wide-eyed, why-me expression. Fatima nudged her in the ribs.

"He'll never get re-elected," Wendell murmured.

"Oh won't he?" Reuven spat. "Six whole Jr. Democrats in the Florida 28th say that he likely *will*. Election tampering says he will for sure. The worst ones always come back, Wendell. It's like a goddam horror movie with Republican presidents. The real bad ones always come back for a sequel, even when you think they're dead."

Fatima nudged Manuela again.

"Alright," Manuela said, standing up. "That's enough filibustering for tonight, Reuven. I know for a fact there are better things you can do with that mouth."

"*Ooh,*" Bruce and Julian cooed in unison.

Manuela took Reuven by the hand.

"I-I'm not finished," Reuven said. "I'll continue this—"

Manuela yanked him into the shadows beyond the glow of the flames. Julian mouthed a *thank you*, which occasioned some nods around the fire pit.

4.

Manuela hauled Reuven into the trees, her iPhone flashlight illuminating the dirt path in front of them. He traipsed behind her.

"Do you have any idea where you're going?" Reuven asked.

"Not really," Manuela said. "I guess that makes two of us, judging from your diatribe back there."

"You know," Reuven said, "you didn't have to interrupt me like that. I was just starting to get somewhere with them."

"Oh you were, huh? Wouldn't you rather get somewhere with me? Somewhere like there?"

"What?"

Manuela tilted the flashlight ahead to the right where the treeline broke. Here stood two log buildings, long and narrow, side by side.

"So?" Reuven asked.

"So let's check it out," she replied, leading him into the high grass off the trail.

"I don't know," Reuven said. "The camp shut down years ago. Those buildings could be really dangerous inside."

"Then why'd you pick this place if you didn't want a little danger? Are the Jr. Democrats that strapped for cash?"

"Well, yes," Reuven said.

"*Ooh*, look at this," Manuela crooned as they approached the entrance to the nearer building. She circled the flashlight beam over the sign atop the door that read GIRLS.

Manuela broke for the door shoulder-first. Reuven firmed his grip on her arm, holding her back.

"Whoa," he said. "You're not going in, are you? There could be squatters in there, for all we know, and—"

Manuela wrenched him forward as she shoved through the door. Once inside, she steadied the flashlight, bathing the interior in wan, whitish light. To their left was a row of ancient sinks, the porcelain caked with decades of grime. To their right were toilet stalls, some opened, some closed. The far wall in front of them bore shower heads.

"So, Reuven," Manuela said. "Didn't you always want to go into the girls washroom?"

"No, not really," Reuven said.

"C'mon, Reuv, work with me here. Can't you just picture all those young nubile camp counselors scrubbing their wet, naked bodies?"

"Actually, I think this was where pre-pubescent children showered, so I can't say that I do."

"Oh, shut up," Manuela said, and pressed her mouth to his.

Reuven mumbled against her lips in feeble protest and then gave in to the kiss. Her tongue was irrepressible in his mouth. At last, her mouth relinquished his.

"I don't know about this, Manny," he said, glancing at the open door.

"Isn't it freaky?" Manuela whispered. "It feels like someone could walk in on us at any second."

"I'm kind of scared, too, to tell you the truth."

"I'm not," Manuela said, voice husky with heavy breath. "I think it's hot."

She lifted the flashlight and shined it around the stalls. Then she pointed it at herself. With her free hand, she lifted her tank top, exposing her breasts to the light.

"How are these for post-pubescent?" she said.

Reuven clamped his mouth down on her nipples. As he gulped, nuzzled, and lapped at her breasts, Manuela whimpered and keened.

Then Manuela's gaining moans were cancelled by a low mechanical rumble. Her flashlight swung wildly, jarring Reuven from his trance-like absorption.

"Holy shit," she hissed. "You hear that?"

Reuven twisted to his right, where in the swirling circle of the flashlight, the door from the farthest stall was bursting outward. It slammed against the wall and Reuven shrieked.

The motorized rumble revved into high gear as a massive shadow charged out of the stall, orange sparks flying from the chainsaw blade that preceded it in outstretched arms.

Reuven tumbled backward into Manuela, pushing her back into one of the sinks. The breath was knocked out of her in a gale-like gust. Reuven slid down the front of her, his tailbone slamming into the gritty floor. He tried to clamber into a crabwalk position. His mouth was split open by another scream as that squalling chain of fire cut through the black. Then the cycling chainsaw blade dived down into his mouth.

A geyser of blood and tongue and brain matter spouted up onto Manuela's naked chest and face. Choking on a scream, her throat emitted only a dry rasp. The blood fountaining up from her lover's sundered face paralyzed her where she stood. The flashlight was frozen steady in her hand, too, locked on the carnage in front of her.

The man with the chainsaw was appraising Reuven's death convulsions. His considerable girth was swaddled in an expensive suit, necktie as vivid in its redness as the blood surging out of Reuven. The face, though—the face wasn't human. It was obscured, downturned. The man-monster raised his vacant gaze to Manuela, and she saw what it was that obscured the face—a mask wrought from simple cardboard. The mask was as hideous as the man. It was Donald Trump. A mask, yes, but the eyes that burnt out from beneath it were empty and evil.

The Trump-masked monster stepped toward Manuela and she did not even try to run. Instead, she sank to her knees. As the monster closed the space between them, she dropped her phone and joined her hands. She started into a whispered prayer, fast and hard.

"Sálvame de este diablo en la máscara del diablo—"

He brought the chainsaw toward her with a gradualness that was almost reverent. She winced as the saw blade sparked and cycled in front of her neck, revving as if the metal teeth themselves were excited by the promise of her flesh. With care, he applied the chainsaw blade to her throat, and then the chunks of flesh began to fly, and the blood gurgled as he moved deeper, and then Manuela's head tipped back and tumbled to the floor, leaving the arteries of her severed neck to make their last, determined spurts. Her headless, kneeling body held itself in tableau, the hands still clasped in prayer.

The monster contemplated this for a moment in the purr of the idling chainsaw. Then he directed the saw blade toward the interlocked fingers.

5.

Fatima tilted forward in her lawn chair toward the dying embers, arms huddled tight over her sweater.

"Am I the only one hearing that?"

Julian raised an eyebrow and lowered his jaw, feigning obliviousness. "What are you hearing? Impassioned screams?"

"Well, sort of," Fatima said, "It sounds like Manuela."

"I think we all hear the passionate screams," Bruce said. "It's one of those awkward situations where you don't want to ask if you're the only one hearing it, but you're pretty sure everyone else is hearing it, too."

Julian leered. "Reuven must be really giving her a tongue lashing."

"Oh, shush," Bruce said, rapping his knuckles on Julian's knee.

Fatima frowned. "It's not just screaming. There's a machine running, too. Can't you hear that?"

"Maybe," Julian said, "Reuven's silver-tongue wasn't enough after all. Manny had to resort to mechanical means."

"Jules," Bruce said. "You have got to shut up."

"I don't think so," Fatima said. "It sounded a lot larger. Like some kind of saw."

"I heard it, too," Wendell said. He withdrew his stick from the reddish embers and rotated it, observing the puffiness of his marshmallow.

"Probably some redneck ripping around on a dirt bike."

"That's hardly reassuring," Bruce said.

"Oh wait," Julian said, pressing a finger under his earlobe. "Hear that? Silence. Sounds like she's finished."

"And I think you're just about finished, too," Bruce said. "Would you like to head in, Jules?"

"All that passionate screaming's giving you ideas, I think," Julian said, standing up and brushing off the seat of his jean shorts. "Glad to know I'm not the only one. Good night to you, Fatima and Wendell. We'll be quieter than they were … or at least we'll try."

"Good night, guys," Fatima said.

Wendell nodded agreement, and then Bruce and Julian headed off in the direction of the Winnebago, disappearing into the black.

"Call me paranoid," Fatima said. "But if there are buzz saws and bikers nearby, I'm worried about Manuela and Reuven."

"That's not paranoid," Wendell said, chewing his marshmallow. "Did you try texting them?"

"Yeah. No reply from either."

"You could call."

"There's no cell service here. If I went and looked for them, would you come with me?"

Wendell popped the last half of his marshmallow into his mouth, chewed, and swallowed.

"I would," he said. "Let's go."

6.

"Well, B," Julian said, peering out the window of the camper. "Fatima and Wendell just left the fire pit together. I guess everybody has officially found a running mate."

"More power to them," Bruce said, unbuttoning his shirt. "Now we can be as loud as we want to be."

"Is that a challenge?" Julian said, pulling closed the orange and brown curtains. "Because if it is, then challenge accepted."

Julian fell back onto the camper bed, landing on the comforter with his arms at full span. Standing before him, Bruce unbuckled his belt. Julian slithered down to the foot of the bed, face hovering around Bruce's midriff.

"Where's *my* screaming machine?" Julian said, reaching for Bruce's crotch.

Julian pinched the bronze pull of Bruce's zipper between his thumb and forefinger and then took his time lowering it. When it would go no lower, Julian gripped at the frayed bottoms of Bruce's cut-offs and tugged them down.

The door to the camper flung open with a slam.

"Occupied!" Julian called out.

"Can't you knock?" Bruce shouted, turning in profile as he scrambled to hike up his jean shorts.

"Seriously," Julian said. "You guys have got to find your own hook-up spot—"

The sight of the intruder's massive silhouette behind Bruce took the words out of Julian's mouth. The dim light of the camper revealed a red tie that matched the bloodstains on the suit coat, along with a running chainsaw and the horrid mockery of a face. Julian screamed.

The scream galvanized Bruce. Wheeling around to face the masked man, he balled his fist and swung a roundhouse right over the top of the outstretched chainsaw blade and up into the intruder's repugnant façade. The cardboard chin crumpled beneath Bruce's knuckles and that permanent, pouty countenance whiplashed back. The chainsaw flung up and Bruce veered away from its cycling teeth.

"Get your ugly ass out of here, dick-face!" Bruce shouted, steadying himself on his feet, fist poised to deliver another blow. "We're gonna call the cops!"

The intruder raised his Trump-masked head again, superior smirk unfazed save for a creased jaw. Beneath the eyeholes, though, the irises spiralled with fury.

"Hit him again!" Julian screamed.

But it was lost under the screech of the saw blade. The man in the Trump mask threw an uppercut with the chainsaw, the blade grinding into the side of Bruce's head, its rusty, rumbling squall dulled suddenly by the flesh and skull. There was a sickening burble as the saw worked its way into Bruce's brain. Flecks of gray matter flew upward and outward, gluing little chips of skull to either side of the camper.

Julian scrambled backward on the bed, convulsing from the screams dying on arrival in this throat. In front of him, Bruce spasmed as he sank to his knees. The Trump-masked man lifted a mud-caked Oxford and stomped it into Bruce's chest, helping him pry the saw blade out of Bruce's skull and brain. With the chainsaw free, the Trump-masked maniac slid his right hand down to the base of the ghastly machine to join with the left one on the rear hand-guard. Like a baseball player, he reared back to take a swing at Julian.

And then the rumbling chain coughed to a stop.

There was the sound of Bruce's limbs floundering on the camper floor, nothing else.

The Trump-masked man stared at the chainsaw, tilting his head as if betrayed. He yanked the starter cord, and the saw chuffed but would not start. He pulled again, harder, letting out a neigh of frustration, but this time there was nothing. He tossed the chainsaw to the camper floor.

That unchanging Trump-face stared down for a long time. The masked man's torso heaved with massive, wheezing breaths. At last, he reached down. He came up with Bruce's discarded belt.

Doubling the belt in his fists, the masked man pulled on either end, producing a piercing *snap*. He looked to Julian.

"N-no! *No!*"

The Trump-masked man gripped Julian's naked ankle in a talon-like hand and hauled him forward on the bloody, brain-speckled comforter. Julian writhed around onto his stomach and kicked and clawed, but the Trump-masked man was too strong. He wrangled Julian's other ankle and, with a commanding jerk, corralled him at the foot of the bed. As he slid off, Julian felt the belt slip around his throat. All at once it tightened, and Julian's eyes bulged out on stalks. He wretched and rasped, kicking his legs out and clawing at the leather strap encircling his neck. Then the intruder's two fingers were pinched over his nose. He bucked and quivered, like a powder keg verging on explosion. Everything was blurred and muffled, even his frantic terminal thoughts. But there was no explosion. His legs gave way to a slow pedaling, and then he gave in to a sinking blackness as he fell dead beside his mutilated lover on the Winnebago floor.

7.

Fatima and Wendell retraced the dark path Manuela and Reuven had taken into the woods. Fatima's iPhone flashlight lit up the left side of the tree line, Wendell's the right.

"It's too quiet," Fatima said. "Maybe they're trying to scare us."

"They're not doing a bad job," Wendell said. "Truth be told, though, my biggest fear is that we'll catch them *in flagrante*."

"Look," Fatima said, spotting the twin log cabins. "There's a light on in there."

From a vent-like opening near the roofline of the closer cabin, pale light crept out like fog.

"Manuela!" Fatima cried out. "Reuven! Are you guys alright?"

There was no response.

"C'mon," Wendell said, starting toward the building. The circle of his flashlight grew larger against the door, which was open just a crack.

"This is your last chance," Wendell yelled. "Pull up your pants. We're coming in!"

He paused and turned to Fatima, his eyes intense and wide, looking for her approval. She nodded. He squared up his shoulder against the door, motioning for Fatima to fall in behind him.

"Don't say we didn't warn you!"

They burst through the door together and thrust their iPhones in front of them. The twin circles lit an unspeakable scene.

"Jesus," Wendell whispered. "Jesus wept."

It was Reuven and Manuela, or what had once been Reuven and Manuela. Reuven was identifiable only by the palm trees printed on his bloodstained cabana shirt. He was set up behind and atop what must have been Manuela in a sodomitic position. There was no way to know for sure it was her, though; she was headless and handless. Reuven's face had been halved horizontally at the mouth. In the hollowed-out remains of his jaw, like cigarettes in a candy bowl, were fingers. Her fingers. The whole arrangement was striped in blood.

"G-gotta get back to the camper," Fatima whispered, stumbling backward to the door. "Gotta get out of here."

"Y-yeah," Wendell said. "The c-c-camper. Goddammit…"

Reaching back, his hand had found hers. He squeezed a fist around her palm and she lead him in a beleaguered mutual traipse out of the shower room. Once they reached the path, they started to run, hand in hand.

The camp seemed miles away. The dark, wooded path stretched on without end.

At last the trees gave way to the clearing where they had set up. There was the fire pit and its dimming cinders, the Winnebago beside the other cars. The camper was stock-still and exuded a pinkish glow, like someone had put vermilion lampshades over all the lights inside.

Fatima ran up to the passenger's side door, pounding on its metal exterior with her palm.

"Bruce! Julian! We've got to get out of here, right now!"

Wendell hammered along with her for perhaps a whole half-minute before they gave up.

"You hear movement?" Wendell asked in a whisper.

"Inside? No."

"Neither do I."

"You want to open it?"

"You open it. I'll go in first."

She opened the door and Wendell, hunkering down in a crouch, barrelled up and in. He sagged to one knee.

"Oh fuck," he whispered.

She stepped up behind him.

"You don't want to see this."

But she was already looking. Together they peered upon the scene impassively, as if the previous atrocity had dulled and numbed and emptied them in full. The inside of the camper looked like a Jackson Pollock painting, the painter having limited himself to just two colors—arterial red and gray-matter gray. The blood-dappled camper walls were accented with the cast-off flecks of ashen bone. Julian, eyes open and bulging, was cheek to cheek with Bruce's defaced head.

"We've got to get out of here," Fatima said, voice wavering.

Wendell slid into the driver's seat of the camper, where the key was still in the ignition. The engine coughed and wheezed but would not turn over.

"Try your car," Wendell said, pushing Fatima toward the door as he vaulted out of driver's seat. "I got your back."

Fatima landed in front of her driver's side door and wrestled in her pocket for the key. A faint breeze moved through the treeline, and all the shadows swayed and rippled as if holding back a deep, wry laugh, as if about to burst with a horrid, saw-toothed punchline.

"Be cool," Wendell said. "I've got your back."

She found the key and wrenched open the door. She let Wendell crawl over to the passenger's side, and then she swung into the driver's seat. She buried the key in the ignition.

It wouldn't turn over.

"But I just filled up…"

"Drained," Wendell said. "That explains the gas smell."

"I smell that too," Fatima said. "We've got to get out of here. We've got to get back to that gas station."

"With the racist redneck?" Wendell said. "He's probably in on this."

"There might be a phone there," Fatima said. "There's no cell service here."

"Where the hell are you going?"

Wendell asked this as Fatima shoved her way out of the car.

"It's our only chance," she said, leaving the driver's side door open behind her.

"Shit," Wendell said, and then climbed out after her.

He followed her as she sped up toward the road.

8.

The signal bell clanged and Purvis loosened his grip on the copy of *Hustler* held firm in his hands. No wheels on gravel, no headlights; just the sound of the bell. Ghost car.

Purvis grabbed the shotgun he kept on his side of the till and then stood up. He crept around the counter and took slow, measured steps through the store toward the door.

There was a man standing at the gas pumps. He was no bantamweight, either.

Purvis held the gun parallel with the length of his body and edged the door open just a sliver.

"Sign says closed!" Purvis yelled.

The stranger didn't move. Purvis brought the door closed again so he could get a good look at him straight-on. He adjusted his eyeglasses to make sure he was seeing correct. The scratched, scuffed lenses settled on his nose and a chill ran from his backbone all the way through to his leg hairs. He was seeing just dandy. The man on the other side of the door was dressed to impress. His face was off-kilter, like he was wearing a mask. And he was carrying a chainsaw.

"I-I said we're closed," Purvis repeated, opening the door again, just a crack.

The stranger reached for the gas nozzle.

"That's full serve, hoss," Purvis said. "You got to get on your way."

The big man turned back to Purvis and started toward the door. Now Purvis could see the face. He'd reckoned right—it was a mask. It was a mask of President Donald J. Trump.

"Now don't go gettin' any ideas," Purvis said. "I got a gun here, and you best believe I will use it…"

With his free hand, the masked man reached into his suit. Purvis raised the barrel of the shotgun, inching it into the space between the door and the frame.

"You're going be munchin' buckshot, buddy, if you don't—"

The masked man produced a wad of cash from his coat and flung it at Purvis. It landed at the foot of the door with a healthy thump. Purvis saw Jacksons—lots of them.

"Christ Jesus," Purvis said.

With the shotgun barrel, he nudged the door open a little further. When he saw the stranger holding his position, he lowered the gun and dropped to his knees.

"There must three, four hundred bucks here. Maybe more…"

Purvis looked up to see the masked man had turned back toward the gas tank.

"Oh, I get it," Purvis said. "For sure I can get that for you. Just you wait!"

Some of the twenties had slipped away from the rest, and, from his knees, Purvis gathered them together, stuffing them into his breast pocket. When he stood up, he saw the masked man had taken the nozzle off the pump, and was lowering himself to the chainsaw. Even in a crouch he was huge.

"I see you got things under control," Purvis said, strolling toward the pumps. "If you need help getting the oil ratio just right, I'd be happy to help with that, seeing as to how generous you've been."

Purvis leaned on the pump, watching the man in the Trump mask fill up his chainsaw.

"It would be my pleasure. I mean, I've got no problem helping out a like-minded individual. That man whose face you're wearing, I voted for him too."

Purvis paused, looked down the highway.

"He's cleaning up the swamp, that's for sure. They must be making it mighty hard for him up there in DC, though, because they haven't let him do much else. I still haven't seen many changes in my backyard. I never did get my job back at the coal plant up in Virginia. You think I wanted to haul ass out here to be pumping gas in the middle of shithole nowhere? Too bad they don't just let the man govern. If things don't change, I might be just as well off to cast a vote for the other party next time around."

The man in the Trump mask twisted his head up toward Purvis in a slow, quizzical tilt.

"Look what I'm saying, though," Purvis said. "Hell, look who I'm talkin' to."

The man in the Trump mask fixed the gas cap back in place on the chainsaw. Purvis just then noticed the crimson flecks splattered across the front of the masked man's suit.

"Course, I could never bring myself to vote for a Democrat—"

The man in the Trump mask yanked the starter cord handle and the chainsaw revved to life.

"Sounds pretty good!" Purvis hollered over the noise of the blade. "But those things could be dangerous near a gas pump and—"

The blade swung around and cut into his shin.

"*Arrrrgh!*" Purvis screamed, his leg buckling beneath him, shotgun flailing up in his left arm as he fell hard onto his knees.

The man in the Trump mask stood up, blotting the night. With a backhand swing, he brought the chainsaw down into the barrel of the shotgun. From a hail of sparks, the shotgun emerged sawed-off. Purvis screamed again. The Trump-masked man kicked the amputated shotgun out of Purvis's hand. Then the chainsaw dipped down once more and the very top of Purvis's forearm flamed with pain as the teeth of the saw ground into his flesh right above the elbow. Purvis collapsed forward, trying to push himself up and out of dodge with the palms of his hands. That gave the Trump-masked man an opening, though, and the chainsaw started back into the wound on Purvis' forearm. In a matter of seconds, the saw blade chewed through the sinews overtop his elbow and into the bone and Purvis, blubbering, hit the dirt face-first.

For a half-second there was no where or when or what the fuck's happening, just stars and black. Purvis had to give his head a frantic shake to see even so much as a blur. There were pebbles embedded in his cheeks and shards of his smashed spectacles in his eyeballs, maybe even some of both.

When the blur tapered off a little, he found himself staring into a severed forearm just inches in front of his face. His heart hammered even harder against the cash bundled in his pocket as he recognized that forearm as his own. Punch-drunk from the throbbing fugue and the blood welling in his eyes, he shifted his gaze to what was left of his left arm, which now ended at the base of the bicep, whence blood was pouring.

"Ah-ah-*ah*," he couldn't even scream. He had to look away.

He watched as the masked man with the chainsaw sauntered over to the detached forearm, its fingers making a slow curl upward. The masked man contemplated the ragged limb for a moment and then knelt to pick it up.

"Puh-please," Purvis croaked.

The masked man stood, chainsaw idling in one hand, Purvis's forearm dangling in the other.

"Please, mister—they can still sew it back on."

The masked man turned to the road and then pitched Purvis's arm toward it. The arm traveled end over end through the night and landed on the road's gravelly edge. The masked man straightened his tie, reassumed his two-handed grip on the saw, and then strolled toward the road.

Purvis felt himself diminishing. He pulled himself forward with his remaining hand, digging the five fingernails he had left into the gravel for traction. His forearm was locked in his sights ahead of him, even though his glasses were smashed, even though everything else was caught in a haze now and fading fast to gray. He dug in tenaciously with those fingernails, feeling them splinter against the merciless dirt and stone. He almost made it to the road like that before the gray faded to black, and his heart ceased beating atop the pile of twenty-dollar bills.

9.

Wendell caught up to Fatima and they ran in stride down the gravel road. They ran until they could run no further. Arm-in-arm, gasping for breath, they trudged up a rise in the moon-lacquered gravel.

"Keep your eyes," Wendell wheezed, "on the tree-line."

His voice was faint over the scrape of their plodding feet.

"Yes," Fatima said. "The tree-line." Her own voice sounded distant, too.

"That motherfucker could be anywhere."

As they made their way down the crest in the road, the GAS sign slid into view on their left.

"I hope," Fatima said, "it's still open."

"Either way," Wendell huffed. "Eyes on the tree-line."

Fatima stopped trudging. Wendell took a few steps past her and slowed before catching on that she was no longer walking with him.

There was a man on the road.

He stood between them and the gas station. He was perhaps a hundred yards away, but Fatima could make out every little fleck and lineament of blood spattered on his suit. His chest heaved with each furious breath he took. He held his chainsaw with its bloody blade pointed out accusingly at the two of them. And as grim as that image was—smeared in their friends' blood, no less—it was the face atop it all that had Fatima petrified. It was the slit eyes underneath the swoop of hair, the smug mouth and the perpetual smooch it offered. It was a mask, yes, she could see that much, but it seemed hyper-real, somehow more truthful in its two dimensions. And it wasn't just terror that coursed through her because of it. That face also infuriated her, even in two dimensions, even in cardboard. That that had been the last face her fellow Florida 28th Jr. Democrats had seen before their deaths was, to Fatima, unspeakable.

The fury sent a tremor through her limbs. She could not stay still.

"Run for the gas," she said to Wendell out of the side of her mouth.

"But—"

"Either run for the gas or come with me."

Fatima charged at the Trump-masked man. As she picked up speed toward him, he thrust out the saw and throttled it, slicing invisible calligraphy in the night air. She was barely cognizant of that rusty, squalling sound against the air rushing passed either of her ears.

The saw flailed out at her as she approached the killer. She dipped low, to the side, and let the madman throw himself forward trying to reach her. She felt the curvature of the saw's tip clip her upper arm. She skidded to a stop as the maniac stumbled forward. He wheeled around, letting out a porcine whinny that was muffled by the cardboard mask. Fatima sprung to her feet, awaiting his approach.

It did not happen.

Instead the Trump-masked man scrambled to his right, stabbing the saw blade out at Wendell, who was trying to flank him. The saw lacerated Wendell's chest, sending out a spray of blood that spattered the Trump mask in crimson. Wendell coughed out ropes of blood, trying to backpedal. The Trump-masked man attempted to slash him across the stomach, and Wendell put up an arm to block it. The chainsaw ripped deep into Wendell's forearm. Wendell fell to his knees. With both arms, the Trump-masked man raised the saw high over his head, braying with anticipation.

Fatima sprinted at the masked behemoth and lowered her shoulder, aiming for the broad span of his exposed gut. She hit him higher than she'd intended, square in the ribs, but it was enough to topple him over. The chainsaw hit the ground hard, spinning away to the side of the road in a barrage of sparks.

The massive madman bucked and squirmed on his back as Fatima mounted him. She brought down a hailstorm of fists into his chest and throat and cardboard face. She reached up underneath the mask, clawing at his cheeks and his eyes. Her fingernails sank into his slack, leathery flesh without piercing it. She made sure to rake her nails across his face as she withdrew them from under the mask. She spread her legs on either side of his quaking, struggling body to distribute her weight and then pressed her forearm down into his neck, trying to suffocate him. Teeth clenched, she pushed deep into the loose neck flesh with hopes of crushing his larynx, driven by that blood-speckled Trump face she stared into, smug even in its two dimensions.

Then, with a decisive convulsion, his struggling stopped.

Fatima could take no more of that repulsive Trump face. She had stared at it for too long, too many years. Even the face of her friends' killer would be better. She pulled off the Trump mask and cast it away into the ditch. Now she could look into…

The same face.

Fatima tremored again, but this was neither simple anger nor hatred nor fear. This was all those collapsing into pure shock, a totalizing torpor that was almost like weightlessness. It was all there, underneath the scratches and the pock-marks: the heavy-lidded eyes, the broad mouth with the lips in full self-satisfaction, and the skin—so slack, so orange. The hair, though greasy and bedraggled, remained styled in that unmistakable sinusoidal comb-over.

Fatima shuddered. She had to look away from that hideous face. It had to be a hallucination. When she looked back, it would be gone, replaced by some predictable middle-American murderer's face, doughy and hidebound. But when she looked back, the face hadn't changed.

She couldn't escape it. She rolled off him and picked herself up, seeking Wendell's plaintive, ebbing moan. Blood was spilling out of his arm with nauseating vigour. It was all too surreal to parse. She had to help Wendell just so she could keep from contemplating the sheer madness of it all. She tugged at her head-scarf, pulling it off. Moving rapidly, she spooled either end around her hands as she rushed to Wendell's side. Skidding to her knees, disregarding the pain, she began to wrap the bundled fabric around his wounded arm.

"I-I'm a goner," Wendell stammered.

"Don't say that," Fatima said. "Everything's going to be okay."

"You're right," Wendell said. "I'm okay with going."

"That's nonsense," Fatima said, pulling the coil of fabric taut so she could tie it tight.

"No," Wendell said. "It'd be great to stay here with you, Fatima. People like you make the world worth struggling through. But anywhere, even nothingness, would be a b-better place—a better place than this."

His head dropped back to the gravel. Numb, Fatima stared at him, waiting for his next breath. It did not come.

"No," Fatima whispered. "No."

Tiny hands clamped into Fatima's neck. She gasped as she was wrenched upward, the arm of a bloody sport jacket suddenly enclosed around her neck. She was thrown down onto her back and then that massive form was on top of her, doll-like hands seizing onto her throat, that horrid, sagging, unmasked face floating overtop it all. He wheezed and chuffed as he choked her, and soon enough, words followed.

"Time for a permanent flight-ban, bitch!"

It was the last thing she made out before her inner ear hollowed out, leaving only muted, heavy sounds. Fatima's vision was fading, too. The face that had turned from orange to red was now getting lost in murky gray. This was how it was going to end, strangled to death on a lonely highway by—

With all her remaining strength, Fatima hurled herself upward, sending the President toppling over onto his side. She sprang up to her feet while he padded on his hands and knees toward his chainsaw. Seeing her friends' killer there, crawling like the slavering dog he was, she screamed into the night, not a scream of fear but a war cry.

She straddled the President's back, reaching around to grab his dangling tie. She twined the fabric around his jowly neck and yanked back on it like the reins of a bridle. The President ejaculated a deep, faltering warble. Fatima screamed again as she pulled, planting her feet on the asphalt to sink all the weight of her body into his back. Finally, the President let out a resounding gurgle, a tempest of spit and phlegm flying from his breathless throat. He hit the asphalt face-first with a meaty splat.

Fatima sat on top of him for perhaps a minute, still cranking back on the tie, waiting for him to move again. He did not. Gingerly, she stood up and stepped away from the President's body, facedown and motionless on the highway.

Looking at Wendell, thinking of Manuela and Reuven and Bruce and Julian, she began to weep. She couldn't look at any of it anymore. She had to turn away.

"F-Fatima?"

Wendell was trying to sit up. She rushed toward him as he pushed himself up to his knees.

The wound in his chest was not as deep as it first appeared. The bleeding in his severed arm had been staunched.

She threw his arm around her shoulder and lifted him to his feet.

Sobbing together, they started down the road past the gas station, toward the promise of sunrise.

10.

They did not stop until they reached the state highway, the junction where Fatima had hooked a right turn into the whole mess. It seemed like a lifetime ago. Four lifetimes.

It was well past dawn when Fatima and Wendell stepped out of the ditch and onto the shoulder of the highway, vehicles flying past them at full speed. They held each other steady as they staggered down the side of the road, an African-American man and a Syrian Muslim woman, each of them soaked in blood. Hours passed before anyone stopped.

The car that pulled over for them was a highway patrol cruiser. Officers stepped out from both sides, their eyes covered with faded aviator shades, their guns drawn.

11.

The President of the United States of America opened his eyes to the dawn. He sat up, realizing he was alone on the asphalt. They were all gone now. Standing up, he stepped over to the chainsaw. It had been scraped in several places. He fingered the choke and then yanked the starting pull and the chainsaw revved to life again. To the comforting rumble of the saw, the President danced. He danced himself to the dividing line of the lonely stretch of highway. He flailed the revving chainsaw above him, letting his momentum spin him around in a pirouette.

The President of the United States danced down the highway eastward, chainsaw screaming its approval.

The U.S. Coast Guard vs Lucifer's Horde

Brandon Cracraft

They thought it was a routine investigation, but found themselves trapped in a slithering hell on Earth!

When I lost the 1970 draft lottery, I joined the marines. The United States Marine Corp shaved off a couple inches of my saffron hair and gave me a pair of glasses that was better birth control than the condoms they shoved in my pockets. I was an overly tall scrawny kid in high school, more interested in books than balls. By the time I was finished learning how to march and discovering how many pushups I could do without my arms falling off, I gained fifteen pounds of muscle.

The straight A's I earned in high school and the handful of courses I took at the community college earned me some stripes. I tattooed my sergeant's stripes under "Semper Fidelis" on my right arm, so devil dogs knew to salute me when I was in my skivvies.

My jungle tour ended in early '72. Nothing made sense is civilian life. I burned through four jobs in five months, ended up moving back in with my mother and baby brother. I was a man in my twenties sharing the top bunk with Tommy's Superman sheets and a half a dozen of his homemade stuffed animals.

Joining the Coast Guard was Tommy's idea. I told him that I loved military life, but I hated the part where pissed off yellow people tried to shoot my balls off. Tommy bought at least ten comics a month, and he liked the idea of his big brother being a "Guardian." I liked it too. He was right. It made me feel like a superhero.

As much I loved Mom and Tommy, the United States Coast Guard felt like home. I kept my stripes, only everyone called me "Chief" instead of "Sergeant," and I got a new job: Maritime Enforcement Specialist.

I branded myself a second time. On my left arm was the Senior Chief Petty Officer insignia right over "Semper Paratus."

"Are we at war, sir?" I said, keeping my eye line straight and my tone even. "I was told the Navy only had jurisdiction over the Coast Guard in times of war." My blue eyes remained unblinking. "Is it the Chinese, sir?" President Reagan wanted us to be afraid of Russians, but I always thought that China was a hell of a lot more dangerous and likely to invade.

The Marines taught me how to remain stoic even when I was terrified or furious. Commodore Wasserstein was obviously never a marine. The slug was sliming his way out of his dress whites. "It's not the Russians," he said, wiping his forehead with his silk handkerchief.

The squid in a skirt wore a lieutenant commander's bars on her blazer, but I knew that she had much more power than the toad sitting behind the desk. She was unnaturally perfect. She tortured her brown hair in the perfect bun. Her pale skin defied the San Diego sun.

"The Navy is not taking control of the Coast Guard, Mister Dodd," she said. "This is a joint operation. We need the support of the coast guard. Even though the Vietnam Conflict was years ago, civilians still panic when the military enters a town."

"You make it sound like we are invading an American town," I said, my tone hiding my disgust and fear.

"I need you to quarantine the town of River's Edge, Oregon." The lieutenant commander kept looking down at her commanding officer, making sure that she only gave me the information he wanted her to say. The Navy believed that "Loose lips sank ships," but the Coast Guard knew that good communication kept people alive.

"Is there some kind of outbreak, sir?" I asked. Even though I maintained eye contact with Wasserstein, I was addressing the lieutenant commander.

The naval officer exchanged a look. There was silence for a few moments, then the commodore nodded to the woman. "There has been an environmental situation, Mister Dodd. I need to perform some tests on the local river and the wildlife." The woman paused as she ironed out her composure. "And the people."

"This sounds like Coast Guard business, sir." My even tone couldn't hide my confusion. This was Coast Guard business. Why did the Navy have their hands in this?

"Which is why the Coast Guard will handle the quarantine and even help me perform most of the tests," the lieutenant commander said. "The only naval officers that will be at the sight will be myself and two young officers who will actually be surveying the rivers and surrounding area."

"The Navy have a vested interest in River's Edge," Wasserstein said. The glare told me that was all he was going to say on the subject.

For the first time, she looked directly at me. I broke eye contact with the commodore to look at her. If I wasn't trained to read fear on the face of a devil dog, I never would've known that the woman was scared. "You will be in charge of most of the operation, Mister Dodd. I will require two medical assistants and a security guard. I am certain that my bodyguard will double as your informant, Mister Dodd."

"I never thought you were a fool, ma'am," I replied.

The lieutenant commander nodded. "I know that you are not a fool, Mister Dodd. This is your operation. Do not concern yourselves with the two ensigns. They are just a couple college boys looking for extra credit. From what I understand, Mister Dodd, you have a reputation for walking over junior officers than having them thank you for the privilege."

"Glad to know that my reputation proceeds me," I said, letting the slightest smile crack my stone demeanor.

"I hope that we can rely on your full support," Commodore Wasserstein said, slowly heaving his bulk up to a standing position. "And your discretion, Chief."

"Of course, sir," I said, reaching out to shake his hand. I pretended to look down at our hands, but I scanned his desk for clues. I wanted to know what was going on. It was obvious that the Navy was keeping their lips sealed.

The file on his desk read *Project: Lucifer. River's Edge, Oregon. June 12th, 1981.* My heart sank and my testicles tried to crawl back in my guts, but I never betrayed my terror. *Project: Lucifer?!* Was *Project: You're Fucking Fucked* not scary enough?!

"Dismissed, Chief," Wasserstein shouted. Out of the corner of my eye, I saw that there was about a thousand other things that the lieutenant commander wanted to say. She clammed up, so I did the same.

As I walked away, my movements even, fear grew within me until it made my stomach ache. The file was dated June 12th, next Friday. Was *Project: Lucifer* what was happening to River's Edge, Oregon or what the United States Navy was about to do to it?

#

The lieutenant commander wore a miniskirt shorter than her lab coat and fishnet stocking with black stiletto heels. She wanted people to stare at her legs, so they wouldn't think about what she was doing. She took out a makeup mirror, nervously adjusting her huge, round glasses that made her look like Lynda Carter in *Wonder Woman.*

"I hope that you will remember to call me Doctor Wakefield, Mister Dodd," she said, putting on some pale, pink lipstick, "and stop calling me lieutenant commander." Her movements were controlled, like she was born wearing high heels. "The commodore believes that I will have a much easier time if the townspeople think that I'm a civilian."

I nodded, trying not to scowl at Ensigns Rowe and Beatty. They dressed the two fraternity boys like Coast Guard officers. That lie burned me. The Navy were not the same as the Coast Guard, and I would love to run those two boys through Basic, so they earned the right to dress as the officers the government allowed them to impersonate.

"I am going to need a bodyguard," Wakefield said, letting her hair out of the bun. Even released, she was in full control of every strand. She probably intimidated the split ends away. "I don't want some kid who doesn't know what he's doing, Mister Dodd. Things could get hostile. My safety is your responsibility."

"I got you the biggest and blackest guy in the Coast Guard." Petty Officer Third Class Matthew Mark Luke John Green deserved high rank, but he would never earn. The six foot seven fellow Vietnam vet was loyal as a dog and could march five miles longer than anyone else. Too bad, Green was terrible at reading, writing, and math. His old fashioned father thought that the only skills a black man needed was knowing how to work with his hands. The draft was a godsend to Green, a means of escape from the Mississippi mud farm he thought of as his own personal Hell.

Petty Officer First Class Miranda Espinoza never stopped glaring at Wakefield. The reservist had five children and a useless husband at home. The medical specialist worked in a hospital as a unit secretary most of her life. She didn't know what Wakefield did for a living, but Espinoza assured me that she wasn't a medical doctor.

"We're almost there, Chief," Tommy yelled. My baby brother surprisingly adjusted well to being Seaman Dodd, remembering to call me by my rank in mixed company. The eighteen year old hadn't gained a pound in Basic. In fact, he seemed to have gotten smaller. The other boy's joked that he stole his uniform from a sea scout.

This was his first real assignment, and it felt good to bring the kid along. The only other eighteen year old was Seaman Delbert Campbell, a corn fed Indiana boy who's main job was making sure that we all had clean skivvies.

Everyone else was twenty to thirty years old. I was pretty sure that Wakefield wasn't a day over thirty, lending credence to Espinoza's theory that she was some sort of scientist and not a medical doctor.

"I guess I shouldn't be surprised that you assigned your brother to be one of my medical assistants," Wakefield said. I tried to read her face, but her civilian disguise created the perfect mask.

"My baby brother is going to be the best nurse in the coast guard, Doctor Wakefield," I said proudly. "He's here to earn money and credit for college. One day, we are all going to be saluting him."

#

Mom went through a lighthouse and covered bridge phase. She drug Tommy and me all over the coast so that she could take polaroid pictures of towns that looked just like River's Edge, Oregon. Most of the buildings were over a hundred years old, including some beautiful Queen Anne mansions. When the salmon farms opened in '75, they started building trailer courts full of rotted, cheaply built mobile homes and a strip mall that contained a bowling alley, a pizza parlor, and a cable TV transmitter.

"The mayor's name is Raymond Fortier," Wakefield said, reading from the typewritten sheet that Wasserstein had given her. "His wife, Beatrice acts as both constable and postmaster. We should probably make contact with them first."

I shook my head. "No," I said, adding authority to my voice, "first, we are going to grab some lunch."

Wakefield crossed her arms. She didn't realize that I was serious.

"If we just march up to city hall and demand to see the mayor," I explained, "we're going to look like an invading force." Wakefield thought about it a moment than nodded. "We need to remind these folks that underneath the uniform are normal folks. Nothing says normal like getting a burger and beer at a local joint. I suppose you want a tab soda. The kids can both have coca cola."

Wakefield raised an eyebrow. "Kids?!" I pointed to Tommy and Campbell. "We don't want to look intimidating. Those two look anything but intimidating. They see that we brought a couple of seaman recruits, and they'll think they aren't in danger." I searched Wakefield's face, hoping to get some clue just how dangerous *Project: Lucifer* was.

"I guess that makes sense," Wakefield said, giving me a nod. This was a woman used to controlling everything around her, but she didn't have a lot of experience with actual command. "So just the four of us?"

I thought a moment than shook my head. "We need to take one of your frat boys. It'll remind them of kids they have in college or lost in the war." I almost played eenie-meanie-miney-moe. Rowe and Beatty looked so similar: same flattop (one light brown, the other dark blond), same shoulders built for football not combat, and same smile that said that the car their daddies bought for them cost more than most houses.

"Take him." It was Rowe. Tommy whispered it in my ear. I already forgot which was which, and I was usually eidetic about names. Those two were just too generic to be remembered.

"Espinoza," I said, and the woman jumped up. "Do you think you can keep these kids in line while I'm gone?"

"Just show me where you keep the whip, Chief," Espinoza said with a smile.

#

"I don't understand why we couldn't bring Mister Green with us," Wakefield said, pretending that she didn't notice that everyone in River's Edge, Oregon was staring at us as we walked the block and a half to Frida's Diner. At least, she kept her cool. Rowe looked like he was ready to get into a fist fight with the entire town.

"Oregon used to segregat," Tommy explained, "Just like the South." She raised an eyebrow and he lowered his gaze to his boots. "People might get nervous if a black man marched into town."

Frida Cavendish was actually the third Frida to own the diner. She inherited it from her mother and grandmother. She still worked as a waitress, putting her teenaged son to work on the grill and making her eleven year old daughter the bus boy.

"Is there a flood coming?" she asked. I didn't know women still wore their hair in a bouffant. I knew that shade of new penny copper came from a bottle.

I looked over at Wakefield. This was her lie. "Well, ma'am," she said, burning through any nervousness with those two words. "We are actually going to be checking for pollution in your river. We did a survey of the coast around this town, and we discovered trace amounts of various chemicals."

Everyone seemed nervous until Rowe asked me if he could have a beer with lunch. The frat boy's nervousness calmed them down, probably reminded them of the first time their teenaged son worked up the courage to have a beer in public with their fathers.

"This isn't about the mayor, is it?" Frida asked, giving Tommy and Campbell complementary extra thick blackberry shakes.

"Is he missing?" Wakefield asked. She controlled her emotions like a gambler, but even the best gambler had a tell. She was nervous.

A new theory bubbled into my mind. Maybe *Project: Lucifer* was some kind of virus. Maybe the Navy accidently dumped some toxic chemicals or even a biological weapon and it seeped into the river.

"Charlie Dunstan brought his troops out there," Frida said. "They've been out looking for Ray and his wife all day." I gave her a questioning look. "Charlie Dunstan's the local scoutmaster. He sometimes acts as Beatrice Fortier's deputy when she needs one."

Wakefield suggested we go look for the boy scouts, but I told her just to enjoy her lunch. There wasn't a person in town that didn't know we were at Frida's Diner. Charlie Dunstan and the boys would find us.

#

When we returned to Frida's Diner for dinner, Charlie Dunstan waited for us with his Boy Scout troop. He wore a scout uniform and kept his chocolate hair short in back and sides and parted to the left, probably the same haircut since kindergarten.

A young American Indian boy and a walking freckle flanked him while the three other boys and a cub scout stood behind him like sentinels. Only the American Indian boy nodded at me.

"What the fudge packer is going on here?" Dunstan said, making a face like he just said the most violent curse.

"Probably nothing," Wakefield said. "We are just investigating a possible chemical spill. We are checking the river and the wildlife." Dunstan ground his teeth. "Unfortunately, I will have to do some routine physical checkups on the people, just to make sure that they don't have any kind of flu like symptoms."

"We found the mayor," Dunstan said. "We couldn't find his wife and little boy, but we found Big Ray Fortier." He motioned to the walking freckle. "Show the lady the picture you took of Big Ray, Horace."

Horace looked ready to cry. He looked to the American Indian boy for guidance, who motioned for him to do as he was told. "Picture's not the best," the twelve year old said. "My hand wouldn't stop shaking."

The image on the Polaroid strained my marine training. Big Ray Fortier looked like he had been chopped up in a wood chipper and then spit out. His arm was mangled and stripped to the bone. Something had eaten his left pants leg than ate the skin off the leg. His face was pale, reminding me of a vampire victim I saw on a late night horror show.

"Jesus Christ!" Rowe said.

I glanced over at Wakefield. Fear twisted my spine. She looked just as confused and shocked as us.

"Well," Dunstan said, stamping his foot childishly. "What kind of fudge packing disease does that to a man?"

"Are you sure that there was no sign of Mrs. Fortier or her son?" I asked.

Horace looked over at the American Indian boy, who lent him some courage again. "Joe Coquille is a genuine Indian tracker. We looked all over the river, and we didn't find anything."

"I'm not an Indian tracker," the American Indian boy said. "I am the troupe leader. I wouldn't be out here if I thought one of my men was still out there.

Little Ray isn't alive. If he was, we would've found him." The thirteen year old looked very serious. He gave me a defiant look that only boys with absent or abusive fathers gave adults. He motioned to his merit badges. "Like you, we never leave a man behind."

"Did you see any blood?" Wakefield asked the boys.

Coquille shook his head. His face cracked with fear, so he looked away as he spoke. "There wasn't any blood anywhere, Chief," the troop leader answered. "We didn't even see any blood on Big Ray."

#

River's Edge Inn offered us eight rooms for eighteen people, which meant that everyone was doubling up and a few people had to triple. I needed to set an example, so I told Tommy and Campbell they were bunking with me.

If there had been a second girl, Espinoza would've volunteered to take cramped quarters. She actually suggested that they let Briggs, who everyone know was secretly homosexual, stay with her, but Wakefield quickly vetoed it. As an officer, she wasn't used to sharing quarters with one roommate, much less two.

Petty Officer Green raised his hand. He convinced half-Black/half-Japanese radio operator Petty Officer Second Class Ken Suzuki and the second biggest man on the team, Seaman Elvis Mahoe, to squeeze into a tiny room with him.

I told the boys to get me some dinner, so that I could have some time alone. My entire body felt cold. I swallowed a lot of fear, and I needed to piss before I ended up wetting my pants. As soon as I was in the bathroom, I let the terror stream out of me. I caught a glimpse at my face, twisted in horror and on the verge of tears. I stayed in the bathroom until I regained control of my emotions and emerged from the bathroom as Senior Chief Petty Officer Dodd.

My baby brother and his best friend had no clue that I felt as scared as they looked. "Campbell!" I yelled, and the thin boy stood at attention. "I'm sending you with Doctor Wakefield and Espinoza."

"I don't have any medical experience, Chief," Campbell said. He tried to remain erect, but his legs were shaking.

"You don't need it, Seaman," I said. "Just do everything that Espinoza says." I needed him to calm down, so I asked, "Weren't you some kind of rodeo champ?"

"Aye, Chief." There was a glint of pride in the boy's green eyes.

"Good," I said, giving the boy a proud smile. "If Doctor Wakefield tries to skip town, I want you to rope her and hogtie her."

"Aye, Chief," Campbell replied, barely able to stifle a childish giggle.

"Tommy," I began. "Seaman Dodd." My little brother smiled when I used his rank. "I need you to keep an eye on those boy scouts. Keep your sidearm loaded and ready. I have a feeling that those kids are going to get into trouble, especially Coquille. I'm counting on you to keep them safe."

#

When I heard someone pounding at my door at three in the morning, I grabbed my rifle and checked to make sure that it was loaded. "Put the weapon down, Chief." Green's keen senses picked up the sound of a weapon. "We got some bad news, Chief."

Green and Suzuki wore tee-shirt and uniform trousers. "They left us," Green said. "I double checked. The Navy left us here." My eyes widened. It took effort to keep a curse from escaping my mouth. "That's not the only bad news."

"They sent you a message, Chief," Suzuki said. "They send it in Morse code. It said *Do your job, Dodd.*"

"That's not a message, Chief," Green said. "That's a threat."

#

The frat boys woke me up just before dawn. Rowe and Beatty stood on the threshold of my tiny motel room wearing nothing but their jockey shorts. It was actually easier to tell them apart in their skivvies. Rowe was the blond. While they were both a respectable height just beneath six feet, Beatty was a half inch shorter.

"Can I help you?" I asked.

When I spoke, the two of them stood at attention. "We needed you to know that didn't know the Navy was going to abandon us, Chief. We wanted to show you that we were loyal to you, Chief." Rowe resisted the urge to adjust his eye line to check the emotions on my face. "We won't betray you."

Beatty held out his fist. "We wanted to give you these, Chief." He dropped both of their lieutenant bars on the ground in front of me.

"Seaman Rowe and Seaman Beatty reporting for duty, Chief." Pride pulsed in Rowe's eager voice. The two of them gave me a salute, and they relaxed when I returned it.

"Get dressed and report for duty, Seamen!" I ordered. Rowe and Beatty walked off, keeping perfect military control of their body. They woke up Mahoe and Briggs to act as security, and the four of them walked out to check the river for chemicals.

Only one of them would return alive.

#

Tommy called me at just after one o'clock. "I need you to come up to the salmon farm, Adam," he said, trying and failing to hide the fear in his voice. "We found the body of Little Ray Fortier." There was a pause. "Charlie, the scout master, took his shirt off and jumped in the river. He said he was looking for Beatrice. I stayed with the kids like they told me." He swallowed a choking sob. "I stayed with the troop like you told me to, Chief."

Espinoza agreed to go with me, but Wakefield insisted on staying so that she could keep testing the townspeople for disease. I made Green and Campbell stay with her. I didn't trust that woman and planned on having a long talk with her tonight.

The eleven year old's body looked nothing like his father. It didn't look like he was attacked by piranha. The boy was blue but his body looked unmarked. He still wore all of his clothes: flannel shirt, white tee-shirt, jeans, leather, waders, and boots.

Horace sat in the corner, with a transistor radio pressed against his ear. Bruce Spingsteen was complaining about his "Hungry Heart," calming the boy down. The front of his shorts was stained with urine. He found what was left of the body of Beatrice Fortier, and no one could find his scout master.

I casually went over and dumped some sea water down the scrawny boy's shirt, causing Horace to let out a high pitched screech. "Old marine trick," I explained. "Now, no one will know that you had an accident."

"Seaman Dodd!" I yelled. "I need you to get these kids out of here." Tommy started to obey, but Horace pulled away and shook his head. "That's an order," I raised my voice, trying to sound authoritative but not frightening.

"Please," Horace begged, "I'm not ready to leave."

Coquille put a hand on the younger boy's shoulder. "I'll look after him, Chief," he said, trying to slurp up snot and tears. "We'll stay out of your way."

"All right," I conceded. "Clean up the poor cub, Dodd. It looks like he got a sick." The youngest kid's entire uniform was stained with fresh vomit.

When most of the kids were gone, I turned toward Espinoza. "Any idea what killed this kid? He looks like a vampire got to him."

Espinoza noticed it first. Something moved. Something slithered beneath the waders and jeans. When the medic pointed it out to me, I jumped back.

"What is that?" I asked, regaining my composure.

"Probably just a salmon," Espinoza said. "It looks like the salmon chewed off most of his mother's skin."

Espinoza took out a pair of scissors then struggled to slice off the leather waders. She finally gave up and just pulled them off. The body of the boy's jeans had been eaten, and we saw several creatures undulating under the denim.

"You kids should leave," I ordered. "It's not safe." Coquille tried to move Horace, but shock and terror froze the boy in place.

Espinoza cut off the jeans, revealing half a dozen eels. The lampreys lacked jaw lines, so they used their ring of razor sharp teeth to attach to the corpse's bare skin. A pair of fangs stuck the flesh repeatedly, searching for the last drop of blood in the little boy.

"Jesus H. Christ!" Espinoza screamed. She then repeated the phrase in Spanish. She tried to bat the slimy beasts away, and they all started to scatter. They slithered as fast as they could back into the water, but not before I was able to smash one under my boot.

I looked over, and one of the monsters attached itself to Espinoza's face. She tried to pull the monster off, but its body was too slimy and its grip to strong. She flailed wildly, swinging her head back and forth. She even tried to stab it with the scissors. The blade couldn't penetrate the tough scales.

When I was a little boy, my dad took me camping and he got attacked by a leech. The old man panicked, and made me burn them off. I hoped that lampreys worked the same way. I grabbed my lighter and held the flame under the monster's mouth. It let out a screech and fell off Espinoza's cheek. She tried to stomp it, but the beast slithered and contorted with inhuman alacrity. I took out my Smith and Wesson pistol and shot the monster back to Hell.

"Are you all right?" I asked, forcing my voice to remain steady. "I never saw lampreys act like that."

Espinoza nodded, but she couldn't stop crying. "I'll be fine, Chief," she said, taking desperate, gasping breaths. Despite their own terror, the two scouts ran to help her. Coquille already had a first aid kid out. "I'll. . .be. . .fine, Chief."

I watched Petty Officer First Class Miranda Espinoza, the toughest person I ever met, faint.

#

"When I was a little boy," I said, feeling my entire body tense. "I used to see lampreys swimming in the rivers. I once even saw one of those bastards attach themselves to a fish." I took a moment to maintain military demeanor. "I have never encountered a lamprey leap up at someone's face. What the hell did you guys spill into the river."

Wakefield was quiet for a while. She drummed her fingers against the wall of her motel room. "Your friend Espinoza is right, Chief. I'm not a medical doctor. I don't even have a doctorate. I have a master's degree in evolutionary biology." She clenched her fist. "Wasserstein read a paper I wrote in college on parasites. He told me that he needed my expertise. I figured there some kind of parasitic or even flesh eating protozoa." She made a face. "You'd be surprised how much microscopic things want to kill you."

"What do you know about lampreys?" I asked.

Wakefield through her hands up in the hair. "Not much. I dissected one in college. My dad once pointed them out to me when we went fishing. I guess Wasserstein thought that one parasite is the same as the other." She took a moment to correct a wayward strand of hair. "Wasserstein didn't know much. He saw my name 'Joan' on the paper, and assumed it was a typo for 'John.'"

"But these eels were *Project: Lucifer*?" I asked.

Wakefield gnawed her lower lip. "No. Wasserstein said that if I didn't have things under control by Friday that he was going to burn River's Edge to the ground." It hurt for her to say that out loud. "He already has an explosive expert in town. They are supposed to make it look there was some kind of explosion."

Before I got a chance to ask her another question, a chorus of hysterical screams erupted outside, some of them belonging to my men. I forgot all about the question and jumped up to run to the door, my hand steady on the Smith and Wesson.

Rowe stumbled down the street, screaming for help. Tears mixed with blood as he drug the naked form of his best friend behind him. Beatty's shirt and undershirt had been shredded and the skin on his back tore off. Rowe had closed his friend's eyes, but Beatty's face remained twisted in agony even after death.

"Someone. . ." Rowe begged, barely able to walk. He tried to say something else, but the only thing that escaped his throat was an animalistic whimper.

When I saw the lamprey attached to Beatty's back, I couldn't breathe. The eel was over fifteen feet long.

#

Frida Cavendish volunteered for Red Cross work in '66, joining her husband in the jungle even though she just gave birth to her first son, Albert. She once fed a homemade brownie to a soldier who lost most of the skin on his face. He was little more than a skull wrapped in cold bandages, but his teeth and tongue were undamaged. Frida felt he deserved a brownie.

She stayed in Vietnam for almost two years, even met and married Lieutenant John Cavendish. If she hadn't gotten pregnant with John Junior, she probably would've stayed until the end.

Frida Cavendish didn't flinch as she forced a ham sandwich into Rowe's shaking hand. When the reservist saw the bottle of beer, he grabbed for it but Frida shook her head. "If you eat every bite of your sandwich, you can have a beer."

Rowe smelled. The poor boy probably soiled himself. He refused to let anyone wipe off Beatty's blood and viscera. His blond hair had been stained black and red. Tears continued to fall, but the twenty year old refused to make a sound.

I put my hand on top of his and he squeezed it tightly. I knew that look, saw it on a hundred marines back in Vietnam. "I'm. . .all right, Chief." It was a lie, but one that Rowe had to tell himself.

The diner was silent except for the sound of Olivia Newton John demanding that her boyfriend get "Physical." Horace kept his radio on, even if the signal was so bad that it was mostly static. He sat in a booth with Troop Leader Coquille, the two never stopped staring at us, stopped expecting me to pull a miracle.

I stared at the wall. One of the boys, probably Coquille, wrote a small RIP with the names: Raymond Fortier (Old Ray), Beatrice Fortier, Raymond Fortier, Junior (Little Ray), Charlie Dunstan, Chadwick Beatty, Elvis Mahoe, Edward

Briggs. I approved. It was good to keep track of the dead.

It didn't matter that it was eels instead of communists, River's Edge, Oregon was officially a war zone.

"That fucking snake!" Rowe suddenly screamed.

"Lampreys are eels," Coquille said. "They're a type of fish. They might look like snakes, but they're actually fish."

Rowe's face burned red. "I know that they're not fucking snakes! I'm a bio major. I know the god damned difference!" He stood up, looking ready to start a fight with a thirteen year old boy.

I stood in the way, letting him know that he would have to take the first swing on me. Rowe's eyes clouded over, and he sobbed as he slumped back down into his seat.

"It didn't act like a fish. Never seen a fish act like that. It didn't care that it couldn't breathe air. It leaped out of the water." Rowe started breathing heavy, and he downed the beer when Frida gave it to him. "I got to remember it, don't I, Chief." I nodded at him and urged him to continue.

"The son of a bitch was nothing but teeth," he said. "It kind of latched onto Mahoe's back and wouldn't let go. We pulled, all three of us. When we finally got the giant son of a bitch off, it ripped off Mahoe's back. Not just the skin. We saw what remained of his stomach, liver and kidneys kind of spill onto the ground."

I got Rowe another beer and a pack of cigarettes from the machine, glancing over at Wakefield. She was taking notes using the napkins.

"Briggs was a tough dude," he said after downing his beer and lighting his second cigarette. "I didn't know that a faggot could be so tough. When that monster attacked again, Briggs jumped on its back and tried to wrestle it. He figured that we had a better chance of killing it if it was on land." Rowe glared at Coquille. "Because it's a fish."

"Hey," Horace said, shaking his tiny transistor radio. The songs were nothing but static. He turned the dial from one to the other. The scrawny, freckled boy took a pair of fresh batteries from his pocket and shoved it in. Still nothing but static.

"Do you have a radio, Frida?" I asked. John Junior said that he had his own transistor radio. Once again, nothing but static. He even plugged it in to make sure.

Suzuki got up and fiddled with both devices. "I've seen this before, Chief. At least, I've seen it in a simulation. They're blocking us."

"Phone's dead," Albert announced.

"*Project: Lucifer,*" Wakefield whispered under her breath. "Wasserstein said that the first phase of *Project Lucifer* would be blocking the radio and phones, making sure that no one could call out." She started to breathe heavily. Wakefield no longer cared about her iron lady persona. She thought she was going to die.

I turned to Suzuki. "Is there any way that you can get a signal to the coast guard base in San Diego? Tell Admiral Jackson that we have the situation under control." The little white lie would keep us alive.

Suzuki shrugged. "If I had a radio, I could do it. Even the squids are smart enough to scramble the receiver they gave me."

Horace raised his hand like he was in a classroom. "I got a ham radio in my garage. My first merit badge was for radio."

I looked over and raised an eyebrow toward Suzuki. "Don't worry, Chief," he said. "I got my merit badge for radio too."

"Well, Horace," I said, "You've been upgraded from scout to sailor. Welcome to my group Seaman Recruit. . ." I waited for him to tell me his last name. "O'Brian." The constellation of freckles parted for a wide smile as he led Suzuki to his house.

"It's only a matter of time before they cut the power," I said, turning towards the toughest person I ever met. "I need a safe space and a makeshift little mobile medic. You think you can handle it, PO?"

Espinoza rubbed at the bandage at her face. "It'll take more than a little love bite to take me out of the fight, Chief." She turned toward Frida. "I don't suppose this town has a doctor or a school nurse?"

Frida answered immediately. "We don't have a doctor, but we do have a veterinarian. Doc Lizzie has to be better than nothing. Also Penny Anderson, who teaches third grade volunteered in '67 to be an Army nurse. I'm pretty sure that Sister Deborah worked as a missionary before she became caretaker of St. Francis Cathedral."

"Can you show me where they are, ma'am?" she asked.

Frida shook her head. "I'm going to be making every ground of coffee and about a thousand sandwiches. My daughter, Gracie, can show you where they live." The eleven year old girl took Espinoza by the hand and the medic smiled. Gracie Cavendish was the same age as her oldest daughter.

I walked over to Coquille and gave him my hat. "You're Acting Senior Chief Petty Officer until everything gets sorted out. There are going to be a lot of panicked people, and I'm making it your job to calm them down."

The Boy Scout stood at attention and saluted. "I won't let you down."

"Green," I said. The huge man immediately stood by my side. "The Navy hired a saboteur. Someone to set fires and explosions. We need to find them." He nodded, lovingly stroking his rifle. He once told me that he preferred sleeping with his rifle to sleeping with a woman.

"Mrs. Cavendish," I said. "I don't suppose you know of anyone new coming into town. It would've been a day or two before us."

"That's the hard part," she said. "This is a fishing town. The salmon farm is always hiring new people. Doug Gray, the manager, he even hired himself a secretary last week. If the talk around the beauty parlor, Wendy Blake, is more than a secretary to him." She looked over at the boys, all of which feigned ignorance about sex.

"That's our man," I said. "Wendy Blake. Young and hot?" Frida nodded. "Way too young for Doug Gray." Another nod. "Wasserstein is a chauvinist, so he thinks everyone is. He probably thought that I would never suspect a woman."

#

John Bledsoe lived in the second biggest house in River's Edge, a Queen Anne built in 1902 designed to be the biggest house in three counties. It was surrounded on all sides by the junked out trailers of the men and women and who worked for him. He built a windmill in his front yard, believing that it would chase away the smell of fish.

Old Ray Fortier was older than his wife, Beatrice, by twenty two years. No one thought he was robbing the cradle. Beatrice Locke Fortier was fifty-five years old, broad shoulders, Bledsoe haired, and she managed to give birth to a healthy baby boy less later than a year she was forced to have a hysterectomy.

Wendy Blake was only twenty years old, not even old enough to drink. While forty year old John Bledsoe no longer lived with his wife, he never actually filed for divorce. The local gossip queens all whispered about the pretty, blond thin girl shacking up with River's Edge's most hated man.

We both knew that John Bledsoe was dead even before we saw that his throat was neatly slit. Green and I both had a lot of experience with dead bodies. "Looks like we got a real professional," I said, not bothering to whisper. "She didn't even get the chair bloody."

Green's senses became alive, and he pushed me out of the way. The bullet sailed into my shoulder. He let out a grunt and then fired his rifle in the direction of the gun. Wood and mortar splattered, but the shot missed a human target.

The second bullet caught Green just above the left ear. He gurgled as his brains slithered down his shoulder and slumped over dead.

I only used a rifle when I had to. They reminded me too much of Vietnam. I was a crack shot with my Smith and Wesson. I didn't think, just pin pointed where pretty little Wendy Blake had to be firing from, and unleashed my entire clip.

\#

With a shaking hand, I added three more names on the memorial wall: John Bledsoe, Matthew M.L.J. Green, and finally Wendy Blake. Since no one was around, I allowed myself a quick cry.

"Chief?" The sound of Wakefield's voice dried me up.

I wiped my eyes and nose and turned around, the picture of military stoicism. "Did you find anything useful from the autopsy?"

"Useful yes," Wakefield answered. "Pleasant no." I urged for her to continue. "That fifteen foot tall beast that Rowe and Beatty killed is still growing, even after its dead. We had to chop that bastard into sushi to make its body stop expanding."

"So you're saying that there is the possibility of a bigger lamprey in the river," I said, grabbing my gun for security.

"There is a full-fledged monster in that river, Chief," she explained. "I would guess that it is at least thirty feet long, possibly longer."

\#

"You can't leave me behind, Chief," Rowe begged. "I owe that son of a bitch. It killed my best friend." He took out his knife. "I want to stab that son of a bitch straight in the heart, straight in the heart."

"I'm going to have to do a little diving in that river," I said. "I could use a man or two on the surface. From what you told me, these monsters aren't shy about staying underwater."

"If you're going in that water," Tommy said. "I'm going with you." I started to argue, but he pulled the first name card. "Adam, I've always been a better swimmer than you. It's the one time me being the short was a good thing."

"Count me in," Wakefield said. "I need to see this thing for myself."

I raised an eyebrow. "Anyone else?" I wasn't surprised when Espinoza volunteered, but I told her that I needed her to keep everything running smoothly at the safe house. To prove my point, the city's electricity suddenly went down.

People started to scream, and I heard Coquille raise his voice, assuring people that everything was under control. The kid knew how to sound confident. He had a future in the military.

"Don't worry," Espinoza said, "we have a generator." When she thought no one could hear her, she whispered, "Come home safe, Chief."

"I'll go," Campbell said. "It's my job to watch the Doc. I've got double duty now that Green's passed on."

I looked over at Frida. "I don't suppose you know where my brother and I could find some swim trunks?"

#

The only swim trunks they could find that could fit me were a pair of swimming briefs. I always loved the feeling of a good speedo, kept my legs shaved so that I could just strip and jump into the Pacific when the mood struck and fight the ways to make it out as far as I could go then slowly make my way back to shore.

I couldn't help but think about Eddie Briggs, the tough Irish faggot liked to test his limits. Whenever he saw me in swim trunks, he gave me a wolf whistle. "How did he die?" I asked Rowe. "You never got to finish your story. How'd did PO Briggs die?"

Rowe stared straight ahead. He was wearing a fresh uniform with the bars and nametag torn off. It was a little big on him. I think it had belonged to Beatty. "He was wrestling that monster, refused to let go. He kept hold of the son of a bitch even after it crushed its leg. We tried to help him, but those eels are slicker than shit. I couldn't get ahold of it. I tried but my arms kept slipping out. That jawless mouth, that mother fucking jawless mouth, was inches away from my face. Briggs grabbed its jaw, and those teeth kind of sawed his hand off. He fell backwards, and I swear to fucking God, Chief, that son of a bitching eel held Briggs under water until he drown."

Campbell double checked to make sure that his gun was properly loaded. The Indiana farm boy thought he was tough, even once told Tommy that he had wished he had been born just ten years earlier so that he could have gone to Vietnam.

Wakefield was wearing Tommy's uniform pants and boots. Unlike me, my baby brother actually traveled with swim trunks. He loved diving, and he looked forward to his first jump from a helicopter into the Pacific. He was born and raised in the pacific.

"I think Chad let the monster take a chunk out of him." It took me a moment to remember that Beatty's first name was Chadwick. "Once the lamprey grabbed hold of him, he told me to pull him. It was like playing tug of war with a battleship. He got that son of a bitch out of the water. He took my hand and we kept walking. He stumbled the further we got out, but he kept walking as long as he could. After that, he had me drag him, carry him. That mother fucker wouldn't let go, just kept sucking his blood." He took a moment to cry again, but Rowe quickly recovered. "I'm not even sure when Chad died."

I turned toward my team, making eye contact with each of them. "This is what we're up against," I said. "Forget Wendy Blake and Commodore Wasserstein's attempt to blow this town up. I don't care what the file says. That was not *Project: Lucifer*. The monster we are fighting is hereby dubbed Lucifer. It might be bigger than Godzilla, but none of that matters." My eyes went cold but my voice became dramatic and inspiring. "We're going to kill Lucifer, because even the Devil isn't tough enough to take on the United States Coast Guard! We'll protect our shores from Hell itself!"

There were some cheers, and I was relieved that not even my little brother knew how scared I was.

#

The river was infested with lampreys. It was like a wall of squirming tails and razor like teeth attached to suction mouths. Their two fangs shot out of the jawless mouth, searching for anything to attach to. A couple of them jumped out of the water.

Wakefield tried to probe the water with a stick. Lampreys swarmed it and pulled it under her grasp. "Lucifer in under there," she said, "somewhere."

"I wish I brought a wet suit," Tommy said. I felt like Tarzan diving into a nest of piranha wearing nothing but a loincloth. Truthfully, I think Tarzan's loincloth provided more protection than our swimsuits.

Rowe stripped off his shirt and undershirt. "You're going to need a third diver," he said. "If you're going to reach the bottom and stir up Lucifer, those little sons of bitches need a third body to attach too." I started to say something, but he kicked off his boots. "I can do this," he assured me. "If you try to stop me, Chief, I'll suddenly remember that I actually outrank you." He hesitated before pulling his trousers off and standing next to us in his skivvies. "Got to give those bastards a good hardy meal, plenty of skin."

Campbell raised his rifle and Wakefield mimicked him. I was the only one who noticed that she was uncomfortable with the firearm. The iron lady had returned.

"My name's Philip," Rowe said, and I gave him a confused look. "Philip Malcolm Rowe, IV, in case you need to write it on memorial wall."

Tommy and I shot at the water. It wasn't enough to injure the lampreys, but it made them scatter. We knew we only had that second. The three of us didn't think about how stupid swimming with blood hungry lampreys were. We just leaped.

It didn't take long for them to attack. The goggles protected my eyes and snorkel my mouth. They lunged at my swimsuit, and I was thankful when they decided that the fabric was enough to detract them. The lamprey settled on my inner thigh. At least, it wasn't sucking on my nuts.

The lamprey on the back of my neck sent pain throughout my body. It must've landed directly on a nerve. I felt the pulse of the fangs.

Even though I told myself not to look back, I couldn't resist. My baby brother was swimming with me amongst these blood suckers, Lucifer's private blood sucking army. All my military instincts vanished. I knew I had to make sure that him and Rowe were all right.

One of the monsters had managed to get inside Rowe's goggles and attached itself to his eyes. Even though he was attacked on all sides by lampreys, Tommy remained a Coast Guard. He was trying to rescue the older boy. Trying and failing.

I swam full speed at them and pulled them up to the surface. At the very least, the two of them needed to be able to breathe. The monsters surfaced, showing their rows of teeth. "Get him out of the water!" I ordered.

"What about you?" Tommy asked.

I pushed them toward the riverbed. "I gave you an order, Seaman! Never question me." Tommy gave me one last regretful look than swam full force toward the river's edge. Rowe tried to help but he was too agonized to think.

The two of the provided me with enough of a distraction. As the lampreys chased the two of them, I dove to the bottom. The current fought me, and several lampreys sawed at my exposed flesh. When I made it to the river bed, I shoved a knife into the muddy floor. The entire river began to move. The lampreys fled, and I knew I had seconds to get out of the water.

"Found Lucifer," I said, pulling lampreys off me. I barely noticed how bad I was bleeding. I was running on adrenaline.

Wakefield and Campbell attempted to use lighters to remove the lampreys. Most of them let go, but the one attached to Rowe's eye was too stupid. It was enjoying the meal too much. "Stand back!" Rowe said, blood dribbling into his mouth. "I'm going to rip this son of a bitch out!" He managed to get ahold of the slippery eel and pulled with all of his might. The hungry monster took the eye with him.

Tommy, wounded in several dozen places himself, began patching him up and covering his eyes with bandages made from Beatty's old uniform. "You're going to live," he said, pretending that he wasn't crying. "We're not going to write your name on the memorial wall. I need to hear you say that." Rowe's voice was slurred and pained, but he managed to repeat the phrase.

"Get him out of here!" I ordered. "Take him to Espinoza. If you two don't save that boy's life, you're both docked two weeks' pay." Tommy nodded and helped Philip Rowe stumble back into town.

Neither of us needed to see Lucifer. We felt his unholy presence. It was Wakefield that turned first. She fired. The first three shots went wild, but the fourth finally hit the gigantic beast.

Campbell could barely speak, but he kept firing. Something animalistic took over. He focused on killing the monster and nothing else. He moved like a robot. Dropping one gun and picking up another.

It was like Vietnam all over again.

I swallowed my cowardice and finally turned to look Lucifer in the bulging black eyes. The rows of saw like teeth were over five feet apart. I couldn't see where it's body ended, but the length between the six gills were longer than me.

The Smith and Wesson fired into the jaw. I actually thought it would be a killing blow, but

Lucifer barely noticed. It writhed a little and then lunged at me. The only advantage I had was speed on land. Lucifer was still a water monster, after all. I managed to sidestep the attack, and Lucifer had nothing but mud.

"You still with us, Campbell?" I asked.

It took a second for the eighteen year old to answer. "Using Rowe's gun, Chief. I think he would've liked that."

"Maybe aim for the eyes," Wakefield said. "That's my only suggestion." There was a shield of sharp teeth between our bullets and the eyes.

Lucifer lunged a second time. This time, he hit his target. The teeth tore off Wakefield's face as she screamed into the monster's throat. She didn't suffer long, because the two pulsing fangs pushed her brain out of the back of her skull.

With its mouth busy, I knew I had to lunge. Bullets weren't doing anything. I needed to take this monster out with a blade. I dug my blade deep within one of the open gill slits. This time, Lucifer noticed. He dropped Wakefield's body and turned his attention to me as I continued to slice deeper. It shook me off and went for the lunge.

Campbell stepped into the monster's way. His rifle was pretty far down the monsters throat when he fired. Lucifer's immense body tensed, so Campbell fired two more times. He wasn't paying attention, even when I screamed at him to retreat.

Lucifer took off the skin on both of the boy's arms and then crushed Campbell's chest with his bulk. I don't know how the boy survived, but I noticed he was still breathing under the veil of blood.

The gigantic lamprey went to attach itself to Campbell's chest. The stupid monster forgot all about me. My knife stabbed deep into the beast's gills, and I used it to pull myself up. I got higher on the beast. High enough to get a good shot at the monster's eye.

It fell on top of me, shattering my left leg. I smiled despite the agony. It took every bit of energy to squirm from beneath the body of the eel. When I finally made it out, I nearly passed out from exhaustion.

My injuries didn't matter. It was nothing. I saw guys get both legs blown off with a well timed grenade. One of my marine buddies literally got his dick blown off. This was war. The rules of war were that you won any battle that you survived.

The only thing that mattered was that I was alive, and Lucifer was dead.

Undying Lust on a Dying Planet
M. Earl Smith

**Their unholy appetites were the only diversion
in the final days on Earth!**

Vincent, caught in moment of lust-filled fury, slammed the head of the fresh zombie against the headboard for a third time, a sickly, wet *thud* announcing that the deed was done. The deceased, nude, chained to the bed, and, until a moment before, lurching forward to bite at the undead flesh of the vampire, slouched like a drunken child, one held in place only by the shackles laced through either side of the headboard.

The vampire, gasping for air that he no longer needed, looked skyward for a moment, as if awaiting an answer on why he had been forsook on this Easter Sunday by a god that had long ago abandoned this place called Earth. Blood, gathered from one of the few fresh human kills left on Earth, covered his face, running down his chest, across finely sculpted abs, to come to an unnaturally even end, signifying where his pants had once been. Pulling his eyes from the sky, the vampire stared at the quickly putrefying mess on his sheets and sighed.

"Oh, Trevor." Vincent looked at his now-flaccid piece and shook his head. "You were such a delightful lover when you were alive. Trembling with excitement, eager to please, willing to do whatever it took to fulfill my desires…and to stay alive."

The deceased offered nothing in response.

Vincent clicked his tongue. "Pity. I hoped that, in death, you'd be just as much fun to fuck. Good lovers are hard to come across these days." Shaking his head, Vincent used a corner of the sheet to wipe the sticky combination of blood, pus and skull bone from his hands. As he worried with a stubborn flake of bone that did NOT want to dislodge itself from between his fingers, he heard a timid knock on the door. There was only one person it could be, of course, but Vincent was more worried about where he was going to procure new sheets than answering the door. Finding material goods was hard, given that ninety five percent of those who used to produce such goods were now walking corpses, content on wandering aimlessly about, looking to eat anything with a pulse.

As to the rest? Another knock on the door reminded Vincent that somehow, five percent of the breathers had managed to survive. A growl of irritation rose as he paced to the door, flinging it open with little regard for modesty.

Tasha Redfeather leapt back, chains rattling as she stumbled out of the way of the heavy door.

Tasha had been one of his best finds, a Native girl from what used to be Wyoming that had wandered off the reservation in search of something beyond the antiquated customs of her tribe. In one of the richest ironies of the apocalypse, Native Americans seemed to be immune to whatever it was that caused humanity to become a mindless, wandering mass of flesh-eating dead. They weren't the only ones. Africa was still a thriving community, now the first world where, a scant thirty years before, it had been the dredges of civilization.

The evolutionary faults of the breathers, however, meant little to Vincent. His tastes ran pale; it was the Europeans, it seemed, that were more than willing to do whatever it took to survive the hell that was now their existence. This was what made Tasha such a delightful exception. Although she was far from dumb, she was uneducated, the product of centuries of neglect and xenophobia carried out by her pasty-skinned counterparts. That lack of education, however, had left her wise in the arenas of common sense and survival. Her primary function was to lure the pale breathers in, with promises of lust-filled trysts and haven from the undead.

They had no idea that what awaited them was an intelligent monster that was far deadlier than the zombies.

If Tasha had time to focus on anything outside of her own survival, perhaps she would have lamented her role in the demise in what was left of humanity. Vincent, however, was a brutal task master, demanding that she not only find attractive males for his unholy trysts, but that she keep their home, an abandoned hunting lodge outside of what used to be Yellowstone National Park, stocked with enough supplies to keep him content. She could have hated him for all this. Hated him for how he led men down a path of deprivation before allowing them to die, only to continue playing his twisted games with their reanimated corpses. Hated how he hoarded the best of the supplies for himself, leaving her with whatever scraps of thread that were left to cover herself. Hated how he left her to fend for herself when his inaction had left her teetering on the brink of death, how he'd left her to be raped by the countless brutal savages he deemed too rough for his own perverted desires, hated how he cared little about what she ate and less about how she felt.

She would had hated him if not for the fact that she was deeply, illogically, madly turned on by him.

That was what had lured her in at the beginning. He was all powerful, unaffected by the plague, willing, at times, to even care for her, even if his tastes had always been slanted towards other men, breathing or no. She wasn't beyond that, after all; seduction was just one of many tools of survival, and if she could have used seduction to escape her situation, she would. Yet the one time she had made such an overture, Vincent had been so repulsed that he backhanded her into a wall, leaving her to wake up three days later, almost dead of dehydration and seeing stars. In retrospect, after seeing how he had treated the partners that had displeased her, she could only be grateful that it had been just that…

"What do you want, girl?" His words sent both a retch of revulsion and a titillating thrill of desire through her, leaving her torn between cowing and preening.

"I-I heard what happened to Trevor…" She kept her voice soft, and the stutter was on purpose. Let him think her a feebleminded fool.

Vincent growled. "So, you were eavesdropping again?"

Tasha flinched, this time in real fear. She had eavesdropped once before, and the beating that followed left her both battered and angry at fate for making her a masochist. "No, Vincent…I heard the chains and the crack and all the sounds of a struggle, so I assumed…"

Vincent placed a cold, pale finger under her chin and brought her mud-brown eyes to his piercing gray gaze. "And when did my pretty little Indian girl start assuming, hm? Isn't that above your pay scale?"

As much as she longed to lean into his touch, she found herself instead pulling away. "You don't pay me anything, Vincent."

A sharp, quick slap followed. "Is your life not payment enough? You should be grateful that I'm keeping you alive long enough to return to your pathetic Sioux!"

Tears welled up in her eyes. "I'm a Crow" she offered, what little defiance she had left creeping into her voice.

The vampire rolled his eyes, and the expression of disdain made her want to reach out and touch him, beg him for just a scrap of affection to feed her misguided desires. "You're whatever I decide you'll be, child. Right now? You're going to be the one to clean up that fucking mess."

Tasha looked past Vincent at what was left of the zombie and winced. "But there's no more sheets, Vincent. I told you that those were the last batch…"

The vampire's hands were quickly around her throat, and as he lifted her off the floor, he could not help but to roll his eyes. "The one thing about you breathers is that you're just like cattle in mating season, whether you want to be or not." An exaggerated inhalation of breath followed. "You stink of need, native. You disgust me."

Something broke within Tasha, brought on by a combination of the dire straits she found herself in and the devastation of having her desires go unrequited once more. He had rejected her advances one too many times. He had insulted her heritage one too many times. He had mistreated, abused, neglected her *ONE TOO MANY TIMES*. Anger welled up in her chest making it heave for the first time in his presence, with something besides primal desire. She made to spit on Vincent's face, but given that his hands were still around her throat, the best she could do was dribble a ball of salvia down her own lip. "I'm going to kill you, Vincent."

The vampire laughed. "With what, a ball of spit on your lip and some silly chant to your sky gods, or whatever you savages believe in?" He let her go, watching with delight as she tumbled into a heap, chains and all, to the floor. "You're going out into the world. You're going to find me someone else to fuck, and you're going to make sure I have clean sheets to fuck them on."

"Fuck you." Tasha muttered.

"Not with that corpse's dick. Oh, and wipe yourself off, Pocahontas. The white boys love it when you're pretty."

It had taken her a month to find the next one, yet what came from the other room was the real drag on time. Try as she might, Tasha could not keep the moans of desire, both from vampire and mortal, from making their way to her ears as she sat, hunched over and exhausted, outside the heavy oaken door of Vincent's chambers. Tonight was the night that Vincent planned on killing the mortal, and she was expected to change the sheets and chain up the corpse before the corpse reanimated.

Not that Tasha would be sorry to see the one that called himself Ted go. Tall, lithe, with piercing green eyes and wavy, shock-red hair, it had been a miracle that the brutal bastard hadn't killed her before they made it back to the manor. Vincent was the only creature alive that had an affinity for rape. Shifting, the bruises on her ass gave her an uncomfortable reminder of the price that she had to pay to get Ted into the clutches of her master. The meeting, however, had been anticlimactic. Ted, unlike most of the living that crossed paths with Vincent, knew from the moment that arrived that his choices were limited, and that he would be better off ceding to Vincent's desires than to fighting a losing battle. This had been the third night that the pair had a go, and from the sticky, slapping sounds that interlaced with the moans of desire, Tasha knew the end was near. Sure enough, in short order, the screams of desire turned into moans of terror as Ted realized what was happening. He was tied with rope, under the guise of bondage, so that when he made to resist Vincent's bite, his hopes of escape were nil. A few shrieks of terror, and a guttural growl from the vampire, and things were finished. Tasha stared at the floor between her knees, unwilling to feel even slightly regretful for leading Ted to his death. There had been guilt before, and somewhere in the back of her mind was the notion that all life that was left was precious, but not this time. She was glad the motherfucker was gone.

The door of the chambers flew open, almost slamming hard against the outer wall, and yet Tasha didn't so much as flinch. The general violence that seemed to pervade every one of Vincent's actions had ceased to scare her a long time ago.

Vincent spoke, yet her eyes never left the spot on the floor she had been staring at for hours. "Okay, Sacagawea, get in there and clean up that mess, and get him ready. If tonight was any indication, he'll be even more fun to fuck dead than he was alive." Her stomach lurched, as it often did, at the thought of a chiseled god such as Vincent fucking what amounted to a pile of rotting, screaming flesh and bones. Hopefully, she told herself, this would be the last time she had that uneasy feeling.

Lost in her own thoughts, her silence irritated the vampire. A blood-soaked rag hit her in the face. "Are you listening, you savage little slut? Get that shit cleaned up, and then make yourself scarce." The sun inched its way across the hardwood, slowly covering the spot she had been staring at, leading Vincent to hiss with irritation. "See that it's done, savage, and make yourself scarce. Hopefully, you get it right. Bringing back Ted, and those new sheets, were the first things you've done right in a long fucking time." Vincent glanced back over his shoulder at the cooling body and grinned. "Tonight's going to be special."

Vincent's fascination with fucking the dead had come about as a happy accident. Scott, a breather that Vincent had been quite fond of, had been the first. Biting had always been a part of the ritual of sex for Vincent, yet he had often taken great care to ensure Scott's survival. While Vincent highly doubted he was capable of love, he prized Scott greatly, and he had always ensured that his trysts with the mortal never left him with permanent scarring. One night, however, while in the throes of ecstasy, things went too far, and Scott died. Hunched in a corner, Vincent had been seething a week over the loss of such a prize when he noticed movement from the bed. The curse, airborne as it was, had taken hold of Scott's once-lifeless body, and in a matter of minutes there was a snarling, rotting corpse, tied up with his legs behind his head and a vacant stare on his face.

Vincent fucked the zombie until it began to fall apart, only stabbing it through the eye when he could no longer derive any pleasure from his former lover. It was then that he found his affinity for fucking the dead. Well, the rotting, walking dead, anyhow.

Walking down the hallway, whistling, he spent a moment adding up all his past lovers. Ten…or was it eleven? His whistling stopped for a moment as he tried to add up all the corpses in his head. Ted would have been eleven, he realized, had he not been so rough with the last and lost it before he had a chance to fuck it. The thought of the dead corpse tied up, on fresh sheets and waiting for him, excited him, and his cock stiffened almost immediately. Fucking the living was one thing, but fucking a mindless, ravenous zombie, one with no idea of what was going on and no way to stop it? It was necrophilia of the highest order, and Vincent couldn't help but congratulate himself on his ingenuity. He had found a way to fuck the dead in such a way that they still moved while he did so.

Shutting the door behind him, Vincent twisted at the three padlocks and secured himself in the room. Although the native often left the property during his trysts, he loathed an interruption today. Ted had been a delightful fuck while living, and Vincent was eager to see what pleasures his reanimated body held.

The zombie, as expected, offered a guttural growl, straining at its chains, unable to decipher that another dead creature was in the room. Ted's gaze wandered aimlessly, looking about for something to eat and little else. Vincent paid him little heed as he made his way to the dresser, pulling out a bottle of lubricant and a half dozen rags. Scavenging the lubricant had been one of Tasha's most useful moments (zombie anuses tended to tear if you didn't lubricate) and Vincent couldn't help but to be grateful for her foresight.

Kneeling on the bed before Ted, Vincent stared at his "victim", allowing his excitement to grow as he lubricated his shaft and gave it a few slow jerks, taking in the moment. He needed this, just as a thirsty man needed water. With a low groan, Vincent entered the corpse, working skin against skin with a few long, slow strokes.

The zombie, bewildered even in its mindless state, hissed and leaned against its chains, looking to bite at whatever it was that violated it. Vincent used a hand to force Ted's head back, even as his thrusts grew deeper and more frenzied. The zombie's teeth snapped at the wrist of the vampire, yet Vincent gave him little notice. He was approaching climax quickly, a rarity for him, and in the back of his mind, he was already planning his second tryst.

Without warning, the zombie's right hand pulled free, just as Vincent reached the cusp. Ted grabbed at the vampire and pulled him down, biting and tearing at Vincent's throat. The vampire howled in anger, pain lacing through his skin and for a moment he could only think of how badly he was going to beat Tasha for this egregious transaction. As he struggled to pull away from Ted, a flash of movement caught the corner of his eye, and a sticky, warm substance splashed onto his back and the sheets underneath him.

Struggling against the dead, Vincent looked up long enough to see Tasha standing next to his bedside. She had hidden under the bed, for hours on end, and in his excitement, Vincent had missed the fact that she was still present.

There was a match in her hand, and as Vincent fought against the zombie, almost free, he realized what was about to happen.

"I told you I was going to kill you." Tasha laughed, tears in her eyes, and tossed the match. "I'm sorry. I love you."

The vampire screamed as he went up in flames, falling back into the zombie's bite as he was engulfed. The zombie was oblivious; although the pair shared their place among the dead, the contrast was apparent. Ted had only sinned in his mortal form, incapable of controlling his own actions in death.

Vincent, however, had sinned as egregiously in death as he had in life. Here, and now, he paid the ultimate price. As the room filled with smoke, Tasha knew that she, too, would pay this price, but it was a small price to pay to revenge love unrequited.

Axe Me No Questions
Sarah Cannavo

For traveling musicians, road trips can be murder!

Blood dripped from the gash in Paul Bloch's left arm as he hurried furtively through the shadows surrounding the motel, blackness broken by the stuttering neon splatter of the Saguaro Inn's buzzing sign. Somewhere inside, the motel manager's body lay crumpled, skull cleaved, his brains and blood staining Paul's black T-shirt, and somewhere out in the darkness was Henry, hunting, axe in hand, and...

Bobbi. Where was she? They'd been running, gotten separated, and Paul hadn't seen her or Henry since then—how long? He couldn't be sure; the minutes were stretching out, hot and soft, and each seemed an eternity, his heart pounding, his arm burning, his stomach a nest of snakes. He wanted to call out to Bobbi, but if Henry was nearby and he heard…

Oh God, Bobbi, where the fuck are *you?*

What if she was—

No. Paul's frenzied mind clamped down on the thought as tightly as he clutched his sticky, blood-slicked arm. *No.* She wasn't dead, she couldn't be dead, things like this just didn't *happen*—it had been a road trip for fuck's sake, just a road trip. How the hell had things ended up here, a string of bodies following what had seemed such a simple, good deed, giving somebody a *ride?*

A hot, dry wind ruffled Paul's hair. To the west, white forks of heat lightning split the night sky.

And then, off in the distance, Bobbi screamed.

"Bobbi!" Paul shouted, skin prickling, heart shooting up into his throat, but the only response was a low rumble of thunder over the desert, and Paul started running.

***

2 weeks earlier

"Bobbi!" Paul leaned on the horn, grinning good-naturedly behind the wheel of the black convertible, a nonpedigree car that had definitely seen better days but would get them from here to there well enough. He hoped. Flicking his dark brown hair out of his eyes, sunglasses on against the California sun high overhead, Paul honked again. "C'mon, let's get a move on! We can't keep our adoring fans waiting!"

Bobbi Kinnear appeared in the doorway of their apartment building, carrying a gift-wrapped box and wearing a tank top and cutoffs that made Paul want to take her right back inside and up to their place; her long, thick hair, of a shade somewhere between dark golden-blonde and light golden-brown, bounced loose around her shoulders as she strode to the car, and she held up the box, smiling. "I can't visit my mother without bringing a gift, Paul."

"Which means if you didn't bring that we wouldn't have to go," Paul pointed out, turning the key in the ignition. "Hypothetically speaking, of course." He tipped his head back with a wide, mock-reassuring grin.

"Oh, of course." Bobbi tucked the gift securely in the backseat, among what bags and musical equipment the couple hadn't managed to fit in the trunk, and climbed into the passenger seat, ratcheting it nearly as far back as tall, lanky Paul had his. He called her The Amazon, and tall, strong, and slender as Bobbi was, the title was well-warranted. Eyes sparkling, she clicked her seatbelt and said, "You know you're not road-tripping to the electric chair, right?"

"Bobbi," Paul said patiently, "your mother hates me."

"She's never even *met* you!"

"And yet somehow that doesn't stop her."

"I love you, but you're insane," Bobbi informed him.

"I may well be," Paul agreed, "but I'm also right. I'm the stranger who took her sweet little girl and introduced her to the strange, corrupting world of indie music. I'm the reason you haven't been home in five years."

"Please." Bobbi rolled her eyes. "I moved to California to be a singer; she knows that. And she told me she's excited to meet you."

"Sharpening her axe now, I bet," Paul muttered, then *"Shit!"* rubbing his arm where Bobbi had smacked him.

"Pussy," Bobbi said, with love. "Anyway, you have three weeks to go before we even get there."

"And I plan to make the most of my last few weeks on this earth, trust me," Paul said, enjoying her smile, the blue sky overhead, the warm breeze on his skin. "Playing our music and making love to you in a string of cheap motels throughout the American Southwest. What more could I ask for before Mama Kinnear comes for me with her meat cleaver?"

"I think you just wrote our next single," Bobbi said, and Paul laughed.

They had been dating for the past five years, and together they wrote and performed their own music as Wine & Roses. Their sound had earned them comparisons to the Civil Wars, Leonard Cohen, and the like, intimate, layered songs and some select covers, and while what success they'd had so far had been low-key, they were both only in their early thirties, "young enough to still be relatively idealistic," Bobbi had put it one day, wondering aloud with a laugh if thinking that way was in fact cynical in itself.

But there was no cynicism to be found today, a bright day in late June, just excitement thrumming like a struck chord. Paul and Bobbi were setting off on a three-week road trip, a Wine & Roses mini-tour of sorts with gigs in several states and room for sightseeing in between: from California to Arizona, New Mexico, Colorado, and Nebraska. After that they were pushing on to Iowa—not because of any gig, but because it was Bobbi's home state, and as Paul had never been there before nor met her mother Allison, she'd talked him into stretching their trip a bit further so she could introduce him to both, although he still wondered how he'd let that happen.

Or—no, he knew, Paul thought, recalling Bobbi in a bra of sky-blue lace, and a bottle of whiskey that'd burned in the best way. But fully-clothed and sober, he wasn't looking forward to that part of their trip—would rather stick his nuts in a toaster oven, if he was being honest with himself. *But if it makes Bobbi happy...*

"You got everything?" he asked her now. "Guitar, assorted toiletries, that sexy black thing you wore on my birthday last year...?"

Bobbi gifted him with a catlike smile. "Guess you'll have to wait and see." She slipped amber-tinted sunglasses on, shook her hair out. "Now drive."

"Photo first." Paul pulled his phone from his pocket and held it high, he and Bobbi crowding the shot smiling. "All right," Paul said when it clicked, stealing a kiss from Bobbi before passing her the phone so she could read off directions as he drove. "The first-ever Wine & Roses U.S. tour has officially begun. Arizona, here we come."

Bobbi whooped, arms in the air, as Paul pulled out of the parking lot, and then they were on the road and rolling, the sun shining down on them and the highway stretching out before them, and neither of them could wait for the good times they were sure awaited them.

"Oh, for fuck's *sake!*" As the clasp of her guitar case snapped, Bobbi dropped down to keep her acoustic guitar from tumbling out; she succeeded, but in doing so skinned her right knee on the hot asphalt of the club's parking lot and fumbled her umbrella, which lay crumpled and quickly sodden nearby, a limp rainbow. The highs of the past few days had been in the nineties, and the storm that had swept in during Wine & Roses' set that night hadn't broken the heat; the rain coursing over Bobbi was warm as blood, soaking her to the skin in moments, and she shut her eyes tight, frustration surging and burning in her chest. With no other outlet for it, ready to explode, Bobbi slammed her first against the convertible's rear bumper and repeated, *"Fuck!"*

"Whoa, easy there, Xena. Another ding like that and the whole thing'll probably fall off." Paul jogged over and held his black umbrella over Bobbi, who sighed as she stood, folding her arms over her breasts.

"Yeah, that's just what we need." She kicked at a cracked chunk of asphalt, sent it skittering into the dark. "And, what?" she exploded, spreading her arms and staring accusingly up at the roiling sky. "The one day a year it rains in Arizona, it has to be on us?"

Thunder rolled lowly, as though shrugging off her words. She pushed her wet hair back from her face and loosed a half-screech into her hands; Paul put his free hand on her shoulder, rubbing gently.

"Hey, Bobbi, baby, hey. It's all right. I mean, I know it hasn't really been, but it will be. Sure, this audience was shit, but at least they didn't boo us, right?"

"You can't hate something you don't pay attention to, Paul. And I wasn't expecting overnight Americana superstardom or anything, but goddammit, is it too much to ask for someone to *listen*, at least?"

"I listen," Paul said, lightning flickering, illuminating his face in a brief brilliant flash.

Bobbi cracked a smile then, small and weary but there. "You have to," she said, leaning in, pressing her forehead to his. "You love me, remember?"

"Always," Paul said, squeezing her hand.

They stood that way for a moment, rain pouring down on the umbrella and puddling at their feet, and then Bobbi broke away with another sigh and a shake of her head. "It's just...I thought this trip would be going *better,* you know?"

"Well, I feel great," Paul said.

"You know what I mean."

He did. They'd been on the road for roughly five days now, and at times they'd been rough days indeed: too many wrong turns on top of each other, not enough A/C in the motel rooms, a memorable incident involving a scorpion and Bobbi's boot. Their gig falling flat tonight was yet another misfortune on the pile, definitely disheartening, but they had over two weeks left to go; things had to pick up at some point, even if Bobbi didn't seem as sure of this as Paul felt when he tried to reassure her. Besides, there *had* been some high points for Paul and Bobbi, if not Wine & Roses.

"Let's just get back to the motel and out of this rain," Paul said, "get you dried off and settle in for another fun, exciting round of Is That the A/C Finally Starting To Work Or Just a Rattlesnake in the Vent?"

"By Fall Out Boy," Bobbi laughed, and a current wilder than any lightning hummed in her blood as Paul pulled her close for a kiss; she half-expected sparks to surge between them when their mouths met, like two currents connecting. Oh, there had *definitely* been some high points this trip.

"There's my girl," Paul murmured against her mouth, grinning, right arm snaked around her waist, and she ground her body briefly against him as thunder grumbled and then crashed in the bruise-black clouds above.

"Let's go," she said, smiling.

"Way ahead of you," Paul said hoarsely, pulling the car key from his pocket.

Once their guitars were loaded into the car, before they climbed in, Paul said, "There's one more highlight you're overlooking here, Bobbi."

"And what's that?"

"We've been in Arizona, what, five days now? And we haven't met up with the Axeman yet. I'd say that's pretty good, wouldn't you?"

Bobbi rolled her eyes. Through their sojourn across the Grand Canyon State, they'd caught reports on the radio and nightly news about a killer dubbed the Arizona Axeman, who'd hacked at least six known victims to death in a trail from Tucson onwards and showed no sign of stopping soon. He haunted cities and small towns alike, desert roads and throbbing metropolises all sprayed with the blood of those he'd butchered, with never a clue left behind but the telltale wounds left by his weapon.

It *was* disconcerting to know he was out there somewhere, to hear another kill announced on the crackling car radio as they drove through a dark, dead-still desert night. And at the last motel they'd stayed at, while Paul got directions from the proprietor, Bobbi had picked up a tabloid lying around the office and found garish, full-color pictures of some of the crime scenes splashed across several pages; morbidly drawn in, she'd studied them even as her stomach turned, the pools of blood, the severed limbs lying scattered, askew, the shattered skulls and pulped bone, and wondered what kind of man could take pleasure in doing that—not just killing other humans, but slaughtering them, as though they were less than animals.

But still.

"The way things are going," Bobbi said, "it'd be just our luck. But seriously, Paul, what are the odds we'd actually run into the Arizona Axeman, out of everybody else in the whole state?"

"Excuse me."

Bobbi and Paul started, turned. Several feet away stood the shadowy figure of a man, irregularly illuminated by the lightning, and then he stepped forward, haloed by the parking-lot lights, and Bobbi relaxed. An older man—in his sixties, if he was a day—his hair white and face lined, but his eyes bright, keen, and there was no sense of frailty about him as he came closer to the couple, loafers soaked dark by the puddle; he was wearing a tweed jacket, Bobbi noticed in amusement, despite the heat, and in his right hand he carried a black briefcase, in his left an umbrella held high.

"I didn't mean to startle you," he apologized. His voice had a distinctive fluid rumble to it, and a British accent to boot; Bobbi felt her eyebrows arch in surprise. "I caught some of your set, and I was hoping to catch you before you left. This may sound odd, but I'd like to ask you a favor."

Paul placed him then; he'd come into the club about halfway through the set, took a table by himself in the back of the dim room and sipped a succession of scotches, briefcase on the seat beside him. Paul had noted him not because of anything out of the ordinary, no inherent strangeness in his mannerisms or attention he'd paid to the show, but simply because his casual entrance had been the first sign of life in the place since he and Bobbi had tuned their guitars and tapped on the microphones.

"Your car need a jump or something?" Paul asked. "Because we'll give it a shot, but we're getting a pacemaker installed in this beauty once we reach Santa Fe."

The older man checked. "No. I don't have a car, actually. That's where you come in. You see, my name is Henry Talbot, and I'm travelling across the country this summer—living by my wits, you might say, if a sexagenarian spending a few months begging rides from strangers can truly be said to have many." He chuckled at his own joke; Bobbi couldn't help but grin back, at ease with the tweed-coated man. "Anyway, after your performance tonight, I couldn't help overhearing that you plan to leave town tomorrow, and as it happens, you're headed the same way I'd like to go, so I was wondering if I might impose on you two to give me a lift, at least to a decent motel."

Bobbi looked at Paul. "I mean, I don't see why not—" she began.

Just as Paul started, "I'm sorry, Mr. Talbot, but—"

Eyebrows climbed foreheads; Paul took Bobbi's arm and said with a smile, "Would you excuse us for a minute, Mr. Talbot?"

Amusement gleamed in his eyes. "Certainly. Take your time."

"What are you *doing?*" the couple hissed in unison once they'd splashed a few feet away, huddling under their umbrellas and staring at each other, incredulous.

"What am *I* doing?" Paul asked, hand on his chest. "Two minutes ago you were all but ready to say 'fuck it' and scrap the whole trip altogether, and now you're not only rarin' to keep going but you wanna haul Leigh Teabing along with us."

"Not all the way to Iowa, Paul. And it's not like we'll have to go out of our way to help him out— he's going the same way we are, he says." Bobbi glanced over at Henry, waiting serenely in the rain, lightning lining his features further. "Besides, he seems harmless enough. What can it hurt?"

"You could probably fill a hospital wing with people who pulled their pants down with one hand, held a gerbil in the other, and asked that question," Paul said, trying to resist Bobbi's grin, her imploring eyes.

"Excuse me," Henry said, and Paul and Bobbi looked over. "I can chip in for gas."

"So you were a professor?" Paul said the next morning as they drove along beneath the hard blue sky, heat lines shimmering above the blacktop under their wheels.

In the backseat Henry nodded. "For thirty years," he said. "I taught agricultural science, which I suspect sounds boring as all get-out, but I grew up on a farm near Dartmouth, so it was well within my realm of expertise. And I truly did love teaching, but when I turned sixty I realized there was so much more of the world than what I'd seen of it, so I decided to retire and do a bit of exploring in my golden years. Travel to exotic lands, meet exciting new people, all of that."

"So you retired from England to *Arizona?*" Paul asked as Bobbi tried to snap a shot of a lizard sunning itself on a rock in the red dirt beside the highway, cursing when it came out blurred. *"Why?"*

Henry smiled. "I was tired of the rain."

Bobbi drew herself into the convertible and laughed, brushing her windswept hair out of her face. Paul smiled, if not as strongly as she did. He had no personal objections to their passenger, odd as the notion of an elderly man hitchhiking across the country like some Deadhead for the hell of it was; Henry Talbot wasn't a backseat driver, wasn't the stuffy, stodgy codger Paul'd worried he might be, at least so far—he was actually pretty cool when it came to things like the music on the radio. And, of course, it helped to have somebody else in the lineup when they pulled up to the pump at the next few Jif-E-Stops.

But still, Paul couldn't seem to summon the sudden enthusiasm for their unexpected guest that Bobbi could. He was doing his best to disguise that fact, though, at least in front of Henry; he wasn't *that* big an asshole.

Whatever, Paul thought, steering wheel hot under his hands. They would be out of Arizona and into New Mexico tomorrow, with no Wine & Roses gig that night, and after that Henry would be out of their hair. He could hold on that long.

When he tuned back into the conversation he found Henry had passed his cell phone up to Bobbi, and she was cooing in delight scrolling through photos of rabbits—Henry's own, Paul gathered quickly, which a neighbor was watching while he was on his grand excursion. Of course Bobbi was losing her mind; she loved bunnies. Photos of her childhood pet, Buttercup, hung among those of Paul and Bobbi in their apartment; an especially artistic shot of him had even snuck somehow into the liner notes of their first self-produced album, *Emptiness and Echoes*.

"Do they have names?" Bobbi asked.

"Of course." Henry delivered the names with gravity worthy of a Shakespearean roll call: "Flopsy, Mopsy, Cottontail, and Sir James Palmerston the Third."

"What happened to Sir James the First and Second?" Paul asked.

Henry shook his head. "Coyotes," he sighed.

"Aw!" Bobbi exclaimed, in dismay this time. "That's horrible!"

"That's nature, Miss Kinnear," Henry corrected, accepting his phone back from her. "And that's something growing up on a farm teaches you very quickly—although it's amply evident everywhere you look. Take the very land we're driving through, for example. Life in the desert is harsh, brutal. The Grand Canyon is breathtaking to behold, and yet how many carcasses have been picked clean in the red miles around it? How many bones lie buried in this sand, undiscovered, bleached and scoured by the wind, the sun? To consider this would disturb a great many of us, to the point where we choose instead to ignore it, bury it as deep and far from our minds as we can." He spread his hands, half-shrugged. "And yet that cycle is in the end only, totally, natural. There are predators, and there are prey."

Henry's voice was sonorous, the even rhythm of it hypnotizing as the highway rolling uninterrupted ahead of them and the miles that had passed behind. Bobbi and Paul sat silent, half-entranced, as he talked, and then he gestured lightly to the car radio and said in a more casual tone, "In fact, this sounds like another update on a rather local predator right now."

Wall of Voodoo's "Mexican Radio" had faded out into a female voice announcing "news every hour on the fifteens," and as Paul turned it up she continued, "—hikers found dead near their campsite in Show Low. Weather conditions have made it difficult to determine a time of death, but police suspect the murders occurred at some point yesterday. They are refusing to comment on whether or not Theresa Gillis and Scott Fitz are the two newest victims of the killer some have dubbed the Arizona Axeman, but the eyewitness who discovered the bodies say the state of the victims leaves no doubt in his mind. Police are urging citizens in the area to be cautious, especially if travelling alone or at night, and if they have any information regarding these or any of the previous murders to please contact—"

A crackle of static swallowed her last words; by the time it passed the broadcast was over and a chipper voice announced A-ROK'S all-eighties weekend, bleeding into Foreigner declaring they wanted to know what love is. Paul snapped the radio off and shared a look with Bobbi.

"Show Low—that's, what, five miles from where we were yesterday?" he asked.

"At most," she said, surprised and worry vying on her features. Neither she nor Paul were ones to automatically associate themselves with disasters or horrific events, the people Paul's college roommate had called "Coulda-Been-Mes": If a drugstore was robbed three blocks from their apartment, they panicked over how it was almost them there, even if they used the CVS across their own street instead of the robbed one; if their sister's best friend's cousin was killed, somehow it was nearly them under the semi's wheels, even if they'd never spent minute one in their company. And even now they weren't so much chilled by any thought that it could have been them killed this time; five miles was still five miles, after all. But it was closer than the last murders had been, *much* closer, and the Axeman, to all appearances, was a nomadic killer, always on the move, so who was to say they *wouldn't* cross paths with him at some point? The idea was enough to start chips of ice prickling their spines, even under the glaring sun.

Birds wheeled and cried out in the distance, dark swooping shadows in the blue sky. Something had died nearby, or was about to, Bobbi thought with a shudder, picturing gobbets of flesh clutched bloody in beaks, bare bones in the sand.

"Well," Henry said mildly, "it seems we all picked a good time to get out of Dodge, eh?"

But a busted back tire kept them in Arizona one more night; Paul could almost hear the dollars in his wallet screaming, stretched as they were. The only upside to the delay was that he and Bobbi didn't have any show to get to that night, and if they set out bright and early and hauled ass they'd still make the next one, their first in New Mexico.

The trio split up once they'd checked into the motel, Henry mentioning something to them about possibly going out that night but promising he'd be back in time for departure the next day.

"What does it say about us that The Elderly Professor decided to head out and enjoy the nightlife while we, two hip young things in the prime of our lives, are hanging out in our motel room, gorging on pepperoni pizza and retro TV?" Paul asked, lounging on the room's double bed, which had an excellent view of all the cracks in the dingy cream-colored plaster of the walls and ceiling, in nothing but black jockey shorts as the A/C wheezed in the corner. Paul's battered black songwriting notebook lay on the weak-kneed bedroom table in case inspiration struck, why he always kept it near at night, and the remote for the grainy TV was in his left hand; Mary Tyler Moore flickered on-screen, and Paul observed, amused, that even the screen's shittiness couldn't dull her smile.

Bobbi was in the stall of a bathroom in a cami and panties the hue of a robin's egg, rubbing lotion into her arms, examining herself in the cracked, stain-flecked glass of the mirror, and doing her best not to bump her shin on the toilet every time she made even the slightest movement. "It says we get to have sex without worrying about waking up the senior citizen in the room two doors down," she called back through the bathroom's half-shut door.

"I like the way you think, Kinnear," Paul said.

Bobbi stepped out of the bathroom, massaging in the last of her lotion; the scent of honey and caramel floated to Paul and he appraised her with a smile: the tan skin her skimpy getup bared, the muscles and lush curves of her long, toned body, her own knowing smile as she sauntered to the bed and dropped down beside him, bedsprings shrieking in protest. "I just figure we're all the nightlife we really need," she said, running her fingers through his hair as he began kissing her neck.

"No argument from me," he murmured against her skin.

He was stiff already; Bobbi skimmed her fingers down the muscles of his chest, his stomach, and stroked him slowly, teasingly, outside his shorts, grinning at the groan that escaped him. When he broke away briefly to shut off the light she reached out and caught his wrist, drawing him back to her. "Leave it on."

"Okay, freak," he grinned, rolling onto his side. His hand stroked her hip, the smooth plane of her stomach; Bobbi's pulse fluttered and her lips parted. Paul knew how to play her body as skillfully as he did his guitar, she often thought, and each time he proved it true; tonight was no exception, as his fingers slipped between the waistband of her panties, lower, and found her wet. He moved a finger, two, inside her and she sucked in a breath, arching her pelvis slightly as he stroked, letting her thoughts blur and fade.

Across the room the ancient TV was still on, meaningless background chatter, at least until the canned laughter of the retro reruns gave way to the blare of the local news, startling the couple on the bed. The lead story was, of course, the Axeman's latest ambush, and the camera panned from the grave, blonde newscaster to the lakeside campsite behind her, where cops and forensic techs were working within a pen of yellow police tape, two black body bags being loaded slowly into a silent ambulance nearby.

"—if confirmed to be the grisly handiwork of the same killer, these murders will bring the total victim count to eight over the past four mon—"

"Oh, for fuck's—" Bobbi huffed, reaching across Paul and fumbling for the remote, clutching it and clicking the TV off.

"This is what you focus on? *Now?*" Paul asked, half-joking, as Bobbi tossed the remote away.

"It's morbid, Paul. I'm not gonna fuck you while somebody's talking about *axe murders.*"

Paul smiled against her skin, kissing her neck again, her shoulder, his skilled fingers starting again. "Don't worry, baby, I'll protect you from the big bad Axeman," he laughed as she gave a soft gasp, moving her lower body in time to his touch. "Besides, it's like you said—what are the odds we'd ever actually run into him?"

The sun was setting when Henry left the motel, a scarlet stain spreading in the west and puddling bloodily over town. It wasn't a bustling, buzzing place, to be sure; Henry suspected that if he stood in the right spot his shadow would stretch from one end to the other. But at heart humans were social creatures, and even the smallest town had places they could gather, so he set off to find one, briefcase in hand, bumping reassuringly against his leg as he walked.

It wasn't long before he found the local watering hole, a dim bar with the simple name Oasis; that night it was half-full of singles and couples, folk older and younger, and he took a seat in the rear of the place as the scene was spread before him, the better for him to survey it.

If he'd had his choice, he would have preferred to be out of Arizona by now; he'd well and truly made his mark here, he felt, and it was time for him to expand his horizons. Ah, but the car trouble wasn't his fault, nor that of the couple who had been nice enough to take him along, and it wasn't as if anyone was after him, after all. So he figured he'd take advantage of the extra time afforded him and have one last bit of sport. *After all, idle hands do the Devil's work, as Gran always said,* he thought, chuckling to himself.

Quickly Henry spotted a promising prospect: a young couple, probably somewhere in their twenties, a laughing, long-haired Asian girl and a fair-skinned, dark-haired boy. His hand was always in hers, and they kept leaning in to talk close and kiss; Henry eyed them carefully yet casually, sipping his drink as they slowly stopped ordering drinks and lingered over what they had left. They'd be leaving soon, he knew, and his blood started to pump harder in anticipation, though he kept his expression composed, right up to the moment they paid their tab and headed off and he did the same, briefcase in hand as he followed them into the night.

They had a car, a bright crimson thing with a tubercular engine and battered rear bumper, but even on foot Henry had no trouble keeping them in sight; they were cruising along, and anyway, Henry's personal fitness was a point of pride. So many others his own age let themselves grow stiff and slow, brittle bones in wrecked flesh, corpses before they realized it was time to lie down for the last time. *Poor saps.* Life didn't have to end at sixty, Henry reflected, drawing in a deep breath of night air, lips curling in a smile to mirror the orange crescent moon overhead. Not if you had something to keep living for.

The red car pulled off onto an unpaved road, isolated, perfect. Henry hung back and watched, breath coming faster, heart dancing against his ribs, his tongue running unnoticed over his lips. Muffled music came from the car's dark interior; shadows shifted and moved within, and a minute after the red car began to rock Henry set his briefcase down, unlocked it, removed the keen-edged axe nestled within, and strode over to the car.

He rapped sharply on the door with the axe-handle, then tucked the weapon out of sight behind his leg as mutters of "Shit!" and the rustle of hasty movement and readjusted clothing issued from inside. No doubt they thought themselves busted, some cop happening by at the wrong moment; the boy's face when he rolled his steam-shrouded window down bore that out. But when he saw Henry, an unassuming old man, so obviously not an officer, he visibly relaxed; Henry could almost hear his guard coming down, and he knew he had them.

"I'm sorry to intrude," Henry said. The girl was leaning over, peering out now too, sleeve slipped off one shoulder and a streak of dark red lip gloss staining her left cheek. "But I'm afraid my car got a flat tire a little down the road, and I'm not getting any cell reception—would you mind helping an old man get on his way again?"

The hormonal glaze was clearing from the young man's eyes; he pushed his hair off his forehead. "Uh, sure," he said, recovering his tongue. "No problem. Wait here for me, Terry, okay?" he said to his girlfriend, whose eyes flicked to Henry before back to the compact mirror she'd produced, complacent.

"Sure thing, babe," she said, wiping away her smeared lip gloss.

The young man pushed open the driver's door and climbed out, sneakers crunching in the dirt. Music spilled from inside the car: A-ROK's eighties weekend, the Cutting Crew doing "I Just Died in Your Arms Tonight" as Henry and the horny Good Samaritan started walking.

"Flat tire, huh?" the young man said.

"Yes," Henry said pleasantly, just behind him. "There was a time I could've changed it myself, but I'm not as young as I used to be." They chuckled together and then, only a few feet from the red car, Henry lifted the axe, added in the same pleasant tone, "For the most part I manage just fine, though," and buried the axe squarely between the young man's shoulder blades.

Blood sprayed from the wound in a red rain, gurgled in the man's throat as he screamed, staggered; his dumbfounded attempts to reach for the embedded blade, pull it free, reminded Henry of a worm on a hook fruitlessly struggling to free itself and a red haze of pleasure enveloped him as he yanked the axe free with a thick sucking sound, blood and gristle glistening in the wound.

The screams had drawn Terry, whose face glowed skeletally in the blue glare of the dash lights, and she watched in horror as her boyfriend staggered forward a few steps, soaked in blood. *"Mike!"* she shrieked, and Mike contorted his agonized cries into something close to "Terry, run" before his spine gave and he collapsed, spasming, to his credit still trying to crawl until with an exhilarated yell Henry buried the axe in his skull. It was a killing blow but still Henry battered and hacked him, pulping bone and brain, muscles burning in release as the pumped and mutilated body twitched below him.

In the ecstasy of the moment Henry almost forgot about Terry, until a shadow flashed past him to the left and his head snapped up, a low snarl simmering in the back of his throat, and he was after her and on her in moments, his red hand a band of iron on her arm. She screamed, almond eyes bulging in their sockets, but he brought the axe down again before she could finish, bashing the blunt edge between her eyes. The satisfying sound of impact sent heat surging up Henry's spine—like an eggshell cracking, but meatier, more *substantial,* more *fulfilling* than that, or the *thunk* of firewood being split back on his father's farm in Dartmoor, and giddily he let her body drop beside Mike's and set about severing, smashing, and rearranging as he liked, undisturbed in the isolated dark.

By the time he finished, he was whistling along to the songs on the car radio— "My Prerogative" as he took clean clothes from his briefcase and changed, wiping himself and the axe down, each movement made with methodical precision borne of both his personality and past experience. When he was clean and sure he'd left no trace at the scene, he shut the axe back in his briefcase and headed back to town, whistling as he went.

Back at the motel, Henry was unlocking the door to his room when Paul passed him, hair rumpled and an empty ice bucket in hand. "Well, well, look who's finally getting in," he said, appraising Henry with a grin. "Do anything interesting tonight?"

Henry smoothed out his shirt. "Oh, you know, this and that."

"Hope you didn't tire yourself out too badly; we're leaving pretty early in the morning."

"You can rest easy, Mr. Bloch; I'll be ready. I'm no spring chicken, but you know what they say: You keep yourself active and you keep yourself young."

Paul gave a wave. "G'night, then."

"Good night, Mr. Bloch." Henry waved back as Paul headed away, then locked the door behind himself, tucked his briefcase under the bed with a final loving pat, and settled into bed and the sleep of the content.

They were up and on the road, Bobbi behind the wheel, by the time dawn turned the clouds pink, and by noon they'd crossed state lines. The convertible held out and Wine & Roses had their first show in New Mexico that night. It went better than the first show in Arizona had, and as Paul finished the last verse of "My Summer Girl" and the audience in the dive bar started clapping, Bobbi's eyes were shining and she was smiling, and Paul felt his heart swelling as he gazed across the small, creaking stage at her. A new song was writing itself in the back of his mind, and in the motel that night Bobbi helped him finish it, in between a few furious rounds in bed and against the wall, and while they were so occupied Henry and his axe were out on the town making their own grand entrance into the Land of Enchantment, a truck-stop hooker and her john their captive audience.

The next morning, breakfast and then back on the road, and the cycle continued through several small towns strung together with stretches of highway, a blur of gas stations and sandstone formations, shows and sightseeing, for a few more days, until Henry announced that they'd been more than kind in taking him as far as they had, but it was time for them to part ways.

"Are you sure?" Bobbi asked in the parking lot of the motel where they were all staying. The concern on her face seemed real; Henry felt a brief tug of affection for her, and his bright eyes crinkled at the corners as he smiled back.

"Quite sure, Miss Kinnear," he replied, a warm breeze ruffling his white hair. "I've imposed upon you for long enough. Enjoy the rest of your trip, and I wish you all the success in the world with your music."

Bobbi made a small noise and then impulsively threw her arms around Henry; for a moment she was afraid she'd been too forceful, that she'd bowl him over, but he stayed steady and hugged her back with surprising strength. The thought slid from her mind, though, as she said, "I'm gonna miss you, Henry."

He chuckled. "As I'll miss the both of you."

"You won't mind if I don't hug you, will you?" Paul asked half-jokingly, with a small grin.

Henry laughed again and stuck out a hand for Paul to shake instead. "Not at all, Mr. Bloch."

"Take care of yourself," Paul said, shaking it. "There's a lot of nuts out there."

Henry grinned broadly, hefting his briefcase. "Oh, don't worry about me," he assured the couple. "I'll be just fine."

"You know, I really am going to miss him," Bobbi told Paul later as they walked through town, sidewalk simmering under their shoes. "He's like a hipper, British version of my grandpa."

"Maybe you should take him with you to visit your mom, then, instead of me," Paul said.

Bobbi laughed, bumping him with her hip. "Oh, so we're back to that now?"

"I'm just *saying...*" Paul held his hands up in self-defense.

"Come on, admit it. You liked him, too. It's okay, I won't tell anyone."

"By the end he *was* growing on me a bit," Paul admitted, kicking a pebble across the cracked pavement. "Any old dude who can sing along to 'Bohemian Rhapsody' like that earns some points in my book." Bobbi nodded her agreement. "Plus, I have to say, at least it gave us a better story to tell than that time we took a wrong turn near Gila Bend."

"You mean when you went behind some rocks to piss 'cause we couldn't find a rest stop and you ended up accidentally pissing on a lizard, who took it the wrong way and started chasing you?"

"While you stood there laughing and filming my suffering, you sadistic bitch. Do me a favor and don't lead with that story when we get to your mom's, okay? Not exactly my proudest moment. *Anyway,*" Paul pressed on. "As I was saying. There might even be a song in the last few days, what do you think? 'The Ballad of Henry Talbot.'" Paul strummed an imaginary guitar and slipped into a Springsteenesque grumble. *"We were drivin' through the desert, my woman and I,/when we came across this old hitchhiking guy/he kinda talked like Magneto, and he raised bunnies, and he asked us for a riiiide..."*

Bobbi shook her head fondly. "You absolute doof." She slipped her arm through his. "C'mon, let's get something to eat."

Paul sighed. "I'm really gonna miss that senior discount of his, I know that."

"The depth of your compassion astounds me."

"What? Man's gotta eat."

"Woman, too." Bobbi pushed open the diner door and they entered, still bantering back and forth.

Meanwhile, their former companion set out later that afternoon to search for another ride. Henry knew it would take some time, and was proved right, but he was nothing if not patient; a good hunter had to be. He approached only those he judged most likely to accept his offer, aware of how strange it sounded in this day and age—strange, yes, but ultimately innocent, which was why, instead of locking their car doors and calling the cops to report some white-haired nut roaming the streets as they sped away like bats out of hell, most people who declined him did so politely, leaving him no problem with them.

Most people.

"Fuck off, old man," one young man said late in the day, flicking his cigarette to the ground and scraping it under his bootheel, scattering a few last sparks in the dirt. His hair brushed his shoulders; he wore a sneer-smile that, like the rest of his style, had been exquisitely lifted from movies that were new before his father first fucked his mother. He exhaled a plume of smoke in Henry's direction and draped his left arm around his giggling girlfriend, whose laugh was as shrill as her colorful clothes. "Why should we take you anywhere?"

"Oh, I didn't mean to imply you had to," Henry replied evenly, more pleasantly than his instincts were whispering he should. "I only asked, that's all."

"'Oh, I didn't mean to imply you had to.'" The boy's handsome features twisted as he mocked

Henry's voice. "What kinda moron runs around asking strangers for a ride, anyway? Whatsa matter, Pops, tryin' to run away before the kids dump you in a home or something?"

The girl, who Henry'd overheard her stereotype of a boyfriend call Maria earlier, nudged him with her leg even as she snickered. "C'mon, Johnny, let's go. I'm bored."

A third young man, in the car's backseat, leaned over. "Yeah, Johnny, let's go already."

"I'm coming, fucknuts. Keep your pants on," Johnny replied charmingly, slinging his body into the driver's seat while Maria let herself in beside him. But Johnny wasn't completely heartless, apparently; as the engine roared to life he looked up at Henry, sunglasses glinting, and delivered some advice: "You know, you oughta be more careful, old man, about picking on people, especially on the road. You never know who the fuck you're getting in the car with."

"Sage advice," Henry said solemnly. "Thank you, young man."

The crew in the car had one more parting gift for him, which flashed in the sun and exploded in glittering brown shrapnel a foot or so from him: an empty beer bottle, tossed from the rear of the car as they sped away. At the sound of impact something exploded in Henry's mind, too, a hot red center that sprayed out pieces every bit as jagged as the brown glass gleaming in the dirt around his feet; they embedded in his brain, throbbed there, and a haze settled over him that left no room for anything else, only one thought, only one thing to do.

Henry watched the car weave back to town, and he smiled.

He followed, and watched, and when night fell Henry went to the window of the ground-floor apartment he'd seen the trio enter but not leave, his shadow rippling black across the glass. Not only was the window unlocked, but it was open, and Henry suppressed a chuckle as he silently popped the screen free and boosted himself onto the sill and into the dark room. They were just *begging* for it, weren't they? Not that he minded the ease of it; a little help here and there was always appreciated.

He set his briefcase down on the cluttered coffee table; moonlight glinted on the axe blade as he drew it forth, reflecting in his eyes as he set off down the hall.

All three were asleep when Henry found them, and skilled as he was at his work, none of them ever stirred: not Johnny, sprawled and snoring in the master bedroom, before Henry brought the axe down on his skull; not Maria, who murmured in her sleep as her boyfriend's brains were bashed in inches from her and Henry raised the axe again, spraying hot scarlet drops across the ceiling on the upswing; not the third friend, the bottle-tosser, who lay drunkenly insensate in a messy twin bed in the guest room, one hand still wrapped around the neck of another bottle and the other limp around his dick. Part of Henry missed the screams, the terror, wished he could have had each one watch their friends die knowing they were next; times like those were more satisfying than any fuck he'd ever had. But while those kinds of kills were suited to more isolated settings, trying it in a populated place like this was an amateur mistake, and he was nothing if not professional.

It was also why he waited until they were all dead to mutilate, to ravage and rearrange limbs, heads, torsos, so he could take his time without worrying about one of his playthings escaping before their turn and alerting someone to his presence, and why he never took trophies of any kind, no matter how tempting the odd earring—or the delicate ear it dangled from—could be. If you kept trophies, you might as well walk into the nearest police station and confess on the spot, Henry believed, and so he left everything behind—in a different place than it originally was, maybe, but still *there.*

He changed clothes and cleaned the matted clumps of blood and hair from the axe in the apartment before he packed the axe back up and let himself out the window, discreetly replacing the screen and slipping away unnoticed. A dog barked nearby and someone hushed it harshly; as Henry started back to the motel, he noticed a snatch of Maria's brown hair clinging to his sleeve and flicked it idly down into the dust. Things had gone well tonight; there was just one disappointment dampening Henry's spirits.

He still needed a ride.

"Try fitting it the other way," Bobbi suggested, watching Paul attempt to wedge his guitar case into the car the next morning.

"*What* other way?" Paul demanded. "This *is* the other way."

"Well, we've come this far, so it has to fit *somehow,*" Bobbi snapped, the dull drums of a young hangover pounding at her temples.

"Would you like some help?" a voice asked behind them, mild, British, familiar.

Bobbi spun on her heel, crushing gravel to dust under her boot. "Henry!" she exclaimed, while Paul leaned, arms folded and legs crossed, against the convertible, sweat cooling on his skin. "What're you doing here? I thought you were leaving yesterday."

"I had hoped to," Henry said with a rueful smile, coming closer, "but alas, my new ride fell through."

"Oh, that's too bad." Bobbi frowned.

"Yeah, too bad," Paul echoed without enthusiasm, knowing what was coming next.

"Why don't you ride with us again?" Bobbi suggested, and Paul rolled his eyes behind his sunglasses. *Got it in one, Bloch.*

"Oh, no. I couldn't—" Henry began.

"But we don't mind, really." Bobbi looked at her boyfriend. "Do we, Paul?"

Paul's smile stretched, his cheeks fit to split. "Mind? No, why would we mind?" He straightened up and started shoving the guitar case with renewed vigor. "The more the merrier, right?"

It didn't take much more of Bobbi's cajoling before Henry gave in. When the old man went to grab his bags from his room, Paul passed by Bobbi and muttered, "You're really going for that merit badge, aren't you, Girl Scout?"

"I thought you said you liked him a bit."

"Yeah, once he left."

"Don't worry, Mr. Grumpy Gills." Bobbi tugged lightly on Paul's belt loop. "I'll make it up to you, I promise." Paul's expression flickered; Bobbi grinned. "That lifted your spirits, huh?"

Paul stole a kiss before Henry returned. "Among other things."

With Henry's help they got everything packed back up and were on the road again before long: it felt, Paul thought, almost as if they'd never been apart, and he wasn't sure how he felt about that. They'd almost been free, after all.

But hey, Paul stewed, remembering Bobbi's words the night Henry'd first approached them. *What can it hurt?*

The Saguaro Inn was a dilapidated faux-adobe structure somewhere outside Grants, with a pink neon cactus waving from the sign and the name of the place in a rainbow array of letters flickering next to it. Dark red curtains covered the windows, and matching paint peeled on the doors; the parking lot was empty aside from the convertible, which seemed to sigh in relief when Paul finally turned the engine off. As far as he knew, Bette Davis had never been there, but she'd summed it up perfectly in one line: "What a dump!"

But it was cheap and they'd been driving almost all day, and it wasn't the worst place they'd stayed this trip, if Paul was being honest, so they checked in. "Pretty quiet around here, isn't it?" Bobbi said to the manager, a short, balding, fretful man in a red vest who'd appeared ready to dance a hornpipe when they'd rung the bell at the front desk and announced they wanted two rooms.

"It usually is," the manager, whose name plate on the desk said Chet, replied. "We're a bit too far off the highway to get much traffic—you guys are the only guests at the moment." He thrust their room keys at them before they could change their minds. "Enjoy your stay!"

That night Wine & Roses played in town, and afterward Paul and Bobbi stopped for drinks in a bar across the street. Bobbi wrapped her long legs around her barstool and her lips around the neck of a bottle while Paul uploaded video from their show, resting his phone on the dark gleaming wood of the bar when he finished.

"Baby, I've been thinking," Bobbi said, drumming her fingertips against her bottle.

"About turning around once we hit Nebraska?"

"You're not getting out of it," she informed him. "But no, not that. What do you think, once we get back to our apartment, about getting a pet?"

"Hmm, let me guess." Paul adopted a look of mock-thought. "You wouldn't mean a bunny, would you?"

"Please." Bobbi draped herself over him dramatically, her hair falling over them both, both of them laughing. "Paul, you know I love them—"

"Yeah, you're a freak for a fluffy tail, I get it. Restrain yourself, woman."

She sat up, smoothing her hair back. "I'm pretty sure we can handle it."

"Do I get time to consider this, or have you already picked out a name?"

"Consider it while I go to the bathroom." Bobbi slid off her stool and kissed his cheek. "And I was thinking Hopalong Cassidy."

Mid-groan, Paul's gaze happened to land on the TV above the bar, tuned on mute to a local news station, and when he saw the headline onscreen he cut off abruptly and reached for Bobbi's arm, gripping it before she could go by. "Jesus, it was just a suggestion." Bobbi looked down in confusion. "What's wrong with you?"

"Bobbi, look at this." Paul glanced at the bartender. "Hey, can you turn this up?"

He did, and Bobbi sank slowly back down onto her stool, Paul's hand loosening slightly but lingering on her arm as together they looked up at the news: ARIZONA AXEMAN ACROSS STATE LINES?

"—denying the possibility that these slayings are the work of a copycat killer," the disturbingly tan newscaster was saying, "which, if true, would bring the total number of victims to fifteen in the past three months. Authorities in Arizona and New Mexico are creating a joint task force in order to—"

Disturbing news enough, but then a list of murder locations appeared onscreen, and as name after name popped up a cold lump grew in Paul's stomach. "Bobbi?" he said in a strangled voice. "Do those places look familiar at all?"

"It's a coincidence," Bobbi said. "It *has* to be."

"Pretty fucking big coincidence," Paul said. "It's everywhere we've been."

And it was; after the sixth victim each murder occurred where the couple had visited, or within a few miles. They'd noticed the closeness of a few, at first, but now that the list was longer and presented so starkly, it was impossible to dismiss or ignore. The timeline, the locations—all, impossibly, matched, and Bobbi locked eyes with Paul, horrified.

"I didn't do it!" she said.

"Well, neither did I!" Paul exclaimed.

The thought hit them both at once. *"No,"* Bobbi said with enough force to break a bone. "No, I absolutely will not believe that."

But Paul looked back at the list, scanning for the spot where their and the killer's paths first converged, and when he found it the cold lump lodged in his stomach became an abyss, yawning, gnawing, heavy and dark. *"Paul!"* Bobbi hissed, swatting his arm. "You can't honestly tell me you think it's possible that Henry is running around *axeing* people to death! I know you're not thrilled to have him along, but that's a pretty extreme conclusion to jump to, don't you think?"

Paul pointed. "That's where we picked him up, Bobbi, and ever since then all the Axeman's murders correspond to places we've been. *Exactly."*

"He's an *old man!"*

"Some serial killers manage to get old. Law of averages, right?"

"Paul," Bobbi repeated, dismayed. "Are you even *listening* to yourself? My fucking God, I can't even—this is *insane!* How do you—what are you gonna do? Go to the police and say 'Excuse me, officer, but I think the elderly professor my girlfriend and I have been road-tripping with is in actuality an axe-wielding maniac'?"

Put so baldly, it sounded even worse than it had in his head, but it was too large a coincidence for Paul to be comfortable with. He didn't want to think he and Bobbi had been seeing scenic America with a sixty-something serial killer chipping in for gas and food, but what were the odds the Axeman had started following their itinerary by pure accident? "No, we can't go to the cops with something like that," Paul said, and Bobbi relaxed until he tossed money on the bar to cover their tab and continued, "But we have to do something."

"What if you're wrong?" Bobbi demanded, following him to the bar door.

He looked back at her. "What if I'm right?"

"I can't believe we're doing this," Bobbi hissed as, after a near-silent and strained ride back from the bar and a couple hours spent waiting in their room for Henry to leave his, she stood keeping watch while Paul tested Henry's door. Unlocked it swung open with a squeal of unoiled hinges, and Paul glanced at Bobbi, eyebrows arching. "What kind of crazed killer leaves his door unlocked when he goes out for the night?" she asked.

Paul shrugged. "Maybe he forgets where he left his axe sometimes, too," he said, far more blasé than he felt, his stomach in knots and a fist clenched hard around his skipping heart. "Look, you can wait out here if you want, and I'll run out screaming if I find any severed heads in the minibar."

"No, I'll come in with you," Bobbi said, her reluctance palpable as she followed Paul and shut the door behind them.

The room was dark, shades drawn, the furniture an assortment of lumps and humps in the shadows; Paul flicked the light on, scattering a flock of shadows and casting theirs warped and towering on the cracked, dusty-pink walls.

The place was orderly: tweed jacket draped over the back of a chair, suitcases stacked in front of the dresser, a tattered paperback copy of *Ivanhoe* on the bedside table beside an empty water glass. Something else was there as well, a framed photo Bobbi picked up and showed Paul accusingly.

"He sleeps with a picture of his *rabbits* next to him, Paul. This is the man you think is Jack the friggin' Ripper." She pointed at him as he opened his mouth. "And if you say Hitler loved his dog I'll hit you."

"You helping me look or not?"

She helped, but kept up a constant commentary on how horrible she felt and how awful what they were doing was; on Paul's part, he would feel bad only if he was proven wrong, which at first it seemed he would be. They worked quickly, unsure when Henry would return, and it took only a few minutes to turn up nothing incriminating among Henry's things.

"Can we go now?" Bobbi asked, stacking one suitcase carefully back atop another.

Paul sat back on his haunches as thunder rumbled in the distance, as it had done intermittently all evening. Something was nagging at him, and keen as he was to get going, he couldn't leave before he figured out what. *Something's missing....*

It hit him a moment later. "His briefcase," Paul said, remembering how close Henry always kept it, from the first time Paul had seen him at the Wine & Roses show back in Arizona. "Where's his briefcase at?"

"Maybe he took it with him," Bobbi suggested, shifting her weight from foot to foot.

"Maybe." Seized by sudden, desperate inspiration, Paul ducked down and looked under the bed. *Bingo,* he thought, sliding it out. "Or maybe he didn't."

"So what? Paul, this is so fucked up, I don't know why we're even doing this," Bobbi said. "We're ransacking the room of a perfectly normal old man, and I think we should just *go* before he—"

Paul got the briefcase open, and the couple stared at the contents.

Nothing but an axe.

"Oh, yeah," Paul managed hoarsely. "That's perfectly normal."

Bobbi's ragged gasp was muffled by the hand she clapped over her mouth, her eyes as wide as those of someone being strangled. The axe, sharp enough to split hairs, nestled motionless in the briefcase, but both of them stared at it like it would rear up and strike any moment—but no, it wouldn't, Paul thought through the shock that was numbing his limbs and making them tingle, muffling his mind like cotton wool. A weapon wasn't deadly on its own; it needed a hand to wield it, someone to pick it up and aim it....

And that person's been riding in our backseat for the past two weeks OH JESUS CHRIST—

"We have to go to the cops," Bobbi whispered, though she didn't move, rooted rigid by the revelation. "Paul, we have to go to the c—"

A clattering crash cut her off and made both jump and look towards the door, which they'd been too occupied to notice opening. Henry stood there, looking as horrified at them as they were at him. Evidently, he hadn't headed out for the night as the couple'd assumed he had, but down the hall for ice; the bucket lay on the floor at his feet, ice cubes scattered on the nubbly carpet, slowly melting and soaking the ground around his loafers.

Henry broke the silence. "Well, this is unfortunate," he said, gazing mournfully at the tableaux before him, and as he walked further into the room Paul scrambled to his feet in front of Bobbi, but all the axeman did was continue, "Very unfortunate, indeed. You see, I *had* intended to let you both live. I've grown rather fond of you two in our time together. But then I go to get a bucket of ice, and stay for a bit to talk with Chet, the manager, about some of the local attractions, and what do I find awaiting me on my return? My new friends, going through my belongings." He shook his head. "I'm sorry it's come to this. I had expected a happier ending for all of us."

The worst thing, the most deranged, psychotic part of this, Paul thought, heart pounding sickeningly fast, was that Henry visibly, genuinely meant what he was saying. "Sorry that doesn't make us feel better," Paul croaked, gaze darting between the briefcase and the slowly-advancing axe murderer.

Henry shrugged. "Understandable. Just as I hope you understand what I have to do now isn't personal, but a matter of self-preservation."

His voice had never lost its cultured precision, making it doubly startling when, as a bolt of heat lightning lit the room with a stuttering flare, he lunged for the briefcase on the floor. Bobbi, though, kicked at it with all the force she could manage, knocking it away from him with the axe tumbling out to the floor.

"Paul, run!" she said, as Henry uttered a frustrated growl and scrambled after his weapon, and as the couple bolted, his hand clutched its handle; Paul and Bobbi had barely made it out of the room before he was on their heels, and Bobbi felt a rush of air far too close behind her as he swung, burying the blade inches-deep in the hall wall, plaster dust spraying as he yanked it free to swing again.

The car keys and cell phones were in their room, and Paul realized too late that in their panic they'd gone the wrong way down the hall; Henry was in their way, and Paul doubted he'd let them pass, even if they asked politely.

Bobbi had realized it too. "The manager," she panted; Paul nodded, and as they burst around the corner the axe-blade followed them, taking a chunk from the wall just above Paul's left shoulder. He turned and shoved hard, sending Henry stumbling back, off-balance, and Bobbi and Paul rushed on. "He seemed so *nice!*" Bobbi wailed.

"Really, Bobbi?" Paul snapped. *"Now?"*

The manager found them before they found him, drawn by the commotion. "What the hell's going on?" Chet demanded, a fine sheen of sweat shining on his head beneath the urine-yellow hall light, looking at them in bewilderment as they began babbling at once, pointing and pulling at his arms and urging him away. *"Axeman?"* Chet said, catching a word or two, eyebrows flying up his forehead. "What are you talking about; what's going on?"

"We have to go," Bobbi said. "Right now, come on."

"I don't understand—"

"We'll explain later." Paul pulled Chet's arm. "If we make it. *Come on.*"

But Chet froze, his body jerking, eyes bulging briefly, and Paul and Bobbi stared in stunned, dumb confusion as something hot, slick, and red sprayed out; some landed on Bobbi's lips, salty and copper. A shadow loomed behind Chet and his body jumped jerkily, puppet-like, and crumpled facedown to the floor; his skull was split like an overripe fruit, and clots of blood and brains sprayed to stain the front of Paul's black T-shirt, horribly warm and wet.

Henry stood there, gore-splattered, axe dripping as he lifted it, held it across his chest. "This was avoidable," he said, shoving the corpse with his foot.

"All of this was. But now…" He shook his head and stepped over the cleft Chet. "But now."

Paul and Bobbi bolted, Henry hard on their heels. At one point Paul whirled around again, struggling with Henry for the axe; a moment later the blade flashed and Paul cried out as the skin of his left forearm split, pain burning down to the bone as blood welled in the gash. As it ran it slickened Paul's grip and Henry wrenched his weapon free, and…

…and pain and fear blurred the next few moments, adrenaline forcing him forward, and suddenly he was outside and Bobbi wasn't by his side anymore and he couldn't see Henry, and before he could stop himself Paul called out "Bobbi!" past his heart in his throat, a rumble of thunder half-drowning his howl out. But if Bobbi could hear him, so could…

"Fuck," Paul muttered, bloody arm pressed to his chest, and he ducked into the shadows as the Saguaro Inn sign spat mouthfuls of neon into the night. His nerves burned, sparks snaking through his skin, as he moved through the dark as quick and quiet as he could.

Oh God, Bobbi, where the fuck are *you?*

What if she was—

No.

A hot, dry wind. Heat lightning in the west.

Bobbi's scream.

"Bobbi!" Paul shouted.

Silence. Thunder.

Paul ran.

"Stop fighting, girl," Henry told Bobbi, one of his lips split and bleeding from a collision with her fist. "You're only making it harder."

He was a fucking tough old bugger, Bobbi had to give him that. Her chest heaved, battered body screaming at her as she lay semi-stunned on the ground, Henry standing over her. She'd managed to wrest the axe from his hands, only to have him knock it from hers; it lay just out of her reach now, her stretching fingers just short of the handle.

"Kind of the fucking point, asshole," she panted, jaw gritted and eyes glinting, and as Henry dropped to grab the axe Bobbi rolled onto her side and drove her elbow up to his chest, so hard she felt her shoulder wrench; Henry wheezed, face reddening beneath the blood streaks, and he and Bobbi grappled, struggling together on the ground. To the sound of thunder they rolled, and then Bobbi was atop him, and off, and the axe was in her hand, and it was, like Bobbi, covered in dirt and gore, Chet's blood, Paul's—

Paul, be alive motherfucker, you have to be alive

—and lightning lit the snarl on Henry's face as he started to his feet, and Bobbi's scream ripped through the desert as she swung the axe. The arc was clumsy, the axe unwieldy in her hand—horror movies made axe murder look so much easier than it was, she thought; she should complain—but the blow still sank home, catching Henry in the juncture of neck and left shoulder.

"Bobbi," he said, looking dumbstruck, and then nothing more as Bobbi yanked the blade free and swung again, catching him with the blunt side square in the skull. As it caved in he collapsed, a last gasp of breath puffing past his parted lips as he slumped to dirt and lay still.

A moment later she heard rapid footsteps running up behind and whirled, her blood still pumping hot in her veins. But it was Paul, and relief surged through her at the sight of him hurt but alive, emotion mirrored on his face when he saw it was her standing there.

And then the full scene hit him—Bobbi holding the axe, Henry's corpse in the dirt—everything crashed down on him at once, and Paul passed out.

Bobbi sat by Paul in the hospital while his gash was stitched up, and when the doctor left the room she rested her head on his shoulder, filthy and exhausted, cement-heavy eyelids sinking shut; Paul laced his fingers through hers and squeezed her hand tight, Bobbi returning the gesture and both their hands still trembling slightly.

"No I-told-you-sos about how you thought picking up an elderly hitchhiker was a bad idea from the start?" Bobbi asked.

Paul chuckled. "I'll wait until after the police take our statements. But Bobbi?"

"Yeah?"

"Once we get back to California, let's not leave the apartment for a while, okay?"

"More than okay." Bobbi nestled close to Paul, and he nuzzled the top of her head with his chin, soaking up the feel of everything, from her body against his to each breath in his lungs. He was still just enough in shock, and he suspected Bobbi was, too, that everything seemed unreal, a nightmare straight out of some late-night movie he'd caught on cable while only half-awake. When the sensation wore off, he'd go batshit crazy, no doubt; until then, he'd enjoy simply having survived.

And maybe one other thing, too. "Bobbi," he said; she loosed a wordless murmur. "I think something good might come from this whole experience."

Bobbi raised her head, stared at him in disbelief. "You're actually trying to find a bright side to this?"

"Yeah." Paul grinned. "After narrowly escaping brutal death and dismemberment at the hands of an axe-wielding psychopath, visiting your mother suddenly doesn't seem so bad."

The Last VCR Made in Hell
James Gardner

The last VCR made in hell spat its cursed self onto the Earth in the mid 80s, hieroglyphics in Enochian, painted across its top with the blood of true virgins etched into the metal with a soldering iron. It smelled of boiled blood, which some found unpleasant and others considered delightful. This allowed the VCR to weed out those who would utterly waste its power and leave it starving.

Its particular appetites led the VCR to be responsible for over 100 disappearances throughout the late 80's. It fed well during the 90's, thanks to the Blockbusters, The Hollywood Videos, but these video stores soon withered away, leaving hollowed-out storefronts in strip malls. The VCR did not experience fear when VHS tapes began to fill first discount bins then landfills. It could not know fear; however, it did know patience, infinite patience. It returned to life when two budding serial killers discovered it in a college AV room.

When it woke after its long slumber, it appeared as scream queen Alana Anderson, today a grandmother doing substance abuse counseling in LA after many years of addiction. "If you're looking at me," she cooed, a fresh-faced cheerleader coed bombshell. Looking down at herself briefly before facing the camera, winking, "then I hope that you're also listening, because you have the greatest innovation in home entertainment right at your fingertips."

* * * *

Inside this apartment, on the second floor, Albie stared transfixed at a TV screen. He was breathing heavily, drawing nearer to the screen while snorting a torrent of air. Real or imagined, Albie *was* smelling the scene before him: the pine needles on which the girl lay, the motor oil and visceral cologne of Mr. Fixit, even the girl's perfume of flowers, sweat, and fear. And there was the girl, the girl with the purple hair, the freckle-dusted nose, the wide eyes that looked not at her attacker, not in fact at anything. Albie wished the girl didn't look so vapid. He had to work his hand a little faster to get his manhood back to full salute.

The girl had said she wanted to make documentary films about fracking, or backpack through South America. Watching horror movies wasn't enough to get her home, they both knew; Eric had to promise to show her the home movies of his fictitious uncle's hike across the Andes. Her breasts bared, Albie saw that one nipple was pierced. And she was incredibly pale, too pale to have ever hiked, pale enough that the blood on her forehead looked shiny, artificial. It shone luminously in the moonlight of this movie forest, even as her body lurched with every pelvic thrust of her attacker.

The camera panned upward to get the attacker in frame. Mr. Fixit's broad back stretched his coveralls tight, so tight that Albie could see the back muscles flex as they pistoned Fixit's hips forward. The camera panned around and down to his massive hands swallowing the girl's tiny wrists as he held her down. His long, lank hair hung like Spanish moss in the corner of the frame as he slowed his tempo for just a moment, then sped up again, jackhammering her hips.

Albie could feel himself not only get back to full sail but he could even feel the electric charge building. He looked in her eyes for signs that she knew this wasn't just a movie she was trapped in. If she'd watched *Fixit Five*, which Albie thought of as an underrated sequel, she would have known that Mr. Fixit never raped his victims, made his victims into gory piles of meat approaching modern art, sure, but he never raped them.

Albie was watching what he called "the doubling effect." One minute, it was the girl his roommate Eric had met in that coffee house, purple hair and freckled skin. Then it was a different woman, one with tanner skin, bigger tits, and a face Eric called Hollywood pretty. Albie watched the two night-and-day faces fight for dominance in his mind, even as they both wore the same cow-eyed, vapid expression. And then Mr. Fixit brought out a large wrench the size of a grown man's forearm. Raised high, it was silhouetted in Movieworld's bright and full moon. Albie heard the leonine roar of Fixit cumming then saw the wrench crash down, again and again, until those two faces became no face, yet another piece of modern art. On the third or fourth strike, Albie could no longer contain himself, the bottle of lightning in his hands finally uncorked. His roar was more of a whimper as the orgasm was rung from his frail body.

"Fuck," Albie said. "Fuck me. Fuck." He was doubled over, breathing heavily, empty from brainpan to ball sack. Then Albie heard the electronic chirping of his phone's alarm. As his phone played John Carpenter's *Halloween* theme on helium, Albie tapped the TV screen.

"You have to get out, Eric," he yelled at/into the TV. The TV was a flat screen, but a sturdy flat screen the size of an oak door, so Albie smacked the screen until his hand stung, calling Eric's name. Then Albie remembered the key phrase: "Eric, you have a rugby game tomorrow."

Mr. Fixit suddenly turned toward the screen. The camera, for some strange reason, zoomed in on the facial deformity, the burned left side of his face, the milky white of his eye, the lips melted and reset into a permanent sneer.

"You have a rugby game tomorrow, Eric."

Mr. Fixit stood up, and the camera panned upward to show his height, a skyscraper of flesh in stained, dirty coveralls he didn't even bother to button back up (no full-frontal male nudity in the Fixit movies until now). The camera zoomed closer to Fixit's wrench to show off its new paintjob of blood and brain matter. Then the wrench was out of frame and coming at the screen was Fixit's empty hand, shooting toward Albie. Albie recoiled as the screen became static. Tripping over his feet and falling backward on his ass, Albie watched the screen of the television stretch like latex as Fixit's hand pushed through, the five fingers forming five little tents in the latex-like surface.

Soon, that hand was followed by a long, apelike arm. The screen became more translucent, more like the thinnest placenta, as the head came through, then the shoulders. Mr. Fixit's upper body forced its way out of the screen like he was literally being born into this world. Albie watched, transfixed, despite having seen this more that he'd seen *Kill All Teenagers*. Fixit's head was coming closer to the floor, and Albie's gaze followed it, which made him notice his jizz on the floor.

"Shit," he breathed and snatched the roll of paper towels from the table. He was racing against time, wiping up the mess even as most of a man's body was now through the screen and drooping just inches above the hardwood floor.

Then the distended screen simply split open. There was no liquid spilling out, only a well-muscled arm, but not the Neanderthal arm of Mr. Fixit. The head that pushed through had a mop of black hair, but it wasn't Fixit's lank, greasy tresses. The face of the young man emerging through the torn screen was handsome, even beautiful, even as it grunted with the effort of pulling the rest of his body through. Finally, a college-aged boy rolled onto the floor. The screen withdrew, becoming the simple glass screen demanded by the real world's physics.

"Eric," Albie said simply, bending down to check on his best friend. Eric rolled into a sitting position, his eyes blinking, adjusting to the sudden brightness of their apartment. Eric's eyes found his roommate's.

"I'm not in your jizz again, am I?" he asked. Albie quickly shook his head no.

* * * *

"This trip into movies?" Alana had explained. "It's like sex, always better with a partner, but unlike sex, it's safer and way less chance of getting AIDS."

"As the owner, getting in's the easy part. It's getting out that can be the hassle, especially if you've gotten all the way into character. That's why it's better to have a partner," she had said, and then licked her lips.

"And I don't mind sharing."

* * * *

Eric pushed himself onto his feet in a graceful way that Albie could never manage. Such athletic feats from Eric, a boy who was shorter than Albie but packed tightly with muscle, came as easily as walking. Albie, on the other hand, was lucky to walk a straight line without tripping over his feet.

On his two feet again, Eric wobbled as though the floor beneath him was moving. Albie sprang into action, was behind his friend before he could fall backward. "You okay, Eric?" Eric stayed on his feet. Albie held up two fingers in front of his face. "How many fingers am I holding up?"

Eric pushed his hand away. "I'm all right," he said shortly. "It's just not easy going from seven feet tall to five ten."

Five-eight, Albie corrected silently.

Eric brushed himself off but there was no need. Wearing whatever skin you choose, whatever person you become, covers you completely, body and soul. The Polo shirt and jeans he wore when he entered were just as clean as when he entered.

"Did you see me in there?" Eric said excitedly. "Man, I tore a door off its fucking hinges. Can you believe that shit?"

"Looked like an old door," Albie muttered matter-of-factly, but Eric didn't take the apparent age of the door as a matter of fact. Albie could see a shadow cross Eric's features. He still smiled but the lips drew back from the teeth, almost bared into a snarl. Albie remembered the rumors about how those teeth had taken off a kid's ear in a bar fight.

"I'm sorry, Albie. Were you there?" Eric asked calmly, almost serenely. Albie was brushing his long hair off his ears, suddenly very protective of them. "Did you actually get a chance to wear Fixit's skin? Or Freddy's? What about Jason's? Or Candyman's? Was I not there during all the times you went in and now you're just the fucking expert on Movieworld?"

Albie stayed quiet. Eric had hit him once, cupping him in the ear so hard that Albie was brought to a knee. Eric had to reach up to hit him and Albie still couldn't stop the blow. He never remembered what the initial disagreement was, but the incident was enough to show Albie that Eric could be just as violent towards him.

"I haven't, Eric." Albie muttered this while looking at the blue TV screen. "I haven't."

The teeth no longer grinding or bared, Eric's smile was once again the charming grin that disarmed many young women and led them to their demise within a medium that was being phased out by the time they were born. "That's right you haven't, pard. But that's all going to change next weekend. You pumped?" He slugged Albie's arm, his knuckle stabbing into a place just underneath the underdeveloped bicep, a bruise being born.

"I-I'm pumped," He stammered, wanting to be in his bedroom, alone. Eric moved Albie's chin so that they were looking eye to eye.

"Listen, you were the one that found the VCR. If anyone deserves to enjoy it, Albie, it's you. And I guarantee you haven't lived until you snapped a girl in half as Jason or appeared like magic behind a bitch and use the Harvester's sickle to cut one in two. In that movie world," Eric said, slapping Albie's neck, "we're the fucking heroes."

The thought of actually getting into the VCR sent his internal butterflies fluttering. It wasn't about the fear of blood, or of death (in fact, the memory of watching Purple Hair's skull cave like a pumpkin near rotting got his cock stirring). Confident, bold, even cocky, Eric didn't really need to be anyone else. Albie, on the other hand, could see himself as Jason Voorhees dropping his machete or tripping while he slow walked toward his victim. Freddy Krueger, with Albie at the wheel, would stumble and fall on his own claws.

Eric threw an arm around Albie's shoulders and pulled him close. "Remember, Albie, the VCR chose us. Alana called our names. *Our* names. It brought us together, created this beautiful friendship. But I think it's time you stepped up, my man." Eric's tone was a big brother's. The arm around Albie's neck tightened. Then he said, "Now what say we watch me harvest some bitches?"

They didn't argue about it the rest of the night. Albie, in fact, wasn't too busy thinking about next weekend to enjoy Eric, as the Harvester, chase down a wannabe animator they'd picked up at a bar a month ago. He'd always be right behind her no matter where she went.

* * * *

"Who do you want to be?" Alana had asked. As she leaned into the camera, the camera was leaning in, as though both camera and star were ready to kiss each other. Her lips were glossy in a way that seemed unique to the '80s, shimmering like a freshly waxed cherry red Ferrari. "You want to be the hero? Save the day? Save democracy?" There was a roll of the eyes. "Or do you want to destroy it? Kill the hero. Not only kill the hero, but torture him until he begs for death? Do you want to date Meg Ryan? Or do you just want to stab her? Or fuck her 'til she's raw, then stab her?"

"Why be the boring old hero and save everyone else," she cooed, "when you can be the Big Bad and just take whatever you want?

* * * *

Just a few days before Halloween night, the Albright Theater downtown was showing a special screening of the *Satan's Toybox* series—the final movie. *Satan's Toybox: Playtime's Over* had the groan-inducing tagline of "This Toy Story is Quite Gory." The toys never stayed small but became actors in pasty white makeup and using whatever sharp instruments lying around (and there were usually a lot). One reviewer from *Fangoria* called the series "psychological torture for those with coulrophobia."

The Albright was all bright colors and giant marquee, a perfect house of worship if your religion was cinematic classics, but it was also nestled in a neighborhood that felt miles away from the coffee shops, microbreweries, and vegan eateries where hip twenty-somethings congregated. Barely a block away from the theater was a gas station with bars on the windows and clerks delivering change and cigarettes from inside a glass partition like they were zoo exhibits. The blocky houses surrounding these were pressed so tightly together someone could reach through a window to punch or even choke their neighbor should they dare to look in at them. Walking on the sidewalk in front of these houses, passersby would quicken their pace, as though the houses, or whatever evil intent lived behind their blackened windows, would pounce with predator quickness.

But the Albright was Eric and Albie's hunting ground. Eric looked around the room for prey, for pretty prey that needed to be told this, for prey that needed someone to pretend to listen and who'd nod at strategic intervals, for prey whose skin would be a canvas and whose twat would be a receptacle.

"Doesn't anybody go out in the sun anymore?" It was intermission and a contingent of Goths surrounded the snack bar. Two concession workers were running about, hands flitting like kung-fu experts, but instead of mantis and snake strikes, they were flinging buckets of popcorn and overflowing plastic cups of beer. Instead of snatching a pebble from the Master's hand, they snatched Debit cards and cash from pale fingers. The sheen of sweat on the worker's faces was as visible as the sheen of spilled beer on the counter. Others were gathered outside to suck the last bit of cancer from their cigarettes or get a brief hit of social media before going back inside.

"Let's find a cunt and give her skin some color. I'm thinking . . . red?" Eric smiled. Quite the comedian, that Eric, the proverbial kid in a candy store. Women of all shapes and sizes, all legs to all tits to all curves, were dressed in black, in jeans and dresses that hugged and even contorted figures, pushing them into exaggerated feminine proportions. Many of them dressed like the Ballerina, their faces covered in bone white powder, their lips smeared with black, but many of them gravitated toward a boyfriend's arm or a girlfriend's embrace. His finger tugged and stretched at the collar of Albie's borrowed *Candyman* t-shirt, which was already stretched by Eric's broader shoulders and neck.

"I think I see a group of gashes over there that might want a good time. Be right back." With a clap on Ablie's shoulder, Eric was soon sliding his way through the crowd, a shark following a blood scent. Albie looked for a corner to disappear into, but there was suddenly a voice to his right.

"Cool shirt. So you're into Mr. Fixit?"

Albie turned, expecting the speaker to be actually talking to someone else. Albie was then overcome with, while not exactly love at first sight, was definitely lust at first sight.

She was tall, almost as tall as Albie with the high heels she wore. But, like a Goya mural, there were many things on her body that drew the eye: the ink-black pageboy haircut, the cat's eye glasses, the black leather dress, the opera gloves covering slim fingers and forearms. There was also tattoos that called out for her attention, from the bat-winged skull taking flight over the mountains of her breasts to a Betty Page looking bombshell dressed as the Grim Reaper winking from the creamy skin of her right shoulder. His eyes wanted to look everywhere, so much so that he almost forgot to answer her question.

She had almost repeated it when Albie finally spoke in a pileup of words, one smashing into the other.

"Mr.-Mr. Fixit. Yeah, I love Mr. Fixit. He's one of my favorite horror heroes."

Her glossy black lips widened into a smile, a very pleasant one. "I know, and he's so underrated. Five movies, five of them and everybody always thinks of Freddy or Jason. It's a goddam crime." She held out her hand, palm down as befitting a woman wearing opera gloves. "Fiona, by the way."

Albie took her hand, wanted to hold it longer than a normal handshake allowed. "Albie," he said quietly. "Short for Albert."

"Albie? Haven't heard that name before. Cool name."

"No, it isn't." Albie cleared his throat, a little loudly for his tastes. "Fiona, though, Fiona, now Fiona is a good name."

"It-it must be." She laughed, appeared to be enjoying the conversation. Albie felt like a tightrope walker, alternating between dizzying exhilaration and mortal fear of fucking up.

He thought of WWED (What Would Eric Do?). Eric had studied and quizzed with him in a way that neither boy did for actual exams, and Eric's voice suddenly came to Albie. *Talk about what she likes. Pretend to listen.*

Albie, though, listened only to the first part and learned that Fiona wanted to be an actress, but would rather play a killer. "I mean, fuck running around and screaming like you're already dying. I want to be the girl that actually does the killing. Where's the fun in just running?" That led to conversation Albie had more natural footing on: how one should stalk a victim, learning their habits, how not to just slash wildly but to go for vital areas (his room had a stash of anatomy texts). Albie was thrilled that he didn't have to pretend to listen or worry about his strengths, or lack thereof, at lying. He could spend all evening watching her hands swirl and dart in the air like planes engaged in a dogfight when she talked. And when they weren't moving, they were touching Albie's hands, his forearms, and each touch made Albie's blood quicken.

Then Fiona's hand swept back and someone had shoved a package of Milk-Duds into it. Fiona stopped talking to look at the package. "Oh my Goddess, Mattie, you are a lifesaver," Fiona said, hooking a long fingernail underneath the box's flap.

"You should probably save it for the movie, Fi," said Mattie in a flat voice. Standing together, it was easy to see Fiona and the other girl as opposites: the new girl was short where Fiona was tall, what a kinder person would call rubinesque instead of statuesque. Her hair was the same midnight shade, but was curled to Shirley Temple proportions. Mattie was all-out cosplaying as the Ballerina, complete with black tutu and corset, clownish white makeup, and a painted grin that stretched around both sides of her face but never touched her actual lips. Her eyes looked hostilely at Albie from the charcoal pits of her sockets.

"Cool costume," Albie remarked, but Mattie simply rolled her eyes toward her friend, as though saying, "Really?" Albie though Mattie reminded him of Wednesday Addams after a series of electroshock sessions (he mentally decided to save that burn for later and only for his own enjoyment). All three were quiet and Albie could feel the crackling energy of his and Fiona's interaction go inert.

"Hey Albie," said Eric, appearing like a white knight, albeit maybe a cockblocking one, to defibrillate this conversation. He looked down at Mattie's cleavage as he asked, "Who are these fine ladies?"

Mattie then gave a ghost of a smile and Albie thought oddly about how, after hearing the Whos in Whoville sing, the Grinch's small heart grew three sizes that day. As Eric was checking out what was filling her corset, she was checking out the muscles stretching Albie's borrowed *Candyman* shirt.

People who were milling about were now moving toward the two sets of double doors, pouring into the theater. Fiona looked over and said, "Everybody's going back to their seats. We better get back." She had reached for Albie's hand, then seemed to realize what she was doing. "Where are you guys sitting? I mean we could all sit together, if that's okay. We could go for coffee or something after."

Albie blinked, unsure if he was simply dreaming this. "Really?"

"Yeah. I want to hear about what you think makes a good horror movie." Fiona asked, directing the question to Albie and not Eric. "You guys up for it?"

Albie could feel his own smile brewing, one sunny and sincere and totally incongruous with the black shirt and jeans he now wore. Eric was still engaged with Mattie in a ritual of mutual objectification, pelting each other with small talk that didn't distract from the view of the other, but Albie still practically shouted "We don't mind" before Eric could answer.

* * * *

"I'm a victim." Alana had talked like she was saying this from behind an AA podium. "But I don't mind, sweeties. I don't mind people lusting after me, don't mind them wanting to see me as life support for a cunt, or just a pair of shoulders to hold up these tits." She hefted her breasts beneath the nightgown. "I also don't mind them imagining me cut up, bleeding out, hanging in a butcher's shed." She closed her eyes and took a deep breath, as though she were settling into a warm bubble bath. "I don't mind because I know it's my purpose to die because in every movie I'm in, *every movie*, I'm a dumb bitch making stupid decisions."

She batted her thick, heavily-mascaraed eyelashes at the camera. "So you do whatever you want to me, hun. I deserve it. Just like the stupid bitches you'll bring home."

* * * *

They all headed back to the apartment with promises of good beer and a viewing of *Autograph*, Albie doing his best to not talk about the torture scenes, fearing he was one conversational tangent from Fiona being utterly horrified. Instead, on the drive over, Fiona and Albie talked about the greatest horror movie hero of all time (Albie loved the fact that she referred to them as "heroes," not "villains" or "monsters"). She also said those dumb movie victims that are always making stupid mistakes (going upstairs, splitting up, etc.) "deserved to get stabbed between their big, fake tits." If Albie wasn't sitting in the back seat of Eric's Corolla, he might have actually fallen at his sex-death goddess Fiona's feet.

The conversation between Mattie and Eric was less scintillating. An example of which is as follows:

MATTIE: You must work out a lot.

ERIC: I do. I run, try not to eat junk. I also play rugby.

MATTIE: Ever break any bones?

ERIC: On me or other guys?

MATTIE: Both.

ERIC: I break more of theirs.

MATTIE: Good, I guess.

Eric tended to hunt for more straight-laced victims and it was showing. Mattie's voice was still a monotone with slightly more life than a robocaller. Albie could already hear Eric's voice, saying how Albie would owe him for "falling on a grenade to get that tall drink of snatch into our place," even though Albie had fallen on more than a few. Thank whatever saint or demon that watched over serial killers that Eric was a tit man.

"I just know that if I wanted to kill someone," she was telling him, "a whole bunch of someones, I'd make sure I wouldn't get caught. No bragging to the police like BTK, no trophies like Gein had that'd be all over the living room. Freddy Krueger, I mean, could at least make someone look like they died in their sleep."

Once again that image of the Grinch's heart growing three sizes came to Albie, but now it applied to him. He didn't think of Fiona's alabaster skin stained red, her skin splitting around and through the artwork that adorned it. Albie was thinking that she could be, dared to hope would be, a muse worthy of Edgar Allan Poe. His Fiona, his Ligea.

Upon entering the apartment, Albie announced that they should "make themselves at home" and Eric looked pleasantly surprised, almost proud. The two girls did as Albie instructed, though with differing levels of enthusiasm. Mattie quietly wiped her fingers across the shelves as though checking for dust (and whatever she found, she wiped onto her tutu), while Fiona looked more like she was in a museum, flitting from one horror movie poster to the next, pouring over his bookshelf full of film textbooks and dog-eared horror paperbacks Albie procured from dusty bookstore bins and yard sales.

In the entertainment center sat the boys' two forms of entertainment: a DVD/Blu-Ray player as well as the VCR from hell, both huddled in their shared shelf, which hid the VCR's demonic etchings.

"Cool place," Fiona said. She was flipping through Albie's copy of *Encyclopedia of Serial Killers*. "I have this book at home." She sat down on Eric's weight bench and began to read. Albie could have stared at her crossed legs for hours, if only to commit them perfectly to memory.

Mattie simply plopped down on the couch. Crossing her legs, she smoothed her ruffles and looked at the couch as though sitting on it with such a short skirt wasn't such a hot idea. Eric held the necks of four beer bottles between his fingers. "Albie buddy, how about you get the movie ready?" Eric pointed at the bookshelf filled to almost bursting with VHS tapes. "It might take him a while to find it."

Albie said quickly before his resolve withered. "Eric, can I see you in the bedroom for a second?"

"You guys have two girls out here, and you're going to the bedroom first?" Mattie asked sarcastically. Albie tensed because he'd seen Eric fly off the handle for less but all he said was "I guess we're having some kind of roommate meeting," cheerful as you please. The bottles clanked together as Eric set them down on their coffee table.

"Just left the movie in my bedroom, ladies. Just need help finding it." He thought to himself, "The Academy Award goes to . . . me!" Albie smiled, looked at Eric, and nodded toward Albie's bedroom.

"Don't have too much fun without us until we get back," Eric said, obediently following Albie into his room. It wasn't until they were actually heading into the bedroom that Albie's stomach felt like it was holding a jumble of surgical instruments. Could he really tell Eric that he didn't want to kill his girl tonight? How could he convince Eric that their tag team could be a trio?

* * * *

"Look at this skin." Alana had raised her nightgown, showing a flat stomach, panties that showed more than covered. "Like a peach, right? A knife would cut right through." She demonstrated. "If you wanted to stab me, fuck my insides with your big, shiny metal dicks, I would bleed so much,

466

give you a bloody O-face. The heroine that survives? She doesn't get nearly enough satisfaction as the whore that dies early." Then Alana Anderson, for her audience of two, had begun to grind her own hips on the bed.

* * * *

Albie thought he gave a debate team worthy presentation of the positives of working with Fiona, even if his words gushed out like water from a spigot. Completely ignoring her hotness, he focused on the practical instead. "She could bring us more victims, male and female, lesbians," he told Eric. "I mean she already said that people in a horror movie who are stupid enough to die deserve it. And she *really* likes blood. I mean she even scares me a little with how excited she is." (It also excited him when she mentioned it, but he didn't think mentioning that would help him sell his idea to Eric). Eric's expression, throughout his pitch, was like he was listening to a wet fart just inches from his face, but Albie persisted. "I really think she could be an asset to the team." Albie mentally patted himself on the back for throwing in a sports analogy. Eric grimaced as though the words in his mouth tasted bad.

"And she'd be on board with this?" Eric finally released those words, each word dripping acidic bile, burning contempt.

"I'm sure she would be. I mean she knows a lot about killing. She even said there are a few people, real people, that just deserve to get killed. She even has a list." A lot of those people were celebrities, not exactly attainable, but she explained how M. Night Shyamalan "needs to spend a few minutes with jumper cables on his nuts. And at the end, you tell him you're going to let him go, but then just take a sharp knife and chop his balls off. That would be a twist ending." Albie really laughed at that, also mentally giving her bonus points for creativity.

"So what exactly does she bring to the group?" As Eric spoke, his smile withered and his voice hardened to stone. "I mean besides somewhere to stick your dick."

Albie stammered. "I-I-I just think there's potential here."

"Potential." Eric spat the word like it was phlegm he was aiming at Albie's feet.

"We can wait. Just let's see where this could lead." Eric stepped forward slightly and Albie took a big step back. "I mean we don't have to kill anyone tonight. We should think about it."

Albie had backed up because of the expression on Eric's face. He could see the rage slowly pulling Eric's facial skin taut, calcifying the hundreds of muscles beneath. When Eric spoke, he did so through gritted teeth, grinding each word that passed through them.

"You know what a big-tittied woman with a bad attitude is, Albie?"

Albie knew the answer—it was a favorite joke of Eric's—but Eric didn't let Albie say it.

"It's a waste of tits. And I've wanted to kill that waste of tits all night. The only thing, the only thing, Albie, that kept that bitch Maddie alive this long is the idea of seeing her get fucking impaled and then being able to watch it over and over again. So is Maddie going to be a potential addition to our team? 'Cause I am fucking vetoing that shit."

"We don't have to bring her." Albie raised his hands. "She's out. We can get rid of her. Absolutely, Eric." The back of Eric's heels were already against the far wall.

Eric stepped up to Albie, eye to Albie's bobbing Adam's Apple. "So it will be just the three of us? You two playing Micky and Mallory while *I'm* your third wheel?" His next two words were punctuated with finger stabs into Albie's collarbone. "Fuck. That." Albie's raised hands did nothing to stop him.

But then he did touch Eric. The nanosecond Albie put his hands on Eric's shoulders, innocent and brotherly as the gesture was, he knew he made a mistake. Albie had a reach advantage, but thanks to Eric's reflexes, he had two fistfuls of Albie's shirt, cementing the level of shit Albie had just stepped in. He didn't even have time to plant his feet as Eric swung Albie like a sandbag, hurling him into Albie's dresser where he crumpled like a crash test dummy. Collectible figures placed lovingly atop it were toppled in the ensuing quake.

Albie's head rang where it struck the dresser. The pain traveled like water down the culvert of his back. It was hard to focus, but Albie could still see his roommate, his friend, looming over him, a 5'8 colossus, his eyes sparking furiously.

"You need to remember something, Albie. I let you be my friend. I. Let. YOU!" He said the last three words like barks from a rabid dog. "If you did not have that VCR, I would not let you be in the same fucking room with me. You need to remember that like you need to remember who's in fucking charge here. If I say those two bitches have to die, then THOSE BITCHES HAVE TO DIE!"

"Whoa!" Mattie said, and both boys' heads snapped to the doorway. Fiona immediately ran to Albie, asking shrilly, "What the hell happened?" She bent down and cradled Albie's head.

Eric's body was rigid. His fists were balled up and practically vibrating with tension. "You cunts just need to mind your own business." Using those quick reflexes, he snatched Fiona's hair. Fiona screamed as all of her hair came away in Eric's hand, not hunks of hair torn from the scalp but the whole thing. Fiona yelped more in surprise than pain, and Albie noticed the white-blond hair pulled back in a skintight bun. Eric looked at the wig, then at Fiona. He squinted in confusion.

Albie saw Eric's expression suddenly go from squinting confusion to eyes-bugged-out agony. The cords on Eric's neck stood out like steel cables beneath the skin. There was no trace of Eric's athletic grace in his spasming limbs. His legs folded beneath him. After Eric collapsed into a twitching heap, Mattie again fired up the stun gun. From his position on the floor, Albie could see the flicker of blue fire, hear the buzzing of angered electronic hornets. But instead of hitting him again, Mattie instead kicked him, sending the toe of her thigh-high boots into his side once, twice, and then another shot from the stun gun.

Albie looked up at Fiona, her hair and face so different now, and it had nothing to do with different hair. A cruel Cheshire Cat smile crept onto her features. Albie could also see the hypodermic needle in her hand, the plunger on it already depressed. Whatever it did contain was now running through his veins, turning his thoughts to molasses.

"Rest easy, sweet prince," Fiona said to him and he took her advice. He had no choice.

* * * *

"So you go out there," Alana had told these two demented psychopaths, "And be the fucked-up bitches that deserve this wonderful piece of technology." Fiona and Mattie had touched the screen; having seen this movie over a dozen times, they knew what happened next. The VCR didn't disappoint, either. Captain Bruce's harpoon impaled her from behind. Alana's body jerked, her head reared back, her mouth hung open, her red lips now a shade of Movieland gore. Alana's thin arms were held out in a crucifixion pose, her face ecstasy as the harpoon lifted her up until her knees were off the bed. Alana's face, in that moment, was final breath, orgasm, and religious experience all at once. The expression recorded perfectly in the brains of Fiona and Mattie as they watched, free to replay in their dreams as they promised their servitude.

* * * *

Eric screamed. A woman with dyed pink hair was pulling at his right arm, her talon-like manicure digging into the flesh, while another with short blond hair was at his left, fangs bared. The sound system was good enough that you could hear them thunk into his meaty bicep. Two more were pulling at his legs. The girl on Eric's right leg had Mattie's dark, curly hair.

"Looking good, Mattie."

"You know it, babe," Mattie said, without taking her eyes off the screen.

All the girls were hissing, their fangs glittering in the moonlight. The camera panned to an overhead shot as each girl began pulling with all their vampire strength.

"You get the right amount of butter?" Mattie liked her popcorn practically drowned in it.

Fiona handed the bowl to Mattie, who didn't even look in Fiona's direction as Fiona moved around the couch and sat Indian style beside her roommate/lover/fellow acolyte. Fiona then got to work on opening a box of Milk Duds.

"Look at that fuckface scream," Mattie laughed, popcorn spilling from her mouth and onto her black T-shirt. The girls were out of their "hunting" attire and were now dressed for movie night: T-shirts and pajama pants. Fiona's blond hair fell limply around her shoulders.

"I know, right?" Fiona said, finally tearing the box open. "I'm just sorry you didn't get to take said fuckface for a ride before sacrificing him."

Mattie shook her head. "I'm not. Dude had a cocktail weenie."

Fiona turned to Mattie. "How do you know?"

"Look where my left hand is grabbing. Oh shit, here it comes!" She tapped Fiona's shoulder furiously as both women turned their attention back to the screen.

All four vampire women pulled at once. Their sound system was so good the girls could hear the tendons and ligaments snapping as they were pulled past their breaking point. Fiona thought she could see tears in Eric's eyes, which was surprising picture quality for a VHS tape.

The extremities being pulled seemed, for the briefest second, to take on the consistency of taffy before tearing away, leaving four geysers of blood uncorked. As Eric's limbless torso hit the ground, the undead women pounced, lapping at the four gory geysers like thirsty dogs.

Both girls suddenly closed their eyes and chanted, "Thank you, Bacchus, for this gift of death, for this gift of life. Glory to you, we sacrifice in your name." Fiona and Mattie then inhaled, breathing in Eric's death, his suffering, letting it travel through their being, giving them strength, as they had done whenever they watched this special edition of *Dracula's Sorority* that was Eric's prison.

Albie and Eric never did figure out all that the VCR was capable of. They never could get past the part of killing without having to dump a body.

"Thank God we got the VCR back. I was looking all of 27," Mattie said. "Would have been a fucking soccer mom before too long."

"I wasn't worried." And Fiona didn't worry. They had owned the VCR for years, and were its most loyal servants. Even after the break-in, Fiona had heard it in her dreams, calling to her in the voice of Alana Anderson, telling her to seek out the kid in the Mr. Fixit shirt.

"Wanna watch your boyfriend next?" Mattie asked.

Fiona thought back to that scene: one frame of film would show Bunny, played by the not-so-virginal Alana Anderson, running from Captain Bruce in high heels. Then it would be Albie wearing Alana's white t-shirt and cutoffs, Albie having considerably less to fill her clothes with. The expression on Alana's and Albie's faces though were identical ones of terror, but Fiona sometimes wondered if Albie was aware. As he minced through the moonlit underbrush on impossibly high stripper heels, having to scream because Bunny had screamed, was he aware that he as Bunny was destined to die with each rewind and playback? Did Albie/Bunny see Fiona's eyes behind the face of Captain Bruce? Fiona thought it was deliciously apropos that Albie/Bunny dies by a very phallic harpoon.

"At least he had good taste in movies." Fiona snuggled closer to Mattie. Both girls were soon watching the movie, partaking of communion with the last VCR made in Hell. The whirring of its rollers sounded like a contented sigh, and it was indeed pleased with its acolytes.

King of the Tortured Dead
Bret McCormick

**A name fom the past ... was he just a joker or
an undying god?**

Conspicuous consumption is the phrase that comes to mind as I think of Reggie Tremblay. When I met him in 1979 he was a soul adrift in the big world, trying to figure out what he would do with his life, in the meantime spending large amounts of his father's money on the finest clothes, restaurants and cars. He'd grown up in Martha's Vineyard. I can't say we were friends. We were classmates at Brooks Institute in Santa Barbara. I was studying motion picture production with the intention of making a career of it, while I got the impression the school was just a passing fancy for Reggie. He'd already begun and abandoned three or four courses of study at well-respected universities. He liked tennis. I recall that vividly. I assisted with one of his student film projects, a comic short featuring a slapstick tennis match. It was during the production of that short film that I got to know him, shared a couple of meals with him and engaged in late night, alcohol-fueled philosophical discussions. We were never close, so I was more than a little surprised when his attorney, Samuel Gibbs-Hewlett, showed up in my offices in Burbank some thirty-five years later.

Ronnie, my receptionist, had ushered him into my personal office and seated him on the sofa opposite my desk. She offered a puzzled shrug as she pulled my office door closed.

"How may I help you?" I asked the thin man whose rigid posture bordered on the comic.

He introduced himself. The man's name, Gibbs-Hewlett, in addition to his stiff pose, aroused my sense of humor. Seldom, outside a Monty Python sketch, had I encountered hyphenated surnames.

"I represent Reginald Tremblay," he said solemnly.

It took me a moment to recall who Reginald Tremblay was. When I did make the connection, I wondered why the attorney hadn't just phoned me. I knew Reggie's family had more money than God and I couldn't imagine how my little independent film production company could be of interest. Especially after so many years. Still, I was curious and willing to hear the man out.

Remembering Reggie, and wondering why his representative was in my office, I may have let slip a confused frown. His solicitor said, "Mr. Tremblay told me you might not remember him. You were classmates at Brooks Institute in …"

"Of course, I remember, Reggie!" I exclaimed, trying my best to seem affable. More to the point, I wanted to move this impromptu meeting along as I had a screening to attend in less than an hour. "How can I help you?"

The man opened his briefcase and removed a DVD in a clear plastic sleeve. Someone had scrawled my name on it with a black marker. "Mr. Tremblay asks only that you agree to watch this video recording," he said, rising from his seat and placing the video on my desktop.

"What is it? A pilot or something?" Naturally, I supposed Reggie was rekindling contact to pitch some sort of movie or television series.

"It's more along the lines of a deposition," Gibbs-Hewlett said, remaining standing at the front of my desk.

"Deposition? Is Reggie dying?" It was the first thing that popped into my head. Even if he was on death's doorstep, I couldn't imagine how that possibly affected me. Surely, I wasn't in his will.

"Mr. Tremblay is living. But he hopes to be deceased in the near future."

I laughed out loud. The guy was putting me on. He had to be. *Hopes to be deceased*?

"Come on," I said. "What gives? Where's the hidden camera? Good one, Reggie!" I exclaimed, looking around my office.

"I understand your confusion," the attorney replied, his face grim and nothing but business, "however, I assure you I am here on a legitimate errand of the utmost importance. May I have your word that you will watch this disc in its entirety?"

He tapped the DVD on my desk with a bony index finger.

I became agitated. "Why should I watch it?" I snapped.

"You are under no obligation. Whether you agree to watch the video or not, Mr. Tremblay has asked that I make a video recording of your response with my cell phone. May I record your response, sir?"

"What the hell is going on here?" Inexplicably, I was more irritated than the situation warranted.

"The matter will be perfectly clear after you watch the video, sir."

So, as Gibbs-Hewlett recorded my answer, I said hello to my old classmate and agreed to watch his deposition. That was, it seemed, all the guy wanted. It was no prank and I could think of no good reasons why I was feeling so put out by the request.

The attorney tucked his cell phone away, offered his hand and vacated the premises. Watching him walk out the office door, I leaned back in my chair and swiveled, my toes digging into the carpet beneath me. I snatched the DVD off my desk and held it a moment, like an intuitive using psychometry to solve a crime. The nondescript disk in its clear plastic sleeve fairly buzzed with some enigmatic energy. I thought of Chandra, the psychic I sometimes consulted on business matters, wishing she was present to give me her take on all this. The temptation to pop the disk into the player and begin watching was powerful, but the wall clock reminded me I had to dash if I wanted to make that screening on time.

After the screening, and some noncommittal chat with a potential distributor, I went for drinks at the Grove. I had dinner at Rodolpho's, then went home.

It was a busy weekend. By the time I returned to the office on Monday morning the video and the mysterious request associated with it were all but forgotten. I was on the phone with my co-producer and sipping a cup of coffee when my eyes fell on the disk. For a brief instant I did not know what it was. I picked it up and then the thing reasserted itself in my memory. The exchange with Gibbs-Hewlett now seemed a distant fantasy. I brought the call to a quick resolution and stuck the damn disk in the DVD player, seated myself no more than four feet from the screen, and focused my full attention on Reggie's deposition.

The first few scenes looked like Super 8mm movie footage of a shoreline somewhere, panning from the water to take in buildings that were obviously not European or American. Voice-over narration began a few seconds into the video. It was Reggie's voice all right. He sounded very much the same as I remembered, his voice only slightly altered by the husky overlay of middle age.

"Greetings compadre!" His jovial tone was forced, unconvincing. "These are scenes from my 1996 trip to Morocco. It really is a different world there, bro. Very different." Reggie's voice generally sounded normal, but every few seconds a strange effect distorted his words. The effect brought to mind a wind tunnel. It was not unlike a treatment that might have been used for a cyborg's voice in a science fiction film of the 1960s.

"This place is where my troubles really started," the narration track declared, as the image on the screen revealed a sort of bistro crammed in among other sun-bleached buildings. The place was located on a narrow street populated by brown-skinned people wrapped in loose light-colored clothing. These locals could not resist the impulse to look directly into the camera's lens. The sign on the front of the place was in a language I couldn't decipher, but it featured a stylized symbol of an eye suggestive of ancient Egypt and the hieroglyphs. "You probably remember, from our rap sessions back in school, that I was pretty obsessed with metaphysics and eternal life and other such esoteric matters."

Now that he mentioned it, I did recall our conversation veering down that path a time or two.

"In Morocco I found what I'd been searching for. But, you know what they say…be careful what you wish." The scene became dark. A rolly-poley fellow in a dirty white suit, wearing a fez, lurked in a shadowy corner. He hunched over a table with a small lamp illuminating his creepy face. The guy looked like a villain in some old movie serial from the 1930s. He clearly had the natural talent to be a movie bad guy. His was a face you instantly despised. "This sinister fellow is Francis," Reggie's voice explained. He emitted a cyborg laugh. "I'm sure you're thinking his name should be Mohammad or Farouk or Akbar or something, but his name was Francis. A prosaic name for a truly dark soul. This guy was a master of the …" long, long pause "… dark arts." An alternate angle on Francis had him flashing a smile which, rather than mitigating his repulsive qualities, only made his face seem more terrifying.

"The," Reggie rattled off a phrase I could not make sense of, but assumed was the name of the restaurant, "catered to a very specific clientele: people like myself who were exploring the edges of reality." At this point my mind flitted back to my original suspicion that Reggie was making a pitch for some weird *reality* TV series. "Francis was a chef of sorts, concocting various edibles to induce expanded states of consciousness or to warp reality in novel ways. I know what you're thinking, dude. And you're wrong. The guy was not a drug dealer. Far from it. In fact, I once saw him put a bullet in the head of a heroin trafficker … but that's another story."

There was a sound like ancient, rusted nails pried from a plank of northern hardwood. Reggie stuttered and heaved a sigh. When he continued, his voice strained as if the act of speaking took every ounce of energy and concentration he could muster. "I want to stay focused. The expanded consciousness Frances created in the minds of his patrons was more along the lines of … sorcery, a word that means nothing to most modern humans. Your mind is probably generating images of Mickey Mouse and an army of dancing mops about now. That's how far our sense of reality, ultimate reality, has been degraded. Sorcery…"

His voice trailed off, replaced by a strange clutter of odd sounds, like a brief audio montage of bumps, scrapes, the blaring of trumpets and maybe the screech of a cat?

The grainy film footage slipped into typical vacation shots of Reggie and a cute dark-haired woman basking and frolicking on a beach, with glum third-worlders looking on from the edges of the frame. "That's Felice," he said, "the love of my life. Back when I had a life. After my transition she couldn't bear to be near me. And she refused to join me. I can't blame her, but still it hurts." The howl of pain that followed on the DVD's soundtrack, jolted me. A sinister chill ran up my spine, setting my hair tingling.

"Damnation!" I exclaimed, drawing back into my chair.

The images on the DVD were now still photographs of Reggie at various locations. "I know none of this makes sense to you. There's no reason why it would," the distorted voice continued. "Still, you're the only person who might be able to wrap his head around what's become of me. It's very crazy stuff, man. Dark, insane, magical stuff like you never imagined was possible."

There was no mistaking the sincere remorse in his voice. I felt it in my chest. The guy was desperate.

"I've known a lot of people. A *lot* of people. When I try to think of someone who will get what's going on with me and take it seriously enough to document it in a responsible fashion, you're the only person who comes to mind. I know you don't owe me anything. I know we're not even friends really. Still, I've often thought of you and the brief time we spent together at Brooks and I'm convinced you're the right choice."

Right choice for what?

I felt like I was being suckered into something I'd regret, but he most definitely had my attention. "What the hell, Reggie?" I muttered as the scene shifted. Still photos of the middle-aged version of Reggie transitioned to a nice library or maybe what you'd call a study in a rich man's home. Sunlight streamed in through windows and French doors in the background. Beyond those could be seen a beautiful garden. An old, haggard-looking Reggie stepped into the scene and seated himself in front of the camera.

"The still photos of me were to fix in your mind that I was once normal," he said. His image flickered and stretched and he was standing at the window, looking out into the garden. Then he was back in front of the camera. "You have no idea how difficult it is for me to focus my mind on a simple task like talking to you." Suddenly Reggie was in three different locations simultaneously. This was followed by one Reggie at the window, then a sort of smeared blur followed by the medium framing of his head and shoulders.

Decent special effects, I thought.

"This is no trick. For the love of …" he choked on the word, "… God, please call me."

The screen went blank. Large white numerals appeared. A phone number. I recognized the area code as belonging to Santa Barbara. Okay, I was hooked. The least I could do was call the guy. If he'd gone to all the trouble of producing this bizarre video, I could certainly spend a few minutes on the phone with him. I wanted to believe it was all a hoax, wanted to laugh about it over cocktails, but the desperation in Reggie's eyes in the last few seconds of the video, the heart-wrenching tone of his voice, convinced me that would never happen. This sort of thing inspired laughter only after insanity had set in.

The Reggie I remembered was many things, but a convincing actor was not among them. My guts twisted with anxiety as I reached for my phone and punched in the number. A man answered the phone and after I identified myself, he said, "Thank you for calling, sir. Mr. Tremblay will be very pleased. I've been instructed to make whatever accommodations are necessary to ensure a visit at your earliest possible convenience."

We talked a few moments, but I got little information other than the fact that they were willing to do anything necessary to get me to Reggie's home in Santa Barbara. By the time I ended the call, I'd agreed to drive up the following day. My planned arrival time was noon.

The grounds were beautiful, perfectly maintained and filled with exotic plants of every description. The winding cobblestone drive led me to the front door where I was immediately greeted by a fortyish man wearing a gray uniform.

"Hello, sir," he said, "I'm Theodore. We spoke by phone yesterday." I exchanged greetings with the fellow, then he gestured toward the open door saying, "Enter this house freely and of your own accord, safely enjoying the hospitality of your host and leaving with unexpected gains."

I stared at him. He stood, frozen in the welcoming posture, indicating the entrance to the house. "What am I to make of that greeting, Theodore?" I asked, shaking off another of those spinal chills.

He stood like a statue locked in his pose. "Mr. Tremblay has very specific requirements, sir. Daily life is highly ritualized here. This is the greeting I must offer to all of our guests. Mr. Tremblay wishes guests to give purposeful thought before entering the house."

I'd already given the entire matter several hours of purposeful thought. After driving all the way to Santa Barbara, there was no way I was going to just turn around and leave. A small part of my mind clung to the notion that this was an elaborate hoax, but the majority of my consciousness had already discarded such hope. "So be it," I said, moving toward the door.

Behind me I heard Theodore say, "You are the first guest ever to respond with the proper words, sir. This is most auspicious." His words made the hairs on my neck rise. Again, I shook off the chill.

He followed me into the house and directed me down a long hallway and into the same study I'd seen earlier in the video. Theodore pointed to a large leather-covered chair. "Please sit here, sir." I sat. "During your visit with Mr. Tremblay, please remain seated in this very spot. For your own well-being it is necessary that you maintain this fixed location." He stared at me expectantly.

"I understand," I answered.

A smile formed on his face. "Again, you have given the precise response. Such a good sign! I will leave you now." Theodore walked away from me. Turning, he made a series of gestures over the threshold and backed out of the room. Leaving me alone in the study, he pulled the door closed as he departed.

I examined the expensive antiques that were scattered around the room in profusion. Any one of them would have been a welcome addition to a museum collection. Then I heard my friend's voice.

"Thank you for coming." Just this, then silence for a moment. I looked around, but saw no sign of Reggie even though his voice had sounded no more than a few feet away. "I so hoped you would accept my invitation." There he was, standing beside the huge windows looking out onto the garden. He was simply there in a flash, appearing from nowhere. He turned slowly to face me.

"Wouldn't have missed it," I said, trying to sound casual. "I've never had an invitation quite like this one."

Laughter.

But, such laughter! It conveyed a genuine sense of humor, but an indescribable desperation as well. Reggie's laugh unnerved me. Then he flickered and split into two images, one a few feet away from where he'd been standing and the other seated in a chair across from me. This was no trick, no hokey Victorian séance performed in shadow. The noonday sun spilled into the study from numerous windows.

"I know my appearance is off-putting," he said. "I apologize. Projecting myself, as a single human entity for you, requires an enormous amount of concentration."

"Why?"

"Yes. I must explain. Francis helped me attain a degree of consciousness one might call godlike." His voice was intermingled with clanks and hissing sounds. The image in the chair shimmered and blurred while the Reggie near the window grew twice its previous size. Both images swept across the room and collided with a soundless explosion of light worthy of a July Fourth celebration.

"I *am* god." As he spoke these three words, his voice sounded like he was whispering in my ear from only an inch away. I jumped and nearly bolted from the chair, but his voice came clearly and with volume from somewhere near the bookcase. "Please remain seated. No matter how challenging this encounter may be to your human sensibilities, for your own safety you must remain within the ring."

Ring? For the first time it occurred to me to look at the floor. Sure enough, a circle had been drawn around the chair with what may have been salt crystals. "Okay," I said unsteadily, "I'm staying put."

"This odd display of shifting images is an unfortunate consequence of my expanded state of being." His voice sounded quite normal now. "Appearing as a man is very hard for me, since I no longer am. Human, that is. Focusing myself into a single timespace location is a bit like a fat lady trying to squeeze her size eight foot into a pretty little size five shoe." Again, he laughed that blood-chilling laugh. "My current state of being is more suited to meeting with prophets on mountain tops and handing out commandments. Impressive, no?"

My stomach tensed and I forced a grunting laugh to acknowledge his joke. Four Reggies now stood in front of me, backs to one another, facing the cardinal directions. Four voices spoke in chorus. "I know this is a bit hard on your nerves, my friend. Forgive me. You're the first guest I've had in many years of your time. The first to last this long in my disagreeable presence."

"They left the ring?" I asked, my mind filling with terrifying possibilities of what might have befallen anyone trying to flee the study.

"Oh, no. Nothing as horrible as that," the four voices answered. "They simply lost consciousness. For humans the most convenient way of dealing with the seemingly impossible is to block it from the conscious mind. Fainting accomplishes that goal nicely."

Now there was a single Reggie seated in the chair across from me, leaning earnestly forward with his elbows on his knees. "You don't know how good it is for me to receive this visit from you. Thank you!"

"You're welcome," I answered, fishing for something more to say. "This will certainly be the most memorable visit I'll ever have with anyone."

"I am honored." Twelve Reggie heads hung in a ring near the ceiling, slowly rotating like a merry-go-round. The twelve heads spoke, one at a time, assembling sentences in piecemeal fashion. "I will explain as quickly as possible so you may be relieved of your discomfort. My evil friend, Francis, played on my ego. He flattered and coaxed me into admitting that I wanted to live forever. Such hubris! I know you realized my vanity. I remember seeing the recognition in your eyes when we were students."

A single Reggie appeared in front of me, hanging upside-down, suspended in the air with arms outstretched, calling to mind the manner in which Saint Peter is said to have met his death. "The hungry darkness in Francis was drawn to the darkness in me, I'm afraid. He made me an offer I only half believed. Eternal life! Ha!" Blood streamed out of his mouth and puddled on the carpet a few feet in front of me. He gurgled as he tried to speak, then he was in the chair across from me once more, looking calm, sincere and completely human. The blood vanished from the carpet. "Forgive me for indulging in self-pity. Getting on with my story; Francis fed me a very special pate which he told me would give me eternal life and knowledge beyond my wildest dreams."

"Pate?" My voice cracked as I muttered the single word. I was not certain I had heard him correctly. My nervous system was on overload.

"Yes. A pate containing a most exotic ingredient." He hesitated. I said nothing, certain that I did not really want to know the specifics of the mysterious constituent. "A human pineal gland," he continued. I'm certain my expression more than amply conveyed my disgust. "Your revulsion is absolutely justified, my friend. I only half-believed it, but even if I half-believed it to be true, I should have steered clear of the man and his dark magic."

"You ate the pate?"

"I did. And it made me what I am today!"

My God, that laughter!

I could not help but cover my ears. It was beyond enduring. The twisted sound echoed through the room and told a tale of infinite suffering and the pleasure of demons, or so it seemed to my human mind.

"Sorry." Again, the whisper in my ear, despite the fact that my ears were covered. Steeling myself, I drew a deep breath and lowered my hands.

Three Reggies on the sofa said, "Do you remember the conversation we had at City Diner that night? We talked of life, death and eternity. We were just barely adults. As I recall, even then you said you were not interested in the survival of your personality."

His words reminded me. When he had asked if I wanted to live forever, I'd thought it was a fool's dream. Who would want to live forever in a single body with a single personality? Somehow, I'd intuited that the human form and mind was a temporary fixture, constructed only for short-term use. Not much more than a novel diversion.

"You were much wiser than I." The word "I" echoed over and over again in the room. The bust of Socrates on the desk took on Reggie's features, its mouth moving. "I am now as close to omniscient as a single personality can be. I am trapped in both heaven and hell. I find it unbearable. I am where no man was intended to be."

"What about Francis? Is there no way to reverse the spell...the magic...whatever it is?" I was sweating profusely. I could feel Reggie's torment. The anxiety increased in me and more than anything I wished to conclude our meeting and leave the house.

"You are strong to endure this," he said softly. "You're a good man. Francis disappeared. When I woke up the morning after my special feast, he was gone. The restaurant was closed, never to reopen. It seems Francis was the servant of another vain fool. His master gained release when I ate the pate."

"I see."

A writhing mass of connected bodies materialized on the floor. The heads said, "To gain the freedom only death can provide, I need someone to eat my pineal gland."

"Your pineal gland? Where is it?"

"My body has been preserved in a cryogenic chamber in the basement of this house. The pineal gland has already been extracted and awaits a willing diner. Know anyone who wants to play god?" The hideous mass of bodies laughed ferociously.

This time I did not cover my ears. I gritted my teeth and tensed until I thought my spine might snap, but finally the laughter ceased.

Reggie took form in the chair across from me. "I am sorry to put you through this friend. I know it's difficult."

"Why do you need me?"

"You have a reputation. A good one. I thought perhaps you could produce a documentary with my funding. Get the government involved. Top scientists, that sort of thing. Legitimize this to the world. I don't want to lure some poor fool into this state of being. I'd like the finest minds to learn of this and see it's real." I shook my head, trying to imagine how such a scenario might play out in what I called the *real* world. His form flickered in and out like a failing light bulb. "Please consider it. I must find release, but I'd rather do it in a way that is not treacherous. I want a volunteer who is fully informed, ready to face the consequences and has at least a chance of turning this trap into some form of service to humanity."

His form exploded and rapidly popped in and out of view in no less than fifty positions around the room. He spoke with many voices. "I've got to stop now. This is too much. I'm losing my focus. Thank you for coming."

Then he was gone.

I released a breath and leaned back into the big chair. Outside the windows, I saw the world was continuing as it always did. Birds hopped around among the vegetation looking for food. The sun beamed down on the plants, feeding them energy. The dim little part of my mind that wanted to cling onto a narrow version of reality, suggested that I'd imagined the whole thing. But I hadn't. There was no way to convince myself it had been a hallucination. I sat there, stunned.

Shortly, the door opened and Theodore came in. "Are you all right, sir? May I fetch you a beverage? Something strong?"

"Yes," I said. "I think I've earned a gin. Neat."

"Right away."

When he placed the drink on the table beside me, he asked, "May I speak candidly with you, sir?"

"Please do," I said, sampling the gin.

"You are a most unusual man. Your willpower is quite strong. I never thought we'd find a human who could endure Mr. Tremblay's presence for such a length of time."

I'd never thought of myself as a person with a great deal of will power and I said as much.

"You are humble," he replied.

"How does a man like you end up in this situation?" I asked, draining the glass. Whimsically, I imagined an ad at an employment agency seeking a butler for a godlike entity.

"I exist at his pleasure, sir."

"I beg your pardon? Could I have another one of these?" I held the glass forward, hoping he'd take it and refill it.

Smiling, he took the glass from my hand. "Perhaps it is easier for you to understand if I say he created me." Theodore crossed to the bar, quickly refreshed my drink and returned it to me.

His statement struck me as absurd. Why? I couldn't say. After everything else I'd witnessed, why would this claim seem particularly challenging?

"I understand it is difficult for you to accept," he said.

"You're right," I answered, forcing myself not to gulp the entire glass of gin.

"All of this," Theodore said with a flourish, "the master created to serve his needs."

I laughed nervously through clenched teeth.

"May I demonstrate?"

"Please do."

Theodore closed his eyes and pressed his hands together in front of his face. "Dear Master, please manifest a beautiful woman in the garden that your friend may believe." No sooner had he spoken the words than a lovely young lady with flowing golden hair was standing outside, rapping on the glass, smiling and waving at us. "Would you care to meet her, sir? Touch her? Speak with her? Assure yourself that she is real?"

I drained the glass. "No."

"More gin?"

"Please." As he filled the glass for the third time, the woman vanished and I asked, "So what happens to you if he finds a willing…" I didn't want to say victim, so I just let my sentence trail off.

"My purpose will have been served. I will cease to be."

"And how do you feel about that?"

He handed me the gin. "I will be grateful to have served."

"I see. So, you're telling me this house and everything in it will cease to be if he is successful?" Theodore smiled and nodded. "And the attorney?" I asked.

"Yes. He, too, is a temporary construct. If I may be so bold, sir, all material beings are temporary constructs, even yourself. My certainty of the fact is merely keener than yours."

I sipped the gin in silence. I felt calm, but not the least bit drunk. I suppose my metabolism had shifted into a previously unused gear. This *temporary construct* wanted the hell out of that place, and quickly.

"The master has asked that you take your time before making a decision. Do not rush. For him a moment is as a thousand years and a thousand years is as a moment. Phone me with your response when you have decided. May I get you anything else, sir? A meal perhaps, before your return journey?"

The thought of the pineal gland pate precluded any possibility that I'd be eating in Reggie's house. "No, thank you," I said, rising. "I'll head back now." I surprised myself with how steady I was on my feet after three gins.

He walked with me to the front of the house. "I'll await your call," he said before closing the door behind me.

I drove slowly back to my home.

For the next few days I stayed away from the office, making lame excuses as to why I wasn't at work. On the fourth day, I received a call from Theodore. "I'm sorry to trouble you, sir," he said, "but, have you arrived at a decision?"

Before I even thought about it, the words came out. "The answer's no."

"Oh," he replied softly. "What will the master do now?"

"Put an ad on craigslist," I snapped. It seems Theodore was clueless about craigslist. After I explained, his tone brightened.

"Thank you! I'm sure Mr. Tremblay will be pleased to have your suggestion."

As I hung up, I found myself thinking, *my suggestion?* I prayed there would be no terrible repercussions if Tremblay followed my flippant plan of action. What had I gotten myself into? Out of curiosity, the next day I checked the ads on line. There it was, under the 'wanted' category: *"Would you like to live forever? Satisfaction guaranteed! One simple dose of our special pate and you will be the god of your own universe. Hurry! This offer limited to one participant."*

I had to go on with my life, but concentrating on mundane, daily concerns became nearly impossible.

I imagined some young Goth kid, covered with tattoos and piercings answering the ad on a lark. And then, living forever. *Forever!* How long, I wondered, had this strange game been going on? Had the original God, if there was one, become tired of omniscience? Had he or she tricked some poor mortal into taking the job of deity? Was the role of God something like a CEO position continually changing hands, while we drones labored on in the company called planet Earth? I was in way over my head. What's more, my conscience ached. I was wracked by guilt. Had I committed a terrible sin simply by communicating with the eternal Reggie?

One day, as I was walking down a crowded street, my ears tuned in to a snatch of conversation. I heard a man's voice say, "The mystic and the psychotic are both in over their heads. The difference is that the mystic is treading water."

That settled it.

I can't say why, but I got in my car and drove straight to Santa Barbara. I arrived there just at sunset. I searched for over an hour and never found Reggie's mansion. I went up and down that street twenty times. I asked the neighbors and they said there had never been a house matching the description I gave.

So now what? Now, I continue my life, hemmed in by the enclosure of a so-called reality I no longer fully believe. Who is God? What is God? Is there a God, or just a series of hapless humans tricked into that office for a time? If Reggie's vast mansion can disappear without a trace, what of these skyscrapers, highways and neighborhoods I see all around me? Will I awaken from this dream of life into a higher state of being or an indescribable nightmare?

Reggie, wherever you are, I hope you're at peace. And whoever took your place, I hope they're at least as benevolent as you were and that they enjoy the position more than you did.

Carnal Harvest
James H Longmore

**His organs were donated to help others –
now he wants them back!**

The pain was excruciating, yet there was nothing she could do to get away from it. Her assailant had administered a muscle relaxant shortly after having spiked her margarita with Rohypnol back at the bar, what felt like a thousand years ago. They had also given her some kind of painkiller, because, despite the searing agony she was suffering through, it was still disproportionate in comparison to what her assailant was doing to her body. Surely that was a sign of compassion; perhaps she had a chance of getting out of this alive after all?

The keen, cold blade of the scalpel glinted as it traced its way down along the faint, white line that ran the length of the paralysed girl's sternum. A thin, red line appeared a fraction of a second after it; fat, crimson beads of blood popped out from the hair's breadth slit and trickled down along the outline of the girl's heaving ribs.

She tried her best to scream, fought in vain against her useless body to wriggle, shift, fight, anything – but it simply wouldn't respond, even when her torturer peeled back the flawless, alabaster skin that covered her chest and cracked her sternum wide open with a hammer and chisel.

The rush of cool, still air caressed her exposed lungs and beating heart, a weird, alien sensation that transcended even the agonizing pain that wracked her body and had her mind begging for the merciful swiftness of death.

But even that grim luxury evaded her; the combination of powerful drugs that swilled around her powerless body conspired to maintain consciousness, and she was all too aware of the fact that she was being dissected like some ultimately dispensable lab rat.

She looked up into the eyes of the person who was destroying her young body, unable to discern if they were a man or a woman, young or old – all she could make out in those cold, dead eyes was something that had ceased to be entirely human a long, long time ago.

A strong tugging, pulling sensation in the exposed organs of her chest, the sharp snipping sound of precise surgical scissors, and the girl found herself staring with disbelief at the pink, spongy flesh of her own lungs as they were held aloft like some sick, twisted trophy, and all she could think of was the opening scene of The Lion King.

She suffocated to death in the end, her failing brain screaming out for the oxygen so cruelly denied following the deft removal of her lungs, her hollowed out chest cavity filling with thick, viscous blood as her heart twitched and shuddered to a complete, final standstill.

*

"What the hell, Joe?" Detective Bob Lyle growled at his partner, "how can you be eating in here? Especially *that*?" He nodded down with disdain to the fat, greasy burger clutched tightly in his partner's hands, a bunch of slippery onions attempting to escape the fat-sodden bun, like the freshly spilled innards of some exotic sea creature.

"I'm hungry," Jonah – Joe to his colleagues – Pemberton replied through a mouthful of half-masticated burger, "and I'm sure she won't mind any." He pointed in the general direction of the corpse that lay spread out and mutilated upon the motel room bed, not phased in the least by the blood soaked mattress and wide, gaping hole in the girl's chest.

Lyle grunted and stalked around the motel bed, his OCD screaming at him that the bed sheets had been less than crisp and starched white before the majority of the young girl's blood had soaked them through, transformed them into a sickly shade of dark crimson. The M.E. had put the time of death somewhere around three in the morning, which meant the poor girl – Lyle guestimated her age at somewhere between nineteen and twenty-three, and that was one piece of detective work Lyle was rarely wrong about – had laid there for the better part of ten hours before being discovered by the motel's one and only housekeeper. The woman, a plump, squat Mexican lady by the name of Guadalupe was still hysterical and was being babysat out in the motel's grubby reception office by one of the beat cops who'd first attended the call-in.

"It's pretty gruesome, Bob," Pemberton stated the blindingly obvious before taking another huge bite at his burger. Somehow, he managed to capture the errant onions in his gaping maw and all but consuming an entire third of the sandwich in one fell swoop.

Lyle treated his partner to his very best Eastwood squint; there was just something about the guy's undisguised glee at the gruesome crime scenes they were forced to attend that made him more than a tad uneasy; Lyle often mused that had Jonah Pemberton not become a cop, he would most likely be out there slaughtering the innocents himself for his own nefarious kicks. Still, with just two more months before the glorious days of retirement, it was far too easy for Lyle to brush Detective Pemberton's ghoulish lasciviousness to one side – just eight short weeks and the man would be somebody else's problem.

"No sign of sexual assault," Lyle said, he always did his thinking out loud. "And the M.E figures she was drugged up to the eyeballs while the perp' did this to her, although we're gonna have to wait for the tox' report to confirm precisely what he used on her."

"You think she was still alive when he cut her open?" Pemberton said as he peered into the gaping gore of the dead girl's chest, at the splintered sternum, and the once beating heart that now lay quite useless and shrivelled up in a slick pool of coagulated blood. "Jeez, that must have been painful," he snorted and pushed the remainder of his lunch into his fat face.

"Looks that way," Lyle replied, disgusted still further at the glee etched on his partner's face; somebody just died here, and in the most horrific way imaginable, *and* she was still in the damn room – was the man so hardened after his six long years in homicide as to have no reverence at all? "She coughed up a lot of fresh blood," Lyle continued, pointing at the dead girl's pretty, blood spattered face, "she'd have to have been alive for that to happen."

"Reckon she was *awake* when he took her lungs out?" Pemberton said as he gulped down the last of his meal, his throat bulging quite alarmingly as the burger slid down. He let out a quiet, gassy belch that wafted across the corpse, and Lyle smelled the sweet stink of grease and onions over the dank, earthy smell of copper and innards that emanated from the dead girl.

Lyle was about to chastise his partner's crassness when his cell phone rang out. It played a stark, tinny version of *Yakkity Sax* – Lyle absolutely loved Benny Hill, considered the comedian to be the pinnacle of sophisticated British comedy – which, given the circumstances, beat Pemberton's gleeful insensitivity at the murder scene hands-down. Flushed with embarrassment – he could have sworn he'd switched the dammed thing to silent before he came in – Lyle stepped into the cramped en-suite bathroom that reeked of disinfectant and stale pee.

"Hello?" he barked into the phone without glancing at the caller ID.

"Daddy?"

"Oh, hi, Sweetpea," Lyle's demeanor softened – his daughter, Tina, may have been a sophomore college student, but she'd always be his sweet little baby girl who'd once upon a time *loved* unicorns and Disney Princesses. "It's not really a good time to –"

"I'm calling to remind you that it's Mom's birthday on Saturday," Tina insisted, "I hope you haven't forgotten."

Lyle huffed. "Of course I haven't forgotten, Tina," he grumbled, "how could I possibly forget my own wife's birthday?"

He had forgotten, of course, just like he did every year – in fact, had it not been for his daughter's annual reminders since the tender age of eight, Lyle's marriage would have long ago gone the same way as so many of his colleagues' at the Precinct.

Tina's light, breezy laughter echoed out through the phone. "Okay, Daddy, that would be a first, but as long as you remember we're taking her out for dinner."

"Luigi's," Lyle butted in, "same place as last year." It was, in fact, the same place as *every* year.

"It's her favorite."

A familiar shape appeared at the bathroom door, outlined by the warped frame and its yellowed, peeling paint. Pemberton tapped at an imaginary watch on his wrist, eager as ever to press on.

"I really gotta go, sweetie," Lyle sounded flustered – he was always the first to admonish cops for taking personal calls on the job.

"Sorry – bye, Daddy,"

"Bye, Tina, and don't forget to take your meds."

Tina's sigh was so loud that even Pemberton heard it. "I'm twenty-two, Daddy, I don't need reminding."

Lyle knew full well that the reminder was superfluous; Tina had been fastidious in keeping up with her immunosuppressant meds since the operation that had saved her life at the tender age of thirteen. But, it made Lyle feel like a good father, and in some ways he hoped it kind of compensated for all the times he'd not been there for his daughter as she'd grown up.

Before Lyle could say *bye,* Tina had hung up.

"All done, Bob?" Detective Pemberton grinned at Lyle, the sheer delight on his chubby, grease-stained face all too plain to see. He'd not dare say anything to his fiery tempered partner, of course, but he sure as all hell was going to wear that holier-than-thou attitude for the rest of the day.

Lyle nodded sheepishly. "Yeah," he said quietly, "let's get out of here."

*

Tommy Rydell was still very much alive when his eyeballs were plucked from their sockets.

"*Pleeeese!*" his voice, high and shrill, was soaked up by the verdant foliage of the dense woods that surrounded him, closing in on his terrified form like some dark, smothering, malevolent creature.

The person sitting astride Tommy on the damp, mossy ground was heavy enough to render him entirely helpless, no matter how much the terrified boy wriggled and fought. His hands, trapped beneath his attacker's sharp, bony knees, felt numb beneath the weight, his trapped wrists feeling as if they could snap at any moment.

"I'll do anything you want!" Tommy pleaded, "just please don't kill me!" He stared at the face that hovered above him, into the cold, staring eyes that burned out from behind the dark gray ski mask. There was a glaring halo of sunlight around the featureless head, created by a persistent shaft of light that sneaked through the canopy high above, and in Tommy's frantic mind, he thought his assailant resembled some kind of evil angel.

If his attacker wanted to do sexual stuff, that was quite alright with him; hell, he was thirteen and all bets were off as to where Tommy Rydell got his kicks; there was just no need for all the brutality and overriding promise of an untimely death.

Tommy had been out stalking around the woods – a popular destination for the older kids who craved a little alone time – as he did most weekends. There was just something special about sunny Sunday afternoons that just screamed *make out time!* Tommy would sneak around the concealing shade of the trees and overgrown shrubs, find himself a frisky couple of high schoolers, make himself comfortable and settle down to enjoy the show. Sometimes, if he was really lucky, a courting couple would get *really* carried away on the soft, leafy ground, get completely naked and go through all of the bases like they were going out of fashion – it was one heck of a way for Tommy to get his sex ed.

Something flashed in the harsh beam of sunlight, reflecting the radiance directly into Tommy's face, it was a cold, metallic glint that hurt his eyes. "*Owww!*" he complained, screwing his face up and twisting his head from side to side – wondering just why the person who pinned him so resolutely to the ground had gone to all the trouble of bringing along a dessert spoon.

The burning sensation the glaring sunlight triggered in his eyes had Tommy crying, and streams of hot, salty tears ran down his wobbling, pock-marked cheeks to sting at the open acne sores that marred his otherwise handsome features. It brought back to him the dreadful memories of the seemingly unending pain he'd endured back in first grade, when they'd removed the bandages from around his head at the hospital and his Mom and Dad had told him that it was all for the best and he'd be able to see properly for the first time in his life.

He'd had to wear those spectacles with thick, heavy lenses that looked like they'd been fashioned from the bottom of those old style Coke bottles and made him the target for so much merciless teasing – if he'd been called *Mr Magoo* once, he'd been called it a thousand times! But, his folks had been right, and once the post-op pain was gone, Tommy's world had become a whole lot clearer – although he could still remember well the times when the whole world had been nothing more than a thick, syrupy white blur.

A pressure on his eyelids, strong fingers prising them open.

"*Nooooo*!" Tommy squealed, hoping against hope that somebody would hear him and come running to his aid at the very last minute, just like they did in the action movies he devoured on a Saturday night.

"Stay still, kid," the gruffness of the voice startled Tommy; this was the first thing his attacker had said since jumping him in the clearing.

"Please let me go," Tommy snivelled, and bubbles of thick, clear snot oozed from his nostrils, "I promise I won't tell anybody –" Unable to do anything else but snivel and plead, Tommy stared up with his forced-open eye at the concealed face, painfully aware that his bladder had let go, with his bowels threatening a similar protest.

And then, all Tommy could see was the spoon.

He yowled like a stuck pig as the spoon slipped between his eyeball and its fleshy housing, the curved edge making its way around all the way to the back of Tommy's socket. Bright, white flashes of startling light set off in his head as the concave metal nudged at the delicate wiring of his optic nerve; it was like Fourth of July and New Years going off in his brain all at the same time.

It was a peculiar feeling for Tommy as the spoon scooped out his eyeball, he got a kind of wibbly-wobbly view of the trees that held sentry above him, much like the camera shake effect they put into the found-footage horror movies in an attempt to make them appear authentic. Tommy felt all too well the tugging, tearing sensation around his eyeball as the thin muscles that held it into place gave way to the harsh probing of the cold metal spoon. And then, his assailant's face grew closer, closer still and Tommy could feel the tepid afternoon air rushing into his denuded eye socket, and the warmth of sticky fluids cascading down his face and into his hair.

"Dammit," that gruff voice again, and Tommy felt his eyeball pop like an overripe fruit and warm, viscous fluid spattered onto his face to invade his shrill scream with its thick, cloying taste

Then, all went black and Tommy felt powerful, insistent fingers prising open his other eyelid.

*

"There are a lot of similarities in M.O.," Detective Lyle lectured Pemberton, his brow furrowed as he thought out loud, "to the Ranier case that came in last month." He pointed to the veritable gore fest of crime scene photos he'd pinned to the battered old cork board on his office wall – no point throwing good departmental money away on a new one, not this close to him walking out of the Precinct for the final time – the victim's mutilated corpse splayed out upon the blood soaked, king-sized bed in glorious technicolor.

After enduring the ghoulish start to his day, it felt good for Lyle to be back in the dingy confines of the precinct, bustling with activity, filled with cop's chatter and where the coffee was thick and black like molasses and tasted like armpit.

They didn't have a name on the missing lung gal as yet, which Lyle found frustrating, she'd used a fake ID to book the room at the motel, and paid in cash, clearly she didn't want anyone to know where she was.

"The liver guy?" Pemberton threw in.

"Yeah, the liver guy," Lyle huffed and tapped a well-chewed fingernail against the photograph of the unfortunate young lady with her chest cavity yawning wide open like some hideous, gaping maw, the pink-white of her split sternum and ribs poking through the ragged meat of her torso, her heart sitting forlorn and deflated amidst her ruined flesh. "Both victims were drugged, but still most likely conscious. Both had one major organ removed – the weapon in both cases is still unknown." Lyle took in a deep breath as he recalled the M.E. telling him that, in his considered, professional opinion, the killer had torn the poor girl's flesh apart with his bare hands while she'd watched.

"So, if it is the same guy, what's his motivation?" Pemberton asked, still accustomed to going through these things by the same old book he'd devoured at the training academy countless years ago.

"Damned if I know," Lyle grumbled. "Could have Mommy issues, quite possibly some junkie out of his tree on Bath Salts or some such – or could be just your plain old, run of the mill lunatic." The detective leaned closer to the board to peer into the dead girl's chest, doing his best to ignore the way in which her no doubt once delectably perky breasts lay flopped either side of her lifeless body upon the bed, still attached by torn flaps of pale, flawless skin. "Perhaps he's building another person piece by piece, from the inside out?"

"Like Frankenstein?"

"Yeah," Lyle said, "or maybe he's eating his way around the human body, one major organ at a time." Thomas Harris had a lot to answer for, the detective mused, with his damned fava beans and nice Chianti.

"So, what do we do? Wait for the psycho to kill again?" Pemberton stood up, his old wooden chair scraping loudly upon the office floor.

"Unless we can pick something out of this goddamned mess, that's just about all we can hope for right now," Lyle told his partner. "We should pull the files of all murders with personal possessions or body parts missing over the past ten years – there may just be something in there."

Pemberton's sigh was audible; by *we*, of course, Lyle meant him. And there'd be a hell of a lot of homicide cases fitting that description, since pretty much *all* serial killers took some kind of trophy home with them.

The door burst open, a ruddy faced, rookie cop stood framed in Lyle's doorway, looking decidedly uncomfortable in her freshly starched uniform, her not inconsiderable chest heaving as if she'd just run a marathon.

"Did they not teach you to knock in basic training?" Lyle snapped, annoyed at having his all too ephemeral train of thought broken.

"I'm sorry, Sir," the cop panted, her pretty face reddening still further, "but I thought you'd want to know straight away." She glanced across the cramped, dusty office at the seemingly random array of ghoulish pictures displayed upon the board above the detective's paper-strewn mess of a desk.

"Know what?" Lyle asked.

"They just found some kid wandering around Devil's Woods with his eyes missing," the cop told him. "He said somebody popped 'em out with a spoon."

*

As it turned out, Tommy Rydell was less than useless as an eye witness – an unfortunate turn of phrase, of course – as he was wildly hysterical, bordering upon downright loony-tunes by the time Lyle and Pemberton arrived at the hospital. The medics had done an efficient job of patching the kid up, his empty eye sockets padded out with cotton balls and gauze, his head wrapped around with a thick swath of bandages that made Lyle think of Boris Karloff.

"Are you sure you can't remember anything at all about the person who did this to you?" Pemberton asked Tommy for what seemed like the thousandth time – the cop was nothing if not persistent.

"You're going to have to leave now," the skinny, sour-faced doctor sounded most insistent. "Tommy needs to rest."

"She took my eyes!" Tommy screamed again, his voice piercing, so desperately high that it fair hurt the ear drums. *"She took my new eyes!"*

Lyle ushered his partner from the tiny, stark white hospital room. He cast a cursory nod in the doctor's direction, expecting at the very least an upturned corner of his thin-lipped mouth by means of a *thank you*.

Nothing.

"*She*?" Pemberton whispered to himself.

"What was that?" Lyle said.

"The kid said *she*," Pemberton scratched at the two-day old stubble that prickled his chin. "His attacker was a woman?"

"It's possible, I guess," Lyle said, "but the boy hardly knows what day it is. Until the shock and the pile of drugs they've got the kid on wear off, we'd be best keeping an open mind on that score."

Pemberton gave a sage nod. "You're probably right, boss."

"There was something, though," Lyle added as they made their way through the intricate maze of hospital hallways. "He said his *new* eyes," he pondered. "What do you make of that, Joe?"

"Like you said, the kid was not in his right mind –"

"What say we do some digging around murder cases involving transplant patients?" Lyle thought out loud once again. "And find out of the Rydell kid had ever had an eye transplant."

"I don't think that's a thing, Bob," Pemberton corrected Lyle, even though he knew damn well the senior detective hated it when he played the pedant. "Something to do with not being able to reconnect the optic nerve, I think – they do transplant corneas, though..." he added the last part to appease the thunderous expression that clouded Lyle's face. "I'll start digging the second we get back to the precinct."

*

"Take a look at this, Bob," Pemberton squinted at the grainy computer screen that perched precariously upon his partner's desk – since the budget cuts, they'd been forced to share the temperamental Dell, so old that it still ran Windows 95.

Lyle leaned across the desk, his reading glasses clinging to the end of his greasy nose, a beige case file clutched in one hand, stale pastrami on rye in the other. He peered over his spectacles, and Pemberton's shoulder, at the fuzzy, badly copied newspaper article displayed in all its monochrome glory on the screen.

"Three weeks ago – it was over in Los Angeles, but the vic' had a kidney taken." Pemberton read from the article. "The victim actually survived the attack and the removal of the organ, but died a week later from an MRSA infection he caught at the hospital."

"Ironic," Lyle grunted.

"They chalked it up to organ farming," Pemberton continued, "happens a lot in LA, apparently; they sell human body parts off to the rich folks.”

“Maybe that’s all it was, then.”

“That’s what I thought, but look…” Pemberton scrolled down the page, the screen moving downwards with jerky, pixelated movements. “At the bottom,” he said, pointing to the article’s penultimate paragraph.

“He was a transplant recipient,” Lyle said, his voice oozing from him like a diseased whisper. “Nine years ago; the perp’ left the old kidneys behind.”

“They leave the sick kidneys in place when they transplant in new ones, unless they’re cancerous, of course,” Pemberton recited what he’d learned from Gray’s anatomy – his wife made him sit through the show, even though he hated it – it was pretty much all they had in common since he made detective. “They just plumb in the new one next to them.”

Lyle slicked back what remained of his thinning, silver hair. It felt greasy, weary, and he honestly couldn’t remember the last time it had seen shampoo. “That could be our man,” he growled, “maybe the heat got too much for him over there.”

“Or woman,” Pemberton said, “Rydell said –”

“– I know what the kid said, Joe,” Lyle snapped. “We need to find out exactly when he had his eye transplant – or whatever the hell it was – and same goes for Ranier and the chick with the lungs.”

Pemberton studied his partner’s face, recognized the look of consternation that dwelled there, like a dark cloud hovering over a grim landscape. “You think this might be the same killer?”

“I’m leaning that way,” Lyle said. “And I have a hunch,” he sat back in the creaky old chair that had been with him through most of his twenty years as a detective, "and a bad feeling about this."

"Didn't know you were a *Star Wars* fan, Bob," Pemberton attempted to inject a little levity as he returned his attention to the computer.

Detective Lyle cleared his throat, and it sounded like a snarl. "I'm not," he said.

*

"I already told you, Detectives, you'll have to get a warrant," Doctor Christoph Pena informed the two surly looking cops who had stormed into his office without so much as a by-your-leave.

Lyle pulled a face, he was pretty damn close to flattening the doctor's thin, pointy nose – world renowned transplant surgeon or not, the man was still an obstinate prick. Since they'd discovered that the guy in LA, Rydell, Ranier, and the lung gal – turned out her name was Sheralyn Braxton, she was all of twenty-one when her life was so brutally snuffed out – had all received their spare parts from the same donor a smidge over nine years ago, Lyle knew they were in a desperate race against time if they were to prevent more death and bloodshed; the murderer was escalating, the time between kills shortening exponentially.

"In the time it would take to obtain a warrant – and we *will* get one – somebody else could die at the hands of this manic," Pemberton tried his best to guilt the good doctor into compliance, but to no avail – the medic remained quite steadfast.

"All we need is the list of names of any other recipients of organs from Jake Cooley," Lyle added, fighting to keep his temper. "Who the hell is that going to hurt, *doctor*?"

It had been easy enough to find out the name of the donor of Tommy Rydell's replacement corneas, since his family had made a big gesture out of thanking the Cooley family for their brave altruism – Jake Cooley had been nineteen years old when he'd gone ass over teakettle through the windscreen of his drunk mother's Corvette. There'd even been a big splash in the local papers, complete with a grainy picture of a chubby Tommy Rydell, aged four and change, with his eyes bandaged up in what Lyle thought was an eerie foreshadowing of what was to come.

The doctor wavered slightly, and Lyle thought he was about to give in. But no. "Do I have to remind you about doctor/patient confidentiality, Detective Lyle?" He looked down his pinched nose at the cop, as if studying some much lower life form.

"Can you at least tell us what other parts of the Cooley kid were donated?" Lyle growled. "Unless of course, the confidentiality you're hiding behind extends to the dead."

Doctor Pena snorted his derision at Lyle's sarcasm. "It does not," he said, grabbing a pristine sheet of pink-tinged paper from the pad on his immaculately ordered desk. He scribbled studiously for a minute of two, before handing the note to Pemberton, a deliberate snub to the older cop who hovered at his shoulder.

"Oh, sweet Jesus," Pemberton said, glancing down at the spidery scrawl that seemed almost feminine; there were nine items on the list.

*

"He's not here," Dr. Pena's assistant insisted, her immaculately made up face reddening beneath the stern scrutiny of the two cops, her ruby red, bee-stung lips pouting like she was about to cry.

"Listen. Miss – Johnstone –" Lyle read the gal's nameplate that sat precariously dead center at the very front edge of her desk, as if it were plucking up the courage to jump. "We have a warrant, and we need to speak to Dr. Pena, so unless you would like to take a trip to the station to chat to us about obstruction, I suggest you hit the button on your intercom and let your boss know we're here." He leaned across the desk to better intimidate, hands planted firmly in front of the terrified assistant, fingers splayed wide.

"H-he left straight after you this morning," the ever-professional Miss Johnstone explained, "and he never came back – I had to cancel all of his appointments and surgeries for the day."

Detective Pemberton eyed the door to Pena's office, noting that there was no light to be seen emanating from the thin crack between it and the polished floor, even though it was already eight at night – either the good doctor liked to sit and work in the dark, or his assistant was telling the truth.

"Is it unlocked?" Lyle asked, following his partner's gaze.

"Yes, but –"

Even as Miss Johnstone began her protest, Lyle was already on his way towards the doctor's office door, crossing the office with long, purposeful strides. "We don't have time for this," he snapped, by means of an apology, "show her the warrant, Joe."

Pemberton slapped the warrant on the secretary's desk and followed Lyle into Pena's office, admiring the grain of the expensive door on his way in – Brazilian Mahogany, unless he was otherwise mistaken.

Lyle sat himself down in the doctor's plush, leather chair with a satisfied groan, the chair was a million miles away from the battered old thing in his office, and his ass felt like it would never want to leave. He fired up the expensive Mac on Pena's desk and stabbed at the intercom with an impatient finger. "What's the password on this thing?" he growled, enjoying the luxury of not having to shout through the door at the top of his voice like they had to back at the precinct.

"I-I don't think I can tell you that," the harangued assistant replied, her voice cold and tinny through the small speaker; she sounded dangerously close to tears and Lyle almost felt sorry for her.

"*Must* we go through this again?" Lyle harrumphed, his finger pressed so hard on the little red button that his knuckle turned white. "We *could* get another warrant, but that would mean disturbing some poor judge out of hours, which really won't go well for you in court – and all the while, there's a killer out there planning his next outing and your stubbornness could well cost someone else their life." Lyle laid it on thick, the poor woman was close to cracking as it was, and he figured that just one more push ought to do the trick. "So, unless you want *that* on your conscience, I strongly suggest you –"

"Jake Cooley," Miss Johnstone blurted out, her voice choked with tears, "lowercase, all one word."

The two words smacked Lyle square in the face, sent his mind spinning in a dozen directions. "Seriously?" he growled as he tapped the doctor's password into the little gray box in the center of the computer screen. He shook his head slowly as the computer whirred to life and there, set as the screen's wallpaper, were the happy, smiling faces of the late Jake Cooley and his exceptionally pretty mother.

It didn't take Lyle long to find what he was looking for, his doggedness at keeping himself abreast of ever-evolving technology never failed to pay off. Pemberton, for his part, wandered around the spacious office, his footsteps silenced by the outrageously thick pile of the beige carpet, poking his nose into the tall, metal filing cabinets that were dotted about the place.

Lyle looked up from the Mac, his face glowing a ghostly white in the screen's light. He pressed the intercom once more. "What happened to the Cooley file?" he barked, imagining Miss Johnstone jumping in her seat at the sound of his voice.

"It's there, under *donors*," the woman replied. She'd composed herself since her earlier breakdown and now sounded cold and detached. "All of the donor cases Doctor Pena worked with are in that folder."

Lyle scrolled down the list, then up again, his keen eye registering that the cases stretched back nine years, the earliest of which was one *Cooley: J.* He tapped on the name again, as if opening the file a third time would somehow, and miraculously, yield a different result.

It didn't.

The file was empty, nothing more than a standard form, each field a virgin white, not so much as a checked box or a note.

"There must be a backup paper file for Cooley," Lyle scrutinized each of the filing cabinets as he posed the rhetorical question to the ever-patient Pemberton. "Could you –?"

Pemberton beat his partner to the punch, yanking open the top most metal drawer of the cabinet closest the picture window – he figured the view across the parkland would be spectacular during the day, but for now it was just cool, still blackness. "It's not here, Bob," he announced, somewhat predictably, "looks like he took it, though." Pemberton rifled through the neatly arranged taupe files that hung suspended within the drawer, making doubly sure that *Cooley: J* had not simply been misfiled.

Lyle let out a huge, weary sigh and leaned back in the chair. His eyes flicked the length and breadth of Pena's PC screen, as if in the vain hope that the information that had been so diligently wiped would magically dissolve back into view. Jake Cooley had been the newly qualified Doctor Pena's first donor preparation, which quite possibly explained the weird attachment the guy had with the kid, quite possibly akin to a cop's fond affinity with his first department-issued firearm.

Unless…

"We gotta go," Lyle barked, jumping from the chair, his knee joints complaining with twin pops that sounded like firecrackers going off. "Get Pena's address from the girl, now." And with that, he marched from the office and towards the elevator, with Pemberton hot on his heels.

*

It hadn't been difficult to extract Dr. Pena's home address from Miss Johnstone; by that stage in Lyle and Pemberton's second visit of the day, she was pretty much broken and just wanted to go home.

"Nice place," Lyle said, looking up at the wide expanse of the Pena house's limestone brick façade. The house, nestled cosy at the far end of an exclusive, gated community estate, was colossal, bigger than some of the exclusive country house hotels that Mrs. Lyle liked to frequent. "I guess I chose the wrong career," he snorted, a wry smile playing about his lips.

The doctor's house was dark, quiet, yet the black Carrera sporting the vanity plates that sat motionless in the driveway suggested that Dr. Pena was home.

Lyle drew his gun. Pemberton followed suit, and the two cops made their way towards the front door in silence, their footsteps swallowed up by the impeccably trimmed, damp grass of the lawn.

"You ready?" Lyle whispered, one hand resting upon the huge brass door knob, the other aiming his Glock at the thick wood, at chest height.

Pemberton nodded, his own gun raised; he'd worked with Lyle long enough to know that the man would merrily kick the door in if it was locked, and to hell with waiting for the backup they'd called for to arrive.

The knob twisted smoothly in Lyle's hand, and much to his surprise, the heavy wood of the door eased open with nary a creak. With a cursory nod at his partner, Lyle slipped inside Pena's house, his slim frame swallowed up by the darkness that dwelled within. He knew that he really ought to have announced their presence, but something deep down in his seasoned cop's gut advised to the contrary, and Lyle was too long on the force to ignore it.

Pemberton wrinkled his nose at the smell that wafted down the long, sweeping staircase. It was an earthy, rank odor, with distinct undertones of something unpleasantly chemical; quite unmistakably the vile stink of death. He tapped Lyle on the shoulder and pointed towards the stairs, indicating that they should make their way upwards – it would be a while before the acrid reek registered with the older cop, his sense of smell had been all but destroyed by years' of heavy smoking back in his younger days. Pemberton fished a small penlight out of a pocket and clicked it on, the narrow beam of yellowish light illuminating the intricately patterned carpet that adorned the sweeping staircase.

Slowly, carefully, the cops made their way to the upstairs of Pena's mansion, alert eyes searching for traces of movement within the inky shadows, ears pricked for tell-tale sounds that may give away any inhabitants.

The hallway at the top of the staircase led off to both the left and the right, stretching away into the lightlessness like some infinite corridor. Following his nose, Pemberton peeled off to the right, the stink growing stronger with every step, and by now, he could see that Lyle's nose was crinkling. Pemberton figured they'd be discovering the doctor's body behind one of the myriad doors that his torch lit up – he hated suicides, there was just something about those who took their own lives that yanked hard on his soul, killing it off one small piece at a time.

The third door down on the left, Pemberton paused, sniffing the air like a well trained tracker dog. He shone his mini flashlight at the door handle, gun poised, with Lyle close behind him. He hesitated; something wasn't right, his heart pounded hard and heavy in his chest, so much so that he wouldn't have been at all surprised if his partner was hearing it.

"Open the damn door already," Lyle hissed in Pemberton's ear, startling him. The cop popped the penlight between his teeth, reached out, and opened the door.

Lyle gagged as the fetid wave of stink hit him full force, the bile rising up from his guts to leave a burning trail all the way up his gullet. He gulped it down, fighting the nausea that washed through every corner of his body. He'd been in the presence of corpses before, many in advanced stages of decomposition, but never in his life had he smelled anything that bad – it stank to high heaven of putrescent flesh, thick, congealing blood, body wastes and the sharp tang of chemicals; he dreaded Pemberton's inquisitive light revealing the source of such an unearthly stench.

With trembling hands, Pemberton directed both the thin light and his weapon towards each corner of the room in turn, ascertaining that they were in a teenage boy's room, adorned as it was with posters of the Texans, Britney Spears, Katy Perry and Miley Cyrus. There was an office chair, a twin bed, and a modest, brushed aluminium writing desk, home to a thick laptop, and laying next to that, as if tossed there carelessly, was a thin, card file that Pemberton thought he recognized.

"Oh, sweet Jesus," Lyle gasped as Pemberton's light hit the bed, illuminating the ghastly figure that rested atop expensive cotton sheets that were stained dark with the ghoulish effluvia that had oozed from it.

The cops stepped gingerly towards the body that lay in the center of the bed, its withered arms by its sides, discolored bare toes pointing upwards.

Fighting against every instinct he had to turn tail and run, Pemberton played his penlight's beam over the desiccated corpse, lighting the atrocity up one ruined piece at a time.

The body had been young at the time of death, Lyle took a guess based upon its height and the Pokemon boxers it wore that the guy had been no more than mid to late teens when he'd shuffled off his mortal coil. His body had been sliced open; gray flaps of emaciated skin draping either side of the body cavity like old, discarded shrouds, to reveal the body's innards.

Glistening wetly amidst the shrivelled viscera that lay deflated and slack inside the corpse's body, the black-red liver shone out in stark, ghoulish contrast, as did the gray-pink loops of neatly arranged intestines, along with the collapsed lungs that nestled within the cracked open rib cage. A kidney lay next to the liver, disconnected from the arteries and veins that should feed it, yet looking somehow *fresher* than the rest of the body.

There were patches of skin here and there, an upper arm, one thigh, a section of the peeled torso, still pinkish, yet turning blotchy as if it, too was rotting. The kid's face was adorned with seemingly random scraps of graying skin stretched taut over uneven the bumps of once prominent cheekbones – as if someone had tried their best to rebuild something irreparably damaged. The unforgiving gleam of Pemberton's light flashed across the corpse's eyes, the cop gasped and staggered back into Lyle, feeling the hard metal of his partner's gun jabbing hard into his spine. One of the corpse's eyes was sunken, oozing, like it had burst, but the other sat proud in the opposite socket, a thin black thread of catgut snaking from its edge, the silver curve of a surgical needle dangling at its end, the eye itself glassy, whole and staring…

The lights blazed on, temporarily blinding Lyle and Pemberton, and mercifully blotting out the horrifying vision of the corpses' fixed, dead eyes. The cops spun around on pure instinct, guns aimed, fingers on triggers.

"Don't shoot!" a terrified voice cried out, *"please!"*

Doctor Christoph Pena stood in the doorway, hands raised, tears streaming down his pinched, pale face.

"What the hell is this?" Lyle demanded, his eyes still smarting from the harsh light.

"She made me do it," Pena sobbed, "I didn't kill anybody, I promise I didn't. She just wanted her son back."

"This is Jake Cooley?"

Pena nodded. He glanced across at the ruined corpse, his eyes red rimmed, shame shadowing his wan features. "I married her after –" the doctor faltered. "After her husband left her, he blamed her for Jake."

"She married the surgeon who took her kid apart?" Pemberton threw in. He clicked off his penlight and sauntered across to the desk, flicking open the beige file that lay next to the unopened laptop. "That's kinda morbid, don't you think?"

"Grief makes people do strange things," Pena offered, as if that was any kind of excuse.

"Like murdering innocent folks so you can reassemble your dead kid?" Lyle growled, his hackles up.

"I didn't kill anybody," Pena protested, "I just –"

"– stitched the parts back together," Lyle growled, "doesn't make you any less complicit, *Doctor*," the cop all but spat out the last word, as if it was a sour taste upon his tongue. "So, where is the delightful Mrs. Cooley?"

"It's *Pena* now," the doctor corrected the cop, as if the detail really mattered.

"Bob," Pemberton interrupted, "you got to see this." He plucked a page from the file on the desk, scrutinized it, his brow furrowed.

"What you got there, Joe?" Lyle kept his gun pointed at the doc's chest, one move out of place and he'd more than welcome the opportunity to blow the sick bastard to Kingdom Come.

Pemberton waved the flimsy sheet of hospital issue paper at his partner, his face so drained of color that he all but resembled Jake Cooley's sorry remains. "It's Tina –"

Lyle's cell rang out, the jolly Benny Hill theme tune a disturbing juxtaposition to the ghoulish circumstances in Pena's house. Without thinking, Lyle grabbed the phone from his pocket, answered the call.

"There's somebody in my apartment, Daddy," Tina's terrified voice squeaked through the miniscule speaker. "I'm scared."

"Stay calm, baby girl," Lyle fought to contain his own panic that rose up from the pit of his stomach. "Did you call 911?"

Tina sobbed, her voice a trembling whisper, "Yeah, but she's in my apartment right now, she keeps saying I stole her son's heart, but I don't even know anybody called Jake – I'm hiding in my closet."

"You stay there, sweetie, you're gonna be just fine..." the words died in the cop's throat; he'd never felt more helpless in his entire life.

And then, Tina Lyle began to scream.

Other HellBound Books Titles
Available at:
www.hellboundbookspublishing.com

The Southern House

There are some places that lie where the barrier between worlds is thin and growing thinner. These corridors are as old as the Earth itself, hidden in dark and forgotten places, waiting to be found. There is a being who stalks these places and travels between those worlds. He was given the name Mr. Shift by generations of children and madmen.

Just as Hickory Grimble hits rock bottom, he inherits his grandparents' farm and believes his luck is changing. He soon finds he inherited more than money and land.

Haunted by his own inner demons, now he has new problems. He begins to see strange creatures on the dark, sprawling acreage, animals that have no business living in middle Tennessee. He also discovers a decrepit, abandoned house in the forest that never seems to be in the same place twice.

Balanced on a razor's edge between, addiction and fate, Hick is now face to face with an ancient evil that has returned once more to claim more of the town's children.

<u>Graveyard Girls</u>

*Female authors –
Horror = something
spectacularly
terrifying!*

A delicious collection of horrific tales and darkest poetry from the cream of the crop, all lovingly compiled by the incomparable Gerri R Gray! Nestling between the covers of this formidable tome are twenty-five of the very best lady authors writing on the horror scene today!

These tales of terror are guaranteed to chill your very soul and awaken you in the dead of the night with fear-sweat clinging to your every pore and your heart pounding hard and heavy in your labored breast...

Featuring superlative horror from: Xtina Marie, M. W. Brown, Rebecca Kolodziej, Anya Lee, Barbara Jacobson, Gerri R. Gray, Christina Bergling, Julia Benally, Olga Werby, Kelly Glover, Lee Franklin, Linda M. Crate, Vanessa Hawkins, P. Alanna Roethle, J Snow, Evelyn Eve, Serena Daniels, S. E. Davis, Sam Hill, J. C. Raye, Donna J. W. Munro, R. J. Murray, C. Bailey-Bacchus, Varonica Chaney, Marian Finch (Lady Marian).

Them

Ray Sanders returns home from Florida to bury his mother.

Soon, the supernatural evidence behind his mother's demise begins to surface in the form of dreams and mysterious happenings.

During all of the madness, Sanders must face his destiny and vanquish the generations-old evil that has plagued his family since the 1800's…

In 1854, Louis Sanders, with the help of Elias Atkins, dug a well to provide water to the family farm. What they did not anticipate was the water to be infested with Odomulites - ancient sins. These malevolent beings - were trapped in our world on their way to the spirit world - formed a pact of protection with both Sanders and Atkins; the families would serve as guardians of the Odomulite nests and in return, a blind eye would be cast when the Odomulites took host bodies to inhabit and feed upon. It was this pact, which in 2016 would propel Sanders and Julie Fontaine - a young woman with a special connection to the Spirit World - into the heart of the last active nest to rid the town of its insidious Odomulite population.

Blood in The Woods

Based upon true events...

For Jody, growing up in the late eighties and early nineties in the small Louisiana town of Hammond with his best friend Jack was filled with wonderful childhood memories.

Time spent playing in the woods, shooting pellet guns, blowing up mailboxes, fighting at school and upon the dawning of interest in the fairer sex, their carefree lives typical of children with few responsibilities and no worries beyond the next pop-quiz or getting to second base. As they grow older together and experience the joys and pains of life, love, family and friendship, they uncover a grim secret that their home town has kept, and through little more than an innocent, idle curiosity, Jody and Jack stumble upon something horrific in the woods and their lives quickly take a most sinister and dangerous turn as they find themselves hunted by an unspeakable evil...

Worship Me

Something is listening to the prayers of St. Paul's United Church, but it's not the god they asked for; it's something much, much older.

A quiet Sunday service turns into a living hell when this ancient entity descends upon the house of worship and claims the congregation for its own.

The terrified churchgoers must now prove their loyalty to their new god by giving it one of their children or in two days time it will return and destroy them all.

As fear rips the congregation apart, it becomes clear that if they're to survive this untold horror, the faithful must become the faithless and enter into a battle against God itself.

But as time runs out, they discover that true monsters come not from heaven or hell…
…they come from within.

Demons, Devils and Denizens of Hell: Vol, 2

The second volume in HellBound Books' outstanding horror anthology fair teems with tales of Hades' finest citizens – both resident and vacationing in our earthly realm…

Compiled by the inimitable P. Mattern and featuring: Savannah Morgan, Andrew MacKay, Jaap Boekestein, James H Longmore, Stephanie Kelley, Ryan Woods, James Nichols, P. Mattern, Marcus Mattern, Gerri R Gray, and legion more…

Shopping List 2: Another Horror Anthology

Once again, HellBound Books brings you an outstanding collection of horror, dark, slippery things, and supernatural terror - all from the very best up and coming minds in the genre.

We have given each and every one of our authors the opportunity to have their shopping lists read by you, the most wonderful reading public, and have the darkest corners of their creative psyche laid bare for all to see...

In all, 21 stories to chill the soul, tingle the spine and keep you awake in the cold, murky hours of the night from: Erin Lee, The Truth Artist, John Barackman, Serena Daniels, M.R. Wallace, Isobel Blackthorn, Alex Laybourne, Jason J. Nugent, Josh Darling, Jovan Jones, Nick Swain, Douglas Ford, Craig Bullock, Craig Bullock, Jeff C. Stevenson, PC3, David F Gray, Sergio Palumbo, Donna Maria McCarthy, David Clark & Megan E. Morales

**A HellBound Books LLC
Publication**

http://www.hellboundbookspublishing.com

Printed in the United States of America